GUARDIANS

Verse Infinitum

iUniverse, Inc.
Bloomington

GUARDIANS

Copyright © 2011 Verse Infinitum

This is a work of fiction. All of the characters, names, incidents, organizations, and dialogue
in this novel are either the products of the author?s imagination or are used fictitiously.

iUniverse books may be ordered through booksellers or by contacting:

iUniverse
1663 Liberty Drive
Bloomington, IN 47403
www.iuniverse.com
1-800-Authors (1-800-288-4677)

ISBN: 978-0-595-40748-4 (pbk)
ISBN: 978-0-595-85113-3 (ebk)

Printed in the United States of America

iUniverse rev. date: 1/3/2011

Acknowledgement

Endless gratitude is owed to a host of people who made it possible for Guardians to be written. I first wish to provide an adhered appreciation to my exceptional mother Elinor who brought me into this dynamic world and raised me and my brothers Rick and Steve who became my closest friends for as long as I could remember. My extended family also deserves every bit of grace like my uncle Peter and Gene and my cousin Mary.

Friends are among the most important value in life. Role models such as Marty Wales made it possible for me to expand my horizon and hope as I stretched my arms everyday to wake up in the morning and wish to thank an enlightened young lady by the name of Teri Ellen who reactivated my inner youth.

From my childhood friends in John Haynes Holmes Towers, Stanley Isaac's Houses and the rest of Yorkville and the Upper East Side of Manhattan to my trusted colleagues in Chelsea Vocational High School and Berkeley College, I salute you!

Teachers and Professors were among the most significant impacts in my life. Ms. Feldman, who taught my 4th grade class in P.S. 190 during the 1976 – 77 year in Manhattan, cheerfully took us to class trips to places such as the American Museum of Natural History that would forever change the course of my enthusiasm. Ms. Stanislaus of Robert F. Wagner Junior High School in the Upper East Side of Manhattan taught, coached and inspired my classmates of 1980 and me to master any subject including English. I also owe thanks to Mr. Adler, Ms. Donner and Mr. Casper for making it possible to graduate with optimism.

I also wish to send my love and ever thanks to the Huffman family of Pennsylvania that showed me all the beauty this world possessed as I enjoyed all the fun during my two week camping trips I took when I was an adolescent in the Fresh Air Fund Youth Camping program.

Mr. Morea, Mr. Weinstein, Mr. Blau, and many others in Chelsea Vocational High School in Manhattan energized my learning experience and fueled my desire to excel in life. I also wish to appreciate all my friends in high school that made my high school years the most fulfilling. I also wish to extend my gratefulness to Dr. Jack Solarwitz and all the brilliance I've experienced in Berkeley College (New York City Campus) from 1995 – 1997.

Since then my perception of life around me changed forever and inspired me to conclude that anything's possible.

What's more is the United States Armed Forces is often the most sufficient source of personal reinvention. In duration of my service in the United States Air Force, my desire to write was reborn. I personally want to thank all the men and women in uniform who became my most trustworthy colleagues anywhere. I wish to thank Sheryll Gomez, Carolyn Neal, and iUniverse for their vital support and encouragement that made this novel possible. I wish to thank all of my colleagues who live and work at Ruppert – Yorkville towers and Knickerbocker Plaza in the Yorkville section of Manhattan for all of the inspiration and invigoration I received for so long.

Most notably, it's my obligation to recognize and thank every person and organization listed in the Special Thanks section of Reader's Aide. I also want to extend my sincere appreciation to you who made a decision to read Guardians…thank you!

Introduction

As a gentle breeze penetrates and caresses our lungs, the enchanting sun sets at the western horizon. A swarm of faint twinkling lights will soon emerge from a veil of daylight. Driving on trails or back roads at a rural countryside is one way you can observe countless stars in the sky. Traveling out to sea on a ship would be another way you can view a small fraction of our Milky Way galaxy. As we're inspired by such a nocturnal splendor in the sky, questions and curiosities of what's really out there continue to mystify the entire world since human society originated!

Recent facts discovered about our own solar system inspire us to explore even further. For example, rocks ejected from Mars by asteroid impacts, traveled long distances through space before landing on Earth. Scientists discovered a fossilized pattern inside that could possibly have been ancient micro organisms within these prehistoric rocks. If such a theory proves to be true, then a new perspective of not being physically alone in the universe would become a household reality! Scientists currently suspect that one of Jupiter's moons called Europa may possess aquatic life underneath its thick surface of ice. Saturn's largest moon Titan also raises possibilities of possessing microscopic life because its rich atmosphere and mineral deposits are physically similar to Earth's during the Precambrian Times, which ranged from 4.6 billion to 600 million years ago.

One of the most compelling discoveries came when the Hubble space telescope conducted a deep space probe to find out what exist at the furthest distance of space ever observed. Scientists detected at least 1200 galaxies within a tiny portion of the cosmos. Further calculations suggested that the number of galaxies is four times the population previously calculated only a few years ago. Theories once considered unchangeable diminished instantly. Since the Hubble space telescope was launched, humanity's concept of the universe has changed dramatically!

Documentaries of the latest scientific discoveries are readily available from an intriguing host of cable and digital network channels such as the Discovery Channel, The Learning Channel, and the National Geographic Channel. My personal confession to all readers is that I've learned more about science and technology from these channels than I've ever learned at high school and college. If it weren't for these exciting networks and other sources, this novel would never be written. The most noticeable programs broadcasted are discoveries made by astronomers and paleontologists. We continue to be amazed by dinosaurs and prehistoric mammals inducted into a fossil hall of fame such as the Rancho la Brea tar pits in Los Angeles. Visiting museum exhibits around the world reinforce our wonder for the past. Fossils found worldwide are carefully preserved by an insulating solution so they could be transported to a museum for assembly and display.

Observing fossils of Earth's past inhabitants enable us to hold our planet in a higher regard. Such complex structures of many fossils inspire us to wonder what Earth's ecosystem was like many years ago. How various prehistoric life forms existed within their ancient habitat? What would it be like to live among these venerable wonders of Earths past and would humanity ever receive an opportunity to observe their natural lives? The truth is; only time can give us an answer.

The Earth and universe continued to inspire me ever since my first class trip to the American Museum of Natural History and the Hayden Planetarium (currently known as the Rose Center of Earth and Space) in New York during my fourth grade class in 1977. Since then, I realized that dedicated paleontologists continue to enlighten us by providing convincing evidence, which unveiled hidden mysteries of Earth's past. I wish to inform every reader that all verbal statements made by broadcast communications including radio, intercom transmission and a loudspeaker would be written in *italic* instead of normal text for greater clarity. All names of all species, subspecies and genera mentioned in this novel would be written in *italic* as well.

Instead of only using the American metric system alone, I've also used the International System of Units (ISU) or Le Systéme International d'Unités (SI) based upon The New American Webster Handy College Dictionary, New Third Edition. When a specific measurement is quoted you'll notice a translation in parenthesis. For example: "This tree is 10 feet (3m) tall." So three meters, which is abbreviated is approximately ten feet. Most translations were rounded to the nearest decimal. I also included a special section called Reader's Aide, which includes a Technology Information section in order to help readers understand a host of fictional devices and gadgets. When there's a change in scene, readers will notice three aligned asterisks seen below:

*   *   *

Such an arrangement will clarify each reader's awareness of any change of scene. Many other novels use this technique to prevent confusion. Reader's Aide will also simplify your efforts to understand this novel by including a Cast of Main Characters section, a Geological Time Frame Chart based upon the International Stratigraphic Chart, Copyright © 2009 by the International

Commission on Stratigraphy. Almost most answers from this Stratigraphic Chart contain a range of years. For one example, the Cretaceous period ended at 65.5 ± 0.3 million years ago, I've decided to list only the main quotes without including plus or minus any time range (i.e. ± 0.3). Readers who wish to pursue further studies would find a wealth of accurate information from various sources such as books, Videos, DVDs and websites.

Although finding answers to our most intriguing questions would pose enormous challenges; scientists and technicians willingly engage into painstaking research over long periods of time despite the fact that there's no guarantee for success. Despite persistent challenges; scientists, engineers and scholars take center stage of network television and broadcast their impeccable wisdom to a delightful audience!

One of the main reasons why programs on the Discovery Channel, The Learning Channel, and the National Geographic Channel became very successful was that scientists revealed their latest discoveries by showing visual enactments that intrigued a vast network of viewers. Detailed computer graphics and video footages of each topic made it comprehensive to the general public. What's more is how each subject was presented without any complex technical terms, which could've intimidated many viewers. Scientists, scholars and narrators present their latest discoveries ranging from unraveling prehistoric fossils to detecting new solar systems with a dose of excitement.

My experience of viewing these channels and others such as Animal Planet inspired me to learn more than ever before. I even could recall the old days of watching In Search Of, hosted by Leonard Nimoy and the Nature of Things as well. Thanks for these exciting cable and digital television stations; science and other educational subjects would inspire a clear meaning and new perspective for many of us! I recommend all of these brilliant networks to be actively presented to every educational institution worldwide. Guardians will be an attempt to perform a similar role. Although detailed graphics shown on these networks would not be available every bit of excitement and intrigue I've experienced writing Guardians would be my sole intention to share with all readers including critics.

Last, but not least a Special Thanks section inside Reader's Aide was developed in recognition of various individuals and institutions for their ever persisting drive to engage into such painstaking research and reveal comprehensive facts that could've eluded us forever. I wish to thank all scientists, engineers, and technicians for their intellectual brilliance and physical resilience of unraveling the mysteries of nature and ourselves. I also wish to express my full gratitude to every reader who decides to read Guardians.

GOSPEL OF DISCOVERY

Broadcast journalists took their seats as technicians tested their communications equipment. U.S. Secret Service agents monitored this assembly inside the Press Briefing room of the White House. All invited guests took their seats with curiosity as they arrived on short notice. A collection of microphones arranged on top of a podium standing on a small stage was activated and tested before all video cameras recorded this event. Invited media guests whispered their curiosity to each other until a humble man wearing a fine tailored suit walked up a few steps at the left side of this elevated stage before he approached the podium.

"Ladies and Gentlemen please rise for the President of the United States and the Secretary General of the United Nations!" the presidential press secretary announced before he departed the stage.

Each distinguished guest witnessed two scholarly figures walk up the steps and made their way to the podium. Members of the audience noticed an unusual facial expression from both public officials who appeared to be surprised. Whispers of speculation within the audience ceased as both gentlemen received their full attention.

"First, I wish to thank everyone for your cooperation. We could only provide brief information and answer only a few questions before we must attend the Osiris 4 Summit." President Russell S. Wilson then provided an opportunity for the Secretary General of the United Nations to speak.

"What we're about to inform you will permanently affect our views in regards to the universe. Thanks to the Humane Space Federation, this new discovery is an inspiring achievement in human history. Secretary General Kufi A. Mobutu announced as the audience's enthusiasm grew. "Until this day of January 17th 2033, we never suspected to make such a discovery.

*   *   *

Radio waves raced from the Earth and traveled to the moon. Once it reached the lunar surface, radio signals penetrated into satellite dishes mounted on top of a Luna research compound. Up to 500 staff members received the news and transmitted the latest information to several lunar explorers scattered at the North Pole region. One of these explorers was collecting small stones on the moon's surface until he noticed a man's voice emitting from earpiece. *"Doctor Ryan, come – in please, Doctor Ryan."*

"Doctor Ryan here," Once Dr. Mack Ryan responded. The voice from the lunar compound transmitted.

"I have vital news for you."

"What news you have Marcus?" Dr Ryan replied.

"We've discovered an extra solar planet that could sustain complex life as we know it." Dr. Marcus Nimbus revealed.

"Where did you get this information?"

"The White House conducted a press conference and transmitted this news worldwide."

"This is the most compelling news I've received since the Hoi-Larson intervention six years ago." Dr. Ryan referred to an asteroid that measured up to two miles or slightly over 3.2 kilometers wide that drifted toward the Earth. Dr. Ryan remembered commanding this mission, which intercepted this asteroid in early July 2027 that was named after two people who discovered this boulder in space before Dr. Nimbus replied.

"Indeed, saving the Earth from impending doom is our first accomplishment. Finding an extra solar Earth is our second."

Dr. Ryan also reflected his experience commanding a crew for which no casualties was ever reported when they captured and asteroid and managed to successfully orbit this asteroid around the Earth and eventually mining it down to a large stone that's placed at the federation's headquarters.

"I can't conceive any possibility that the federation will neglect this discovery." Dr. Ryan affirmed.

"Neither could I," Dr. Nimbus agreed. *"As a matter of fact, I wouldn't be surprised if the federation makes this latest discovery the top priority of our mission's objectives."*

"Huh…wishful thinking; I wish the federation would pursue this discovery aggressively."

"Well, in that case, your wish is my command," Dr. Nimbus replied. *"I've just received official word that a summit will be held immediately at federation headquarters."*

"Send me the news transmission so I could view it on screen." Dr. Ryan requested before he view of the lunar surface transformed into a full view of the White House press briefing room along with President Wilson and Secretary General Mobutu revealing the news and answering questions.

"Equipment is ready, power supply is adequate and we're ready to raise the launch pad." Dr. Ryan confirmed into a microphone before a retractable dome directly above them began to slide apart.

"Well…this is it!" Dr. Nimbus said to Dr. Ryan when they saw a swarm of bright subtle lights twinkle as the platform rose the transporter above the opening. Thousands of stars provided faint insights of a possible future for humankind. Both men knew that the sight of these distant stars was only a fraction of what truly exists in distant space. However, they received an official confirmation that could change their lives forever!

"You're ready for take off, best of luck!" The woman's voice from the compound complemented over a loud speaker.

Dr. Ryan thanked her over the radio before Dr. Nimbus activated the ship to vertically lift off the platform of the lunar hangar before ascending above the ridgeline of a large crater the compound nestled inside. Its twin engine generated a mild vibration when they saw their physical altitude rising. Widows equipped to protect the crew from the sun's luminous rays, darkened as they saw the sun. Once they've ascended 120 feet or over 36 meters, Dr. Nimbus activated a propulsion switch before adjusting his accelerator forward. Dr. Nimbus commanded all three landing gears fold into their storage bays before he activated the autopilot flight mode before leaning back on his adjustable seat. The ship's artificial gravity made their journey convenient as Dr. Ryan stared directly ahead.

"Mack…what are you thinking about?"

"You remember the space telescope my father developed?" Mack brought to his colleague's attention.

"The Illuminator, what about it," Marcus responded.

"If I'm not mistaken, I think I left a copy of the Illuminator's data disk inside one of the other rooms?" Mack hoped to be true.

"Do you have written data or the interactive video?"

"I have the video," Mack smiled before he unbuckled his seatbelts and walked over to the main facility behind the cockpit.

Marcus waited until he suddenly heard a cheerful shout of the word "yes" followed by sounds of approaching footsteps. Marcus then turned his head and upper body over to his right hand side and observed his colleague and friend holding an American dime sized silver disk secured inside a clear plastic shell case. He tenderly removed this tiny disk from its case and pocketed the plastic shell case. He then carefully placed this tiny disk into a compartment of a 360-degree, four-dimensional holographic telepresence projector, which the fourth dimension represents time.

Additional verbal commands from both explorers placed the ship on alert for incoming space debris before they closed the cockpit's entrance door, while the windows' built-in solar protection shades darkened until all windows were black. Mack made additional verbal commands to deactivate panel display lights and adjust their seats. Miniature projectiles would collaborate in order to produce a 360 degree vision that's known to be the most vivid virtual reality simulator ever created.

Once Dr. Ryan verbally activated this virtue reality system called Clairvoyance, both men were in complete darkness before they noticed being suspended in simulated space with nothing else but their seats. What immediately caught their attention was a gigantic bright star located directly in front of them. Mack estimated this star to be about 300 times wider and 5 times more massive than our sun or five solar masses. Marcus felt suspicious as he noticed dust and gas sporadically ejecting off its surface. An intricate balance between this star's enormous gravity and strong nuclear fusion activity at the center of this star's interior would soon topple.

This red supergiant couldn't fuse iron, which caused it to shred its last layer of burning gases and material as a final gesture that gravity will contract this star's size before it will release enough energy to fuel human society for centuries. Modern astronomers suspect that such a supernova would end a star's luminous lifespan. Rays of light escaped from the surface of this giant star, which began to contract itself from the center. A raging shockwave suddenly escaped an ever-increasing gravity of a shrinking stellar mogul. Intense gravity made the red supergiant implode as they witnessed a powerful explosion of material ultraviolet and X-rays raging out in a fiery conquest. Everything in its path would be annihilated including a visible Jupiter like planet and its moons. Modern scientists and scholars currently estimate that a similar fate will happen to our sun around five to six billion years into the future.

An initial shockwave stripped this planet's atmosphere and began to evaporate its liquid surface into steam. A visible, orbiting moon suddenly disintegrated into pieces before its core ultimately dissolved into dust! Such intense brutality of this bright light of stellar expiration fervently engulfed sparse remains of a former gaseous giant planet until it vanished from their view!

"What a ferocious way for a world to end! The planet and its moons blew away like a pile of ash." Marcus could barely believe such a disaster at cosmic proportions.

"You want to watch a different star?" Mack asked.

"Sure," Marcus felt more enthused.

Mack then said "next scene" before a new simulated situation was displayed before them. Once again they noticed being suspended elsewhere in space and in view of another massive red star. This star was referred as a red hypergiant, federation members and visiting retirees. This recognizable figure could only be none other than Dr. Donald Netherland!

"*Welcome back gentlemen! Congratulations on the research center.*" this legendary figure said from inside an LCD screen.

"Thank you sir!" both replied simultaneously to a tall man with white hair and hazel eyes.

"*What you've heard is only part of the story.*" Dr. Netherland informed them.

"*You're the best we have! It's my honor to invite you to the Osiris 4 Summit at headquarters.*" Both men listened to Dr. Netherland's encouraging message.

"What would transpire from this meeting?" Dr. Ryan asked.

"*This summit would permanently alter the federation's policies.*" Dr. Netherland smiled as both men viewed his image with inspiration and intrigue.

"Umm…so we won't return to the lunar research station anymore?" Dr. Nimbus enthusiastically asked.

Dr. Netherland leaned back on his tall leather seat and rested his hands on both enlarged armrests before he decided to provide rare information. "*Since you've successfully intercepted the Hoi-Larson asteroid and completed our first lunar research compound, the entire chamber including myself are convinced that you would be the best candidates for our next objective.*"

Their eyebrows rose as their hearts pumped more rapidly due to their intense speculation of conducting a key role in the federation's new goal while Dr. Netherland waited patiently for their response before Dr. Ryan said; "We're honored to attend sir!"

"What about the federation's plan to terraform Mars?" Dr. Nimbus wondered.

Dr. Nimbus referred to humanity's second mission to Mars that would be the federation's first attempt to convert Mars's atmosphere over long periods of time. He knew that terraforming requires increasing the average surface temperature of Mars before introducing extremophiles to Mar's surface that could thrive under such an environment while producing valuable oxygen and nitrogen. Water would become available from Mar's melting Polar Regions necessary to give rise to plant life. Eventually, the most complex life forms including humans would settle permanently on Mars when its terrain and atmosphere becomes suitable.

"*Gentlemen…our goal of returning to Mars would no longer be our priority.*"

Once Dr. Netherland verbally confirmed the federation's change of plans, both men were surprised to discover such an ambitious organization losing interest in pursuing the most significant mission in human history. While

Dr. Nimbus continued to think of possible reasons, Dr. Ryan decided to ask his long time mentor what inspired the federation to redirect its prime objectives.

"Sir...what convinced the Chamber regarding this new planet's importance and why would this mission be more challenging than humanity's second mission to Mars?" Dr. Ryan wondered.

"We received convincing evidence that this extrasolar planet is capable of sustaining complex life, just like our Earth. In fact, we originally thought that it could be similar to Saturn's moon Titan; however data from Adam and Eve reassured us that this new world deserves our full attention."

"What did we find sir?" Dr. Nimbus requested.

Dr. Netherland raised his right eyebrow and wittingly smirked by Dr. Nimbus's question. *"You'll find out at the summit. Although I don't wish to tell you over an insecure transmission, I'm certain that you'll come to a simple and logical conclusion of this planet's prospect for further research. I look forward to seeing you at the summit. Oh...by the way, the best times are clearly ahead for all of us!"*

Dr. Netherland displayed a fervent smile before his transmission ended. Once both men viewed a blank screen, curiosities of the federation's new role flourished. Silence dominated the cockpit room enabling both men to feel a rush of blood flowing through their veins and arteries. Marcus and Mack continued to stare at this capital ship awaiting new goals while vital components are being added by orbital technicians working on a space platform.

OSIRIS 4 SUMMIT

"*Welcome Air Force One, you're cleared for landing.*" Air traffic control confirmed before the flight captain announced their descent to land at a geographically remote operations and administrative installation with formidable security.

Located at a secluded area of a rocky desert, this obscure installation served as the current headquarters of the organization. President Wilson and Secretary General Mobutu left the aerial conference room, so they could find their seats and buckle up for a safe landing. Only a runway, air traffic tower, and hangars were noticeable when they peeked out their window from the presidential plane that made a soft landing. The squadron of fighter jets that escorted Air Force One landed after the president's plane and made their way to an available hangar. Armed guards were summoned to an orderly two line formation and faced each other across a red carpet as Air Force One was taxied on the flight line before it parked next to a portable stairwell the ground crew connected to the plane's front side exit.

"Attention!" a voice shouted before all armed guards in formation simultaneously clicked their heels together and stood tall to formally welcome both distinguished visitors.

A sealed door of the aircraft hatched open before the visiting dignitaries waved to their hosts before walking down the aluminum steps. A sincere hail of salutes from armed guards welcomed all visitors as they walked on a red carpet. This bright red carpet guided them to limousines that transported all visitors to an entrance site of an underground facility. One of two armed guards posted dialed a combination of numbers on a panel post before all invited guests noticed a massive circular vault door opening.

President Wilson held precious memories of when he became the first director of Intelligence for the federation when it was founded fourteen years ago. A dose of passion ignited when he saw headquarters for the first time in years. He received a sense of joy as he reflected his glorious memories.

Additional encouragement was felt when he noticed a slim man with black hair and a dark complexion approaching him.

"Welcome back Mr. President!" Dr. Malik Abdullah al-Saud expressed a warm smile before he embraced his long time friend.

"Doctor Mobutu, Doctor Garcia! It's been a long time." were additional comments from Dr. al-Saud as he welcomed his guests.

Dr. al-Saud wore his white formal uniform known as dress whites along with rows of medals. He also wore an elegant pair of white patent leather shoes. Sunlight reflected off his silver buttons as both silver ensigns on his shoulders sparkled. Dr. al-Saud cheerfully guided all visitors inside headquarters.

*   *   *

Soon, a space transporter became visible to the naked eye. Muffled propulsion engines enabled this spacecraft to vertically dock to a signaling landing pad. Shocks and struts of each landing geared enabled a soft landing. Idled engines deactivated before the craft's hatch opened before a chute latter was lowered to the landing pad. Guards and technicians watched both men climb down from inside the spacecraft before greeting them. Dressed in their finest uniforms, Drs. Ryan and Nimbus felt the Earth's embrace by its strong gravity that welcomed them back home. With the exception of periodical medical breaks and vacations, both men have spent five years in space executing various tasks from mining an asteroid to exploring the Moon's North Pole Region and ultimately constructing the lunar compound.

Drs. Nimbus and Ryan remained patient as they anticipated meeting the founder of this facility. A gust of dry air accompanied both men as an orange tint of the rocky desert reminded them that they're home once again. Distant rolling hills, mesas, and cliffs reflected a warm reception.

Once they climbed down the chute ladder of the transporter, two young guards then, secured the spacecraft. Another young guard arrived with a transporter, which appeared and operated like a golf cart; transport them to the main entrance. Dr. Ryan noticed new construction while Dr. Nimbus remembered his earlier experience at headquarters when he noticed a group of old hangars and the air traffic control tower, which remained unchanged. Mack recognized additional structures including six large dish antennas, which replaced an outdoor physical training site.

A hot and dry climate of Groom Lake, Nevada enabled them to relax and feel relatively at ease. Arid soil remained suitable to dozens of different cactuses and thorny bushels. Security agents drove white four door sports utility vehicles to patrol all perimeters of the installation. With the exception of two newly constructed four story tinted glass office buildings, a state of the art radar system and a formidable security apparatus, this obscure establishment appeared to be geographically isolated from the outside world.

"There's the Hoi-Larson." Mack said once they entered the spacious lobby.

Both men walked over to a large stone placed on an elevated platform at the center of the main lobby. Dr. Ryan stared at the boulder as he recalled his memory of successfully preventing this giant boulder from landing on Earth. Both returning astronauts were recognized by Dr. al-Saud, who stood at the opposite side of the boulder along with Dr. Garcia.

"Gentlemen…welcome back!" Dr. al-Saud announced before showing a warm smile as he embraced them.

"Long time no see!" Dr. Nimbus said before they talked about their latest accomplishment at the lunar compound.

"I'm glad you made it. The president and secretary general arrived here earlier with their advisors." Dr. Garcia announced.

As they continued their conversation, Dr. Nimbus immediately noticed two attractive and intelligent women cheerfully talking to each other as they stood twenty feet or six meters away from his position. His heartbeat accelerated with excitement when he realized they were invited to the summit. Dr. Nimbus remembered them well due to their memorable reputations.

Both ladies stood five feet, seven inches (1.7m) tall and were in excellent physical shape. Dr. Ryan appreciated the famed psychologist's dark wavy hair that extended down past her shoulders. Her eyes appeared sincere and her triangular shaped face was in perfect harmony with her nose and cheeks.

Dr. Nimbus respected a master engineer who prized her smooth hair with a mixture of individual black and blond hair that reached her shoulders. He also remembered her sincere expression of her face due to her keen brown eyes. Dr. Nimbus was impressed by her bronze complexion as he noticed a new pair of platinum earrings.

Both wore their dress whites that included knee length skirts. They also wore numerous metals pinned across their chest as formal symbols of their achievements. Once Dr. al-Saud engaged to speak with Dr. Garcia, Dr. Nimbus instantly called for his colleague's attention.

"Mack, Mack."

"What?"

Dr. Nimbus then whispered his soft and quiet voice into Dr. Ryan's ear. "Look over your right shoulder."

"Oh…it's Lucy Rosalila." Mack displayed seldom modesty as he referred to the renowned psychologist.

"Meena Singh is here." Marcus added.

"I never told you this but I remember Lucy evaluated me during our annual clinic. I felt nervous. I would equate it to stage fright." Dr. Ryan revealed.

"I love how Meena styled her hair! I've tried several times to talk to her but I suddenly become muted for no reason." Dr. Nimbus revealed a similar experience.

"Lucy's more beautiful than ever…it's good to be back from the moon!" Dr. Ryan concluded before he noticed an African American couple approaching them.

"Gentlemen, long time no see!" An inviting man wearing his formal dress white uniform was surprised to see two longtime friends.

"Harold! Alicia! Great to see you again," Mack felt energized to meet two colleagues he hasn't seen for a long time.

"How you been?" Dr. Nimbus wondered.

"I'm testing these new spacesuits we recently developed. Alicia currently instructs explorers." Dr. Harold Nevins provided their most recent activities.

"Who's working with you now?" Dr. Nimbus wondered.

"I'm working with Dr. Haru Nakamura and Dr. Viktor Ivanov." Dr. Harold Nevins told them.

Dr. Ryan learned the latest news. "I haven't seen Viktor and Haru for years! How have they been?"

"They're great! Everyone here misses you." Dr. Harold Nevins felt rejoiced to see both of them once again.

"I'll never forget the Hoi-Larson Intervention. It seemed like it happened yesterday. It's amazing how six years passed by so fast." Dr. Alicia Nevins told everyone.

Dr. Nimbus noticed both women looking in their direction as they quietly exchanged comments to each other. When Dr. Garcia returned into their conversation, Dr. Nimbus was determined to reveal the news by tapping his right hand on Dr. Ryan's left shoulder to get his attention.

"Mack, don't look over but both of them are looking over and whispering to each another. They may be talking about us?"

Dr. Nimbus showed his subtle smirk of excitement and intrigue while Dr. Ryan's modesty wrestled his enthusiasm. A layer of moisture covered his palms as he used peripheral vision to see both women whispering to each other. Mack's hair rose at the back of his neck when he thought he overheard Lucy saying his name. Mack's body temperature elevated once he saw them giggle quietly and inconspicuously before looking directly at him. His instincts made it possible to turn a blind eye and reengage into the conversation.

Dr. Ryan then heard a soft voice calling for their attention. He looked over his right shoulder and noticed an Asian couple wearing their formal attire waving and calling for their attention as they approached him. A hollow sensation inside Mack's body was felt when he discovered Lucy and Meena escorting them.

"Marcus…Mack!" The Chinese male known as Dr. Fan Zhu praised he arrived.

A sudden numbness was felt in their feet as they felt physically stiff and experienced shortness of breath. Dr. Ryan thought about the best topic to discuss while Dr. Nimbus covered up his usual signs of shyness. Although an upbeat enthusiasm in part of both ladies initially complicated their confidence, Dr. Nimbus subconsciously thought about the best words to say while Dr. Ryan decided to be himself and maintained his professional bearing for Dr. Zhu's initial hospitality.

"Gentlemen…you're back at last! It's great to see you." Dr. Fan Zhu was happy to greet two returning astronauts. "You remember my wife Ying?" He added before she smiled and showed her friendly gesture.

"Of course! I'm glad we're back." Dr. Ryan replied.

"Gentlemen, I wish to introduce you to Drs. Lucy Rosalila and Meena Singh." Dr. Ying Zhu presented to two nervous men who felt that this was one of the most pivotal social event since they've originally met Dr. Netherland.

"We heard so much about you. It's great to meet you." Dr. Nimbus introduced himself enthusiastically.

"It's amazing how you intercepted that wandering asteroid." Both men appreciated Dr. Rosalila's remarks.

"Thanks." Mack smiled.

"I remember the last time I saw you," Lucy told Mack. "It was at the diagnostic center?"

"Oh yes…I remember." Dr. Ryan mumbled.

Dr. Ryan never suspected her to recall his visit so soon. He knew he had to come up with an alternative that would refocus on a new topic to discuss. As their conversation continued Dr. Ramon Garcia reappeared in the main lobby and told the entire group to be prepared to receive their official call to enter the conference room so this historical summit would begin.

Dr. Ryan felt lucky to be interrupted that successfully broke up the conversation as everyone made their way toward a historical meeting. Lucy and Meena talked with each other casually while Mack and Marcus proceeded instantly to the conference room. Once they entered, three men and three women instantly recognized both returning astronauts.

"Marcus! Mack! I can't believe it, it's you," a cheerful voice from one of the six individuals cried out; as both returning space researchers from the Moon were grateful to see them.

This voice was a British accent from a tall blond haired man with blue eyes. His reputation as a long time engineer and a main participant of the Hoi-Larson intervention, earned him a position to direct Engineering. His witty personality and sincere knowledge would be a usual reference to a man by the name of Dr. Stuart "Art" Remington. Born in London, he was intrigued to develop new technology and explore outer space. The same age as Drs. Nimbus and Ryan, he never thought within 35 years of his life that such a summit could ever take place until Dr. Netherland told him about this latest discovery. He also felt this surprise was the greatest experience since his wife Doris accepted his proposal five years ago.

Dr. Doris Remington is a licensed pharmacist and registered nurse born at the outskirts of Sydney, Australia. She missed the Australian outback where she would view the center of the Milky Way galaxy during a clear night. While she used her green eyes to see the shape of the galaxy, it never occurred to her that one of these 200 billion stars in the Milky Way galaxy would have a direct impact in her future. A future she'll learn more about once they enter the main conference room. She adjusted her blond hair as she approached the others with her husband.

"My goodness! It's a pleasure to see you again!" An endearing Dr. Doris Remington was happy to see everyone.

"It's been a long time! I can't believe we're all together once again." Dr. Nimbus cherished such rare gatherings of close colleagues as everyone exchanged their stories.

The Remington's, the Zhu's and the Nevins reengaged their conversation with Drs. al-Saud and Garcia. Drs. Ryan and Nimbus continued to socialize with Drs. Singh and Rosalila. As their talks continued, two more invited guests arrived from the university complex at Papoose Lake, Nevada, where they received the latest news.

Dr. Antonio Marino was born in Rome, Italy and developed extensive skills that earned him a valuable reputation for years. Antonio was muscularly built and worked for Intelligence for over a decade. He groomed his dark hair along with an olive complexion along with brown eyes. He was six feet (1.83m) tall, while his wife Dr. Tracy Marino Tracy stood five feet, seven inches (1.7m) tall and along with a fine physique and gorgeous dark red hair. Her latest style was fashioned short and curved in when her hair reached her shoulders. She stood next to her mentor Dr. Malik al-Saud, who studied medicine since his college years in Saudi Arabia. While their conversation continued, another couple approached the congregation.

He possessed a thin built and a light complexion and grew brown hair along with a thin mustache. He appeared to enjoy the great outdoors and appreciated nature for all the wonders he studied. He also stood six feet (1.83m) tall while his wife was only three inches (7.6cm) shorter. Dr. Ryan then invited

Dr. Arnold Weinstein and his wife Esther into the group conversation. Arnold and Esther were both Jewish and met in Tel-Aviv. He worked for Intelligence for twelve years and currently directs this division of the federation. Arnold was known for his relaxed personality and opened mindedness.

His talented qualities and charm were reasons why his current wife, Dr. Esther Weinstein fell in love with him sixteen years ago and married him two years later. She was well organized and worked for the executive offices of the space federation better known by insiders as the Chamber. She directs and coordinates plans and programs along with Dr. Deborah Reynolds. She always cared for her smooth brown hair that was short and in compliance with the latest trend. Her hazel colored eyes and her light complexion made her appear young rather than a 12 year veteran of headquarters. Like her husband Arnold, she was happy to see two Hoi-Larson heroes back from a long absence from Earth.

"Mack! Marcus! I thought I'll never see you again come over here." Dr. Arnold Weinstein cried out before he embraced his long lost friends.

"I'm glad to see everyone!" Dr. Ryan cried out in return.

"I miss this place, I miss everyone here." Dr. Nimbus acknowledged as he hugged his long time friend.

"You remember Esther?" Dr. Weinstein asked.

"Certainly," Dr. Nimbus responded with his friendly gesture before Dr. Garcia received a signal from Dr. Netherland who stood forty feet (12.2m) away before entering the main conference room where this historic meeting will be conducted.

"Ladies and gentleman, this summit will now commence!" Dr. Garcia announced before curiosity inspired the crowd to enter the main conference room.

All federation members wore their formal dress attire except Secretary General Mobutu, Dr. Garcia, President Wilson and his advisors. Each participant recognized an oval shaped conference table measuring about 100 feet (30.5m) long and ranged up to 40 feet (12.2m) wide, which accommodated fifty seats. President Wilson and Secretary General Mobutu sat next to each other on one end of the table as other guests sat on both long sides. Dr. Donald Netherland who was an official host of this summit, sat at the opposite end of the conference table from where the President and Secretary General were seated.

He planned to use a holographic virtual reality simulation inside a giant white domed shaped conference room to transcend all guests into a virtual simulation of a four dimensional image of the latest information for a select group of attendees. Dr. Netherland inspired the Engineering division to develop this visual illusionary technology that could record events from the

Adam probe and its four detachable planetary terrain rovers known as the Eve probes. President Wilson prided this simulator, which will reveal the data received.

Dr. Nimbus and Dr. Ryan knew that this edition of the Clairvoyance holographic telepresence projector was much more advanced than the cockpit version they recently operated. Once everyone was seated, a single light at the top center of this dome shaped room suddenly turned off before a clear hologram of an extrasolar planet suspended in deep space. This visual display showed details of what the Adam space probe observed. The new world as it appeared three years ago, due to signals taking as much time to reach Earth from its location three light years away.

Dr. Netherland displayed a mild temperament while the entire panel recognized continental land formation. "What you're seeing is the only planet in the known universe that resembles Earth! We finally discovered Earth's fraternal twin."

"Physical characteristics such as geology, atmospheric pressure, weather, and water is compatible to Earth's. What's more is there's no evidence of industrialization or urbanized activities, which was why we're convinced there's no current evidence of any intelligent life we know." Dr. Netherland advised all spectators.

"What's the name of this new planet?" President Wilson asked.

"We originally named it Osiris 4. However, I advise that we call this planet, Isis." Dr. Netherland suggested.

"Isis? That's a perfect name." President Wilson smiled as he agreed because he knew about ancient Egypt and a mythical relationship between two primeval deities known as Osiris and Isis.

"As far as I'm concerned, it's the most appropriate name I could propose." Dr. Mobutu agreed.

Dr. Netherland then, stood up from his seat again before he verbally emphasized his next suggestion to a panel of 50 participants. He emphasized this new discovery as everyone else continued viewed faint points of lights known as stars dominate a 360 degree holographic display of deep space.

Dr. Nimbus rose from his seat when he made visual contact with a potentially habitable planet. Dr. Ryan stood as his doubt of finding such a planet was reconsidered. Dr. Fan Zhu and his wife Ying were captivated to see such a planet while Dr. al-Saud witnessed the greatest achievement since the World Peace and Progress Summit held ten years ago at Geneva. Dr. Weinstein wondered what possible life could live on such an untainted world while Drs. Art Remington and Anthony Marino shared Dr. Weinstein's confidence of this planet's ability to support life.

"Well...this is it!" Dr. Netherland announced as he sat down again.

"What we currently know is that it has two small orbiting moons which makes the planet's rotation about twenty four hours or so. We've discovered three inner planets that range in size from the Moon to Mars, which the second and third planet have boiling atmospheres. What's even more interesting is the fact that there are five larger gaseous planets located on the outer portion of this particular solar system!"

"Why they're such an important contribution to this planet's current condition?" Dr. Mobutu asked Dr. Netherland.

"All Five outer planets act as a shield against incoming asteroids and comets. Their strong gravitational forces would attract and filter out any possible threat to Isis's wildlife."

"Just like when Jupiter intercepted Shoemaker-Levy 9 in 1994." President Wilson replied. "This could be a significant factor of survival to whatever exists on Isis."

"Definitely…the less outside threats you have the less mass extinctions would occur. I'll show you more data." Dr. Netherland offered to reveal more facts.

"How long did the federation knew about this discovery?" Secretary General Mobutu asked.

"This planet you're viewing was originally discovered on September 1st 2023. The orbital space telescope Illuminator was the first device to detect this new world." Dr. Netherland displayed pride of the federation's latest achievement.

"The following year after Osiris 4 was detected, you've sent the Adam and Eve probes?" Dr. Garcia remembered.

"Yes, it took over 10 years for these probes to reach their desired location. Once they've made it, these probes instantly transmitted data back to Earth, which took approximately three years." Dr. Netherland told each panelist around the federation's main conference table.

President Wilson then wondered. "When did the federation initially received data?"

"We began to receive data three weeks ago." Dr. Netherland informed a stunned council. "We're continuing to obtain valuable information regarding this planet's habitability as we speak."

"I heard that the federation ship was upgraded. It is true?" Secretary General Mobutu wanted to know.

Dr. Netherland noticed all of his colleagues leaning over to listen to his next comment. "The Humane Space Federation Starship Guardian was modified to actively transport equipment and personnel between Mars and Earth. However, additional provisions were considered so it could travel long distances at high speed and exceptional hull durability."

"What provisions you're talking about?" President Wilson was surprised of Dr. Netherland's new intentions.

"Before I specify any changes, I wish to show you what inspired us to enhance the ship." Dr. Netherland claimed before he verbally requested "Eve number one."

A clear hologram of this newly discovered planet instantly transformed into a simulated habitat. All participants were intrigued by their telepresence of a grass surface of a continent. Everyone heard sounds of birds and felt a gust of wind blow across the conference table from emitted air originating from behind screened walls. Panelists scented impeccably fresh air as they recognized that they're located where one of the four Eve probes landed, which was at the outskirts of an open prairie of tall grass and weeds dotted with bushels.

As panelists monitored the area, Dr. Ryan noticed a tall batch of shrubs blocking his view of the open prairie. He focused his attention to a tall shrub and became estranged as he suspected to see what appeared to be raspberries accompanied with protective thorns attached to each branch.

"Whoa...these shrubs moved!" Dr. Nimbus observed.

"Maybe it's the wind?" Dr. Ryan thought before he noticed that these shrubs actually tilted in multiple directions "What the hell?"

Other panelists heard their discussion before they focused their full attention to this area. Dr. Nimbus witnessed something move from behind these shrubs. "Whoa...did you see that?"

"I was just about to ask you the same question myself." Dr. Ryan saw something flap from the left side of this batch.

"There's something behind it." Dr. Nimbus emphasized once he saw a long, thick and pointed white horn peeking out the left side of this batch that was positioned roughly 30 feet or over nine meters away from the conference table.

A once mature shrub ripe with berries was toppled over by an enormous animal that used a long thick trunk to grab branches of berries that fell to the ground. Panelists didn't utter a single word when everyone stood from their seats and witnessed a gray skinned elephant-like creature emerge through this shrub. Two flapped ears waved back and forth similar to modern elephants.

A pair of thick, straight tusks that measured 10 feet (3m) long was accompanied by a powerful trunk. Judging from one of four Eve probes physical size and ability to measure an object's size and composition, this browser stood up to 17 feet (5.2m) tall at the shoulder, which is a similar height of an adult female giraffe! This giant walked gently across their simulated view. All eyes stared at such a colossus heading over to bordering woodland where this male could find more leaves, twigs and natural fruit. An abundance of vegetation and tall weeds was necessary to fulfill such an appetite of a maturing male estimated to weigh up to eight tons or 7.2 metric tons, which exceeded the mass of an adult *Tyrannosaurus rex*!

"Who ever wish to identify its species, you may look at your digital display tabloid." Dr. Netherland announced before spectators viewed their own tabloids.

Each digital tabloid in front of them was a result of this Eve probe's built-in Identification Detective device used to trace DNA and skeletal structures of living organisms before conducting a match making process by comparing this particular life form's identity to all available information stored into a massive computer database called Soul Mate. Once Dr. Ryan read his tabloid, he noticed this animal's official species was known as *Palaeoloxodon antiquus*, also known as *Elephas (Palaeoloxodon) antiquus* and commonly referred to as the Straight-tusked elephant. Modern paleontologists discovered the Straight-tusked elephant lived in Europe within the Middle and Late Pleistocene or roughly 781,000 – 50,000 years ago. Despite their moderate sized ears and straight aligned tusks, this giant elephant behaved much like modern Indian Elephants This lone male held close family ties and possessed their own complex language.

"Ladies and gentlemen, you've witnessed the Straight-tusked elephant similar to how they were on Earth hundreds of thousands of years ago." Dr. Netherland demonstrated his pride as this massive male gently walked past the table and headed toward nearby trees.

Dr. Ryan's mouth dried as his heart felt suspended in thin air as he could barely believe he's viewing the most complex life outside Earth. Both men were completely taken by surprise as this male walked into the forest to find an abundance of leaves inside.

Once the prehistoric elephant disappeared from their view, Dr. Netherland stood up to discuss this matter further. "Ladies and gentlemen, I understand how you would feel about such unprecedented circumstances. However, we can't deny the facts. What we're viewing is completely authentic."

"You have any more data?" President Wilson's asked.

"Eve number two." Dr. Netherland responded before he introduced more data.

Spectators recognized a different location near the center of an enlarged plain during the same day. Observers were completely surprised when everyone instantly noticed what appeared to be a horned dinosaur walking over to their simulated position. Panelists subconsciously stood up from their seats as they estimated this female to extend up to 17 feet (5.2m) long with an agile ability to search for food. Dr. Ryan was impressed to see a convex pattern of long spiked horns attached to her neck frill mounted above and behind her head.

The largest horns that extended over three feet (1m) were located at the center of her crest, while shorter horns were sequentially mounted on both sides. Her tough thick skin appeared reminiscent of a Black rhinoceros in Africa.

When Dr. Nimbus viewed his personal display tabloid, he read that this species identified as *Styracosaurus albertensis* migrated across Alberta and Montana during the Late Cretaceous period, which ranged approximately 99,600,000 – 65,000,000 years ago. Dr. Nimbus learned that despite tough plants as their main diet, this horned dinosaur and others were thought to possess powerful jaws capable of slicing through stubs, roots and tubers.

After Dr. Nimbus viewed his digital tabloid, he focused his full attention to this stunning female approaching his seated location. Her enlarged nasal horn and two miniature horns above each eye made her appear fierce especially when observers noticed that her frill eventually revealed a conspicuous surface pattern. Dr. Ryan thought blood accelerating through numerous vessels inside her frill caused this female's frill to swell. A mixture of daylight and rapid blood flow together transformed her neck frill into visible color patterns intended to intimidate potential predators and as a gesture to attract mates.

"Why is this female so intense?" Dr. Nimbus wondered as she used her two nostrils above her toothless beak to sniff the probe.

"I hope she won't destroy it." Dr. Ryan felt concern to lose such an important source of data.

"Don't be worried about the probe. She's more intrigued than agitated." Dr. Netherland revealed.

Styracosaurus tilted her head over to her left side before it shifted over to her right as her eyes twitched. Once this female realized this probe remained stationed, she veered left before approaching a batch of tall bushes. Dr. Ryan looked over to a smiling Dr. Netherland before realizing that he already studied this new data before presenting it to all participants inside the conference room. While all spectators watched *Styracosaurus* walk away, Dr. Ryan glanced over to the opposite direction and was instantly captivated to see a gigantic hornless rhinoceros-like creature with a long neck walking over to their simulated position. "Look at that!"

Once Dr. Nimbus heard his friend's response, he immediately looked over to view this spectacle. "Whoa it's tall!"

Dr. Nimbus's response prompted the others to focus their attention toward a gray skinned herbivore gently walking past the conference table as though all participants are physically present at this location, three years ago when it was recorded. Spectators realized how this adult male was able to stand over 18 feet (5.5m) at the shoulder and was able to lift his four feet (1.2m) long head up to a whopping 26 feet (7.93m) above the ground. Thumping footsteps on the ground proved this remarkable mammal weighed at least 18 tons or 16.2 metric tons.

"Ladies and gentlemen you're witnessing a living resemblance to *Indricotherium*, also known as *Baluchitherium* and *Paraceratherium*. If you would read your tabloid you'll learn that this genus existed in southern Asia during the Oligocene Epoch." Dr. Netherland estimated that *Indricotherium* existed on Earth from 33,900,000 – 23,030,000 years ago.

"I never though we'll ever discover anything like it!" Dr. Nimbus continued to monitor *Indricotherium* for which is an ancient relative to modern rhinos in Africa and Asia.

Dr. Ryan watched as *Styracosaurus* indulging into her chosen batch of bushes nearby while *Indricotherium* walked over to a tree located forty feet (12.2m) ahead. "The skin of both animals resembles a rhino's."

Dr. Netherland heard their discussion. "If you think that's amazing? Keep looking at the same direction."

"What's over there?" Dr. Ryan could barely wait to see what Dr. Netherland already discovered.

Dr. Netherland lifted his left eyebrow and deliriously smirked due to such suspense. "Umm…you'll find out very soon."

Dr. Ryan learned that his mentor didn't want to spoil his surprise as he looked back into the open plain. Once *Styracosaurus* walked away, panelists noticed a heard of giants emerge from a group of trees that blocked their view.

Barely a sound uttered as everyone stood up once again to capture a better view of two female sauropods walking around five miles or eight kilometers per hour. Although one was a bit larger than the other, the larger sauropod dinosaur possessed a neck that stretched up to 24 feet (7.3m) long along with an enlarged tail that extended up to 46 feet (14m) from their 15 feet (4.6m) long torso. The larger female weighed about 15 tons or 13.5 metric tons. Both females appeared similar to one species of sauropods that existed around 150 million years ago or within the Late Jurassic.

As they approached the panelists' view, everyone recognized that their two rear legs were much longer than their two front legs, which tilted their stance down from their rear hips. Their tails appeared stiff from the base and rose up above their hips. Each elongated tail sloped up until its midpoint where it gradually became more flexible. The last 20 feet (6.1m) of their tail length waved randomly in all directions.

Dr. Ryan then read his tabloid before learning that for the first time in his life, he saw *Diplodocus carnegii* alive! His muscles stiffened as all six giants that stood over 20 feet (over 6.1m) tall at their hips migrated gracefully past their main view. Air inside the conference room felt thin as witnesses could see their casting shadows cover open grass. As faint vibrations resonated across the open plain, Mack remembered when fossils of *Diplodocus carnegii* were discovered in Wyoming.

Dr. Ryan thought about a world renowned industrialist and philanthropist known as Andrew Carnegie, who financed an excavation during the nineteenth century in order to fulfill his quest to enlighten the world through education. One interesting fact exhibitionists discovered were their light skeletal frame and a pair of anvil shaped beams at the underside of each vertebra of their tails, for which the phrase; double beam, is an English meaning of *Diplodocus*. Dr. Ryan understood that philanthropists like him made an enormous difference in research.

A grunting vibration echoed across the plains as two of the largest females called out to distant companions. As they continue to trek past everyone's view, Dr. Netherland smiled as he watched four smaller females emerge as they were following the two older sauropods. All six individuals didn't detect the Eve probe and wasn't aware of an audience three light years away.

"This is the greatest news I ever received." Dr. Ryan felt hollow and light as all six bold females continued their migration to greener pastures away from the northern border of the open plain.

"Projector off," were Dr. Netherland's verbal command before the visual panorama was replaced by a second of darkness before a bright light at the center of this domed room reactivated.

President Wilson was almost out of breath when he leaned back on his seat. "I don't know what to say? Based upon the facts you've showed us, I think this planet is remarkable!"

"It's amazing how peaceful this planet could be?" One panelist concluded before Dr. Netherland contracted his lips as he raised his eyebrows as his personal gesture of more facts to reveal.

"Ladies and gentlemen, I wish to show you more data from Eve number three. But before we begin, I wish to inform everyone here that this data I'm about to show you would not be easy to watch. For some, it may be unsettling; for others, it may even be disturbing. Does anyone wish to leave the conference room?"

Once Dr. Netherland received unanimous desires to view more data, he verbally called for "Eve number three," which was located at the southern border of the steppes.

Spectators noticed several impressive vultures identified as *Teratornis merriami* of North America during the Pleistocene epoch (2,588,000 – 11,700 years ago). These giant vultures stood up to five feet tall (1.5m) and stretched their wingspan up to 23 feet (7m) wide. They pecked into a carcass while a group of fearsome carnivores raced out from behind a row of bushes.

Each panelist witnessed 10 powerful mammals with massive skulls, well developed jaw muscles and thick bone dissolving molars. Their average size was six feet (1.83m) long without including their bushy tails. Dr. Nimbus suspected these monstrous marsupials weighed up to 600 pounds or over 272 kilograms.

All of them approached the carcass as a feeding mob, which never established any formal hierarchal relations when they engaged into this feeding frenzy. Pairs of forward facing eyes and wide muzzles made them look and behave like a hybrid between a Tasmanian devil (*Sarcophilus harrisi*) and a Grizzly bear (*Ursus arctos horribilis*). They all possessed powerful neck and shoulder muscles. An Identification Detective device inside this Eve probe identified this genus as *Borhyaena*, which existed in South America (Patagonia) during the Oligocene epoch that lasted from approximately 33,900,000 – 23,030,000 years ago and during the Miocene epoch that ranged from 23,030,000 – 5,332,000 years ago. They stood flat-footed and managed to maneuver rather well despite their stocky limbs. It was most likely that *Borhyaena* ambushed their prey and often searched and scavenged for carrion as well.

Borhyaena belonged to a family group called Borhyaenidae, which means gluttonous hyenas although these ancient marsupials are not related to modern hyenas. This family group ranged in physical size from fox sized carnivores to bear sized mongrels. Marsupials are animals, which each female possess a pouch where their young would be able to suckle inside because of their premature births. These pouches will protect their offspring until they're fully developed.

Panel members were surprised by bold expressions of their powerful physique. Drs. Rosalila and Singh felt that they would be in serious danger if they ever came face to face with such massive meat-eating marsupials of South America's past while Dr. Fan and Ying Zhu were intrigued by how fast they could consume the carcass. Panelists were ever grateful that this image was only holographic, especially when they noticed another group of strange, but frightening looking carnivores approaching them.

"What are they?" Dr. Nimbus wondered as six potential rival predators continued to approach these giant marsupials.

All 10 feeding fanatics were prepared to confront all six powerhouses of the Permian period (280 – 225 million years ago) of South Africa, China and Russia identified as a suborder of therapsid identified as *Gorgonopsia* that's also in the Gorgonopsidae family. They appeared to measure 10 feet (3m) long, which included their short tail that measured only about one foot (30.5cm). Like *Borhyaena*, their heads were large, approximately 30 inches or 2 ½ feet (76cm) long and matched the giant marsupial's terror! Observers noticed a sleek muscular physique. *Gorgonops longifrons* weighed at least 700 pounds (318kg) and possessed pin sharp, flesh shredding teeth as their upper canine teeth measured up to four inches (10cm) long!

They appear to possess some mammalian features such as their legs being tucked under their bodies instead of being slanted out. However, their claws appeared like talons and their forward facing eyes were mounted on the sides of their Komodo dragon shaped heads. Their skin was covered with minute gray scales. Modern paleontologists called them gorgons because their names were derived from a legendary Greek mythical monster known as Gorgona. Her appearance was so dreadful that a person could turn into stone by simply observing their horrible sight. Gorgons were reputed to be one of the most ferocious apex predators to exist before the age of the dinosaurs! Panelists at the opposite side of the conference table stood from their seats, so they could find a better view of this malicious maelstrom.

Psychological tensions escalated as two rival predators grew more antagonistic toward each other. The desire to defeat their carnivorous rival was all they had in common. Various intimidation methods and poise tactics were utilized by both species. Although this stalemate didn't persuade either group to retreat, the 50 panel members felt a deep sense of fear and danger to their impressive size, unparalleled valor and their overt display of pulverizing power! Dr. Ryan knew that rival predators would fight for territory, water holes or kill a competitor's offspring in order to reduce future adversity. He watched this battle over a carcass of an giant herbivore with two giant bony knobs mounted on its snout identified as *Brontops,* which appeared to have died of old age. *Teratornis* made repeated attempts to reclaim the carrion but were fended off by this ferocious feud. Dr. Netherland knew that modern predators and scavengers seek descending vultures in order to pinpoint the exact location of any hidden carcass. He also knew that the largest predators would confiscate carrion from smaller, more agile hunters as an additional means to survive.

A vicarious conviction of each invader and sincere vigilance of all defenders would be perfect ingredients for catastrophe. An adult male *Gorgonops* suddenly lashed out toward a rival *Borhyaena* to provoke a battle. This adult gorgon bit a defending male marsupial across his face that triggered a violent reaction from an infuriated marsupial that successfully freed his head from the provocative protomammal. Another gorgon tackled a female *Borhyaena* before biting her abdominal. *Teratornis* realized it was their best interest to stay away from this cunning clash before spreading their wings for a strong gust of wind to lift them off the ground and glide to nearby trees. Pin sharp teeth of *Gorgonops* and dense molars of *Borhyaena* were used as offensive strike weapons to scar or even kill each other.

Some witnesses turned away as an adult female *Borhyaena* charged against a male gorgon before clamping her jaws into his lower right flank, while others were impressed to see such persistence of both rivals. Dr. Netherland once contemplated how such intensity could last for so long. Disturbing growls, snarls and seething annoyed some members inside the board room while others were fascinated to watch both species rolling and wrestling with each other.

"This is more intense than any conflict we saw at the Serengeti National Park." Dr. Ryan whispered to Dr. Nimbus.

"Imagine viewers watching this on the Discovery Channel or the National Geographic." Dr. Nimbus asked as he could barely notice which species achieved a tactical edge over the other.

Two gorgons managed to slip away from this intense standoff before racing over to the carcass before dunking their heads inside the abdominal and used their teeth vigorously to bite off chunks of flesh. Ten carnivorous marsupials vigorously retaliated against four fighting intruders. Spectators noticed a male and female *Borhyaena* toppled a young *Gorgonops*, causing this male to be disoriented as his back pounded the ground before both defending marsupials aggressively chewed into his chest.

"Deactivate scent." Dr. Netherland verbally commanded the Clairvoyance telepresence projector to suspend its ability to produce a foul odor from the carcass as its audio components continued to emit sounds of rage and pain, while spectators viewed blood seeming through fur and scales of both species.

Once this old male escaped his rivals' relentless assault, he made a wise decision to retreat. Other gorgons immediately recognized their choice before withdrawing from a never ending assault. Dr. Nimbus viewed two remaining invaders with blood soaked heads from the carcass before being ransacked by 10 vindictive marsupials. Both gorgons had no better choice than to flee for their lives.

Borhyaena eventually chased all six invading marauders out of their food domain. Each individual within this defending feeding mob licked their own scars as a natural procedure to heal wounded flesh. All remaining victors wasted no time to race back to the carcass and to aggressively reengage into their feeding frenzy in order to fulfill their appetites before any other rival predators appear.

"Well…if you think you had enough…take a look at this!" Dr. Netherland then requested "Eve number four."

Silence was a result of deep sympathy the panel felt toward an elderly male herbivore the Identification Detective device referred this dignified genus to be *Iguanodon*. This once dominant male stood approximately 16 feet (4.9m) tall as he walked of all four legs and stretched up to 30 feet (9.15m) long and weighed about five tons or 4.5 metric tons. *Iguanodon* was part of a family group called Iguanodontae, which migrated across continents in large herds 100 million years ago or near the end of the Early Cretaceous in Europe, Africa, Asia and North America.

Observers noticed this elder's emerald skin and along with pairs of long bright white stripes ranging from the base of this male's skull to the end of his tail. One pair covered his spine as others marked both sides of his ribs. Panelists suspect mammalian as well as reptilian characteristics of *Iguanodon* as they recognize this elder developed a tough but smooth skin. Since this male's hind legs were twice the size of their fore legs and his thighs were longer than their shins, spectators suspect that this dinosaur is able to run on his rear legs to sprint away from predators.

The Iguanodontae family of dinosaurs was recently discovered to possess a pattern of diverse evolution in surprisingly short periods of time, unlike reptile families such as crocodilians (crocodiles, alligators, caimans and gavials) that remained almost completely unchanged for 250 million years. This family group of dinosaurs showed rapid adaptation in diverse environments.

Various species within this family of Iguonodonts ranged worldwide except South America. This family group even migrated north of the Arctic Circle when Earth possessed a warmer climate. Although no sufficient ice sheets covered this region during the Mesozoic era (225 – 65 million years ago) Iguonodonts most likely migrated south to greener pastures and possessed adaptation features to deal with changing conditions including sparse sunlight during the winter where it would be burdensome for reptiles to adapt to short days and long nights. Although Dr. Ryan never suspected these dinosaurs to possess a physical anatomy like cats or dogs, he suspected they possessed both reptilian and mammalian features similar to cynodonts, which was a group of extinct therapsid reptiles whose spinal chord shifted as they walked and laid eggs similar to reptiles but grew fur, lived in burrows and were active at night that's similar to mammals.

Dr. Nimbus read the tabloid that revealed these herbivores diet of horsetails and various ferns that was most likely located near lakes and rivers. The tabloid also stated that both front legs could function like arms with four appendages this male could use to hold branches along with a solid sharp spike where their opposing thumb would be located. He then read that these solid spikes were most likely used for defense, display for mating and as a means to obtain food. Dr. Nimbus was also impressed to know that *Iguanodon* lived an active social life and communicated often with other members of migrating herds. Everyone soon felt sad as they eventually witnessed a veteran dinosaur collapse for the last time, before he gently rested his head on the ground and exhaled his final breath.

Silence became interrupted by bizarre noises from various directions. Some panelists recognized high pitches while others noticed a low rumble. Snarling, growling, hissing was heard before some spectators saw bright reflective eyes moving behind nearby bushes. Meanwhile other guests discovered sinister looking silhouettes manifesting at the background of their view during a late afternoon sunset.

Observers were able to distinguish hyena shaped mammals appeared from the shroud of nearby bushes to inspect the carcass to ensure this individual has died. Spectators identified this gigantic ancient relative of the spotted hyena as *Percrocuta giganteus*. Dr. Ryan remembered reading about how these ancient hyenas could weigh up to 400 pounds (182kg) or more. They measured up to 10 feet (3m) long and stood five feet (1.5m) above the ground! The larger *Percrocuta* led six of her companions to the carcass. Dr. Nimbus was glad he never encountered them in China during the Miocene epoch or from around 23,030,00 – 5,322,000 years ago when he learned that adults was able to grew up to the size of an adult male lion of Africa (*Panthera leo*). *Percrocuta* developed powerful jaws capable of penetrating bones of elephants, buffaloes and rhinoceroses.

Shortly after, five white and gray colored felines manifested. Each feline showed no concern about the giant hyenas feasting on the carcass due to their own imposing size. The Identification Detective identified this species as *Panthera leo spelaea* that was also known to be the great Cave lion of Europe, Asia, Africa and North America! Dr. Nimbus discovered that they grew up at least 11 feet, 6 inches (3.5m) long, which is estimated to be around 33 percent larger than the largest modern lions. He watched all five individuals indulged to feast the carcass similar to how it was done during the Pleistocene epoch (2,588,000 – 11,700 years ago). European cave paintings revealed an ancient story of the great Cave lion existing up to 2000 years ago in Southeastern Europe.

"Mack...I wonder how our ancestors handled them? There's no way we could've overpowered lions like them during prehistoric times." Marcus whispered.

"The only way is to out smart them by using traps or other weapons such as spears and archery." Mack responded as Dr. Rosalila listened covertly to their discussion and was impressed of how Mack responded.

Restless noise generated by two bitter enemies was one reason why more rival predators were attracted to this location such as three meat eating creodonts that grew larger than any modern rhinoceros or hippopotamus. Late afternoon daylight made it possible for Dr. Ryan to see three humongous carnivores with a head like a wolf and a body shaped like a leopard's that grew elaborate yellow fur along with bright red stripe patterns riddled across their fur. Two young females measured 13 feet (4m) long and an older adult male measured an incredible 16 feet (4.9m) in length! Dr. Nimbus suspected their thick fur was capable of resisting punctures. These heavily built carnivorous mammals stood at least six feet (1.83m) at the shoulder as their heads extended over three feet (1m) long. Each creodont was capable of weighing over a ton or over 900 kilograms.

Dr. Ryan noticed their feet were cushioned and he also recognized that all three curious giants grew thick flattened nails instead of long pointed claws. Panelists recognized that all three individuals appeared similar to what lived in Mongolia during the Eocene epoch or approximately 55,800,000 – 33,900,000 years ago. Dr. Netherland watched all three creodonts racing toward the carcass.

"I can't believe at the size of them! What are they?" Dr. Singh asked Dr. Rosalila.

"My tabloid reads; *Andrewsarchus mongoliensis*." Dr. Nimbus responded to Dr. Singh's inquiry.

As these gigantic creodonts instantly used their massive mouths to clamp down on a mouthful of flesh before employing their body strength to pull back until a piece of flesh tears off. Members of the panel realized that tensions would only escalate as the other two competing scavengers didn't appreciate such intrusive manners of *Andrewsarchus*. Everyone inside the conference room realized that the great Cave lion and the giant spotted hyenas of prehistoric China decided to unleash their resentment toward three mighty marauders of Mongolia!

Feasting was no longer an option for three invading creodonts once a young female *Andrewsarchus* was attacked by two female Cave lions. Spectators were surprised to see this female creodont engaging into this battle before she repelled both Cave lions. The other young female successfully prevented herself from immanent injury from three tormenting hyenas before chasing one of them around the carcass. After a resilient struggle with both rival predators Dr. Ryan noticed the fur of the older male *Andrewsarchus* standing tall on his shoulders before inciting a counter attack. Dr. Remington was grateful for the audio and visual quality of the holographic projector while he continued to see such a fearsome feud between three prized predators of Isis. Such convincing stimulus of visual, audio and scent accuracy along with its ability to produce compatible temperature, wind and daylight transcend conference members to this sight as this clash continued.

Dr. Nimbus remembered *Andrewsarchus* was named after Roy Chapman Andrews, who lead an expedition at Mongolia, which excavated fossil remains of this majestic mammal! He continued to see this sincere struggle between *Andrewsarchus*, *Panthera*, and *Percrocuta* incited concern among all spectators when a giant feline pounced on top of the male creodont's back before biting the rear of his neck. Dr. Ryan watched one of two female creodonts bit the aggressive Cave lion before pulling this female off of her father's back. Once the Cave lion slipped off, the young female instantly chased the marauding Cave lion relentlessly. Dr. Netherland waited patiently to view two species of vultures appear within their field of view. Panel members were impressed to see both species of vultures hovering above. President Wilson read his tabloid to learn that *Teratornis merriami* of North America lived during the Pleistocene epoch or from 2,588,000 – 11,700 years ago, before he read how the larger *Argentavis magnificens* managed to survive in Argentina during the Eocene epoch, which ranged from 55,800,000 – 33,900,000 years ago.

Dr. Nimbus was compelled to see how *Argentavis* managed to stand up to five feet (1.5m) tall and achieved a wingspan of up to a whopping 24 feet (7.3m) wide. Dr. Ryan stared at these animals in absolute awe. Dr. al-Saud never thought he'll ever see such a robust natural habitat as he watch each individual vulture pecking and screeching at each other. Recorded footage from the Clairvoyance telepresence projector suggested that both species of vultures concentrated on specific organs of the carcass. As their bald, featherless heads and necks were soaked with blood one of these giant vultures looked at the opposite direction of the panel before all scavenging birds instinctively fled the carcass by jumping off and flapping their wings frantically to escape a new threat racing toward the carcass.

Dr. Nimbus and Dr. Ryan were surprised to discover a 26 feet (7.93m) long reptile estimated to weigh up to two tons or 1.8 metric tons, which matched the weight of a rhinoceros. The Identification Detective device referred the species of this giant mature male as *Megalania prisca*, which was an ancient relative of the modern Komodo dragon (*Varanus komodoensis*) of Indonesia. Dr. Netherland suspected that *Megalania* possessed multiple types of harmful bacteria inside his saliva, due to their broad diet, which includes germ infested rotten meat. Dr. Singh recognized an intricate mixture of brown and green scales that made him appear like the largest Komodo dragon she ever seen as *Megalania* revealed rows of sharp serrated teeth to reassure his true demeanor!

His neck swelled and before witnesses hear a high pitched seething as a clear warning to all other spectators to stay away from this carcass or they'll ultimately become one. As soon as he delivered his message *Megalania* instantly used his powerful jaws to clamp into raw flesh before swaying and tugging his head to tear off a piece of meat. *Megalania* then lifted his head toward the sky so torn flesh would sink into his mouth. The giant relative of the Komodo dragon conducted this procedure several times similar to how they done it at Australia during the Pleistocene epoch.

Megalania prisca suddenly appeared suspicious of his surroundings once the giant lizard stopped feeding and scanned the area only to discover three creodonts defying his earlier warning as they surrounded *Megalania* to attack! The giant Komodo dragon lifted his massive tail before curving it up and winded it to his left side. *Megalania* swung his tail in response when the *Andrewsarchus* leaped from behind to tackle the giant lizard. Panelist heard this reptilian's tail pound into this young female creodont's body before seeing her lose balance and falling on her side. Dr. Nimbus noticed saliva dripping from the giant lizard's mouth and believed that harmful bacteria were principal ingredients.

Dr. Ryan was impressed to witness such courage in part of *Andrewsarchus* when he noticed all three individuals preparing for another attack. Dr. Nimbus was surprised to see the right side of *Megalania* become slightly wounded. He then discovered the tenacity of the giant reptile as he rolled over to fend off all three attackers. All three creodonts regrouped for their third relentless assault against this respectable reptile.

Megalania felt his body temperature rise and established his new priority to cool off, which was why charged against one of female creodonts. One recovering young female *Andrewsarchus* watched as this huge reptile utilize his superior size and weight in order to run directly over her sibling just before *Megalania* raced toward a river at the right side of everyone's holographic view. Both female creodonts were shaken by their encounter while the fathering male remained unharmed. He caressed his two daughters to reassure their dignity before encouraging his maturing offspring to indulge into the carcass. Secretary General Mobutu read his tabloid to learn that even in the twentieth century, some people claimed to have witnessed massive lizards weighing up to 1000 pounds or over 454 kilograms living in Australia particularly Victoria and Queensland!

This simulated day continued into the early evening as the felines returned for their own piece of their prize. A thunderous call from each ferocious feline warned *Andrewsarchus* to leave the area or be leveled by this prominent pride of Cave lions. All three creodonts wisely consumed as much as they could before more confronting pride members arrived. Once the older male *Andrewsarchus* discovered an opposition of seven females and two giant males ready to attack, he instantly commanded both youngsters to flee. Dr. Ryan was certain that all three creodonts were satisfied, which was why they lost much of their aggression. Although *Andrewsarchus* withdrew from the carcass, a father and his two daughters departed with dignity by gallantly walking away as they grunted their defiance to all nine Cave lions.

Panelists discovered a frenzy feeding in part of *Panthera* to maximize their consumption within the least amount of time. Dr. Netherland understood that most predators or scavengers consume their food source rapidly insure their fulfillment before rival carnivores appear along with their desire to fulfill their appetite to the point of attacking rival carnivores.

An undeniable sense of accomplishment was shared among this pride as they dutifully engaged into a frenzy feeding session that appeared like an internal competition against each other to fill their stomachs first. Although they growled and snarled at each another, Dr. Netherland suspected all pride members to be cautious in injuring each other due to mutual survival because of a large pride population. Dr. Nimbus noticed a familiar group of giant hyenas known as *Percrocuta giganteus* returning to the scene.

Low frequency vibrations were in unison with their deliberate display of bone crushing teeth. Although the giant lions of Africa, India, England and California appeared to satisfy their hunger, none were willing to give up something so valuable without any effort. Twelve clan members warned them for the last time before lowering their heads toward the ground as a sign of an impending attack while their shaggy mane rose from behind their necks.

Dr. Ryan whispered to Dr. Nimbus. "This scene reminds me of a video documentary by the National Geographic."

Dr Ryan realized that when any of Isis's living inhabitants were hungry; their precautions are superseded by a desire to maul a rival regardless of mounting hazards and considerable risk. Before he could interpret what would happen next, both rivals collided into combat! Most observers managed to cope with disturbing footage of a deep seeded hatred among two instinctive adversaries.

Dr. Nimbus saw green pastures of the grass bathed in blood. This bitter feud continued as they used their powerful teeth and jaws as dangerous weapons to wound or even kill a competitor. Dr. Ryan was convinced that an injury would be immanent during this ferocious fight. The female Cave lions decided to move away while the two larger males maintained a defensive stance a little longer before they eventually withdrew from the stalemate.

Miraculously, none of the contenders were seriously injured. The massive felines left diligently while the giant hyenas gorged themselves by consuming this corpse's remains. Although these Cave lions measured at least 11 feet, 6 inches (3.5m) in length and stood five feet (1.5m) at the shoulder, Dr. Ryan learned that sated cats would be described as anything other than a threat toward an orchestrated clan of hungry hyenas! For now the giant spotted hyenas known by the Identification Detective device as *Percrocuta giganteus* mastered their dilemmas just like the same ancient species achieved in China long ago.

"Where exactly this event occurred?" President Wilson asked before Dr. Netherland verbally requested the Clairvoyance telepresence projector to end this simulated scene before everyone noticed a flat map of planet Isis draped across the domed ceiling.

Witnesses noticed three main continental regions. Dr. Ryan noticed one continent at the center of this map that was noticeably larger than the others. This continent matched the size of Europe, Africa and Asia combined.

THE MOMENT OF TRUTH

"All four Eve probes are located at this area of land I refer to as the Central continent." Dr. Netherland used his laser tipped pen for spectators to focus their attention to this massive continent. "As far as I'm concerned, it's the most active habitat known. This is the largest of the three known continents."

"Quite an impressive area of land," Secretary General Mobutu concluded. "We discovered well over 100 planets outside of our solar system and none of them could compare to this.

President Wilson used a handkerchief to wipe off his forehead before leaning back on his seat. "Who would ever suspect to find a planet so lush?"

"I felt the same as you do when I viewed this information for the first time. I've measured this planet's composition; the truth is that we're viewing another Earth.

President Wilson and Secretary General Mobutu paused as they thought about Dr. Netherland's conclusion of this planet's habitability. Participants learned why Dr. Netherland decided to wait until this summit before releasing confirmed data that inspired the Chamber to rethink their original goals. President Wilson took a deep breath after he became convinced that the Mars mission should be suspended indefinitely.

"The Central continent's habitat is more robust than I ever suspected. However, the federation's highest priority is to ensure that every living species on Isis remains a living species and its environment should never be influenced by human activity!" Everyone sympathized to Dr. Netherland's affirmation.

Dr. Ryan noticed Dr. Netherland signaling to the president and secretary general before both men approached him from the other side of the conference table. Dr. Netherland whispered into their ears before he informed other panelists that they will talk outside for a moment.

Once all three men left the conference room, curious whispers echoed across the conference table. Speculation as to what Dr. Netherland would privately tell President Wilson and Secretary General Mobutu manifested inside everyone's mind.

"Mack...what do you thing they're talking about?" Dr. Nimbus wondered since he noticed Dr. Netherland's discreet signal to both distinguished public officials earlier.

"I'm sure he's revealing his strategy to them in order to earn their support." Dr. Ryan felt a strong hunch.

"More probes could be sent to the Central Continent and the other continents as well." Dr. Garcia believed as he studied a flat geographic map of Isis gleaming across a domed ceiling.

"We could only send so many probes. However, if we could program an inconspicuous blood sampling robot then we could obtain precious DNA of most life forms and if a returning space craft could transport these rare molecules back to Earth, then we could decode compatible DNA to Earth's prehistoric life." Dr. al-Saud speculated as gentle whispers intensified.

"I would've never suspected an opportunity like this in a million years. We shouldn't ignore Isis for one minute!" Dr. Art Remington agreed.

"Personally, I can't think of a reason why the Chamber would redirect their attention elsewhere? I'm sure more funds would be appropriated for further research." Dr. Antonio Marino said in conviction as his wife Tracy listened.

Dr. Antonio Marino was also an explorer and possessed similar enthusiasm to his colleagues. His wife Tracy was excited because the Identification Detective device traced and illustrated various molecular strands of every living creature on Isis. She's about the prospect of deciphering DNA codes of Isis's inhabitants and shed new light on the mysteries of Earth's past inhabitants. Isis will establish a new perspective of science like never before!

"With living creatures instead of fossils as our source of information, I'm convinced that science as we know it would never be the same again." Dr. Ryan told his co-panelists.

*   *   *

All three men conveyed outside the conference room before Dr. Netherland guided them down the main corridor. The president and secretary general anticipated a formal proposal of how to explore this new natural wonder further. Both visiting public officials suspected to find out after Dr. Netherland removed a set of keys from his front trouser pocket to open an entrance door.

"Gentlemen, this is it. I'll discuss the federation's latest objectives as well as our preferred options to focus more attention to this new world." Dr. Netherland invited both men inside of an empty room with a small conference table and only eight seats. This 20 x 40 feet room that contained a fifty inch LCD flat screened HDTV attached to a wall.

All three gentlemen took their seats before initiating their discussion. "I can't believe what I saw! We must approve more funds. This has to be the greatest day in my life." Dr. Mobutu's heart pounded his chest as joy raced through his nerves.

"Donald…I could barely contemplate what you just found. I thought finding another Earth can't be done." President Wilson commended his long time friend.

"That's why we must collaborate in order to fulfill our next objective." Dr. Netherland emphasized.

"What objective do you have in mind?" President Wilson anticipated.

"Before we discuss our strategy, I wish to release previously classified information. What you'll about so see was only viewed on a need to know basis."

Dr. Netherland then activated this room's Clairvoyance projector. Although this image lacked an action packed pandemonium of the wild they've experienced inside the main conference room, this new image revealed an exceptionally rare footage, which only a few people within the inner sanctum of the federation know its content. Both men began to view a deserted area of the Nevada desert.

Both men viewed a clear image of Dr. Netherland wearing a blue buttoned shirt and a pair of jeans while standing at a rural area of the Nevada desert. A mild steam of air streaked across the immediate area. A warm sunny afternoon along with a clear sky comforted him while talking toward the camera. Both visitors leaned forward from their seats when they saw something appear above Dr. Netherland.

"What the hell is that?" President Wilson wondered.

"This is our other great accomplishment."

"When was this video made?" President Wilson asked.

Dr. Netherland responded. "This video was made two weeks ago. It's classified as Top Secret and was only known by some Chamber officials.

"Good heavens…I never suspected the federation was able to accomplish such a feat." Secretary General was impressed.

Dr. Netherland then revealed his newest proposal of the federation's strategy of refocusing their attention to this new discovery of Isis. Two former astronauts who currently serve the public had no doubt of Dr. Netherland's credibility. President Wilson knew Dr. Netherland for 25 years and had unshakable faith in him. Secretary General Mobutu admired Dr. Netherland and knew him personally for over two decades and always respected his ideas. Both visitors felt intrigued as Dr. Netherland answered numerous questions regarding tactical details. President Wilson and Secretary General Mobutu ultimately supported his strategic goals.

All three gentlemen used their wristwatch devices called Watchdog, in order to contact leaders of every nation and their ambassadors of the United Nations within a secured global communications network. Secretary General Mobutu provided a combination of codes and verbally set up an emergency meeting at the United Nations while President Wilson verbally sent his message to the United States Senate and House of Representatives.

*   *   *

Dr. Ryan continued to contemplate what all three men talked about outside the conference room. He thought more probes would be sent to unravel DNA (Deoxyribonucleic acids) samples from various animals. He suspected that Adam & Eve would remain at Isis while the federation would send advanced probes to travel across this planet's continents. Dr. Ryan wondered how economically feasible Isis would be while Dr. Nimbus thought about the full extent of life on Isis. Since he saw animals that once lived in various timeframes of Earth's history, he suspected Isis to possess superior air and water quality along with an abundance of vital minerals. Other participants around the conference table just wanted to see more of Dr. Netherland's latest findings when he'll return with the president and secretary general. Drs. Ryan and Nimbus concluded that exploring this planet at its current condition would change the course of human civilization forever knowing that there's more that one Earth in the universe and humanity would no longer be limited to one habitable planet!

Marcus's muscles subconsciously twitched once he saw the entrance door hatch open to let Dr. Netherland and his two colleagues reenter the conference room. Silence replaced excited conversations as all three world leaders took their seats. Secretary General Mobutu noticed everyone's tense desire to know how the federation will respond to this discovery because they believed that all three individuals made a final decision.

"Ladies and gentlemen, may we have your attention please? Dr. Netherland will provide mission directives to the entire panel." President Wilson continued the conference.

"After viewing our latest findings, I'm certain everyone here is convinced that this new planet calls for our full attention to pursue this new discovery further. Before we continue, I wish to show everyone the Humane Space Federation Starship Guardian, which is our latest technological achievement." Dr. Netherland stood up before displaying a confident stance.

Dr. Netherland exerted his verbal command for the conference room's light to turn off before requesting "Guardian." Only a few seconds past before the entire council noticed being suspended in simulated space overlooking Earth's orbit. Spectators around this table noticed rays of light reflect the moon as the sun peeked from behind the right side of Earth from their simulated view. Each participant leaned back on their armchairs as they viewed a giant space ship in orbit being assembled on a space platform.

"Ladies and gentlemen, I wish to present you the Humane Federation Starship Guardian." Dr. Netherland proudly displayed the organization's latest prototype.

People rose from their seats as they observed a clear hologram of a two mile (3.2km) long ship made from carbon nanotubes. Drs. Nimbus and Ryan realized this ship was equipped with multiple engines and reactors. This new model revealed a bronze exterior as sunlight reflected off its surface. Invited guests to this historic summit noticed orbital satellites and other probes attached to the top of the ship. Pairs of sliding trap doors on the roof of this newest model showed where several Transcend orbital shuttle crafts were parked inside.

"In regards to your previous question of specific modifications Mr. President, we've decided to enhance its propulsion system by using antimatter technology. We also equipped it with an agricultural system capable of supporting up to 2000 people. If you look closer to both wings, you'll notice wavelength receptor cells capable of receiving radio waves, infrared, light, and a host of stronger waves such as ultraviolet, and X-rays. Transducer reactors will receive energy from space and convert it into electrical power and remaining energy would aid propulsion. Our hibernation chambers are based upon advanced cryonics."

"Huh...this ship would be able to transport personnel to Mars within weeks instead of almost a year, why would this ship need hibernation chambers?" Dr. Ryan replied.

"This ship isn't destined for Mars!" Dr. Netherland announced before all participants silently leaned forward.

"In regards to the Mars mission, we wish to supersede our original goal and establish our new goal of sending one thousand, five hundred of our most qualified and resourceful people to Isis." Dr. Netherland's told his co-panelists who were instantly overshadowed by this awe inspiring surprise.

Dr. Netherland continued to describe how a perfectly suitable atmosphere of nitrogen, oxygen, and traces of carbon dioxide along with a compatible atmospheric pressure would make Isis an ideal mission for humans to explore. He also explained why terraforming Mars would be postponed.

"When did you expect this new planet to be similar to ours?" President Wilson asked with a smile.

"When we first went to Mars, the original prototype of the Adam probe was tested when we pointed it toward Earth and measured its composition from our orbit around Mars." Dr. Netherland stated. "When the Adam probe entered the fifth planet's orbit around Osiris, the Adam probe then measured atmospheric conditions of Isis and sent us results that confirmed my suspicion of Isis being Earth's fraternal twin!"

"Whoa, that explains why you were convinced of Adam's credibility." Secretary General Mobutu's faith flourished as he read his tabloid that showed how similar Earth's data was in comparison to Isis based upon the Adam probe.

"Once we received initial data from Adam, I knew we had to take appropriate action." Dr. Netherland told his colleagues.

"So you found extra time to modify the ship for deep space travel, that's amazing!" President Wilson laughed.

While everyone felt intrigued by this new challenge, Dr. Garcia performed calculations using his pad, pen and calculator. "Sir, I've made some calculations and estimate that if this ship could travel up to forty percent the speed of light, then if would take at least eight years to arrive and another eight years to return to Earth."

Dr. Netherland acknowledged his advice. "I wish to inform everyone here that who ever choose to travel to Isis would be obligated to settle there permanently."

Nerves twitched while body heat intensified from a rapid flow of blood cells racing through the veins and arteries of all invited guests. Dr. Ryan felt like a hollow balloon once he interpreted his mentor's words. Although he knew Dr. Netherland would not take such a particular discovery like this for granted, he never expected him to pursue this discovery so aggressively. Dr. Nimbus wondered if such a mission was survivable and thought about psychological consequences. However, everyone's muscles tightened as they looked at each other for their response to Dr. Netherland's suggestion.

"Doctor Ryan, I'll need to speak to you privately." Dr. Netherland requested.

Dr. Ryan felt a burning sensation on his skin as he followed him out of the conference room. An empty corridor outside was an appropriate area for their discussion. After he closed the entrance door, Dr. Netherland approached his most trusted protégé and placed his right hand on top of Dr. Ryan's left shoulder.

"Mack, I'm sure you're aware of your reputation and credentials."

"Yes, I am."

"Your contributions were important for humanity and your integrity is imperative." Dr. Netherland added.

"Thank you very much."

"Personally I though this new world would never be discovered in my lifetime. The truth is that we're all fortunate to find such an exceptional planet." Dr. Netherland explained further.

"I agree."

"I'm confident you'll understand what I'll tell you." Dr. Netherland stated before he added. "Mack...this is the most significant challenge to human existence. Let's face it...I'm lucky to be alive to experience this exceptional era of human history."

"I can't conceive anyone who's not excited about another Earth existing." Dr. Ryan agreed.

"I have a proposal for you."

"Yes sir?" Dr. Ryan listened intently.

"You're the best the federation has to offer regarding our next objective. I wish to appoint you as commander of the Humane Space Federation Starship Guardian, which will travel and settle on this new world of Isis." Dr. Ryan listened and interpreted every word Dr. Netherland said.

"I want you to think it over?" Dr. Netherland advised him.

"This mission to the new world has challenges as well as rewards. If anyone refused to go, then I completely understand their concerns and consider their reasons not to travel to Isis." Dr. Netherland maintained an open mind.

"Ever since I received news of this discovery, I feel my life changing for the better. I don't consider this mission to be an ordinary job; I consider it to be the grand purpose of life for a sentient species like us." Dr. Ryan professed before he added; "I'm honored to accept this exceptional role in human history.

"I'm certain your attitude toward this mission will persist." Dr. Netherland reinforced his faith in him.

Dr. Ryan felt a bit tense when Dr. Netherland informed him that he would be commanding officer of the first manned mission to this new world. He then perceived the sparse chances of humanity accomplishing another discovery such as Isis will ever be achieved within his lifetime and despite such unforeseen responsibility of leading this mission; Mack concluded that no other discovery could possibly compare to planet Isis.

Dr. Ryan knew his time has arrived. Less than twenty four hours ago, Dr. Ryan suspected Osiris 4 was a world of liquid hydrogen, helium and methane accompanied with a thick atmosphere of carbon monoxide. He also concluded that planet to be a smaller version of the planet Neptune. What's more Dr. Ryan never suspected any interstellar ship being developed, much less commanding this vessel.

"Let's go back to the conference room." Dr. Netherland led him back into the conference room to rejoin the others.

Once they reentered the main conference room, Dr. Netherland signaled to President Wilson and Secretary General Mobutu before they acknowledged him. Once Dr. Ryan returned, he remained calm, but quiet when he took his seat. Dr. Nimbus looked over to his friend only to experience silence. Dr. Ryan stared into his tabloid and read the information about this unprecedented planet, which prompted Dr. Nimbus to suspect that something important took place outside. As tempting it was for him to ask his colleague for any specific details, he decided to wait until this conference was over.

Dr. Rosalila realized Dr. Ryan's silence and thought he received startling news from Dr. Netherland. She suspected a serious conversation due to their recent departure and seeing Dr. Ryan behaving inconspicuously as he read the tabloid. She tried to analyze what Dr. Netherland could've possibly told him, but since he kept silent, she couldn't find out any possible answers.

Dr. Nimbus looked at him and noticed he was intensely thinking to himself. "Mack, are you alright?"

"Umm...yeah, I'm fine," Dr. Ryan whispered in return, as his friend's suspicion grew.

Dr. Netherland confirmed that humanity is technologically capable of traveling three light years away to another solar system while attached landers will settle on the planet's surface. Revisions and modifications were necessary to prepare this space ship for long distant space travel. The width of the oval shaped main fuselage of the starship was 1320 feet or over 402 meters wide. While the total width of the extended wings stretched up to three quarters of a mile or 3960 feet or around 1.2 kilometers at its widest points.

Dr. Ryan reflected two primeval rulers of the Nile Delta, who've transformed Egyptian society. He remembered Osiris was born from his father Geb, who was worshipped as a god of the Earth and his mother Nut, who was worshipped as a goddess of the sky. He also recalled Osiris becoming lord of the dead as well as the god and presiding judge of the afterlife.

Mack Ryan felt sentimental regarding the star Osiris for which became the first star system the Illuminator studied before discovering an exceptional planet. He also recalled hieroglyphics of the green face of Osiris that symbolized rebirth that instantly become a literal translation of new life at another star system awaiting 1500 chosen Earthlings. Mack learned that the goddess Isis was the beloved sibling and spouse of Osiris as Dr. Netherland displayed his pride for planet Isis, which was named after a goddess of fertility, motherhood and magic. He also claimed planet Isis possessed numerous favorable climatic and topographic conditions that made it possible for life to flourish. Dr. Netherland was excited to realize that the federation will spread human civilization beyond the confines of their celestial birthplace.

"In all my years in science, I never felt such excitement." Dr. Netherland said before he verbally ordered the Clairvoyance telepresence projector to deactivate and reactivate the conference room's lighting.

"We're due for a press conference outside." Dr. Garcia told President Wilson before he led him and the others outside the main conference room.

*   *   *

Excitement and suspense was felt outside the main complex of headquarters. A flock of visiting aircraft parked inside hangars as more continued to land on the main runway. Journalists and broadcast technicians installed their equipment as they anticipated a press release of a lifetime! Scaffolds were erected in order to mount a projection screen to view the contents of Isis. Microphones were carefully positioned while attendants prepared a mahogany conference table and five black leather seats. Uniformed band members tested their musical instruments and made final adjustments for their orchestration.

A row of twelve guards stood on each side of a red carpet that stretched from the main entrance and reached the table and all five chairs. Although the media broadcasted discoveries and breakthroughs in the past, but none could compare to what would soon be revealed to the general public for the first time ever.

"How much time we have left?" One journalist asked.

"One minute." a producer responded before the director signaled to the band's composer to orchestrate traditional folklore music as the first indication of this ceremony's commencement.

Video cameras recorded five distinguished people emerge from the underground facility. As these confident figures walked up the entrance ramp, photographers adjusted their zoom lenses so they could take the best photos. News correspondents attached their microphones on to their blazers before taking their assigned places. Media technicians broadcasted all five historic figures worldwide. Scaffolds were used to suspend a temporary projection screen above and behind the conference table while security forces were positioned to ensure a safe event. Once all five honorary speakers were lined up, the public relations director of the federation will formally introduce all five individuals who would reveal this new age to an estimated three billion viewers worldwide.

"*Ladies and gentlemen, I present the Secretary of Energy, Doctor Julius Ramon Garcia!*" loudspeakers called out his name before a warm applause encouraged the first panelist to sit at the far left seat.

"*Please welcome Secretary General Kufi Mobutu of the United Nations!*" Observers continued to present a humble welcome as Dr. Mobutu proceeded to sit next to Dr. Garcia's left side.

"*Ladies and gentlemen I present President Russell Wilson of the United States.*"

Cheers and waving from observers encouraged the president to acknowledge his warm reception before he eventually sat at the center.

Viewers leaned toward their television set or raised the volume of their radios once all three men congregated. A heat of passion ignited inside all spectators as they heard more names called.

"Please give a warm welcome to the founder and chairman of the Humane Space Federation Doctor Donald Netherland!" Guests and observers cheered as he waved to everyone before sitting next to President Wilson.

"Everyone give a round of applause for the former commander of the Hoi-Larsen Intervention and director of the Lunar Research Center, Doctor Mackenzie Ryan!"

Persistence of gratitude from an appreciative audience provided assurance for him to greet an entire crowd. The temptation to ask Dr. Ryan about the Hoi-Larson experience was felt by most journalists who prepared their lists of questions. Dr. Ryan sat on the last seat at the right side of the conference table next to his mentor Dr. Netherland. A composer suddenly ceased the band's music before President Wilson initiated this presentation.

"My fellow human beings, I wish to share our most remarkable discovery ever. January 17th 2033 is the day we agreed to pursue this new world by selecting our brightest scientists and engineers to travel three light years and land on this planet."

"It's official! 1500 men and women will be carefully chosen to travel across space and bridge humanity into a new settlement age." Journalists were shocked at Dr. Mobutu's verbal agreement.

"The Humane Federation Starship Guardian will be capable of interstellar space travel in less than five months. Were convinced this new planet can support complex life including humans. As the first crew of 1500 departs our solar system, the Humane Space Federation will maintain distant communications and support." Dr. Netherland announced.

"Leave our solar system? Would researchers live there permanently?" One reporter wondered before a deliberate statement from President Wilson was intended to confirm his question from the press.

"That's affirmative! People will settle there for life."

"Mr. President! You're Excellency! Do you mean this planet is just like Earth?" Another reporter shouted out before she asked; "Could that be possible?"

"It's absolutely true!" Dr. Mobutu boldly stated.

"Gentlemen, what name you assigned to this new planet?" A veteran journalist asked this five member panel.

"Since this planet is located in a solitary star system known as Osiris and since it's the fourth closest orbital planet from its parent star, we originally called it Osiris 4." Dr. Netherland announced before saying "We now call this planet, Isis."

"Mr. President, you stated at the White House that there's no convincing evidence of an intelligent extraterrestrial civilization on this planet." Another journalist asked. "What kind of life forms exists?"

"I'll show you." Dr. Netherland then told the public relations director to present their findings.

Daylight of an early afternoon didn't complicate images of raspberry-like berries on shrubs before seeing a gigantic Straight-tusked elephant from England known as *Palaenoloxodon antiquus* browsing near a horned dinosaur identified as *Styracosaurus* from Alberta and Montana. Spectators were also amazed to see *Indricotherium* walking past their view. Dr. Netherland leaned back on his seat anticipating how people would respond once they discovered these 26 feet (8m) tall hornless rhinoceros browsing like a giraffe in order to tear off leaves and branches from the treetops. Spectators couldn't believe seeing a spectacular migration of Late Jurassic giants of North America recognized as *Diplodocus*.

Video airwaves traveled to almost every household on Earth. Newspapers, information pagers, and word of mouth would notify the rest of the world within days. Little thought was required for particular reasons why the Humane Space Federation diverted their original plan of a settlement mission to Mars and preferred to travel all the way to Isis instead. As *Diplodocus* migrated to join another group of companions, observers realized Isis would be the only planet ever discovered where humanity could live without being confined inside space suits or air tight capsules.

Viewers were horrified to see a relentless battle between *Gorgonops* and *Borhyaena*. Many were barely able to view such a disturbing clash over carrion. Graphic details of this event prompted personal safety concerns of settling on this new world as both stout fighters ridiculed their rival's right to consume the carcass. Spectators felt a deep sense of sadness seeing an elderly male *Iguanodon* collapse for the last time. Various participants that scavenged the carcass afterward convinced a civilized world that there's so much more in life than anyone's daily routine and personal pursuit. Observers realize the Central Continent's flourishing megafauna will change their perspective of life!

Once their projection revealed what panelists viewed earlier inside the main conference room, journalists were barely able to believe that such a robust habitat exists outside Earth. When this projection screen became blank once again, Dr. Netherland offered to answer questions from observers.

"Doctor Netherland," a veteran anchorwoman asked. "Since announcing this new discovery, not a word was mentioned about your earlier goals of terraforming Mars?"

"I'm glad you asked that question. Since we received favorable data on Isis's behalf, we cancelled our original plans for Mars and decided to modify the Humane Space Federation Guardian in order to successfully travel out of our solar system using anti-matter propulsion technology designed by Engineering. Doctor Garcia received and evaluated the full report."

Once Dr. Netherland referred to Dr. Garcia, the media focused their attention toward him. "After a careful review of blueprint diagrams and viewed this ship orbiting Earth, I'm convinced that we have the required technology, which includes 1500 proven hibernation chambers capable of long distance travel. All 1500 individuals will be divided into ten shifts while the rest will hibernate. This process will continue until they reach Isis."

Dr. Netherland offered to answer more questions before he selected another journalist. "Sir, when will all 1500 individuals leave Earth for the last time?"

"All selected individuals will be trained intensely for approximately five months before their departure. The federation will maintain a direct private line with the media in order to establish a secured communiqué while I'll personally maintain direct contact with President Wilson, Secretary General Mobutu and other world leaders."

"Doctor Netherland, would you leave Earth and command this interstellar mission to Isis?" A young reporter wondered as he held an electronic notepad waiting for his response.

Dr. Netherland smirked as he chuckled before he responded. "Unfortunately for me, due to my uncompromising obligations to the federation, I must remain on Earth. However, after careful scrutiny, I've chosen Doctor Mackenzie Ryan to successfully lead this mission into a new settlement age."

Representatives of the media asked Dr. Ryan numerous questions. "Ladies and gentlemen I am honored to accept this supreme responsibility and I will be prepared to lead all 1500 scientists, engineers and other personnel to this new world and settle there for the rest of our lives. Although we would always feel homesick for Earth, we will propel the starship Guardian to travel to Isis. *Homo sapiens* will become the first known species to travel across space and become an interstellar civilization! I've selected Doctor Marcus Nimbus to be vice commander of our mission, who'll assure our mission's success."

Dr. Netherland approved Dr. Ryan's decision before journalists made initial contact with studio executives and editors. As all five panelists rose from their seats, journalists continued to present their report and broadcasted their news of a discovery that was once thought to be impossible or even ludicrous.

By the end of the day, almost the entire world would learn and become part of an unprecedented time in human history. All distinguished gentlemen at the press table knew very well that billions of people are observing this event. By the time all questions were answered, all five panelists stood up from their seats before greeting willful supporters and close friends as humanity enters an Era of Isis!

FAREWELL TRUE GUARDIAN

A deliberate smirk of Dr. Ryan's reflection in a mirror showed relief after five months of intense training. He also appreciated quiet moments inside a dressing room where he pinned on his last medal on his chest. A soft ringing inside his ear proved to be a temporal haven from the media and ever excruciating demands from the Chamber. After months of brainstorming, a subtle moment reassured his confidence as he placed a silver, star shaped pin above his rows of medals. When a wall mirror reflected a man wearing his formal attire, Dr. Ryan reflected his life on Earth.

Intense training included observing images of various herbivores and predators of the Central Continent of Isis. The Identification Detective devices attached to each Eve probe made it possible to observe various animals conducting their daily activities. All data from Adam and Eve probes were permanently stored in memory banks for future study. The federation learned new strategies to adapt to this new environment despite this planet's similarities to Earth.

Dr. Ryan continued to learn what was required to lead a unique role in federation history. Dr. Lucy Rosalila remained receptive to Mack's opinions for the last five months and appreciated his qualities and personality. She was confident of Dr. Ryan's psychological profile and professional attitude. Although she was part of the medical staff known as medics, she reported directly to the Chamber by providing confidential analysis of each potential candidate.

Lucy thought about her Mesoamerican ancestry, which included the Aztecs, the Mayans, the Zapotecs and the Olmecs as well. Although her ancestors including the Hopi people possessed an uncompromising desire to explore the cosmos, she never thought she'll participate in such an assignment that would literally take her to one of these points of light dotted across the sky.

Dr. Ryan lost 15 pounds and felt younger as he buttoned the top button of his blazer revealing his physical accomplishment. Dr. Rosalila noticed how he focused most of his attention to his rigorous workout schedule and intense studies. Lucy listened to Mack speaking to the mirror as a means to prepare for another press briefing. She peeked inside his dressing room with curiosity as he inserted both hands into a pair of white cotton gloves. She gently knocked on the opened door.

"Mack?"

"Hi Lucy!"

"You're preoccupied?"

"No, not at all…please enter."

Dr. Rosalila walked inside as he looked into the wall mirror before adjusting his bottom row of medals on both sides of his chest before straightening out his neck collar attached to the top of his double breasted blazer. "You look great. You're ready for the press conference?"

"Yes. Today's an important day for all of us."

"I agree. President Wilson and Secretary General Mobutu are here along with the media."

"It seems like I just saw them yesterday." Dr. Ryan reflected his experience at the summit five months ago.

As they continued to talk, both heard someone else knock. "Doctor Ryan, the media's ready…hello Doctor Rosalila."

Dr. Ryan took a deep breath. "Well, this is it."

Dr. Rosalila stared at Dr. Netherland leading Mack out of the dressing room before she said, "good luck."

Both men walked through a hallway before they encountered President Wilson, Dr. Ramon Garcia and Secretary General Mobutu. All five gentlemen exchanged their excitement and were ready to walk through a nearby door that led them on a stage. Once the pair of swinging doors hatched open, a congregation of news correspondents and technicians provided a warm applause when they approached an oval conference table with five seats placed behind the table.

Dr. Ryan took his seat at the audience's right view of a mahogany table as Dr. Netherland sat next to him. President Wilson sat at the center while Secretary General Mobutu sat next to the president and Dr. Garcia sat at the far left side of the conference table. Dr. Ryan received a signal from Dr. Netherland to initiate this press conference before he stood up from his seat and approached a podium with a microphone. Holding a wide screen palm pilot provided by Dr. Netherland, Mack gracefully approached the podium as journalists leaned forward from their seats anticipating his speech. Dr. Netherland leaned back on his seat showing his pride of an astronaut standing on stage.

"Ladies and gentlemen, friends and acquaintances, five months ago the world received the most fascinating news ever announced in human history! Only one day before this official discovery, none of us ever believed an Earth analog existed outside of our solar system. Ever since we recognized Isis's existence our basic concepts of the universe has altered forever. Modern science has developed a new perspective, while humanity will continue this new era with open mindedness and understanding."

Silence inside the assembly room of the Humane Space Federation's headquarters at Groom Lake, Nevada persisted until media journalists and reporters aggressively injected more questions regarding their mission to Isis. "Doctor Ryan, how many life forms on Isis resembled Earth's prehistoric life?

"The most compelling fact is that we've discovered dozens of life forms resembling Earth's extinct inhabitants and some even appear similar to Earth's living specimens such as, insects, lizards, snakes, birds and small mammals."

"We know that Isis is a world untainted by human activity. How will the federation prevent environmental damage due to human habitation?" Another reporter asked.

"Utilizing the most environmentally friendly technology and applications are mandatory in this mission. Gas emissions would be forbidden along with hunting activities. Our latest technology would be a technological leapfrog because fossil fuels such as coal, oil and gas would not be pursued. All types of waste would be recycled and pollution would be curtailed. Our environmental impact on Earth should warn us that our mistakes on Earth shouldn't be repeated on Isis."

"Doctor Ryan, how do you feel about not coming back to Earth ever again and what strategy you will endure to settle on Isis permanently?" Another veteran journalist asked.

"I will miss everyone here. I'll miss Secretary General Mobutu, President Wilson, Doctor Garcia and all of my colleagues and acquaintances especially Doctor Netherland. However, I know that I won't travel three light years alone. I'll be accompanied by some of the most reliable and assuring individuals anywhere."

"Doctor Ryan, how can you assure us that the safety of the crew including yourself can survive in such an unpredictable environment?" A young reporter asked.

"All four Eve probes provided sufficient awareness of what's out there. We're learning survival techniques on an extrasolar planet from the brightest experts. What's more we're learning how to overcome loneliness and prevent space madness," Dr. Ryan told and intrigued group of honorary guests. "We're ever more certain that by observing modern living relatives on Earth and evaluating the facts collected from all four Eve probes would make it possible for us to make educated decisions, which would reassure not only our survival, but our prosperity as well."

Once Dr. Ryan answered his question, a young female captured his attention as she waited patiently to be called. "You mentioned before that you had environmental friendly technology to protect Isis's environment. What are they?"

"Engineering developed a personal transporter called Drifter, which emits no exhaust fumes and is capable of traveling over 70 miles or over 112 kilometers per hour in an event that we're ever pursued by any potential danger. The Feral Sentry device that could be carried or attached to each Drifter transporter is designed to emit various frequencies that could complicate or even repel most attacks by producing repugnant signals undetectable by humans, which is not lethal and causes no permanent harm to any animal. I also advise that all landers will not settle anywhere if it disrupts natural activities such as migrations. Our principal goal is to never interfere with nature's way." Journalists and other spectators appreciated Dr. Ryan's pledge.

Dr. Ryan then reassured his faith in this mission to all who observed his presentation live or via satellite network. The world then learned more about a flagship made by Carbon nanotubes similar to the composition of an elongated cable used for the space elevator that's being designed by the federation's Megaprojects Development Center at Kapustin Yar located in Astrakhan Oblast, at southern Russia. This interstellar ship that was designed there as well, extended two miles or 3.2 kilometers long, while much of the surface contained protected solar power and frequency range receptors.

"Doctor Ryan, what are your final words?"

He paused for a moment of silence. "First I wish the entire world all the best in peace, security and prosperity. Although we won't be able to physically be with you anymore, we'll always maintain communications by using a device called Mercury one. This newest prototype could teletransport light into a receiving model on Earth, while the federation possess a similar model that would send light signals to our receiving unit. It'll send and receive light patterns similar to a nineteenth century telegraph. It would teletransport light patterns and instantaneously receives and deciphers sequential signals before a decoder would translate it into any written language. May all forms of goodness prevail on Earth and God bless humanity."

Once his presentation ended, Dr. Ryan received a standing ovation from all spectators inside the assembly room including his colleagues on stage. He acknowledged this warm response by waving to a joyous crowd. Once he made his last acknowledgement, Dr. Netherland then stood up and approached Dr. Ryan.

"Great speech…congratulations!"

"Thank you sir." Dr. Ryan said and felt grateful.

"I'll meet you back outside within a half an hour." Dr. Netherland asked him.

"Certainly," Dr. Ryan agreed before leaving the assembly room and proceeded to his living quarters to prepare for his formal departure. After packing essential supplies and valuable belongings, Dr. Ryan left his temporary living quarters for the last time, he noticed four men approaching him as he closed the entrance door.

"Mack, I'm glad I could see all four of you together." Dr. Netherland told him before Dr. Ryan followed him along with Dr. Nimbus, as well as Drs. Derrick Grace and Karl Gruber into a control room adjoined to the main lobby.

All five individuals wore their formal dress white attire as they contemplated their departure. Dr. Netherland carried a small attaché case as all five gentlemen entered the room. Dr. Netherland suddenly raised his small attaché case before he placed it on a countertop. He opened it before removing four keys. Three of them appeared identical but the fourth one was noticeably larger and distinctive.

"Here they are gentlemen." Dr. Netherland stated as he handed out each of these four keys to each individual.

All three identical keys were distributed to Drs. Nimbus, Gruber and Grace. The fourth key was given to Dr. Ryan before the palm of Dr. Netherland right hand embraced Mack's left shoulder. Dr. Ryan suspected that his mentor made a special arrangement regarding a role for these four keys.

"These keys contain microscopic disks inserted inside. They're the only keys in the world that could open a heavily armored safe inside a guarded vault room aboard the Starship Guardian." All four men acknowledged Dr. Netherland's instructions.

"All three identical keys must be inserted into their respective locks and turned simultaneously to open a single vault where Dr. Ryan's key will be stored. Your key will then open another vault, which a memory disk will be stored inside. This memory disk could be played on either a holographic projector or any disk player on board the starship. Miniature prongs would emerge at the side and tip of each key in order to open each vault. There's a guest list of everyone who must attend this assembly according to mission directives available at the command and control center." Dr. Netherland instructed them.

"Sir…what does this disk contain?" Dr. Ryan wondered.

"You'll find out in the future. Be advised that X-rays inside the vault containing the disk would destroy it if anyone attempts to open any vault before its scheduled moment." Dr. Netherland said.

"Heavens forbid, what if any of us couldn't be physically present at this event?" Dr. Grace wondered.

"The fourth and last vault was programmed to open automatically at a certain time in the future if the original objective can't be accomplished. Inside the fourth vault has alternate information stored inside another memory disk inside. Once that door opens, vault number three's disk will be destroyed by X-rays. Dr. Nimbus, the instructions pertained on the other disk would be exclusively made for you if the disk in vault number three is gone." All four men heard from Dr. Netherland before he led them out of the room and into the main lobby.

Five men entering the lobby appreciated inviting sounds of applause and whistles. The crowd once randomly scattered inside approached and joined all five of them. A graceful smile of Dr. Netherland, Secretary General Mobutu and President Wilson were a delight for all who will depart mother Earth for a historical journey to Aunt Isis!

Dr. Ryan remembered a cherished custom of the federation for all working crews to form a complete circle before every mission; regardless how many astronauts/cosmonauts will participate. Dr. Ryan usually calls for this circle of scientists and engineers to initiate an expression of teamwork and interdependency. The entire crew eventually stood next to each other, held each other's hands and formed a complete circle that surrounded the mounted boulder. They focused their attention toward what remained of Hoi-Larson before closing their eyes and bowing their heads in complete silence.

This bow of silence lasted a few minutes. Silence was soon replaced with a soft exchange of words once they raised their heads. Dr. Nimbus noticed two men and a woman entering the lobby from outside. All three coordinators will direct each person to depart the lobby before journalists greet each pioneer as they'll walk between rows of people on both sides. A red carpet will lead to one of 10 orbital space planes parked at the flight line. Excited spectators were relentlessly seeking to view all 1500 departing representatives of Earth. Once a commentator announces the name of each individual over a loud speaker, than he or she will walk outside. All three coordinators lined up every individual before their names were called.

A voice emitting from loud speakers announced the first name before Dr. Netherland embraced the departing individual before she left the lobby and walked on a red carpet. As more names were called, an ambitious cheering crowd whistles and waved while more ascending astronauts emerged from inside headquarters. Dr. Netherland appreciated all the smiles, laughter and waving hands seen everywhere. An awe-inspired feeling from the general public propelled more astronauts and cosmonauts to emerge before acknowledging the world's desire to greet all who'll propel the human race into an interstellar civilization. Dr. Netherland is proud to know that humans will become the only species in Earth's history to travel to another solar system.

"*Doctor Marcus Nimbus*" was called over the loudspeaker, which prompted Dr. Ryan to place his left hand on Marcus's right shoulder as he shook his best friend's hand.

Before Dr. Nimbus departed, Dr. Netherland bestowed his best wishes. "Doctor Nimbus you'll succeed Doctor Ryan if he's no longer able to command! I wish you all the best!"

Dr. Netherland embraced his protégé. "God bless you!"

Once both gentlemen separated, Dr. Nimbus gracefully walked outside before a tidal force of applause and vocal cheer echoed inside where Dr. Ryan and his mentor faced each other while President Wilson and Secretary General Mobutu looked on. "Mack, it's very difficult for me to see you, Marcus and the others leave for the last time. I will miss you dearly. This is one of the most difficult situations I'll experience for a long time!"

"This situation isn't easy for me either. I never told you this, but when you've gone to Mars, I've admired you ever since."

"Everyone at the Chamber honor you! Personally I'm convinced that you, Marcus and the others are among the best candidates the federation could appoint." Dr. Ryan heard encouraging words from Dr. Netherland before they hugged each other as their bold expression of an integral personal bond between an altruistic mentor and a loyal protégé that would never be severed by distance and time!

Once Dr. Ryan's name was called from the loudspeaker, he instantly felt a bit of reluctance to physically let Dr. Netherland go. As soon Dr. Ryan physically released his role model he embraced President Wilson before he hugged a sobbing Dr. Mobutu. Dr. Ryan subtly walked away before he looked over his left shoulder to see all three men with his naked eyes before departing. Such a cheerful expression of Dr. Netherland's face proved that long years of mentorship proved worthy while Mack became an instant role model for the world. Secretary General Mobutu and President Wilson have immense confidence in every participant who's receiving one last hurrah from society.

June 18th 2033 will be Dr. Ryan's last ordinary day. What he once accepted as a cultural norm will ultimately be challenged. Due to limited communications with humanity, he thought how it circumstances would be if he settled on the most geographically isolated place on Earth. Mack wondered how he'll experience breathing air of another planet and drinking its water. He realized that life as he knew it would not be the same again.

Emotions grew as Dr. Ryan was the last person to walk down the red carpet. Dr. Netherland, President Wilson and Secretary General Mobutu remained inside the main lobby as Dr. Ryan continued to receive praise from people standing on both sides of the red carpet. Once he walked up the aluminum steps, his overt wave captivated the public one last time before boarding one of ten space planes that will transport 1500 people to the orbiting ship.

Since orbital space planes were developed, people no longer have to lie flat on their backs and face directly up before launching. Passengers are accommodated similar to traveling on a commercial airliner. These prototypes could transport up to 300 passengers and cargo from Los Angeles to Tokyo within three hours. A conservative estimate of four hours before their arrival prompted him to think this flight would not be like any other passenger flight. He understood that once the space plane departs this runway he'll never stand on Earth again!

Broadcast airwaves continued to saturate the Earth's atmosphere when Dr. Ryan entered the space plane and disappeared from the public's view. Dr. Ryan felt a strong sensation as he thought about walking on the surface of a world with its Ozone layer intact along with the freshest air and cleanest water conceivable. Mack's chest tightened as he thought about looking up into a cobalt blue sky while he feels a steady cross breeze pressing against his body while listening to gentle waves meeting the shore and gentle rays of light emitting from Osiris reflect off his face. Dr. Ryan thought about how life would be living on a fraternal twin of a cherished planet that cradled his existence.

When crew members fastened their seatbelts, Dr. Ryan realized that had it not been for the Earth, mentors like Dr. Netherland and true friends like Dr. Nimbus, then all of his historic achievements of the Hoi-Larson Intervention and developing the lunar research center would've never happened. When all orbital space planes lifted off the runway, a modern symbolic moment of pioneers leaving their sheltered nests were felt and shared among all eight billion people all over the world including the lunar research center. Once occupants inside each orbital space plane felt additional gravity as they ascended up into the sky, everyone either viewed personal photographs of family and friends or used one of their telephones to call family, friends and acquaintances while leaving the Earth.

"Well Mack, this is it. Months of intense training finally led us to this moment." Dr. Nimbus announced.

"I was thinking of a typical late afternoon view of the sky of Isis. I could barely imagine what it would be like to see Osiris descend beyond the horizon." Mack wondered.

"I know what you mean," Marcus responded. "I'm thinking about viewing cirrus clouds directly above and some stratus clouds meeting the horizon."

"Both the Adam and Eve probes repeatedly indicated that Isis Mediterranean climate is similar to southern California and northern Mexico.

"I'm thinking how bright the stars would be on a clear night on Isis." Mack professed is curiosity. "You'll think you're able to touch them."

"I'm excited to find out how our sun would appear as a distant star." Marcus cherished his though. "I would be fascinating to see our own sun looking like a tiny point of light in the sky and reflecting the fact that despite our sun appearing like any other star, that point of light is the reason for our being."

"I think for the first few weeks we'll subconsciously confuse our settlement location as a place on Earth." Mack said as he detected the space plane's speed declining.

When each orbital space plane approached the Humane Space Federation Starship Guardian, the main propulsion rockets ceased and retrorockets activated to prepare the passenger transport plane to dock. Propulsion engines managed to position each transporter to successfully dock into an entry port of this flagship. When the air pressure inside the space place and orbital starship matched the space plane's hatch opened. The crew then detached their seatbelts before taking their necessary belongings and approached an exit. Airtight ensured both ships maintained their oxygen supply as the artificial gravity mechanism made it easier and even pleasurable to stand up.

"Okay, everybody ready?" Dr. Ryan asked before he received a favorable response before he became the first individual of the entire crew to enter the Humane Federation Starship Guardian.

After each crewmember entered the star ship, Mack never suspected such a contemporary design. He learned that all living quarters and laboratories were accommodating. An artificial gravity field generated from numerous floor rods was compatible to Earth's. These artificial gravity generators produce 99 percent of the Earth's native gravitational strength in order to comply with the crew's physical and psychological needs.

No other spacecraft in human history enticed a congregation of pioneers. Their entertainment needs were addressed by possessing data of every single movie and sitcom episode ever created in human history. The crew was able to view any sporting event within the last 80 years of broadcasting history. Scientific research presentations stored inside the computer memory banks ranged from astronomy to zoology. Crew members were impressed to see demonstrations of various holographic stage show studios designed to view Broadway shows and concerts. Another way to enjoy their leisure time is to view events using the Clairvoyance telepresence projector. Similar to the main conference room at headquarters, any individual can verbally request to be completely surrounded by a high definition virtual reality supplied by each Eve probe.

Although entertainment and recreation could help prevent loneliness and boredom, workplace instruments were never more advanced. Some equipment was new such as Mercury One, which would be the first interstellar communications system. All four planetary landers were attached to the main ship that was capable of commuting passengers and equipment between, a planet and the flagship. What's more was that each lander could rest on almost any terrain including water. What's more is they could accommodate up to 300 settlers comfortably. Each lander will be converted to the original settlement center known as Town Hall. Designers, builders, and technicians inspected all components as additional orbital space planes continued to take their turn to dock and unload passengers into the starship. As scientists and technicians boarded the vessel, inspectors debriefed all travelers regarding numerous features and safety advice.

Hibernation chambers based upon modern cryonics were shown how it's used and when to use all 1500 capsules aligned in aisles. Each crewmember was issued a times table of when and which chamber to use. Living quarters were designed to make any crewmember feel at home. Physical fitness facilities were readily available, while the vitamin rich oval tablets would supply all necessary nutrients to maintain maximum physical energy. What's more is each capsule could fulfill the crew's appetites.

As for personal hygiene, recycled water would be the main reason why scientists will use a soap solution that would use body sweat as a resource instead of spring water to remove any form of bacteria and undesirable elements. Various water vacuums located inside shower stalls were designed to remove suds and clear the skin of any unwanted dirt. Mucus is then trapped into a compartment until it's full before they would be used for carbonated fuels. An invention called Aqua-Spring was developed to desalt, detoxify and recycle fresh water from any substance including urine. Carbonate containers could use manure as a means to help fertilize planted vegetation on board.

Fire safety is a priority for all inspectors who demonstrated a new central fire safety system called Air Thief. Receptors located in every single room of the starship will detect fumes or smoke. A loud room alarm with a flashing light will be activated to warn occupants to leave the area. Twenty seconds later, each entrance equipped with a regular door also has an airtight slide doorway that will close and seal. All slide doors and its sealant mechanism will be used for emergencies only. Vents inside each room will suddenly extract oxygen from any ignited room causing the fire to cease. Conditions inside a room will remain until a fire technician arrives to the emergency area to deactivate the Air Thief. If anyone is trapped inside, then there are assigned air masks, which could prevent smoke inhalation and supply life saving air. These devices are located inside every room of the ship.

The finest medical doctors, surgeons and nurses were necessary to operate an on board hospital and clinics. Onboard emergency response personnel were trained to rescue and recovery. Dr. Ryan noticed a red line drawn on the floor of all corridors, halls, and passageways. If an emergency ever occurred that particular line would be used to guide gurneys. All new occupants were trained and drilled to place themselves against a wall so emergency personnel can pass through. This procedure will last until the main alarm and flashing lights are deactivated.

Dr. Ryan endured himself to feel such ultimate freedom as he inspected the starship with Dr. Nimbus who shared similar views. Drs. Arnold and Esther Weinstein appreciated its fire proof wall paneling while Drs. Martin and Angela de la Vega were pleased to know of all amenities. Dr. Ying Zhu and her husband Fan liked the air quality inside the ship. Drs. Antonio and Tracy Marino felt their hopes come alive, while Drs. Art and Doris Remington were impressed with numerous safety features. Drs. Malik and Ada al-Saud were confident of this ship's technical abilities while engineers conducted final tests before relinquishing full command and control of this starship to its permanent occupants.

Once everyone was officially on board the starship, their first task was to meet and place their designated key into an assigned safe inside the vault room. Drs. Nimbus and Ryan gathered Drs. Gruber and Grace. Dr. Nimbus directed the others down a long corridor until they approached two tall security guards standing on each side of a reinforced steel vault door.

"Hello gentlemen." One of the guards acknowledged them.

"How are you Mike?"

"Fine, how are you?"

"I can't feel any better," were the words of Dr. Nimbus as Mike's partner Dave pressed a series of buttons on a panel attached to the right side of the stainless steel frame.

Dave dialed a code before he opened a door that was one foot (30cm) thick. When the door was opened, Dave's next task was to use one of his keys to slide open a barrier gate. A center ceiling light activated once Dave opened the gate and entered a small room with four small vault doors left ajar. Mike waited until everyone entered the vault room before he guided their attention to all four opened vaults that would conduct an imperative role in this mission. He requested all witnesses present when he placed one memory disk inside a protective cubical container. Mike placed the container inside safe #3. Dr. Ryan utilized his specialized key to lock safe #3. Mike also closed safe #4 that contained another disk inside a storage case.

Dr. Ryan placed his key inside a protective case before placing it inside safe #2. Drs. Nimbus, Grace and Gruber used their identical keys to lock this vault simultaneously. Once safe #2 was secure, all three men placed their keys inside their cases with their individual names printed on them. Once all three keys were placed inside vault #1, Mike then closed vault #1.

"Gentlemen, Doctor Ryan's key would open either vault number three or four when the designated time arrives. His key is not capable of opening both vaults. The vault that will be opened contains the playable disk while the other disk will be destroyed inside the sealed vault by X-rays." Mike advised all participants.

Mike guided them out of the vault room before the ceiling light deactivated. When everyone departed, they heard a heavy sliding gate and strong impact of a vault door closing. All four gentlemen walked through this corridor until they arrived at the other side, where they entered the command and control center. Crew members felt subtle vibrations as the interstellar ship propelled ahead for the first time. Dr. Ryan sat on the command seat while Dr. Nimbus was sat ahead of him. Four specialists sat alongside Dr. Nimbus who propelled the ship to leave Earth's orbit. Silent emotions were a common expression when departing emigrants saw their precious view of the Earth one last time!

"Mack! I'll miss you always! The Chamber will miss all of you on board." Dr. Netherland said over a LCD screen.

"God bless you always," were the soft sobbing words from Dr. Ryan before he saw Dr. Netherland's image disappear from his miniature screen of his Watchdog device!

Besides the most advanced technology inside of the most conforming spaceship ever built, Dr Ryan learned about the human potential that founded the Humane Space Federation and created an interstellar ship. He realized that the human potential also supplied 1500 of the finest men and women to travel to this new world. He was grateful of their extensive education and considerable training, and experience. Although Dr. Ryan has a tough time contemplating how humanity's distant ancestors managed to survive and thrive, he often felt indebted to his ancestors for making it possible for him to exist. He thought about how he'll handle similar circumstances his distant ancestors experienced when he arrives on Isis.

"Headquarters, come in headquarters, starship Guardian will make our final orbit around Earth, over?" Dr. Ryan announced over a microphone and being viewed by a video camera inside the command and control center.

"*This is headquarters, over.*" The voice over a radio communicator responded.

"The federation starship is on course." Dr. Ryan informed them over his communicator.

"*You're ready for take off! On behalf of Earth, the Federation wishes you to live long and happy always and forever!*" An affirmed and subtle voice stated before the crew paused for a moment before closing their eyes and gently bowing their heads.

Video monitors on board displayed numerous channels broadcasting live footage of people at various places worldwide waving a loving farewell to all who looked out of a window to see a planet full of friends. A full circle of the Earth's orbit was a final gesture before leaving the confines of their nest to travel into unknown territory on their own. Conditions were silent, while deep breathing and occasional tears traveled down their faces of the crew. The departing crew felt as though they were brave universal citizens who've undergone a tedious challenge of departing mother Earth.

For as long as he could remember, Dr. Nimbus fantasized what it would really be like to walk next to living specimens of Earth's dynamic past. He only dreamed of witnessing such evolutionary elegance in action inside forests, steppes, seas, and plains. He understood that even the highest mountain summits and the deepest ocean floor were no exception of being a part of Earth's natural art, which continues to inspire human creativity. For all selected individuals who'll travel to planet Isis will be privileged to be able to experience the past and the future being one and the same!

"Well, I hope nobody forgot anything?" Dr. Nimbus chuckled as his colleagues appreciated his uncompromising humor.

A mild jolt transcended the Starship Guardian beyond Earth's orbit and pursued its first objective; Jupiter. Although, Dr. Nimbus and Dr. Ryan knew that penetrating the asteroid belt that orbits the sun between Mars and Jupiter inherits certain risks; however, the vast majority of asteroids and meteors are millions of miles away from each other and all individual boulders would be located and illustrated to navigators so the ship could avoid collision.

Drs. Lucy Rosalila and Meena Singh whispered to each other inside the command and control center, where Mack and Marcus tested computer terminals. Both women wanted to inform them of their true feelings they had for two veterans operating an interstellar ship. Unfortunately they couldn't decide when to reveal their secret and had no clue of how Mack or Marcus would react if they were ever informed.

Drs. Harold and Alicia Nevins were communicating with headquarters by providing information regarding the ship's condition and propulsion. Intelligence reported to their assigned work places while Engineering arrived at various laboratories and propulsion rooms. Dr. al-Saud called Dr. Ryan and informed him that the onboard hospital is ready.

"Mack, Marcus…can we both join you?" Meena asked them with Lucy standing next to her looking on to them.

"Certainly," Marcus responded while Mack smiled intently but kept his sensitivity to himself to prevent Lucy from noticing his modesty.

"Great!" Lucy responded before all four people merged into one group and proceeded to look outside of one of the observation windows inside the command and control center.

"What's strange is that Dr. Netherland once estimated that up to 50 billion people existed throughout known human history and at least two million living species of plant and animal life exist on Earth." All three compatriots heard Dr. Ryan's words before he stretched his right arm and pointed his index finger toward Earth.

Each window contained a tinting device capable of blocking harmful ultraviolet rays. Once these protective layers cleared their view, the crew saw a rotating sphere that was responsible for the crew's existence. Dr. Ryan realized that he watched the true guardian of every living specimen including all who'll see this big blue motherly marble for the last time before pursuing empty space!

LESSONS TO BE LEARNED

Four months felt like an eternity since they departed mother Earth. After all they've accomplished, neither Lucy nor Meena revealed their true feelings toward two oblivious men. Lucy was hesitant because she thought if she was rejected then she'll feel embarrassed within a small social circle of only 1500 permanent colonists. She felt that her professional impact to this mission will be complicated. She's confident that Meena was the best person to keep her secret. Although Tracy Marino and Ada al-Saud would've been sympathetic, she didn't want rumors to spread among the crew and had no desire to live with such a reputation.

"Lucy, I have some startling new data from one of the Eve probes. You want to see it?" Mack asked.

"Yes, of course." She smiled before they walked to an empty domed room with a glass floor.

They sat on the middle of the floor before Mack provided a verbal command of "Eve number three" to deactivate the center light and transform a dull white dome shape room into a detailed visual telepresence simulation of the central continent's surface. A panorama of lush greenery of the northern steppes appeared calm. Lucy leaned on Mack's right side as he submitted himself into live action holograms of a heard of 8 gigantic bull bison roaming the grasslands. Their horns were impressively long and thick as bulky shoulders enabled them to maneuver their heads. Their muscular limbs were able to support their one ton physique equivalent to 908 kilograms. Most of the older males appeared much heavier.

"I can't wait to see them in person." Mack cried his elevated excitement when seven feet (2.15m) tall bulls approached the area where they were sitting. Mack watched them find a desirable area before they actively consumed grass.

"It seems that there's two different species of buffaloes roaming across the vast open steppes. What are they exactly?" Lucy asked.

"Two larger bulls are known as *Bison latifrons* of North America during the Pleistocene epoch, which consisted of the Earth's last Ice Age. Both of their long horns achieve a width of eight feet or almost 2.5 meters, while six other giants with curved horns are the legendary Steppe Bison or *Bison priscus*, which lived in North America at the same time period." Mack answered Lucy's question as both noticed the Steppe Bison appeared more robust than their larger companions."

"What's emerging from behind that congregation of trees?" Lucy wondered.

"You have to be kidding me? This can't be?"

"What are they?" Lucy asked.

"You're won't believe this but these elephant size shaggy rhinos were identified as *Elasmotherium* of Russia during the Pleistocene epoch. Each horn could grow over six feet in length.

"What about the four smaller rhinos?" Lucy guessed.

"All four smaller rhinos are *Coelodonta*, better known as the legendary Wooly rhinoceros of the last Ice Age. The name *Coelodonta* means hollowed horn. Mack explained as Lucy placed her left arm on his right shoulder. "They lived in Europe and Siberia during the Pleistocene epoch. They're larger and more powerful than most modern rhinoceroses."

Lucy was surprised to see two species of giant deer emerge from behind nearby shrubs. Based upon their antler patterns, she suspected they were two different species. Both species of deer could raise their heads eight feet (2.44m) high and possessed antlers that weighed 100 pounds or over 45 kilograms or more. The sole difference between these two species of deer was that *Megaloceros* of Europe and Asia existed during the Pleistocene epoch has developed elk like antlers, which was one reason why they're commonly mistaken as the Irish elk. Mack learned that *Megaloceros* was more closely related to the fallow deer and continues to be impressed with the span of their antlers that extended up to 12 feet (3.66m) wide!

The other group of dignified deer possessed antlers with a different pattern. These antlers of *Eucladoceros* were six feet (1.83m) wide, they grew vertically and stood up to six feet (1.83m) above their heads and the highest tines were able to reach 14 feet (4.27m) off the ground, which matched the height of an African elephant! Their two giant antlers held over a dozen tines or points! *Eucladoceros* of Italy migrated across the opened steppes during the Pliocene epoch that ranged from 5,332,000 – 2,588,000 years ago and the Pleistocene epoch or 2,588,000 – 11,700 years ago.

Both species of giant deer grazed on grass and monitored their surroundings for any possible danger. Lucy noticed the Wooly rhinoceros becoming alert. A rapid twitching of their nostrils indicated that they scented something disturbing. Soon afterward, *Eucladoceros* and both species of giant bison appeared antagonistic. Sensitive ears of *Megaloceros* and *Eucladoceros* pivoted back and forth to listen for any sounds from a forest that bordered the open steppe.

"What the hell is that?" Lucy wondered as she tightened her grip on Mack's shoulder.

"That's the North American Short faced bear, also known as *Arctodus*! They lived across the northern regions of Canada during the same time period as the other mammals." Mack answered as they witnessed two gigantic and strange looking male predators peeking out of the forest edge surveying physical health and endurance of each herbivore.

The splendor of *Eucladoceros* and *Megaloceros* swiftly ended as they darted through a wide grassy trail that pierced through the northern woods. Lucy was impressed to witness both species of deer leap up to thirty feet or over nine meters without their hooves touching the ground. Lucy never thought she'll see a Short faced bear appearing like a crossbreed between a bulldog and a lion. She also observed their dark brown fur that insulated all 1500 pounds (681kg) of their flesh from frostbite during the coldest and darkest winters of northern Canada, particularly the Yukon region.

Their slim build was possible for them to stand five feet (1.5m) at shoulder and was able to stand on their hind legs that raised their height up to 11 feet (3.36m) tall. Commonly known to terrorize the coldest highlands of the Western hemisphere, these bulldog bears were equipped with long spines that provided them enough flexibility to burst into a rapid sprint toward any unsuspecting prey. Not only was the Short faced bear leaner than modern Brown bears (*Ursus arctos*), *Arctodus* ran faster and was much more carnivorous. Lucy placed her head on Mack's shoulder to limit her view of what she anticipated and attempting to distract Mack's own self induced hypnosis of this natural scene. Both Short faced bears agility enabled them to maneuver more like tigers rather than modern bears.

Although the handsome deer were gone, the brawny bison and rugged rhinos were well prepared to settle their dispute and used their nostrils and vocal chords to verbally warn the big bears from the forest to run away or lose their ability to walk anymore! Mack knew a situation like this all too well. *Arctodus* bobbed and weaved and employed distraction methods to complicate their defending prey's concentration.

The Bulldog bears didn't have pigeon toes like modern grizzly bears (*Ursus arctos horribilis*). Instead they evolved straight toes like a lion. Mack suspected these bears intended to cause a panic among the group so at some point during this stalemate one of their swinging horns or hooves would accidentally injure a member of the defending group. He knew such an accidental injury caused by friendly fire would give the predators a distinct advantage. The injured victim will be selected while the others are encouraged to flee. Mack understood that once the injured victim is separated, then both bears would then launch a full scale attack to kill the injured loner. He knew such vigilance was necessary in order to fulfill their monumental energy requirements to survive a long winter ahead. Mack studied various defense techniques of each animal along with their stern body language, timing and group communication.

Lucy continued to watch Mack's full scale concentration to the holographic telepresence projector rather than her physical presence. "Mack, are you okay?"

"Huh...oh...umm...yeah," Mack stuttered as he witnessed a group of plant eating titans of the taiga exert a firm warning toward their carnivorous counterparts.

To simplify matters even more, *Elasmotherium* decided that they had enough before they charged toward both barbaric bears just like they would have done against any threatening predator in Russia during the Pleistocene epoch that ranged from 2,588,000 – 11,700 years ago. Mack learned that the name *Elasmotherium* means plate beast, due to their flat cheek teeth that grinded together as they pursued the giant bears. Dr. Ryan was skeptical that this stalemate ended as both bears maintained their defiance. He wondered why both bulldog bears remained persistent despite mounting opposition.

"Why won't they leave?" Dr. Rosalila was unaware of why they didn't flee.

"You see how slim they look?" Mack emphasized.

"Yes."

"Starvation would be a sufficient reason why they'll subject themselves to such dangerous risks. They would've dispersed much sooner if they were only moderately hungry."

"Oh...so you mean that mounting hunger would constitute a greater resilience to catch prey?"

"Of course, that's exactly what I think." Lucy felt intrigued to learn how various individual circumstances influences personal behavior of every species including humans.

Mack also mentioned other possible factors including an unbridled obligation to feed offspring or facing pending harsh winter they must be prepared to comply without any exceptions. Lucy recognized such persistence once Arctodus ran around both giant rhinos to antagonize the others before they discovered that an older and more fragile male Steppe bison fled from the group.

Lucy showed no enthusiasm to watch both bulldog bears race toward this elderly male before one of them disemboweled the buffalo's rear legs tenaciously while the other male clamped his jaws into the bison's throat. The old male bison struggled defiantly until his energy depleted. Mack knew that the resulting outcome would be an imminent end for a long living bison that migrated across the steppe numerous times. Despite such overtly demands, *Arctodus* achieved their kill without being fatally injured. If the Short faced bear ever suffered torn flesh or broken bones, then their consequences would be nothing better than eventual death! Mack witnessed what Dr. Netherland once theorized that all life forms live by an abstract set of natural rules that influence their general behavior and govern their lives.

Don't get sick or injured; is one of the rules Dr. Ryan learned. The fact is that there are no hospitals, veterinarians nor paramedics to heal any wounds or ailments. Mauled flesh and broken bones constitute an inescapable end of life. If an herbivore encountered a serious injury, then they wouldn't be able to keep up with their migration. Any potential predator could discover their condition and take advantage of a rare opportunity of an easy kill. If a predator ever experienced an injury, then they would not be able to hunt and if they were part of a group, then they would ultimately be rejected and permanently forced out of a pride, clan or pack causing further mischief. Any disabled predator who can't hunt would surely die of famine. Not to mention if an injured predator encounters rival predators. The consequences would most likely be curtains for any wounded rival predator that strays into enemy territory.

Each dominant male and female of every social group are well versed with this rule. If a dominant individual endures physical limitations then a powerful competitor would challenge their supremacy. If an injured leader's social status ends then the former leader would most likely become a loner and the only companion any former group leader would ever have is the injury that got them in this undesirable predicament in the first place!

Such persistence of *Arctodus simus yukonensis* became a magnet for Dr. Ryan's attention. Mack remembered Dr. Netherland lecturing about how experience mixed with the most dominant gene pattern would be imperative to comply with the second rule, which is to intertwine the best or most dominant pair of genes for the next generation. In most cases, the Alpha males and females would be suitable to mate and produce promising offspring. Dominant genes are a principal ingredient to insure survival for any species or extinction could be inevitable. All life forms must inherit the best physiology for each new generation over the course of millions of years so they could adapt to nature's unmerciful demands.

"Mack." Lucy squeezed his shoulder.

"What?" Mack lost his focus before he looked over to her.

"I wanted to tell you how much I appreciate," were all the words Lucy said before an instant manifestation of a dark humanoid silhouette appeared before both of them.

Soon after, they witnessed more of these humanoid shaped silhouettes emerging. When each figure appeared, they willfully approached them. Mack realized these familiar humanoid figures were friendly and their clothing was well tailored. While they approached, Mack noticed the identity of each silhouette approaching them. Lucy felt interrupted as she lost her opportunity to reveal her important news to a blue eyed astronaut. Lucy tilted her head back in disbelief of such bad timing to reveal her message to Mack.

"Hi Mack, hi Lucy," Marcus cheerfully said as he accompanied Meena, Martin, Angela, Ying, Fan, Harold and Alicia.

"Hey everyone, I'm glad you showed up. Join us!" Lucy stared at Mack with growing frustration as Mack encouraged the others to accommodate him. Lucy reluctantly cooperated as she welcomed all the others including Arnold and Esther Weinstein who just entered the Clairvoyance room.

"How many more of these asteroid clusters we have to pass?" Harold asked.

"There's only one group of asteroids left." Marcus answered before saying "Then we'll approach Jupiter!"

"Anyone wants to see Eve number two?" Mack asked.

"Sure…Yes…Of course," were mixed responses before Mack verbally commanded "Eve number two" before spectators noticed a busy habitat. Everyone enjoyed their generous view of each living specimen fulfilling their particular niche. A mild breeze provided a fresh scent inside the room. The crowd observed an area, which appeared to possess a warm climate. Being able to see vast open grassland extending as far as the horizon was a fair description of the Great Plains that excited the group inside the Clairvoyance projector room. Forest trees bordering open grassland indicated that Eve number two made it to the outskirts of the open plains bordering the woodland.

"Look at these beautiful birds." Angela was impressed to see a group of four giant land birds known as *Emeus crassus*.

These chirping charmers stood five feet (1.5m) tall and weighed over one hundred pounds or over 45 kilograms on average. Along with their gold plumage, each individual grew as large as a Greater rhea (*Rhea americana*) of South America or an emu (*Dromainus novaehollandiae*) of Australia. They appeared to develop powerful legs but walked slowly into the open plains searching for any possible food source such as seeds and insects.

"Wow! Look at that over there! I can't believe it! This can't be?" Fan wondered.

"What do you see?" Marcus joyfully wondered.

"I saw an adult Sabre-tooth cat walking away from behind these set of bushes." Fan answered before the group of people felt stimulated by his remarks including his wife Ying who was equally excited of what they just saw.

"It's *Smilodon*!" Arnold told everyone before his wife Esther informed the group that *Smilodon* existed during the Pleistocene epoch.

Ancient California and Argentina were places they prowled and pounced on unsuspecting prey. The crew was amazed to see a lion sized feline possess such a short stocky tail along with a perceivably powerful physique along with bulky neck muscles! Her hardened shoulders and chest showed how this stabbing cat used her long upper canines to penetrate the throat of buffaloes and other large prey to slash the esophagus or coronary arteries.

"The only other true saber tooth cat I know of is *Megantereon*." Arnold said before two more human shaped silhouettes appeared before their view until everyone recognized Victor and Nina.

"Whoa…I don't want to miss this." Victor said as he and Nina found their preferred area to sit.

Dr. Viktor Ivanov was born in Kiev and his wife Nina was originally from Moscow. They conducted space studies in Russia, Ukraine and Kazakhstan. Both shared their extensive experiences at the Megaprojects Development Center at Kapustin Yar test range in Russia. Viktor pursued his life with Engineers, while Nina enjoyed her work with Intelligence. When both of them became captivated with the open plain, Lucy and Meena glanced over to each other and recognized their common frustration of delivering their sensitive message. Lucy gave Meena a subtle facial signal to leave the projector room. Once both women stood up, Lucy told Mack that they would be right back before leaving the room. Once they were outside, the long corridor was silent and deserted, which was a perfect time for both women to speak.

"I can't believe it! I tried to get his attention several times, but all he does is study various life forms either in the library or at one of the Clairvoyance rooms. He's fascinated with this new planet." Meena whispered as Lucy continued to insure that nobody else would hear them by looking in both directions.

"I practically squeezed him like a stuffed teddy bear and he barely looked at me. He was lecturing me about the Grand Steppes before everyone else showed up." Lucy revealed to Meena as she rolled her eyes.

"Personally, I think they're obsessed about Isis." Meena suspected.

"What we should do is wait for the right time." Lucy emphasized. "You should wait until you're alone with him."

"I'm sure he'll know soon enough," Meena pledged before they decided to head back to the projector room and reunited with their close colleagues.

When both women returned, they saw everyone focused upon watching the Great Plains before Mack verbally requested "Eve number four" that viewed an unusual area that was the located at the center of the continent. Observers noticed giant bull bison, rhinos and mammoths appearing uneasy as they raced past this undesirable area due to an array of scattered bones, and visible scent markings on the barks of dead trees.

As a thunderous resonation of racing footsteps echoed the area, a full grown male bear emerged from a patch of thick bushes. Lucy and Meena couldn't believe the sheer size of his shoulders, flanks, loins, and padded paws. Weighing in excess of 1800 pounds or over 817 kilograms and stood 12 feet (3.66m) tall on his hind legs. This bear had an unusually large forehead that added more masculinity to this maturing male. His jaws appeared powerful and his incisors and canines were thick. As ferocious he appeared, the irony was that this male was primarily a vegetarian! He fulfilled a primary diet of nuts, berries, acorns and vegetables.

"Wow! This male's shoulder is as tall as me." Mack praised as Meena and Lucy shared little enthusiasm for his hypothesis.

Observers were impressed by such intelligence of *Ursus spelaeus* when he stood on his hind legs and used his wide muzzle to scent for fruits on an apple tree. Better known as the great European Cave bear, he found what he wanted he then pressed his paws against the tree and used his strength to shake it. Soon after, a hail of green apples fell to the ground. The Cave bear then used his tongue and lips to pick up and chew on some fallen apples just like this species has done in Europe, Russia and other parts of Asia during the Pleistocene Epoch (2,588,000 – 11,700 years ago).

A mature masculinity of this male attracted another cave bear from a distance. Mack noticed faint twitches of his large nose before he raised his head and turned to his right side to find the source. A cheerful reaction in part of this giant male could only be a warm welcome for a beautiful, well groomed female with dark brown eyes. Subtle hymns coming from this mature adult male reassured his friendliness to her. She slowly approached the larger male with caution. Although he discovered the female of his choice; his attention suddenly focused toward another animal that was approaching the female Cave bear from behind. He suddenly sounded an alert signal to warn her of imminent danger, as he diligently pursued this potential problem!

A giant male North American Short faced bear known as *Arctodus simus yukonensis* apparently stalked the female cave bear for some time. However, an intimidating form of resentment this male Cave bear expressed to the Short faced bear would constitute his demand for battle! Rapid maneuverings of the thinner, more flexible Short faced bear enabled his first strike. A wide bulky body shape of the Cave bear was capable of absorbing bites and blows like he received during an initial clash. *Arctodus* inflicted another hard bite to the Cave bear's shoulder before being fended off by his defending rival. Bobbing and weaving in part of *Arctodus* enabled him to confuse his opponent so he could pursue a third strike. This time the Bulldog bear's front right paw swung in order to hit across the left side of the Cave bear's face.

"Wow, can you believe such physical agility of both of them?" Mack said with invigoration.

"They're magnificent!" Marcus announced before he cheerfully stated. "So far, Eve number four showed us the most ferocious clashes on Isis!"

Meena and Lucy looked at each other before they smirked and rolled their eyes to grimace about two fascinated friends. The vast attention both men provided to simulated data continued to annoy both women who didn't share such enthusiasm.

The female Cave bear witnessed her chosen male stand erect before he swung his gigantic left front limb and pounded his heavy paw across the right side of the Bulldog bear's head. The impact made him lose balance before falling on his left side. An antagonistic male Cave bear in season, full of testosterone instantly attacked his menacing rival!

This angry Cave bear sought to get on top of his opponent and bite his bitter adversary voraciously at his throat. It wasn't long before the female cave bear decided to unleash her resentment toward her enemy by biting the bulldog bear's rear leg while the male used his paw to press against the Short faced bear's head until the perpetrator slipped away free. Both Cave bears chased *Arctodus* into nearby woodland. The Short faced bear's long legs were firm enough to narrowly escape death or dismemberment. Ever since birth, each life form on Earth and Isis inherited and learned evasive techniques to escape overwhelming danger.

Dr. Ryan recalled how Dr. Netherland lectured him about how such superb species of Earth and Isis live in full compliance of another abstract natural rule such as life forms employ an abstract balancing scale and weigh in the potential risks and rewards, which influence an individual's decision making process. The main reason why the giant North American Short faced bear decided to leave was because the female cave bear joined into this ferocious feud. If the rival Short faced bear didn't leave, then both European Cave bears would've inflicted torn flesh or maybe a broken bone that would ultimately mean the end of life for *Arctodus*!

Sometimes life in the wild appears to be a constant choice. But if an individual makes wise decisions, then full benefits of safety and security along with other rewards would be perfectly suitable for any for of biological life to enhance sensory, judgment, and timing abilities. Such skills are mandatory to live long enough to become the most suitable candidate for mates when they reach maturity in the future and would be the one who'll transmit their genes into the next generation.

Dr. Nimbus, Dr. Ryan and others were amazed of how a single planet could sustain such a diversity of dynamic creatures. Also their greatest surprise was how dinosaur-like inhabitants could coexist with their fellow Tertiary era mammals. Although various speculations were exchanged among the entire group, most were confident that Isis could be a planet lucky enough to avoid some cataclysmic events during the planet's natural history.

Such catastrophic events that caused major extinctions such as the K-T Boundary, which was the timeframe when an asteroid penetrated the Earth's atmosphere and struck the Yucatan Peninsula approximately 65 million years ago; striking a final blow to an already severe environmental circumstance of the dinosaurs on Earth. Perhaps Isis may have been lucky enough to experience only regional meteorite showers instead of a doomsday asteroid that ended the dinosaurs' long struggle with drought and famine.

Marcus recognized how smaller life forms of the Cretaceous period managed to survive drought, famine, plague and an eventual asteroid impact. Once the largest herbivores and the top predators of the Mesozoic era (225 – 65 million years ago) perished, while smaller mammals flourished. Dr. Netherland referred the K-T Boundary during his lectures as evidence of another abstract rule animals are obligated to comply, such as each living species must adapt or face grave consequences! Natural selection is an imperative process of mastering environmental challenges and stern competition from rival males for mates for the sole purpose for reproductive success.

Dr. Ryan and others knew the Central Continent was a special place for such activity. Its location and landmass was ripe with evolutionary opportunities. This land of natural wonder was previously estimated to match the geographic size of Europe, Africa and Asia combined while the Great Plains, Grand Steppes and Principal Prairies were each the size of half the continental United States. Lucy and Meena felt annoyed as they watched Drs. Ryan and Nimbus became space faring fans of planet Isis.

Some herbivores or plant eaters prefer certain soft bay leaves while others enjoy lush grass. Roots and tubers are favorable for some herbivores as others prefer fruits and vegetables. Seeds, wild nuts, acorns, cashews, almonds, and grains are also appreciated by many. Some even include algae and moss in their diets. Marcus was impressed how smaller and more athletic browsers followed slower moving giants and would wait until a large branch or set of twigs fall to the ground in order to consume their precious leaves that would've been inaccessible by their sole efforts.

Insects were important for life on Isis and Earth because pupa or baby beetles consume dung and maggots or baby flies eat meat to reach maturity.

Others consumed vast microorganisms including bacteria and viruses. A sheer abundance of food is a blessing for flying and walking birds, rodents, small creodonts and hoofed mammals known as condylarths and animals that consume insects classified as insectivores. Parasites were also available for birds and small amphibians. Lizards, frogs, and other animals that possess a spinal chord referred as vertebrae live and comply with another abstract natural rule they obey.

Mack remembered Dr. Netherland claiming that every life form is interdependent and interconnected to each other for collective survival. Plant and animal life coexist and compliment each other much more than the naked eye can see. Every time we breathe out, plants and trees receive life giving carbon dioxide and breathe it in. Plants continue to release vital oxygen appreciated by all animal life! Even volcanic dust and ash benefit plants over long periods of time.

A plant's existence will be sacrificed to satisfy an herbivore's hunger while dung will be a prime component for fertilizer that'll make it possible to grow once again and even reproduce. Dung, sunlight, rainwater, fertile soil and carbon dioxide are all reasons why plenty of young plants emerge before displaying their ripe crops. A complete cycle of dependency will be repeated throughout the year to insure a mutual partnership between plant and animal life continues to maintain a planet's ecology!

Dr. Netherland lectured how predators play an important role within an intricate balance of nature. Persistent preying removes sick and injured animals so healthier individuals could survive due to reduced competition. If predators didn't exist then all plant eaters will multiply and become overpopulated. Soon after, food would be scarce and lack of nutrients would impede all necessary energy required to migrate and find more food sources. It would most likely be that herbivores would multiply to the point of mass starvation. Dr. Ryan recalled Dr. Netherland's lessons and learned to appreciate his mentor's discoveries.

Drs. Martin and Angela de' la' Vega evaluated each species. Dr. Fan Zhu studied relationships among local residents and migrating herds. Dr. Alicia Nevins was impressed with Isis compatible weather while Drs. Arnold Weinstein and Harold Nevins suspected the Central Continent would be the best place to settle once they arrive to this new world.

As crew members discussed this giant continent, Dr. Ryan thought about how every living individual has an origin and will physically decease. He recognized another natural rule plants and animals obey. Although birth may encounter complications and death may be delayed, Dr. Netherland claimed there's no exception to this rule. However, Dr. Ryan learned that even lifelessness gives rise to other life. He observed animals consuming flesh and others crushing bones to extract nutritious marrow at their center. Mack discovered insects and microorganisms will consume the rest. Only a few bones remained intact and would ultimately fossilize.

Dr. Ying Zhu thought about using the Dove and Condor miniature planes in the future to detect as much information of this new world as possible. Both miniature planes were unmanned and are controlled by radio frequency from a control station inside each lander craft that'll be converted into Town Hall once the landing crew who'll settle on the Central Continent. All members of the landing party examined these abstract rules that influence the behaviors of all natural life.

The Watchdog device Mack wore around his wrist activated when all four miniature antennas spontaneously extended before a holographic screen illuminated. A familiar, trusted colleague appeared within the small screen. Mack recognized Dr. Haru Nakamura's hologram. He worked for Engineers for over a decade. His accomplishments justified his impeccable reputation. Ever since he was born in Hiroshima, he dreamed of space travel. For many years, Dr. Nakamura actively participated in designing and developing many new inventions within the federation.

"*Mack, come in.*" A youthful facial expression requested.

"Haru, how are you?"

"*Fine, were approaching a collection of asteroids straight ahead.*" Dr. Nakamura revealed.

"We'll view the asteroids from the Clairvoyance room, but maintain an evasive course." Dr. Ryan said before he provided a verbal command to end this natural scene before activating the holographic telepresence projector.

After a split second of absolute darkness, the crew inside the 360-degree, 4 dimensional projector room was instantly suspended in animated outer space. Faint twinkling stars were everywhere. Its clarity was clear enough to distinguish various distances of individual stars. Speakers, air ducts, and rotating fan blades built inside the walls of this domed room provided additional authenticity of gently approaching a collection of asteroids to every spectator inside the room. This group of asteroids increased in size as the starship Guardian approached with caution. Dozens of meteors ranged in size from small rocks up to one mile (over 1.6km) wide! However, the seven asteroids were much larger in size ranged from over a mile or over 1.6 kilometers long, to the size of Manhattan, which is approximately 13 miles or almost 21 kilometers long, and up to about 2 ½ miles or over 4 kilometers wide. Most of these asteroids appeared spherical in shape and all of them possessed a rugged surface. Mack noticed several oval and irregular shaped meteors as well.

"Umm...they're much too far away to see a clear image; I'll zoom-in for a closer look." Dr. Ryan then pointed his index finger toward the distant asteroids before saying "zoom in" before the projector propelled the crew closer to this congregation of boulders until they were less than fifty surface miles or over 80 kilometers away from center of this flock of drifting boulders.

Dr. Ryan decided to travel toward the right side of their visual position. He then instructed Dr. Nakamura to used extreme caution for space debris. All meteors are a classification of small asteroids from the size of pebbles up to one mile (over 1.6km) long or wide. An asteroid would be classified when an object is larger than one mile. Meteors become meteorites when they land on a planet. All of these meteors and asteroids were reminiscent of a time when Dr. Ryan and the others were called to save the Earth from an asteroid over six years ago.

"Look at the size of this one." Dr. Ying Zhu said as they proceed to pass by a Manhattan sized asteroid, located on their left hand side based upon the angle of the projector.

Mack was aware that these cosmic boulders viewed by the Clairvoyance telepresence projector could end the existence of all known life on Earth and Isis combined! Rare minerals such as iridium, titanium and platinum were abundant on many asteroids, which would benefit humanity in various ways including space travel. The crew watched these boulders drift aimlessly in space as the starship Guardian continued its scheduled route to Jupiter.

"Haru, do we have any more clusters ahead?" Mack asked.

"No, it was the last one." Dr. Nakamura confirmed as they passed by the last three meteors.

After the last meteor passed by their simulated view, Dr. Ryan quietly and discreetly yawned before he rubbed his eyes. As inclined he was to the Great Plains and Grand Steppes, Mack felt exhausted. He finally found the right opportunity to rest. His next task will take place ten hours from when Dr. Ryan's stood up and informed everyone that he intended to go to sleep for several hours until the starship arrives at the outskirts of Jupiter's magnetic field.

"Well everyone, I need to get some rest." Mack said when he stood up and stretched his arms and legs. "Jupiter is only a few hours from now."

"I feel exhausted too." Lucy responded before she stood up from the glass floor.

Lucy and Mack quietly departed the simulated space scene inside a domed shaped room. They walked down the corridor discussing their recent observations inside the Clairvoyance room. Although Lucy was waiting for the right time to talk to him, Mack seemed too exhausted to even discuss anything else.

"Hey! Wait up." Marcus said as he was running toward them along with Meena.

"I'm glad we passed through the asteroid belt." Mack said as Marcus and Meena caught up to the others. All four of them walked together to their individual quarters to rest.

"We must be careful when we slingshot past Jupiter." Marcus added as they continued to walk down the corridor.

"Well...this is where I get off." Mack rubbed his eyes when he reached the entrance door to his living quarters. As soon as he opened his entrance door, he gave his long time friend a handshake before he collectively greeted Lucy and Meena before entering. Marcus was assigned next door to Mack while both ladies were just across the hall. After he entered his quarters and closed the door, he heard faint sounds of three people entering their living quarters nearby. He changed his clothes before brushing his teeth inside his bathroom. When he reentered the bedroom, he turned off the lights, except for a lamp attached to his right end table next to his full size bed. His final task was to turn off the lamp before he lied on his back and fell asleep.

THE PLANET OF THE
GODS' TRAJECTORY

Mack shifted to a preferable resting position on his full-sized bed. His quilt nestled him, while both pillows suspended his head. He eventually lied on his back before staring up to the ceiling. In order to abide by his schedule he requested the time.

"Earth's time at headquarters." Mack mumbled inside his living quarters.

Within seconds a simulated voice stated the time of 10:00AM in the morning. The official time would correspond to the Humane Space Federation headquarters' time located at Groom Lake, Nevada. He stumbled out of bed and bathed before he proceeded to a closet before he got dressed. A two-piece jumpsuit was well tailored for a perfect fit. Mack heard a new message revealed from his intercom. He recognized a familiar voice speaking through a small loudspeaker.

"*Mack...come in, over?*" a voice of Dr. Nimbus requested.

Dr. Ryan approached the intercom and pressed a button to respond. "Send it...Doctor Nimbus."

"*Mack, I have great news! We're approaching Isis and it's within visual range.*"

"I'll be up in two minutes." Mack affirmed as he collected a few more personal items before he then turned off his lights before leaving.

He paced through a long corridor as he dutifully placed his belongings into his front pockets of his trousers. It was necessary for him to walk 200 feet or 61 meters until he arrived at a pair of sliding doors where he could press a nearby button to call for an onboard elevator to arrive at his level. Once both sliding doors opened, Dr. Ryan joined Drs. Malik al-Saud and Fan Zhu inside the elevator. Dr. Ryan greeted both of them as the doors close and before all three researchers went to the command and control center upstairs.

"Mack…did you hear the news?" Dr. Malik al-Saud asked.

"Marcus told me everything." Mack smiled.

"I'm grateful that we made it!" Malik cheerfully shouted.

"Just think of the air quality." Dr. Fan Zhu shared his excitement with all three crewmembers of the H.S.F.S. Guardian, as they willfully approached their desired level.

"First, we'll meet Marcus. Then we'll head straight to lander one destined for Eve number four's location." Mack said.

Once they reached the upper level of the ship, they met Dr. Nimbus inside a busy room where numerous windows revealed an Earth analog waiting for their arrival. Dr. Nimbus wasted no time to approach and follow his three other companions into the on board elevator before all four of them headed down several levels where they'll board a lander, which will be their future home and workplace everyone refers to as Town Hall.

As they progressed to this lower level everyone felt a deep passion as they made final preparations to land at the very center of the Central Continent. It felt like an eternity for the elevator to reach their desired level. Once the elevator doors opened, all four of them met more friends. Dr. Ryan met Drs. Angela and Martin de' la' Vega at the terminal, while Dr. Zhu noticed Drs. Alicia and Harold Nevins anxious to be a part of such a historic event. Dr. Claude Moreau from Paris couldn't wait to land on the surface of Isis. Dr. Moreau worked for Intelligence while studying archaeology and primatology. He originally met his fiancée Dr. Zarina Ansari from Tehran to operate supercomputers and inspected computer mainframe terminals along with Ying Zhu, Meena Singh and others at Engineering.

Everyone filed a single line and followed Dr. Ryan inside. Each level had ten feet (3m) high ceilings from the floor. Sixteen levels and reinforced hulls extended this unit to measure 180 feet or 55 meters high and up to 300 feet or over 91 meters wide at the center. An elliptical shaped lander had stout legs attached to the bottom to maintain a firm foothold of the surface of their chosen region.

Dr. Ryan secured himself into his assigned seat along with two hundred other associates. Dr. Ryan ordered the lander to be released. Dr. Nimbus knew how to pilot this craft just like any other craft such as Transcend, which several of them were parked inside spacious docking bays of the flagship. Advanced avionics simplified this potentially monumental task.

Rapid speed of descent penetrated the atmosphere and vibrated the craft. Members of this landing crew braced themselves as they continued to descend toward the planet's surface. Geographic data showed the crew their desired region was located between the Great Plains, Grand Steppes and Principal Prairies.

"Mack what name should we call this region?" Arnold wondered.

"Based upon its geographic location we should call it Bull's Eye." Mack proudly suggested."

"Bull's Eye...I love it! I couldn't come up with a better name myself." Arnold laughed as they descended to the surface.

Judging from fitted edges of both seacoasts, it appeared that the land formation matched that of the neighboring continents ranging five hundred to seven hundred miles (804.5km – 1126.3km) away from each other. This could only mean that the Central Continent was once physically connected to the Eastern and Western Continents long ago, similar to how Earth's continents were once combined to form a super continent known as Pangaea, which is also spelled as Pangea.

Apparently, three main natural forums known so far was the Great Plains, Grand Steppes and Principal Prairies, which were all located at the Central Continent. Each one of these open fields was at least the geographic size of half the continental United States. The Bull's Eye region was recently estimated to be as large as Texas, Oklahoma and New Mexico combined. The Bull's Eye region, where Eve #4 landed became known as a scattered woodland region with hills, kopjes along with two main rivers with lakes and several water holes.

"Mack, the northern mesa is directly underneath our position." Dr. Weinstein told everyone after he found the geographic location of a rocky mountain with an unusually flat top.

The crew will maintain their intended aerial position as they gently lowered their altitude. Receptor knobs located at the bottom of the lander absorbed the planet's gravity waves, while circular plates at same locations, will generate and generate repelling magnetic polarities to the planet's magnetic field. Thus, the craft that weighed thousands of tons or metric tons would weigh only ounces or grams so they could drift toward the ground without using its retrorockets.

Dr. Nimbus adjusted its position directly above the flattened summit adjacent to independent rolling hills. Dr. Nimbus reassured everyone that they were in perfect position as he carefully lowered it to the top of this mesa. A laser was used to determine their altitude from the mesa's surface to make a soft landing. They continued to reduce their altitude from the ground as four hydraulic landing legs emerged from underneath. A monitor showed Dr. Nimbus that they were only a few feet or meters away from the surface before he gently lowered the craft. All four legs achieved a firm grip before struts and shocks of all four legs gently lowered it until a firm, flat center at the bottom of the lander gently touched the smooth surface that ranged up to half a mile wide.

Everybody ready?" Dr. Ryan asked over a microphone before all two hundred pioneers cheerfully responded.

Some power generators were turned off before the ship was programmed on station mode. Key personnel instantly went to the lobby before a few buttons were dialed to unseal and open the hatch. Stimulation of adventure was felt everywhere as inviting rays of daylight from an orbited star called Osiris, penetrated the interior of the lander. Once a hatch opened, people from all over the world experienced a new world for the first time, as they were able to see a panorama due to their higher elevation.

For all who came to this world, people like Marcus from Los Angeles and Martin of Mexico City and his wife Angela, who was born in Rio de Janeiro, gathered to see an unprecedented alternative to ordinary life. Dr. Doris Remington sympathized her joy with the others unlike she ever did since she was born in Sydney, Australia. Her husband Dr. Art Remington originally from London gave her a warm embrace and told Doris that he loved her. Dr. Harold Nevins who was born in Chicago hasn't felt so happy since he was twenty five and traveled to South Africa where he met his wife Dr. Alicia Nevins.

The scattered woodland appeared like a natural convention hall for a diversity of inhabitants. A pistol shaped device known as the Identification Detective (I.D.) was used to emit various short bursts of wavelengths ranging from radio up to X-rays, which can trace patterns of bones and detect DNA composition. A small built-in LCD screen at the top rear end of this device would display a match making process in conjunction with a massive computer information database known as the Soul Mate, which finds a perfect or suitable match to what the I.D. device scanned. Once a skeletal formation matches with known assembled fossils, then an artist conception of either a dinosaur or any other prehistoric life form will be displayed on the screen. However, if any life form shows no resemblance to any fossil or known living species then this device would display its closest genetic relative.

"Everyone...look at them!" Angela brought a group of six migrating giants to Dr. Ryan's attention.

Dr. Ryan then used his I.D. device to find out what identical species had a long suspended neck and tail. Once his results were completed, he saw an artists rendering of *Apatosaurus* formerly known as the *Brontosaurus*. *Apatosaurus* had black hides with green patterned stripes and once lived in North America during the Jurassic period (about 193 – 136 million years ago). All six of them approached a large swampy waterhole. It appeared that they had no difficulty moving a physique that measured up to 65 feet (20m) long, and up to 33 tons or 29.7 metric tons.

"What's that over there?" Dr. Fan Zhu was surprised to see two large mammals emerge from the waterhole in response to an arrival of all four giant sauropods of the Jurassic approaching.

Dr. Ryan enthusiastically wanted to find out what was originally submerged that walked along the river's edge. Once he used his device, he was surprised to notice that a life form that was able to weigh at least 5 tons or 4.5 metric tons existed in North America during the Miocene epoch (23,030,000 – 5,322,000 years ago) was identified as *Teleoceras major*. This massive herbivore measured at least 13 feet (4m) long and could easily stand six feet (1.83m) at the shoulder.

All four short stocky legs supported massive shoulders and a barrel shaped body that nearly touched the ground. Although *Teleoceras major* was an ancient relative to the modern rhinoceros both of them appeared more relevant to a modern hippopotamus. The only sign of their true relations to rhinos is a small triangularly pointed horn at the edge of their snouts and thin tails with thick hairs at the end.

Dr. Ryan noticed a hill adjacent to the mesa. He ordered a group of transport devices to be dispatched so a select group of explorers could ride down this annexed hill to reach the open plain where they'll conduct their first exploration of a foreign world. Moments after Dr. Ryan ordered engineers to dispatch transporters. Dr. Fan Zhu along with his wife Ying, Drs. Nimbus, Martin and Angela de' la' Vega rode down the ramp with five all terrain vehicles or ATVs known as Drifters, which were powered by various sign waves ranging from radio to X-rays.

Such an efficient source of power would propel this sporty ATV that possessed no exhaust system. A dense coil located at the rear axle was designed to generate enough power to rotate a built-in, electromagnetic propelled generator, which rotated both rear tires. Two front wheels that were used for steering were the same size as the rear. Dr. Ying Zhu climbed off of her transporter she brought out before encouraging Dr. Ryan to get on the first time. He then tested this transporter to ensure its mechanical condition before all five explorers made their way down a rolling hill.

Dr. Nimbus was aware that the mesa was located at the center of this scattered woodland region. He also knew that being in the center of it all and landing on top of an elevation would provide the best of both objectives, one being able to explore various life forms through easy access and the other was to prevent human activity from interfering with of Isis's natural habitat.

"Okay everyone we'll activate our devices. We'll maintain a close proximity and Watchdog devices should be activated." Dr. Ryan wanted all wrist watches on for instant communication.

Drs. Angela and Martin de la Vega accompanied their colleagues down the hill. Each explorer pointed their Identification Detective devices toward every living specimen they saw as they approached this swampy lake. Dr. Martin de la Vega noticed a fearsome looking boar like omnivore. This powerful female appeared like a known entelodont that existed in North America during the Miocene Epoch or roughly from 23,030,000 – 5,322,000 years ago, identified as *Dinohyus hollandi* also known as *Daeodon*. Her physical anatomy resembled a hybrid between a bull buffalo and a wild boar. Her legs were heavy and had used two functioning hooves on each of her four feet with a third laterally reduced hoof she never used at the rear of each leg.

This female developed a gray, thick shaggy mane mounted behind her head and traveled down the top of her neck and shoulders. Hair also grew at the tip of her tail. This female stood over five feet (1.5m) at her shoulder and weighed approximately 1700 pounds (772kg) while males could weigh up to a ton (908kg). Her most distinguishing features were a pair of bony knobs at the base of her jaws and an impressive set of teeth with large canines that were suitable for an extensive diet from roots to rotten meat.

"You ever heard of pig sticking?" Dr. Nimbus asked.

"Sure...what about it?" Dr. Ryan wondered.

"Meena told me her ancestors rode horses and hunted wild boars in India carrying spears. Imagine hunting this female?"

"She'll topple your horse before sinking her teeth into you."

"Mack...look at that!" Dr. Angela de' la' Vega shouted frantically as she saw a meat-eating dinosaur studying them.

"Oh no! Let's get the hell out of here...fast!" Dr. Ryan wanted to record their identity before they fled.

Unfortunately the Identification Detective revealed bad news when it showed a picture of a well known carnivore that was fixated to stealth and pouncing on unsuspecting prey during the Late Jurassic and Early Cretaceous or from around 161,200,000 – 99,600,000 years ago in North America, Africa and Australia. Dr. Ryan couldn't believe the fact that an appalling male *Allosaurus* showed how easy it was to dodge bushes and trees similar to how an ostrich would avoid ditches. Dr. Ryan applied maximum speed to his transporter to disperse. Mack heard faint footsteps and heard heavy, but controlled breathing from behind.

Dr. Ryan's concern for survival flourished when he heard these faint footsteps intensify. Heavy bellowing from a persistent predator disturbed him even more as he continued to flee. The transporter's springs, struts, and multiple shock absorbers of an independent suspension system, managed to keep all fleeing explorers from being snatched off their seats. Dr. Ryan was determined to catch up with the rest of his crew once he noticed the *Allosaurus* losing interest to pursue them anymore.

"Mack, we could pursue this river straight ahead." Dr. Angela de' la' Vega persuaded him.

Dr. Ryan insisted that he would go first and advised everyone to be exceptionally careful and alert of his or her surroundings.

As each explorer approached a wide river, they noticed a charming horse-like species that possessed a gray base coat along with long black stripes. This prehistoric zebra-horse was soon identified as a genus called *Hipparion*, which was widespread in Africa, Asia, North America and Europe from the Mid Miocene to the Early Pleistocene or from around 15,970,000 – 781,000 million years ago. This bachelor male used only one hoof on each foot while two others was noticeably reduced and was suspended high off the ground. The crew saw this mature male drink from the river.

This male was as large as a domesticated horse and convinced Dr. Ryan that he was capable of detecting danger. While he continued to drink, Dr. Nimbus noticed something strange peeking out from underwater near the shore where *Hipparion* drank.

"Retreat!" Dr. Nimbus shouted out to his unwary colleagues as a gigantic carnivorous amphibian instantly manifested from under the waters surface.

An immense size of this particular individual was rarely achieved. This male was as large as a full grown *Tyrannosaurus rex* and estimated to weigh as much as seven tons or 6.3 metric tons of sheer terror. This full grown adult was most likely living well into his second century who feared no rival, which was rare during the late phase of this giant crocodile's life!

"Terrible crocodile" is the official English translation of a genus called *Deinosuchus*, which narrowly missed his target. *Phobosuchus* is another name meaning 'horror crocodile' referring to ancient expert ambushers that used the shroud of a docile river to conceal their deadly intentions! *Deinosuchus* terrorized Texas during the Late Cretaceous period or 99,600,000 – 65,500,000 million years ago.

Africa's Nile crocodile (*Crocodylus niloticus*) is known to adapt a similar hunting strategy in modern times. This giant ancient saltwater crocodile instantly focused his attention to one of the explorers. Each pointed tooth was as long as an adult man's finger and his head measured at least 6 feet 6 inches (2m) long! Suddenly, a symphony of raging heartbeats inside Dr. Ryan's chest coincided with thundering footsteps of a cunning giant approaching Dr. Zhu.

"Retreat everybody...retreat!"

Dr. Ryan witnessed a fifty feet (15.2m) long carnivore use his massive mouth to snatch Dr. Fan Zhu from his Drifter before he flipped Dr. Zhu into his bristled mouth before swallowing his long time colleague within seconds. Dr. Ryan and others were horrified as they couldn't see their companion inside this reptile's massive mouth. Pandemonium didn't end, due to the fact that the suspect of Dr. Zhu's death pursued to catch Dr. Ryan as his next goal!

This ruthless man eater rapidly made his way toward him with his jaws cocked wide open. Timing was important for Dr. Ryan who found himself only a few feet or meters away from his own death! Thumping footsteps accompanied by air passages venting through this male's esophagus frightened everyone trying to escape. Dr. Ryan found an open passageway between stones and streaked through this narrow trail to accomplish a greater distance.

Suddenly and quite surprisingly, *Deinosuchus* abruptly slowed down before he stopped. When Dr. Ryan looked back at this giant reptile, he noticed a keen and devious expression of his two reptilian eyes as his gigantic mouth showed an empty white interior. Despite his narrow escape, Dr. Ryan had to deal with a disturbing consequence of losing his long time colleague under his command. His first thought about his liability for the death of his trusted officer and his obligation to explain to Dr. Ying Zhu and others about how he was responsible for Dr. Fan Zhu's fate.

"Mack! Are you alright?" Marcus wondered.

"I'm responsible for Fan's death! Dr. Ryan cried, as he must acknowledge that his future relations with his crew would change permanently for the worse.

"Listen to me! There was no way you could have fended off *Deinosuchus*!" Marcus tried to help his friend understand that he wasn't liable despite Dr. Ryan's insistence otherwise.

"He's right...nobody knew there was a giant crocodile in the river? If we knew then what we know now; none of this would've happened!" Angela agreed with Marcus.

"I brought them here. I could have told them to stay back. It's my fault I should have pulled him away."

"Mack, how the hell would you able to pull a person away from a seven-ton saltwater crocodile?" Martin stressed while something at the edge of the forest edge monitored their conversation.

While colleagues tried to condone Dr. Ryan's mischief, Dr. Angela de' la' Vega looked behind only to see a group of three bird-like dinosaurs with feathers and extended arms pounce toward her direction before they've landed on her. "Oh my God...No!"

Dr. Martin de' la' Vega looked over to see three large raptors leap from behind a tall cluster of bushes and shrubs before he saw his wife being tackled off her transporter by one of three organized group of skilled hunters. Once he saw her on the ground it was too late for him to respond when the first pack member used his powerful jaws to clamp tight on her right shoulder, while a second one had a firm grip on her left thigh.

"Angela!"

By the time Dr. Martin de' la' Vega cried out her name, a third hunter bit tenaciously into her abdominal. A panicking scream of agony from his wife was all he was able to hear as her dismembered body was pulled in a tug of war by two raptors before they tore her in half above her pelvis. Blood rushed out of her lifeless corpse and sprayed all over their red plumage that developed black diamond shaped patterns.

"Let's get the hell out of here!" Dr. Nimbus knew it was hopeless to save her from three carnivorous dinosaurs known as *Utahraptor* meaning Utah robber, which stole Angela away from Martin and the entire crew.

Utahraptor looted many specimens from their existence in Utah roughly 125 million years ago within the Early Cretaceous. Their physical anatomy was compatible to *Veleciraptor*, but this species was much larger and possessed a more powerful sickle shaped claw that measured up to 15 inches or 37.5 centimeters at their second toe, which was the largest and located between the first and third toes. Mack also learned that their fourth toe was unilaterally reduced and located at the rear of each foot.

Escaping the frenzy feeding of *Utahraptor* became the ultimate goal of the crew. Dr. Ryan wanted to head back to Town Hall. Drs. de' la' Vega and Nimbus agreed before using a meadow to reach the wide river. Only a short distance to Town Hall would save all three surviving explorers except they're required to travel past or around four enormous bachelor bull buffaloes becoming suspicious as they explorers approached their position.

"Look at the size of them. They appear just like Africa's Cape buffalo." Dr. Nimbus noticed while Dr. de' la' Vega continued to sob over his devastating loss.

Dr. Ryan cautiously used his Identification Detective device to identify four bachelor males that were able to stand at least seven feet (2.15m) tall at the shoulder and weighed 1.5 tons or 1.35 metric tons each. Their black hides and dark eyes made them appear intimidating. But their most convincing feature were a pair of enlarged and powerful horns that spanned up to twelve feet (3.7m) wide that were attached to the top of their skull.

"We better be careful." Dr. Ryan warned the others.

"What's the matter?" Dr. Nimbus lacked sympathy for what lied ahead and blocked their path to Town Hall.

"That's *Pelorovis antiquus!*"

"So what, we must return to Town Hall!" Dr. Nimbus replied as he also attempted to comfort his friend Martin as he continued to sob over his devastating loss.

"They're distant relatives of the Cape buffalo. They must have short tempers." Dr. Ryan learned that *Pelorovis* lived in East Africa during the

Middle and Late Pleistocene epoch or around 781,000 – 11,700 years ago. "We have to find an alternate route."

"Where could we go?" Dr. Nimbus became impatient.

"We could go into that wide open trail penetrating the bordering woodland. We should be able to emerge from the other side of the mesa." Dr. Ryan pointed to an alternative route in order to avoid any confrontation.

"There could be something inside that trail. What if we're ambushed?" Dr. Nimbus was reluctant to take his friend's advice.

"We can't pass through the bulls. It's too risky."

Martin de' la' Vega looked straight ahead with reddened, watery eyes and soaked cheeks. He remained silent when he wiped tears from his face as he became despondent. Before Dr. Ryan could finish his statement, Dr. de' la' Vega abruptly accelerated as he continued his course toward four bachelor bull buffaloes!

"Where the hell is he going?" Dr. Nimbus was shocked to see him stand on his transporter while approaching the bulls.

Dr. Martin de' la' Vega continued to approach them without any evasive maneuvers or reduction in speed that captured one bull's attention. Tiny particles of mist and carbon dioxide raced out this bull's nostrils as this male exerted a deep breath before charging in rapid speed before lowering his head and aiming one of his two enlarged horns. Heavy steps of a galloping bull soon increased as he accelerated into a full stride.

"Martin! No!" All Dr. Ryan was able to do to help was place his hands around his mouth and scream as loud as possible.

Dr. Ryan's loose jaw lagged open as he saw the center of this bull's right horn collide into Dr. de' la' Vega's abdomen. He was lifted off his transporter before being tossed twenty feet (6.1m) into the opposite direction. Dr. Ryan heard a faint cracking of bones coming from their friend's spine during impact before he slammed onto the ground. Dr. de' la' Vega barely moved his arms and head but his legs remained physically motionless.

"Oh my God...I think he's paralyzed!" Dr. Ryan cried out.

Although Dr. de' la' Vega lied on the ground, this bachelor male became more aggressive as he lowered his head and pointed his flamboyant horns toward him again. All both men could do is watch *Pelorovis* use his left horn to pick him up and toss his battered body into a nearby shore of the swampy waterhole.

Such mayhem provoked three other bulls to focus their attention to both observers as they tried to call for their friend but they couldn't get any response from a lifeless body lying at the waters edge. Their only alternative was to ride away from three other pursuing buffalo bulls as they raced to the entrance that led inside the wide grassy trail. A dark canopy of trees became an inviting haven for Dr. Ryan as he moved ahead.

"Marcus, are the bulls following us? Mack wanted to be sure they evaded all four giant bulls.

"Marcus?" Silence was the only response Mack received for his verbal inquiry.

Dr. Ryan didn't even hear a faint but unmistakable sound of a vibrating engine of the terrain transporter, which struck a terrible chord with his nerves. "Marcus! Marcus!"

His heartbeat accelerated while body sweat formed beads across his face. He raced in the opposite direction to find his best friend. Dr. Ryan felt to be in a loosing battle with maintaining his professional bearing due to his mounting frustration. He initially suspected the bulls caught up to Dr. Nimbus and battered him ruthlessly. When he continued to move back toward the end of this trail, he found an empty transporter lying on its right side with no sight of Marcus and the bulls.

"Marcus!"

Although he felt relief of the bulls, Dr. Ryan soon heard a heavy cackling sound of crushing twigs and shattering tree branches originating from dense woods located at his left side of the trail. Amplified belching and groaning vibrated through the woods and Dr. Ryan's nerves. A disturbing combination of retched sounds and an empty transporter let him to reluctantly believe that the chances of his friend's safety or even survival were bleak at best!

Dr. Ryan noticed a large dark silhouette moving inside the woods but was unable to identify it. He instantly froze once he witnessed a gigantic meat eating mammal emerging from behind a row of trees bordering the trail dragging Dr. Nimbus in his mouth. His black fur and dark sinister eyes made this male appear deadly. Dr. Ryan couldn't believe how this male with a head shaped like a hyena's and body shaped like a leopard's, stood almost six feet (almost 1.83m) at the shoulder. His length was estimated to reach up to 13 feet or 4 meters long and believed to have weighed a ton or 900 kilograms! He may have been the largest carnivorous mammal that ever existed. Libya and Egypt experienced a grim reaper of land carnivores during the Miocene epoch or from over 23 million to over 5.3 million years ago. Larger than any rhino, this meticulous male's skull measured beyond three feet (1m) long and his enormous jaws was used to fulfill a diet that any slow moving giants including mastodons!

Dr. Nimbus bled profusely while his right shoulder and chest was nestled inside of this creodont's spacious mouth. Dr. Nimbus struggled to reach his left hand out toward Dr. Ryan before this giant creodont identified as *Megistotherium osteothlastes* applying even greater pressure of his powerful jaws to crush his upper torso. Flesh and blood ruptured out of both sides this creodont's wide muzzle as Dr. Ryan heard Dr. Nimbus's ribs and spinal chord be crushed into pieces. His friend's arm and head instantly lagged toward the ground indicating a dreadful end for a pioneering compatriot.

With no hope of saving his friend, an enraged Dr. Ryan got off his transporter before he lifted a nearby rock and threw it toward the giant creodont. A disturbing blow on male's shoulder provoked him to drop a mutilated carcass and focused his resentment toward Dr. Ryan, who was climbing back on his transporter. Without any warning *Megistotherium osteothlastes* exerted his rage by pursuing him. It was imperative for Dr. Ryan to move rapidly on his transporter once he heard heavy thumping steps from all four enlarged padded paws. Blood stained teeth were inevitable when Dr. Ryan looked at a ferocious reflection from his left side view mirror. A sole surviving explorer had no choice but to pursue this strange trail that could easily lead him to the end of his life!

Dr. Ryan was shocked once he saw three gigantic primates that resembled gorillas exceeding 650 pounds or 295 kilograms pounced from bordering woodland at his left side ahead before seeing them charge *Megistotherium*. Each adult male stood around 10 feet (3m) tall while standing on all four limbs and possessed the strength of at least twenty Olympic weightlifters! This species was the real life King Kong of Earth's natural history from the Late Miocene to the Mid Pleistocene or roughly 11,608,000 – 126,000 years ago in China, India and Pakistan. Some people currently claim that *Gigantopithecus blacki* still exists inside the most remote areas of the Himalayas and could possibly be a natural explanation of a mysterious modern primate known as the Yeti.

All three handsome primates clashed with *Megistotherium* for their own purpose of patrolling their mountain passé. Loud roars echoed across the vicinity as Dr. Ryan darted through an uncertain trail until it was safe enough to slow down. Dr. Ryan felt emotionally exhausted as he contemplated how disastrous this mission will be for his crew. Dr. Ryan thought about such pain until an unexpected jolt of a sudden stop threw him off ten feet (3m) ahead of his Drifter. Dr. Ryan was lucky to be uninjured as but felt shaken as he gently got back on his feet. When Dr. Ryan stumbled back to his Drifter, he reluctantly noticed a severed right front tire lodged into a ditch. Unable to reattach the front tire, he had no better choice than to cross this trail and enter a bordering forest at his left side hoping that they'll be another way back to the mesa. Dr. Ryan stumbled over logs, rocks, and twigs to avoid *Megistotherium osteothlastes* which is part of an extinct order of carnivorous mammals known as creodonts (order creodonta) that means meat eating tooth.

Creodonts had two family groups called Hyaenodontidae and Oxyaenidae.

The main difference between creodonts and modern carnivores is that creodonts had smaller brains; no bone at the center of each ear, the skeletal structure of their feet weren't attached to their ankles and had grooved nails instead of claws. A creodont's pattern of were well suited for meat eating purposes. At their first molar pairs developed sharp pairs of carnassials while their rear molars were capable of crushing flesh and bones. All large creodonts had jaws capable of exerting over 1,000 pounds (454kg) of pressure per square inch in every bite, which crushed bones instead of slicing through flesh. Since Dr. Ryan's transporter was beyond repair, he decided upon himself to hide inside a bordering forest from the pursuing creodont or anyone of the gigantic primates. Dr. Ryan became paranoid while hearing a distant resonation.

"Town Hall…come in! Town Hall…come in!" Mack shouted out for any desirable response. However, he captured the attention of something else.

However, a swamp inside a forest didn't make matters for Dr. Ryan much easier. Dr. Ryan heard a hissing tone coming from the edge of a gray misty shroud above the swamp. He wasn't able to find out what could cause such a disturbing gesture as he continued to maneuver through trees and bushes. Despite efforts to avoid this swampy lake, he suspected this possible source was closer to him than he originally estimated as this hostile verbal expression became more intense.

Dr. Ryan became more nervous as he listened to cackling sounds of nearby rattling bushes and breaking twigs in compliance with a sequential pattern of footsteps. He decided to move away from the source to avoid what ever he heard penetrating through thick bushes. As he entered an open clearance inside the forest Dr. Ryan paced across soft soil before looking back in order to see what would emerge.

A gigantic rodent revealed itself when it penetrated a batch of bushes. It appeared like a gigantic beaver with a massive tail in conjunction to its body shape. Unlike modern North American beavers this giant grew as large as a black bear and weighed up to 1000 pounds or 454 kilograms. Thick chocolate brown fur made this male look heavier as his well-adapted limbs could propel this massive mammal to move rapidly and even swim.

Dr. Ryan remembered Dr. Netherland owning a statue of such a prehistoric beaver that appeared much like their modern counterparts. Although this rugged rodent didn't make dams like modern beavers, *Castoroides ohioensis* was able to adapt to land as well as various bodies of water. This powerful male measured seven feet, six inches (2.3m) long and despite their fossils proving their coexistence with early humans, there's not much evidence of *Castoroides ohioensis* ever being perused by hunters, despite their thick fur. *Castoroides* means "beaver-like" and this brave male was able to fight much larger predators, similar to how his species survived at North America during the Pleistocene epoch, which ranged from 2,588,000 – 11,700 years ago.

Dr. Ryan knew his best option was to gently move away and show no form of aggression toward the giant beaver, because if he did, than *Castoroides* would retaliate. This male demonstrated some curiosity as he saw Dr. Ryan leave his vicinity by blending into the woods. As he dodged trees and jumped over rocks and logs, Dr. Ryan didn't hear this male follow him anymore. He continued to pace through the forest as he felt more relieved.

Additional reassurance was felt when he saw Town Hall on top of a visible mesa only 200 yards or 183 meters from his location. Dr. Ryan reached the edge of the woods and discovered another open grass trail spanning across his path directly ahead. His only known objective was to cross this trail and penetrate a forest that bordered it at the other side. Dr. Ryan walked exhaustively across this open trail to reach the other side. Up to 80 feet or over 24 meters of open space left to cross provided a safe haven until he noticed something pouncing toward him from the edge of the bordering woodland he wanted to enter!

Dr. Ryan soon discovered what it took to fulfill a natural role of emperor of the Earth's ecology during the Late Cretaceous period or roughly 99,600,000 – 65,000,000 years ago; and mastered of their surroundings of North America and Asia! Acute senses and a forward binocular vision with possible zoom lens helped this king of carnivores ambush a petrified commander similar to how modern crocodiles would pounce upon unwary prey drinking from the edge of lakes and rivers. Rather than raging out of water, this female hid inside an open pocket behind a row of bushes and trees so she could wait for anything that crossed her path. The "tyrant lizard" or *Tyrannosaurus rex* was among the largest and fiercest meat eating life form ever to walk on land. The largest *Tyrannosaurus rex* grew to an astonishing fifty feet (15.25m) long! Such carnivorous dinosaurs don't stand fully erect. Instead a typical *Tyrannosaurus rex* would stand horizontally from head to tail in order to maintain a perfect balance on their giant legs. Despite their stance this species stood 20 feet or over six meters tall at the hips and weigh up to seven tons or over six metric tons!

A six-ton (5.4 metric tons) adult female patiently waited for her opportunity. An overt display of banana sized teeth measuring up to six inches (15.24cm) long made Mack freeze, which was why *Tyrannosaurus rex* was inspired to pounce with her mouth cocked wide open. Her giant muscular jaws widen vertically as she lowered her massive head toward the ground to fulfill her desire to consume a commanding officer. Mack wasn't able to do anything when he was snatched from the ground before being embedded inside this female's massive mouth. Her massive jaws, which exceeded four feet or 1.2

meters long devoured Dr. Ryan's flesh and crush his bones. Suddenly a vortex sucked him inside the esophagus of this female's "S" shaped neck as a gesture of final destiny. Mack continued his futile efforts to struggle until he frantically unraveled a draped blanket that covered him.

Once Dr. Ryan tossed his blanket off his bed and regained full consciousness, he sat upright before he took a series of heavy breaths. His body was covered in sweat as his hair became moist. He maneuvered toward the edge of his bed before his feet touched a carpeted floor. He reached over to a lamp to turn on his lights. Dr. Ryan then approached his intercom to answer an audio message activated inside Dr. Ryan's living quarters.

"Doctor Ryan come-in please," Dr. Nimbus transmitted.

"This is Doctor Ryan!"

"We're approaching Jupiter's moon Callisto."

"Move the ship toward the planet's right side and pinpoint the nose of the ship away and accelerate thrusters, so we could maintain a safe distance." Dr. Ryan instructed before Dr. Nimbus acknowledged his instructions.

Dr. Ryan walked into his bathroom to clean and remove body moisture before drying himself with a cotton towel. Once he put on a new pair of boxer shorts and a white undershirt, he then approached a closet and took out a blue jumpsuit and a pair of black boots. Once he was completely dressed, Dr. Ryan made his bed, turned off his lights and departed his living quarters.

Dr. Ryan proceeded through a long corridor and approached a mechanical elevator. A slow moving elevator arrived once a set of double doors opened. Mack entered before he pressed a button before the elevator transported him to his desired deck.

"Mack, you must see this," was the first group of words from an excited Dr. Nimbus, who was captivated by such a majestic presence of a massive planet.

An artistic blend of red, white, gold, brown, and orange, colored clouds covered this entire planet. Different shapes and swirls of clouds at various layers of the planet's altitude created a three dimensional visual effect. The planet of the gods became an appropriate reference of the giant Jovian planet as the starship made its way past one of Jupiter's satellites called Io and continued to approach a planet that was almost a star itself. Emitting more energy than it receives from the sun would be one reason why the starship vibrated when this planet's powerful gravitational force tugged the starship toward it. Seatbelts and a set of verbal commands were necessary to prepare all 1500 men and women to brace themselves to be propelled like a sling shot.

"It looks imposing…I thought I'll never encounter a splendid spectacle such as this!" Dr. Ryan professed.

"What's the latest news about Europa?" Dr. Ying Zhu asked.

"The federation's launching probes to Europa. Once this destination is reached then a miniature submarine explorer known as Diver will search underneath its blanket of ice and explore possible liquid water below," Dr. Arnold Weinstein responded.

"Speaking of water, Mars once again pose more evidence of water existing in the past and now finding traces of its molecules today." Dr. Antonio Marino said to the crowd.

"I heard about that a long time ago, Dr. Malik al-Saud responded. It's amazing how neutrinos are so small in physical size; they could physically penetrate the Earth's surface and come out the other side of the planet without touching anything!"

"Has anyone remembered Dr. David Suzuki's statement of how small Superstrings could actually be? Dr. Ryan asked.

"Tell us." Dr. Ying Zhu wanted to know.

"I heard that he once stated that the size of individual superstrings is so small that if you compare the physical size of an atom in comparison to a superstring, then the atom would have to be the size of our solar system in order for the individual superstring to be the size of an atom." Dr. Ryan's colleagues were fascinated to hear such startling news.

"You remember when astronomers discovered a black hole and a pulsar merging? Dr. al-Saud asked. Scientists estimated that the energy involved during this fusing event could've fueled all of modern human civilization until the end of time!"

"Speaking of black holes, how about the primordial black holes that wander through the universe? They're so dense, that they're physical sizes range from atoms up to a living cell. Yet, they could have the mass of a mountain range!" Dr. Fan Zhu told the crowd.

"I learned how devastating it could be if a tiny black hole entered Earth." Dr. al-Saud recalled Dr. Netherland's lectures.

"A minor cosmic catastrophe would be a supernova of a star, causing an entire solar system to be destroyed. However, a major catastrophe would be a collision of two or more galaxies! Also, when a galaxy becomes active and become a quasar or even a blazar, it would become a menace to many neighboring galaxies. The word quasar means quasi stellar radio source." Marcus reminded everyone how an intense electromagnetic phenomenon received its name.

"I was shocked of how gamma ray bursts are thought to last only a few seconds but could outshine our galaxy for hundreds of years! Gamma ray bursts are suspected to be the most violent natural phenomenon ever observed by astronomers!" Dr. Fan Zhu impressed everyone.

"I remember Doctor Netherland lectured us about the Great Attractor.

It's an elusive region of space but it's pulling hundreds of galaxies including our own toward it. Doctor Netherland suspects it's an exceptionally massive black hole that's tens of thousands of times more massive than our galaxy." Dr. Ryan said.

"Dr. Netherland showed us a map of the universe. Each point of light represented at least one thousand galaxies. He revealed how the structure of the entire known universe would appear based upon modern cosmology. Millions of galaxies were aligned together in a long formation that extended billions of light years across known as the Great Wall, which were separated by enormous areas lacking any galaxy became known as the Great Void. The whole structure appeared like a spider's web, which was why cosmologists called it the Cosmic Web!" Dr. Nimbus revealed to the group.

"Think about this…our sun and Osiris could last ten billion years. A typical blue giant star only exists for about a few million years or so. However, a red dwarf star could remain intact for at least a trillion years!" Dr. Singh added into the conversation.

"One lesson I'll never forget was the time I found out that Jupiter was so large; you could fit one hundred Earths inside of it. The sun is so large; you could fit one million Earths inside." Dr. Rosalila participated into their discussion.

"I was very surprised what I learned about Saturn. The planet itself is so light, that if there's ever an ocean large enough, Saturn could actually float on it. Not to mention that Saturday was previously called, Saturn's Day," Dr. al-Saud commented.

Everyone felt subtle vibrations originating from a planetary giant. Soon afterwards, the ship's vibrations intensified as Jupiter's inner magnetic field belt was breached. This planet that possessed 1300 times' greater volume and over 317 times more mass than Earth expressed its wonder and intimidation to the entire crew. The gravitational force rapidly increased above the normal gravity force or G-force. A single G-force is equivalent to Earth's native gravity level. However Jupiter's gravity is approximately 2.34 times that of Earth's. So if a two hundred pound (91kg) adult man stood on the equator of Jupiter, he would weigh a whopping 468 pounds or over 212 kilograms!

While Dr. Nimbus and Dr. Ryan freely exchanged their knowledge of the universe, Drs. Singh and Rosalila listened to the group conversation and through about two men they increasingly admire. Both women whispered to each other as the others exchanged their understanding of the universe. What impressed them most wasn't how much they knew, but how humbly they've expressed their wisdom. Both women agreed that Dr. Nimbus and Dr. Ryan's cheerful attitude were most attractive of all.

Everyone was pressed against their cushioned seats holding armrests for personal stability. Some instantly noticed the entire ship was shaking as a result of penetrating Jupiter's awesome magnetic field. Once all of the lights inside the command and control center blackened out Marcus looked out the exposed ceiling and front windows and see a clearer view of gas formations riddling Jupiter's sky.

"Hold on everybody this could be intense," Dr. Ryan shouted.

"I'm glad we're passing Jupiter only once!" Dr. Nimbus infused his brand of optimism.

As they approached this perplexing planet, the crew inside the command and control center recognized faint flashes of light originating from deep inside Jupiter's clouds. Various compositions and altitudes of this planet's clouds displayed multiple layers of colors and patterns that entertained all who observed Jupiter's amazing atmosphere. The starship Guardian darted forward, causing a whiplash effect among the crew.

Feeling such a thrusting force of a cosmic roller coaster ride would seem to match the description of their gravitational trajectory past Jupiter. It was easy to notice visible storms that appeared like gigantic hurricanes. These white oval shaped monsters were the size of the planet Mars. Mack saw dense equatorial clouds intertwine as currents from underneath moved them into many directions. Between these gigantic hurricanes and violent eddies made these thick colorful clouds reflected an image of splashed paint on a clear canvass surface. A collection of various colors fascinated everyone on board.

A legendary hurricane located at Jupiter's southern hemisphere, appeared a like gigantic red eye that could engulf two Earths inside. The Great Red Spot symbolically kept its mighty oval shape by consuming other storms including minor hurricanes such as neighboring white spots that would travel too close. Dr. Ryan and others stared at this surreal storm with awe.

Jupiter's rapid rotation and gravitational force accelerated the starship's speed evermore. A cosmic work of art that expressed its atmospheric panorama of swirled clouds and colorful gases dominated their view. Jupiter's imposing gravity propelled the Humane Federation Starship Guardian through a natural projection out of its orbit and ultimately beyond the solar system. Dr. Ryan and his crew expected the most intense portion of this propulsion would soon end as they witnessed these colorful clouds transform into a black sky of nocturnal blight. The sun's rays ceased as Jupiter's dark side entered their view.

Although fine details of Jupiter's splendorous sky vanished, the dark side revealed another compelling phenomenon. Bright flashes of light were easily detectable. These flashes of light inside Jupiter's nighttime sky were powerful lightening bolts as intense as atomic bombs. Each bolt of lightening was powerful enough to incinerate a midsized city within a single strike. Dr.

Ryan knew that Jupiter was named after the arch Roman god as it showed off its symbolic and literal might. He also understood that the Roman God of Jupiter of the sky and thunder was also the son of Saturn and was a sibling of Neptune and Pluto. His sister and wife Juno gave birth to Mars. He though about such mythological history as the Starship Guardian maintained its course.

"I still remember when I was studying Jupiter's electrical storms at the university." Dr. Ying Zhu mentioned. "Doctor Netherland presented an active portrayal of massive lightning bolts striking the surface almost constantly."

"How could I forget? It startled me when he informed us that it would be equivalent to a continuous nuclear war in duration of Jupiter's natural history." Dr. Fan Zhu recalled.

If any one of Jupiter's lightening bolts would strike the surface of Earth, the energy released could annihilate even the most fundamental life forms including single celled organisms within a city sized area! Despite Jupiter's immense size, the planet's rotation only takes 10 hours to complete, so at the equator it's rotating approximately 22 times faster than Earth. Such a rapid rotation, which is the fastest of all the planets in the solar system, is one cause of such formidable weather patterns.

A sense of relief was felt among the crew when all lights inside the command center reactivated that assured Mack of the ship's structural integrity. Lucy noticed a broader scope of widespread activities of flashing lights as they moved further away from the dark side of this storm plagued planet. Dr. Ryan watched Jupiter shrink in size as vibrations among the starship weaken until the ship's hull became stable once again.

"Okay everyone, let's go to debriefing." Dr. Ryan announced before delegating command to Dr. Karl Gruber before departing with his trusted colleagues.

Dr. Ryan guided his companions into an elevator that brought them down to their desired deck. Everyone followed him out of the elevator and walked through a long corridor until they opened an entrance door that invited them into an auditorium. Dr. Martin and Angela de' la' Vega joined the others as they've entered. All lights inside a small auditorium activated once they entered. Drs. Fan and Ying Zhu sat at the front row with Dr. Nimbus. Dr. Ryan walked up on the stage's steps at the right side of the audience's view before he approached a podium and activated a microphone. Other researchers eventually entered the assembly room and took their seats behind the first row. This debriefing will discuss the next phase, which regards initial procedures for their suspended animation. Dr. Ryan is assigned to the first crew, which completed their shift and will be relieved by the second crew.

"Before we begin there's something I wish to share with everyone here,"

Dr. Ryan announced before he decided to reveal an important message for his crew. "Eve number one."

Although action packed detailed graphics of the 360-degree, four dimensional holographic projector wasn't available, a giant flat plasma screen illustrated a high definition display on a rectangular screen that measured 60 feet (18.3m) across and up to 30 feet (9.15m) tall so the entire audience could see a clear image of a gigantic Komodo dragon gently walking through tall grass and weeds toward a river.

"Does everyone have a clear view of the screen?" Mack asked standing behind the podium at the center of a stage that was three feet or almost one meter above the aisle surface.

Dr. Ryan received a favorable response. "We received new images of Isis. What's more is that every single life form we detected is widespread in the Central Continent."

"Is that what I think it is?" Dr. Fan Zhu wondered.

"It's *Megalania prisca*." Mack confirmed Dr. Zhu's suspicion.

"What does *Megalania* mean?" Dr. Harold Nevis asked.

"Ancient great roamer." Mack responded before closer images of his legendary lizard impressed everyone similar to how their fossils inspired paleontologists worldwide.

"Eve number two," Dr. Ryan requested another scene.

This next scene revealed a robust livelihood within an open plain. Dr. Ryan pointed to a group of browsing hornless rhinoceroses browsing treetops up to 26 feet (7.93m) above the ground! Elongated legs enabled this gray, leathery skinned herbivore to stand over 18 feet (5.5m) at the shoulder, as their extended necks helped them to consume short bushes and high branches of tall trees as well.

Their skulls estimated to measure up to 4 feet, 3inches (1.3m) long, it appeared small compared to their 16 tons (14.4 metric tons) of monumental flesh. "Giraffe rhinoceros" is an English translation of *Idricotherium* for which Dr. Ryan verbally described this genus of magnificent mammals.

"Whoa...what's that over there?" Dr. Angela de la Vega asked when she saw a bold mammal inspecting the immediate area.

"That's *Archaeotherium*," Dr. Ryan replied as this name of this genus literally means "ancient beast" and grew as large as a cow.

Members of the audience were surprised to see this large female lead her young, which grew four feet (1.2m) long. Spectators inside the auditorium were shocked to see a living specimen that appeared similar to an extinct family of pigs called Entelodontidae (Entelodonts) that were distant relatives of modern pigs. Although it's almost impossible for Paleontologists to obtain enough measurable data to know the exact fur, skin color and specific social customs of many prehistoric animals, however, their persistent study of fossil records, geographic origins along with observing living relatives with the aid of computer animation made it possible for modern scholars to unravel the mysteries of Earth's prehistoric life.

Drs. Viktor and Nina Ivanov noticed stocky limbs that resembled a buffalo instead of a pig because Archaeotherium grew two toes on each foot. They noticed their enlarged heads along with a muzzle like a crocodile's that contained two bony knobs attached to the rear of their jaws and located directly under each eye. Archaeotherium developed impressive jaws and hard teeth capable of consuming just about anything including carrion. They evolved a long spine; the height of their shoulders was noticeably high due to dense muscles attached to their vertebrae in order to support their massive skulls.

"Eve number four." Dr. Ryan said before another scene of scattered woodland with leafless trees.

It was easy for the audience to notice a familiar appearance of a bold and beautiful group of horned dinosaurs walking to a nearby waterhole to drink. Elongated pairs of brow horns above their eyes and a smaller nasal horn made each of them appear formidable. Many members of this audience recognized *Triceratops horridus* of North America during the Late Cretaceous period or from 99,600,000 – 65,500,000 years ago. This spectacular species was estimated to measure up to 30 feet (9.15m) long weighed 11 tons or around 10 metric tons.

Ever since Othniel C. Marsh originally named this life form in 1889, the legacy of *Triceratops* continues though modern times as Dr. Nimbus noticed them maneuver similar to rhinoceroses or large buffaloes. The Late Cretaceous was a time when *Triceratops* was the largest, heaviest and most populated genus of all the great horned dinosaurs! Their neck frills emerged from the rear of their heads and was made of a hard layer of bone. It appeared to act like a shield to protect their neck vertebrae and to anchor their powerful jaw muscles. Their neck frills could fulfill a role of a solar receptor designed to absorb sunlight to warm a network of blood vessels. Their heads measured over 6 feet 6inches (2m) long as their fine physique stood up to 16 feet (4.9m) tall!

Dr. Martin de' la' Vega noticed all four mature bulls approaching a fresh water hole, while others noticed a group of pterosaurs circling above all four males. One of these flying reptiles landed on the shoulders of one of the horned dinosaurs before pecking his spinal chord. Marcus identified *Sordes* of Kazakhstan devouring insects and parasites before resuming flight similar to how this task was accomplished during the Jurassic period, which ranged from 193 – 136 million years ago.

Possessing an 18-inch (45.7cm) wingspan, Sordes pilosus was capable of hunting insects, parasites and scavenge carrion of large animals. Such a unique method of landing on a large animal's back to remove annoying insects and parasites evolved into a remarkable hunting niche for many small pterosaurs. One distinct advantage of small pterosaurs was their ability to scavenge on corpses, which were inaccessible for large land carnivores because they're trapped in deadly tar pits or mud pools. Modern birds such as the Red-billed Oxpecker (Buphagus erythrorhynchus) of eastern and southern Africa extract insects and parasites from Elephants, buffaloes and rhinoceroses. It's possible that small pterosaurs even scavenge insects and small animals that were stepped on by dinosaur migrations similar to how Black back gulls (Larus marinus) of modern North America consume vulnerable insects and small mammals stampeded by migrating bison.

Pterosaurs most likely possessed hair on their torsos and blood vessels within both wings, enabling their body temperature to be controlled both internally and externally similar to Cynodonts (meaning dog teeth) that possessed reptilian and mammalian characteristics. In other words, it's possible that pterosaurs including *Sordes* used their wings to receive the sun's rays into a plexus of blood vessel inside. Their plumage insulated their torsos and legs from cooler temperatures and maintains their body heat from within. Dr. Ryan and his colleagues were amazed to learn more fascinating facts of this ceremonious spectacle!

"Marcus! What's that behind the tall row of bushes?" Dr. Fan Zhu asked.

"I don't know. But I saw something move behind it too."

Although Dr. Nimbus wasn't certain what it was, all four male *Triceratops* abruptly stopped once the audience noticed their nasals squinting frantically. Dr. Ryan suspected that these mature bulls detected a discomforting scent. All four matured males initially bellowed as they repeatedly tilt and swayed their heads before repeatedly snapping their massive jaws. The audience felt compelled to hear jet streams of air raced out of a male's nostrils as a verbal warning to what ever could possibly be behind a row of tall shrubs and bushes nearby.

"I know there's something behind those bushes." Dr. Nimbus's suspicion was finally confirmed as he was instantly startled to witness an enormous bipedal dinosaur rise above the highest point of the bush.

"That's *Giganotosaurus carolinii*." Dr. Nimbus claimed.

"What does the word mean?" Dr. Ying Zhu wondered how such a spectacle exceeds the length of an adult *Tyrannosaurus rex*!

"Giant southern lizard," Dr. Nimbus responded as they were face to face with a sheer symbol of Southern supremacy during the Cretaceous period

(136 – 65 million years ago) when this female showed her bitter rebuttal toward *Triceratops horridus*.

All four horned dinosaurs resented what grew up to 52 feet (15.9m) long and weighed 8 tons or 7.2 metric tons of monumental flesh with enlarged spikes on her back and tail. Once this matriarch looked toward the audience, Dr. Angela de' la' Vega recognized a pink tint or shade riddled across her bristled mouth, which revealed a fine alignment of strong serrated teeth that extended up to 5 inches (12.7cm) long. Dr. Ryan recognized her powerful jaw inside a sleek skull estimated to measure around 6 feet (1.83m) covered with red skin.

A thunderous verbal outburst from *Giganotosaurus* provoked all four mature males to deliberately urinate on the ground as their unmistakable gesture to an irritated queen carnivore. Once this heated exchange of verbal bitterness escalated, Dr. Nimbus noticed the female's damp face due to water she drank from a nearby water hole. Dr. Nimbus was convinced that *Giganotosaurus* intended to rest and claim this waterhole as her valuable resource instead of ambushing prey.

Empathy for any intentions of *Giganotosaurus* wasn't the mature bull's priority because all four were more concerned about claiming this particular waterhole for themselves! Dr. Ryan and others saw tensions reach a climax when two larger males instantly charged toward this objective carnivore. Dr. Ying Zhu could never forget seeing one of the brow horns of a male *Triceratops* puncture her abdomen before she used her "S" shaped neck to lash her head forward and bit this male at his giant crest. Dr. Derrick Grace observed a second male *Triceratops* use his exceptionally powerful jaw to leap up and biting the left shoulder blade of their rival.

The audience saw the carnivorous female retreat back behind the nearby bushes before she began to evaluate their immense cheeked beaks with grinding teeth inside and an array of enhanced horns. A powerful resonating scream of verbal threats helped *Giganotosaurus* defending herself as she backed away cautiously to discourage four males to charge. The audience felt deep toned vibrations emitted from an agitated female that was startled to see *Triceratops* since she'd reawaken.

Dr. Ryan observed a mild trace of dried up blood across her flesh shredding teeth that indicated a previous engagement with consuming prey. He suspected the female was resting before she was interrupted. Theropod dinosaurs walked on three large toes that have sharp claws. They walk like modern birds. Theropods commonly possess brawny legs and small arms along with an "S" shaped neck and a rigid horizontal tail. Most theropods including this female had evolved follicles of plumage and even feathers. Her immense size and strength didn't overlap her wise decision to temporarily retreat. Despite her being rudely awakened from an apparent nap, this female ended up only 50 yards (over 45m) away from what Dr. Nimbus suspected to be her lair.

Miraculously she only suffered minor injuries, which was less of a burden than her current complications of defending her territory. Despite an eventual triumph of *Triceratops*, the giant southern lizard doesn't like losing even the tiniest fraction of her vast territory, which would be hundreds of square miles. What's more is rare resources such as a stable waterhole produced from underground springs would be imperative for this female's survival. *Giganotosaurus* will wait until one of these thirty feet (9.15m) long maturing bull *Triceratops* roam alone so she'll make an attempt to ambush any one of them. This process will be repeated until she's ready to launch a counter attack in order to reclaim her territory!

Dr. Ryan remembered when Rubén Carolini explored Patagonia and discovered fossils of *Giganotosaurus carolinii* in 1994. To his surprise, Rubén Carolini unearthed an almost complete fossil skeleton of what was estimated to be the largest land carnivore ever to exist in Earth's known history! Unearthed in Argentina, these fossils reveal a dinosaur with a slimmer built and possessed curved serrated teeth unlike. Dr. Netherland referred this particular incident to his protégés during lectures to prove that miracles is a part of reality and no human being should ever be excluded from experiencing the extraordinary.

"Ladies and gentlemen! That's all for now." Dr. Ryan announced before he informed the audience that a full time medical staff would monitor individual hibernation chambers for safety and security in duration of their suspended animation.

No astronaut or cosmonaut ever experienced modern cryonics like what's aboard the starship Guardian. However, their repeated reassurances that the end of this long journey will result in being reawakened alive and in good health. A previous estimate of eight years in suspended animation would feel like a long night's sleep in contrast to remaining awake that would feel like a life time. Their path to paradise started once three nurses entered the assembly hall to guide everyone to the chambers.

The entire assembly stood from their seats and followed all three nurses to a room, which contained rows of individual capsules. These prototype cryopreservation chambers succeeded previous models originally used during the twentieth century as a prolonged device to cure fatal diseases. If an individual would be diagnosed with an incurable disease or virus, then he or she would use a hibernation capsule and remain in a deep freeze until a cure is discovered then he or she would be reawakened for their life saving medical treatment. Neurotic activity inside a person's brain would become less active. Blood flow would be docile but stable. His or her digestion process will be temporarily suspended as well as hair growth and cellular death and rejuvenation. An individual will be completely unconscious and will not feel any stimuli in duration of his or her long sleep. Drs. Ryan, Nimbus, Weinstein and Marino were part of the first shift that will experience this rare procedure. Nurses and technicians briefed all safety precautions. Dr. Fan and Ying Zhu made final preparations along with the Remington's to be separated for years by entering a hygienic care room. Drs. Alicia and Harold Nevins followed the others to this room. Drs. Ryan and Nimbus saw the al-Saud's walking inside as they discussed their objective with the Drs. Martin and Angela de la Vega.

"Mack," Lucy said as she rubs her right thumb on his left palm.

"Yes?"

"I'll meet you just outside the washroom." She kissed him on the cheek then proceeded to the ladies washroom. Meena gave a similar gesture to the Marcus before she followed Lucy inside. The two long time friends were taken by surprise by unprecedented hospitality of both women. Neither Marcus nor Mack said a single word as they stared at each other.

"Did Meena do what I think she did?" Marcus wondered.

"I think so, because Lucy did the same thing to me."

"Umm…we're spending too much time in the Clairvoyance projector rooms." Marcus emphasized to his colleague.

Both gentlemen then made their way into the washroom before their moment of truth arrived when they met Lucy and Meena again. Everyone wore orange body suits that covered everything except their faces. Mack thought about when they'll reawaken, the Humane Space Federation Starship Guardian will be approaching this new world! After members of the first shift were successfully cleaned and prepared for their initial hibernation process, only four individuals stood outside their hibernation chamber. Once their safety briefing was over, all four reengaged into their conversation.

"Mack there's something I wanted you to know." Lucy felt as though this would be a good time to inform him of how she felt and to be sure that he would be receptive.

"Sure…go ahead."

"My father told me about when you attended the Papoose Lake campus of the university. He said that you were his student when he taught space travel.

"Of course…I remember."

"I knew you commanded the Hoi-Larson intervention and learned that you're responsible for our first lunar compound. What I really wanted you to know is that I've always admired you for a long time. I wanted to tell you several times but there were so many interruptions." Mack's eyebrows rose higher than ever before as she stood in front of him waiting for his reply.

Mack's curled lips made him appear stunned and shy. But his inviting smile reassured Lucy of a warm response she desired for a long while. Mack finally admitted that he was too nervous to approach her because she was so attractive and immensely intelligent. Mack still remembered his curriculum at the federation's university. He remembered the first time professor Rosalila introduced his daughter during a session. Lucy then lectured the class and Mack was in love ever since. So much time has passed until Mack's love for was revealed to Lucy.

"I've always since the first day I saw you during your father's lecture. I've been in love with you since." Mack confessed before they warmly embraced each other before they eventually loosened their grip before separating.

Meena revealed to Marcus how much she loved his autobiography called; Mastery: Inside and Out. She also told him how his mission with Mack initiated her long lasting impression of him and she was nervous to propose a relationship because she feared rejection because she conceived Marcus as a workaholic.

"I never thought you ever felt anything for me…heck, I didn't think you read my autobiography. I didn't think I could even get your attention. If I only knew…" Marcus said before Meena interrupted him by placing her four left fingers horizontally across his mouth while pressing her left thumb under his chin.

"You know now," was Meena's response before she smiled and continued to stare into his surprised eyes.

Marcus's soft dry hand caressed the hand that prevented him to speak any further. He gently removed her hand from his mouth and told her "From now on, everything will be much better both of us…all of us!"

A mild mannered French kissing of two inspired couples dissolved their long lasting social barrier. The last four space explorers entered their assigned modules. Careful preparations was assigned to each patient before the airtight door of each chamber was sealed closed to initiate this deep sleep process that will awaken them to a new Era of Isis!

Extraterrestrials from Earth

Subtle dreams and faint images stimulated each person who remained in suspended animation. Over eight years of loneliness inside an enclosed module transcended Dr. Ryan into his dream world. He imagined what it could be like to live on Earth without any presence of human civilization except his crew? During his long term hibernation, Dr. Ryan realized that human activities must be monitored on Isis more carefully than on Earth. He knew that life will be robust but its natural habitat would be sensitive.

Dr. Ryan reflected the potential dangers of Isis. He never forgot his nightmare of being eaten by a *Tyrannosaurus rex* before he awakened inside his living quarters or eight years ago. A gravity control mechanism maintained his suspended position inside the module. Bioplasma receptors inside their jumpsuits detected faint stimuli from his skin in duration of his time inside the chamber. Extreme cold temperature inside these capsules made them almost clinically dead until the awakening process. These orange jumpsuits along with head and face gear were worn during their hibernation. Every participant was subjected to extreme medical supervision in duration of their confinement.

Engineers and technicians monitored data from each bio-monitor jumpsuit and adjusted temperature and air pressure inside every chamber when necessary. Members of the last or tenth shift prepared all medical facilities and physical therapeutic centers for an important phase of this mission. Hibernation chamber control technicians adjusted panels as paramedics, specializing in post cryonic recovery care waited patiently to remove all members of the first shift from their long hibernation that finally ended. Interior temperatures of each module gradually increased and took approximately 48 hours for suitable conditions inside the capsule to be completely stabilized.

The most important phase involves physical therapy of each chamber's occupant. Once conditions inside each module stabilized, soft sounds, mild odors and faint lights stimulated their senses for the first day of recovery. This awakening phase require the most attentive supervision. Gravity generating rods inside each capsule will be activated.

Flexing and maneuvering limbs was required to regenerate weakened muscles. Soon after, more gravitational pressure will be applied to strengthen muscles even further. Artificial heat from insulating suits would warm up over time so this recovery process could successfully reawaken each occupant. A continued gradual increase of gravitational force would eventually enhance a person's physical strength.

Once a qualified physician certifies each individual, gravitational rods inside each module will generate enough gravity to match the same G-force as the starship. Air pressure and temperature would be adjusted to match similar conditions outside before a team of paramedics rushed into the hibernation chamber. After eight long years in repose and 48 forethoughtful hours of preparation, a faint sound of an air tight, latch was heard when chamber room technicians opened the first capsule. A team of trained emergency personnel wasted no time to help this individual out of the capsule. This man laid passively on a gurney as paramedics rushed him to sickbay. A light cloth was placed over his eyes to prevent visual shock. The federation's medical staff carefully orchestrated this procedure to transport this patient to the Emergency Room. Due to being barely coherent and devoid of physical energy was one reason why emergency response personnel verbally assured his return to full scale consciousness.

"Doctor Ryan, it's good to see you sir." Paramedics rushed Dr. Ryan over to sickbay as they discouraged him to speak in order to prevent vocal stress.

"Transport him to ER One." One nurse told them before directing them to an ER specializing in post cryonic recovery.

Nutrition and physical conditioning were a central focus of the medical staff. Physical therapists handled his strength and cardiovascular training, while dermatologists maintained an accurate record of Dr. Ryan's skin, hair, and lip condition. Field computers continued to monitor his heart, blood pressure, and body temperature. Monitoring devices used circular abrasives to connect a receptor to his chest. Attached wires will transmit data from this abrasive patch, to multiple monitors. A registered nurse would monitor each recovering patient constantly. Cameras and microphones monitored the progress of each individual including Dr. Ryan. Technicians monitored his condition throughout this recovery process. If a medical emergency ever occurred then doctors and technicians would intervene to recover any patient.

A couple of months of physical and psychological therapy served Dr. Ryan well. Muscles and joints readapted to simulated gravity on board the H.S.F.S. Guardian, which is currently inside the solar system of Osiris! A new phase of this mission began when a blond haired Argentinean woman entered Dr. Ryan's hospital quarters before she approached him. Her white lab coat and long time experience confirmed her role as a registered nurse.

"Doctor Grace, is it you?" Mack wondered.

Dr. Julia Grace was born in Buenos Aries and was inspired by two revered paleontologists known as Rodolfo Coria and José Bonaparte. Both seasoned veterans unraveled a collection of dinosaur fossils, which includes *Gigantosaurus carolinii* and a super massive sauropod dinosaur known as *Argentinosaurus huinculensis*. Both could be the world largest land predator and herbivore in Earth's history! Fossils of *Amargasaurus* and *Carnotaurus* were also discovered in Argentina.

"Long time no see." After months of recovery, Dr. Ryan felt he'd never hibernated when he dialed a button on a handheld panel before his adjustable bed raised him to sit upright.

"Good heavens...we made it. We made it!" Dr. Ryan cried.

Recent discoveries within Patagonia inspired Julia to be a registered nurse and loved studying fossils as a hobby. Patagonia consists of the southern region of Argentina and Chile. Julia's colleagues from Bolivia, Columbia, Chile, Uruguay and elsewhere shared similar enthusiasm with her and were on board the H.S.F.S Guardian. Julia still remembers her days at the University of Comahue at Neuquén, Argentina where she unearthed an ostrich like herbivore dinosaur that stood over five feet (1.6m) tall. Her group excavated fossils an elusive species called *Patagonykus puertai* while she conducted field research for the university before attending medical school.

Her husband Derrick came from the other side of the Western hemisphere. Born in Ottawa, Canada; Dr. Derrick Grace was a notable lecturer, author, naturalist and researcher. He received a global applause when he unearthed the most complete fossils of *Tyrannosaurus rex* and other large dinosaurs in Alberta, British Columbia and inside American states such as Montana and South Dakota. Although he officially worked at the Chamber, Dr. Grace loves the great outdoors and learned critical survival skills since childhood. Although he must interact with nothing he ever seen before in his life, Dr. Grace is the only individual from the Chamber who accompanied Dr. Ryan and others through the jungles, steppes and plains of Isis. Dr. Grace's life changed forever when he first met his wife Julia during a conference at Buenos Aries ten years ago. Both eventually fell in love and were married two years later.

Dr. Julia Grace confirmed to Dr. Ryan that his therapy was complete and he was ready to get dressed. After she left his room, Dr. Ryan bathed and wore his blue jumpsuit before gathering his belongings and walked to the command and control center located at the bow of the starship. Once he arrived; Dr. Nimbus was already there and greeted his colleague he hasn't seen in six years.

"Welcome back Mack!" Marcus embraced him.

A distant world was seen for the first time. A blue aura enveloped this planet with signs of a healthy atmosphere with its ozone layer intact and predictable weather patterns. Dr. Ryan was impressed to notice the polar regions contained only small patches of land covered with ice, while all three massive continents were position outside these regions. He realized such additional habitable land made Isis even more exiting as Earth's fraternal twin. Dr. Nimbus felt a special privilege, as they'll be the first to explore a world full of action and adventure!

A feeling of splendor embraced everyone inside the room as clear details of Isis's terrain provided ample clues of possible places to settle. The first command affirmed by Dr. Ryan was to activate an onboard planetary tracer located at the bottom and near the front portion of the ship, which would transmit an infrared laser toward the planet. Satellite signals will reflect off this planet's surface and return directly to the receiving unit. The Planetary Indicator device was programmed to measure and calculate geographic ranges. Data will then be stored into a vast computer memory storage system called; Soul Mate.

"I can't believe that I'm seeing Isis within my naked eyes." Dr. Ryan felt ecstatic of his observation.

"Isn't she magnificent?" Dr. Nimbus asked as the members of the Humane Space Federation Starship Guardian calmly watch this blue sphere grow larger is size. Noticeable green pastures covered most of Isis's continents. Spiral patterns and jet streams of white clouds riddled this lavishing wonder of a world.

"Its blue oceans and green land reflect Earth! I can't believe it was ever possible." Dr. Ryan responded.

Various colors of land shapes revealed a hidden beauty to every spectator onboard. Canyons, cloud forests, valleys, plateaus, grasslands, and multiple temperate zones! A cosmic craft of art proved that a pristine atmosphere and ripe surface is repeatedly possible. Everyone once believed that Earth was the only suitable planet; however our universe is capable of repeating such an achievement of creating and evolving another Earth!

The ship suddenly received data of Isis's surface. The Planetary Indicator immediately revealed new data shown on a hologram of the planet inside a darkened room for Intelligence to evaluate. The Planetary Indicator also specialized in detecting tectonic activities and monitoring its climate. What's more, this build-in scanner can work alongside another device called the Geographic Indicator so more precise details of Isis's terrain could be revealed for Intelligence to evaluate. The planet will continue to rotate while the Planetary Indicator sends infrared and radio waves so questions regarding Isis's terrain would be answered. Isis's terrain will recorded and would be available for future reference.

Dr. Ryan's next command was to activate an interstellar communications relay system in order to maintain contact with Earth. Dr. Ryan then ordered to send an encrypted message through Mercury One. Earth and the Starship Guardian have a sending and receiving terminals. Beams of light would be produced and instantaneously teletransport this beam across three light years in sequential timing patterns similar to superposition of electrons. Once a pattern is deciphered by the receiving terminal, then a computer translation mainframe will decode any cryptic light pattern and convert it into legible writing. Although it may be time consuming to accurately translate the message, however the time it takes to receive a message is sparse compared to three years it would've taken to reach Earth.

Dr. Meena Singh and others of Engineering tested Mercury One. She along with Drs. Ying Zhu, Art Remington and Haru Nakamura of Engineering developed new inventions and modified existing wonders of human innovation. Ying Zhu and Art Remington developed the Feral Sentry along with Dr. Derrick Grace who provided them with accurate consultation on wildlife and environmental issues. Dr. Grace advised engineers in regards to how their prototypes affect natural life and other ecological factors. Dr. Derrick Grace consulted the Chamber and advised the federation in regards to environmental issues.

Drs. Remington, Singh and Rosalila thought about an early theory of ancient astronauts. During the advent of many civilizations worldwide, written passages tell a story of benevolent beings descending from the sky and come into contact with humanity's ancestors. These non indigenous spacefaring beings who've originated from the stars were believed to inspire the invention of the wheel and were suspected to be the source of ancient wisdom. Some crew members wondered why Dr. Netherland lectured about a theory of ancient astronauts. Once all 1500 pioneers reached Isis, everyone realized that the basis of his lectures revealed that the federation's pioneers could possibly become ancient astronauts themselves once they arrive at Isis!

Drs. Nimbus and Ryan thought about the fact that there could be a hominid species that could give rise to descendents that could eventually become a civilization on Isis, similar to human evolutionary history on Earth. Although both men found it strange to become ancient astronauts, they clearly remember Dr. Netherland's pivotal voice as he suggested that if they ever encounter an emerging intelligence of indigenous sentient beings, they have uncompromising rights to a sovereign existence. He also suggested that the federation should not interfere with their society's progress.

Dr. Ryan selected numerous landing sites minutes before Dr. Karl Gruber entered the command and control center. Dr. Gruber will be in command of the orbiting vessel while Dr. Ryan and his close associates made their way to the elevator. Dr. Gruber was born in Berlin and posed enough commanding experience to take charge of the orbiting Starship Guardian. He taught astrophysics at the federation's university campus at Papoose Lake, Nevada. All nine of Dr. Ryan's close friends entered the elevator and headed down where all four landers were located. Dr. Nimbus along with Drs. Arnold and Esther Weinstein accompanied by Drs. Derrick and Julia Grace, while Drs. Malik and Ada al-Saud proceeded to the terminal with Drs. Antonio and Tracy Marino. Drs. Singh and Rosalila met everyone else there as well.

Dr. Zarina Ansari was enticed to enter a state of the art lander with her fiancé Dr. Claude Moreau who showed similar enthusiasm. Dr. Singh also informed Drs. Nimbus and Ryan that this new prototype could move over water so their craft could settle on an island off a coast of the mainland. Drs. Singh and Ansari assured them that this new transporter could hover over any surface including water!

By the time their inspection was completed, the entire Central Continent team entered the lander. Suspense occupied their thoughts while searching their assigned workplaces. Dr. Ryan's heartbeat accelerated as he took his assigned seat. He contemplated endless scenarios of possible events as he completed his final inspection of the landing craft. Both of the de' la' Vega's, Drs. Kepa, Yilmaz and Aliyev were prepared for departure from the flagship.

When two technicians sealed the hatch door, Dr. Ryan took his seat and activated the communications array to maintain steady radio contact with the parent ship. The Starship Guardian will permanently orbit Isis and communicate with Earth. Dr. Ryan preferred to settle in a region of the Central Continent that would possess a Mediterranean climate and a manageable topography for agriculture.

Once all technicians left, the terminal entrance hatch was sealed before the Central Continent team felt the lander separate from its docked position. The crew felt an initial drop when they initially descended from the mother ship. Video monitors enabled them to view an eye catching spectacle of Isis as a mild glow from Osiris reinforced a warm welcome to a group of strangers from far away. Dr. Ryan became startled to see his original view of twinkling stars be replaced by a panorama of blue oceans, green plains and rugged mountain ranges with white summits.

"Starship Guardian," Dr. Ryan requested over an onboard communicator.

"*Doctor Gruber here.*" A sincere voice responded.

"Have you found any suitable landing spot?" Dr. Ryan asked.

"*I found a perfect spot that's equivalent to Earth's 20 degrees latitude north of the Equator and 90 degrees longitude west of the Prime Meridian. Continue your present course and you'll see an extended, sheltered bay located at the west coast of the Central Continent.*" Dr. Gruber revealed to the landing crew.

"Mack...I see the region. We're right on target." Marcus noticed a group of flat, treeless islands inside this bay.

"Great! Thanks Karl!" Mack said in praise.

"*Anytime.*" After Dr. Gruber's last response, Marcus focused his attention toward this geographic location.

"That's interesting; if not amazing, 20 degrees latitude and 90 degrees longitude...that's the Yucatan Peninsula of Mexico?" Dr. Nimbus recognized during their descent.

"Come to think of it, your right! Were making an ancient, historic landing on this exact geographic location on Isis where an asteroid pounded the Earth's crust. It's amazing how at this very same spot on another planet our landmark descent will occur. Dr. Ryan expressed his realization.

"What's even more significant is that we should not become that doomsday asteroid by any means." Dr. Nimbus emphasized.

"We must find either a group of islands off the coast so we would minimize our chances of interfering with the environment. We received immunization shots and brought field vaccination to prevent any spread of disease passed on by humans. Also, we can not interfere or intervene in any natural activity. What's most important is that we didn't bring any lethal weapons with us. Therefore our ability to inflict harm would be curtailed in order for us to protect this planet's environment." Dr. Ryan stated.

Drs. Rosalila and Singh overheard their conversation. Their faith in both gentlemen was reinforced as they proved to be willing to preserve planet Isis as they would do for their own homeworld three light years away. Although settling on this new world presents challenges to a qualified crew, their wise and subtle nature would be imperative in order for human achievement to continue.

Dr. Lucy Rosalila's experience in psychology and therapy sessions with post traumatic stress patients was one of many reasons why the space federation hand picked her as their answer to any potential mental health dilemmas this historical crew would encounter. Although Drs. Arnold and Esther Weinstein were originally nervous of their hibernation process, both of them realized their daunting challenge was over. Enchanting memories of their recent vacation to the Serengeti National Park in northern Tanzania and southern

Kenya convinced them that Isis would be an amplified version of any national park or game reserve.

Drs. Derrick and Julia Grace didn't have to think much when they were offered this mission of a lifetime. Derrick's compassion for the environment and Julia's adventurous goals to settle on this new world would be fulfilled once they land. Drs. Malik and Ada al-Saud were concerned about medical consequences and took every precaution necessary such as additional immunization shots to provide additional protection against alien viruses. Vaccination is also required in order to prevent any spread of disease caused by humans. This obligation is strictly enforced so no incident of outbreaks would harm Isis's natural habitat. Dr. al-Saud knew that careful consideration was necessary for this mission's success.

Dr. Taina Kepa adored the tropics including her homeland known as the Fiji islands. She's certain that she'll love the Central Continent as well. Her fiancé Dr. Haru Nakamura felt riveted to record geographic details of Isis's terrain using his newest version of the Geographic Indicator that's commonly referred to as G.I.

Drs. Martin and Angela de la Vega chose to spend the rest of their lives on this new world. Both were grateful to have pursued a career in space exploration and discovered a habitable extrasolar planet favorable for life. Dr. Harold Nevins missed Chicago, but he knew that settling on this new world with his wife Alicia would be a successful alternative to everything he'll miss on Earth. Ever since the days of their intense training, crewmembers contemplated the moment they'll stand on the surface of another planet without wearing spacesuits and using air masks.

Drs. Fan and Ying Zhu felt absolutely delighted to be descending to their new home and were excited to be assigned to the Central Continent! Ying was confident that the Feral Sentry device would be safe against dangerous fauna. She invented an enormous computer database called the Soul Mate with Dr. Art Remington and his wife Doris were the most patient of all excited settlers landing on an uncharted landscape. The crew's excitement flourished once they felt a stronger sense of gravity when the lander penetrated layers of clouds. Monitors showed and confirmed their intended position above the west coast!

Drs. Antonio and Tracy Marino noticed more vivid details of forests and rivers. A destined congregation of islands located inside an extended bay was easier to monitor while they continued their descent. Drs. Moreau and Ansari felt all four extended legs of the lander extend until the felt a soft and swift thump from the base of the lander foretold its first contact with Isis's surface. Drs. Viktor and Nina Ivanov felt all four legs brace the ground before the lander gently lowered itself down to the surface of a large flat island that appeared to be a barrier reef at one time. Not a decibel was heard once the bottom center of the lander gently rested on the ground.

Dr. Nimbus whispered to Dr. Ryan. "We're secured."

"Ladies and gentlemen, welcome to planet Isis!" Dr. Ryan announced to his colleagues over a microphone before two hundred of the finest astronauts and cosmonauts cheered in celebration for entering a new era in human history.

For years the Humane Space Federation planned, studied and executed the most daunting task. No one could possibly forget such treacherous and demanding work required to finally land on a foreign world. However, despite paramount challenges, the crew's unbridled passion of their assignment would be a driving force the crew needs to settle on this new colony. September 4th 2042 was the day when everybody realized that their unconditional compassion for planet Isis and each other were the most sufficient reason for their greatest achievement!

TERRA INCOGNITA AND MARE INCOGNITUM

Dr. Gruber selected a perfect landing target for Dr. Ryan's crew to call home. As soon as their Lander settled still on this empty island, it instantly became Town Hall. Although this Lander was up to 100 yards or 91.5 meters wide and stood 180 feet or 55 meters tall, an elliptical shaped Lander could accommodate all 200 crewmembers. Dr. Nimbus was glad to land on the center of an island, which lacked trees and bushes.

"Ladies and gentlemen this is it." Dr. Ryan provided his first order for the entire landing party to collect valuable components before entering a stairwell and walked up or down to the main entrance of the lander at level three.

Dr. Ryan pressed one of two buttons on a wall panel next to a detachable wall that hatched out before swinging down. Pressure joints attached on both sides of this hatch gently lowered this expansive loading ramp before it eventually connected to the ground. Dr. Ryan along with Drs. Nimbus, Fan Zhu, Martin and Angela de' la' Vega gracefully walked down this thirty feet (9m) wide converted ramp until the heels of their jackboots merged with a collection of sharp, narrow stalks of short green grass.

"Do you hear that?" Dr. Nimbus wondered.

"It seems to be coming from inside the main entrance?" Dr. Fan Zhu was curious as he looked up the ramp.

"It must be the latest ATV model Meena told me about earlier. She was quiet about the details, but assured me that this new model phased out the older models." Dr. Martin de' la' Vega said.

"Whoa!" Dr. Angela de' la' Vega was shocked to see Dr. Singh and other engineers gliding down the ramp before approaching her.

"What the hell?" Mack wondered when he saw four floating vehicles that appeared like Jet Skis or even snowmobiles.

"How could they hover three feet above the ground?" Dr. Nimbus saw no wheels, legs or any other physical apparatus suspending these new transporters above the ground.

"Here's our latest prototype!" Meena said as she parked her hovering device next to all five explorers.

Marcus kneeled down and took a better look underneath this prototype. He couldn't believe no visible apparatus suspended it from the ground. He also noticed a sequential pattern of minute plates with emerging rods. "How could it hover without touching anything?" Marcus asked after he stood back up.

"Miniature dome shaped rods absorb the planet's gravity waves as a source of energy before a transducer reactor utilizes the flat plates to produce a repelling magnetic shield to lift the craft using Isis's magnetic field and maintain midair suspension similar to how a boat would float on water. It could even hover above lakes and streams." Meena revealed her latest accomplishment.

Each personal transporter measured eight feet (2.5m) long and estimated to be over three feet (1m) wide. Movement was possible by a miniature turbine rotors at the rear of this vehicle with the aid of intake valves located at the front. This personal transporter is able to rotate the air turbines like a rudder in order to maximize steering and handling.

Storage compartments were installed on both sides of this unit's rear. A small trunk was built-in directly behind a black vinyl passenger seat designed for up to two people. This prototype was designed for easy motion due to an accelerator handle at the right end of a handlebar and a brake pedal that was located at the left. The brake system worked by cutting off acceleration from the rear and activates two smaller retroturbines installed at both sides of the front end, enabling it to decelerate to a full stop. Computer and electronic display panels including LCD screens were positioned placed between both handles and below the handle bar.

"Try it." Meena proudly presented her newest development as she stood from her idled transporter.

"This is amazing!" Mack was impressed as he felt a timid aerial height adjustment once he sat on this new transporter.

"It feels like sitting on a boat." Marcus was fascinated by its gentle suspension and comfortable accommodations.

"This feels better than a snowmobile I tried at Colorado." Fan admitted as he sat on one of the other Drifters.

As all prototypes were shown, Lucy, Esther, Derrick, Alicia and Arnold noticed these new prototypes and approached the group to get a closer look. Soon after, Alicia's husband Harold arrived with Doris, Viktor and Nina, along with Haru, Taina, Zarina, Tracy, Claude and Julia. Malik and his wife Ada eventually arrived at the scene to witness a technological marvel.

"I suggest we test these prototypes before we depart." Mack said before the others agreed before testing the accelerator before conducting evasive maneuvers to get acquainted with its velocity. Dr. Ryan also learned to balance himself while making sharp turns.

Martin de' la' Vega and his wife Angela felt enthused to ride a craft that's capable of detecting rocks and other obstacles and could automatically adjust its height to avoid collision. Drs. Nimbus and Ryan were convinced that this prototype would make it possible to survive this challenging megafauna, which would decimate their chances of survival if they hiked the Central Continent. Once explorers became aware of their abilities to travel on this new transporter called Drifter, Mack decelerated until he stopped before he climbed off his transporter. He then verbally requested his colleagues' attention.

"Well, this is it. Want to tell everyone this and I mean this from the bottom of my heart." Mack soberly stated.

"As long as I could remember, I've always dreamed of a new era in human history. I've wished for a global golden age when there's unity within our diversity. A golden age when you think that a challenge can't be accomplished, but someone else would show the world otherwise. Such a golden age when truth would be accepted as authority and not authority accepted as truth. I've dreamed of the human mind mastering philosophy and not philosophy mastering the human mind. I've also wished for a time when we would only benefit from the truth and never be disturbed by the truth. This global golden age is now! This golden age will become the new age of Isis!" Mack Ryan proudly professed.

Lucy soberly approached him after he revealed his feelings to a close knit crew gathered on a grassy island on this historic day. She then used her right hand and touched the left side of Dr. Ryan's head before her hand progress to the rear of his neck. Her compassion encouraged Mack to raise his head to and revealed his watery eyes, moist dimples and sense of gratefulness. She knew he deserved a warm response, which was a reason why she anchored her right arm before wrapping her left arm behind his shoulders before embracing him diligently. Mack placed his face directly on her right shoulder while she rested her chin on his left shoulder.

Meena then approached Dr. Nimbus and embraced him in a similar manner as Lucy. Subtle tears cascaded Dr. Nimbus's cheeks as he felt her warm dimple rested on his cold ear. Meena ensured Dr. Nimbus of her full appreciation for a man she held high regards. Dr. Nimbus was too shy to tell Meena how much he was in love with her; and was too nervous to admit it.

Meena's embrace was the reason why Dr. Nimbus suddenly felt a boost of confidence from her revelation.

Claude approached Zarina and passionately embraced her as he kissed her, while Viktor and Nina did the same. The rest of the crew followed suit and revealed each other's appreciation for their solid relationships. The Marino's, Weinstein's, Nevins's, and de' la' Vega's shared a similar feeling towards each other and felt lucky to be in love with someone special. Dr. Haru Nakamura approached Dr. Taina Kepa and told her that he loved her before he embraced her then thanked her for all the love she gave him.

After each couple embraced, Mack requested the whole group to form a circle. Each participant held the next person's hand and faced each other. Once everyone held hands and formed a huddle, everyone's head bowed for a moment's silence. Prayers, meditation, wishing, hoping and good intentions were shared among everyone with this formation.

"Good luck! God bless! We love you! I hope you'll be safe! Be careful!" everyone encouraged Drs. Ryan, Nimbus, Zhu, Angela and Martin de' la' Vega sat on their individually assigned Drifters before they waved for the last time. Dr. Ryan used his wrist to twist his accelerator before moving toward the shore of this island that symbolized a new chapter in human history.

Everyone felt a slight tug as each transporter slid down a small hill until they reached the shore. Cobblestones and brown soaked sand covered the outskirts of this deserted island. Faint sounds of mild waves and riptides caressed the shore as conceivable encouragement for all five explorers to propel directly ahead into uncharted territory just like when ancestral human population spread beyond the Olduvai Gorge in Africa to explore unknown regions until humanity's habitation ranged worldwide! Dr. Ryan thought how his generation will be the first to settle on a new planet, which is now referred as the New World of Isis.

Everyone felt a faint vibration as they traveled over water. Dr. Nimbus was stunned to see a group of sea birds with long narrow wings gliding over the sheltered bay. What made them unique were their enormous size and bright white feathers with beautiful black edges. Each one had an average wingspan of between 17 – 20 feet (5.2m – 6.1m) wide, which is an average size of a modern hang glider. The Identification Detective device Dr. Nimbus used displayed a picture of *Osteodontornis orri* of California during the Miocene epoch (23,030,000 – 5,332,000 years ago) on its screen.

Paleontologists were certain that this species of sea birds evolved tall bony ridges at the rim of their three feet (91.4cm) long beaks to catch squid and fish. Their heads, necks and beaks display characteristics of a pelican. *Osteodontornis orri* also had a heavily built body with legs and feet similar to an albatross. The crew watched as they circled an area of the bay before diving down toward the surface of the bay.

Whoa…it's amazing how they could glide over water." Dr. Nimbus realized how these prehistoric birds searched for potential food that would move near the surface of the bay.

While *Osteodontornis orri* maintained their distance from the waters surface, Dr. Ryan directed his team to travel one mile (1.6km) to the shore of the mainland. Although these beautiful seabirds were a sight to see, Dr. Ryan focused his full attention to what he saw through his binoculars.

"Mack…what is it?" Fan wondered.

"Be careful everyone, I see some scary looking crocodiles on these shores!" Mack explained when he pointed his pistol shaped Identification Detective and pointed it toward one of four reptilian giants resting on a distant shore.

An enormous database located at Town Hall referred as Soul Mate was used originally as a reference encyclopedia, dictionary and thesaurus. The Soul Mate worked in unison with the Identification Detective device to conduct a match making process before finding a similar reference and display results on a LCD screen of the I.D. device. Dr. Ryan felt surprised and nervous when he witnessed a display of a crocodilian genus known as *Deinosuchus*, which meant, terrible crocodile. These giant crocodiles were also known as *Phobosuchus*, meaning horror crocodile. Dr. Ryan read that they've reigned in Texas during the Cretaceous period (136 – 65 million years ago). Their diet consisted mainly of dinosaurs, but a few explorers would suit them just fine. All four sunbathing giants reminded Dr. Ryan of his horrible nightmare he experienced before the Humane Space Federation Starship Guardian reached Jupiter's orbit.

Dr. Ryan activated his Watchdog device wrapped around his left wrist to contact Intelligence and inform them of a foreboding presence; so this scary sight could be documented on record as a permanent reference. He cautiously guided his crew to the shores of the Central Continent. None of the explorers could believe their massive size and intimidating expression as two smaller ones, estimated to be up to 42 feet (12.8m) long, while two larger ones were believed to be a whopping 49 feet or almost 15 meters long!

Dr. Ryan also learned their heads could grow up to seven feet (2.15m) long and they weighed up to 8 tons or 7.2 metric tons. Their massive mouths were cocked open so they could receive and absorb a maximum amount of sunlight. One of the two larger ones laid on a pile of boulders so heat from these giant rocks could warm this mongrel's abdomen faster as this old male stretched his front limbs.

Interactive currents and riptides wobbled Dr. Ryan's transporter until they arrived at the edge of white sand. Everyone kept one eye focused toward the giant salt water crocodile coming ashore before searching for a place to sunbathe.

"We made it!" Dr. Nimbus noticed white sand transform into green grass accompanied by low level plants

It wasn't difficult to notice lizards, snakes, beetles, and other insects climbing trees or crossing the surface. Additional Birds were detected as they flew off branches of trees bordering the grassland. Dr. Fan Zhu pointed his Identification Detective to a group of fleeing birds, which appeared like a healthy sea tern possessing a large head and bill. Dr. Zhu was surprised to notice this species actually existed during the Late Cretaceous or approximately 99,600,000 – 65,500,000 years ago, which were well accustomed to active flight all over Texas and Kansas. An athletic ability of *Ichthyornis dispar* enabled this toothed bird to swim and walk rapidly over land. Dr. Ryan continued to observe these charming birds that stood eight inches (20.3cm) tall with beautiful white feathers around each eye accompanied by black feet, beak and cranium feathers on top of their heads. Cobalt blue feathers covered the majority of their bodies including both wings.

"I see an opening inside the forest. It could be a trail?" Dr. Ryan proceeded ahead to inspect his latest finding.

"Starship Guardian…be advised that we've made it to the mainland and we're heading toward a trail." Dr. Ryan stated.

Dr. Ryan was intrigued to see a clear open trail penetrating dense forest. Branches of tall trees overlapped the trail, creating a canopy that blocked much of Osiris's starlight. Dr. Ryan noticed this trail extending as far as his blue eyes could see. He estimated that this particular trail was approximately forty feet (12.2m) wide. Dr. Ryan suspected cross country migrates commonly use these long trails to cross the continent.

"Town Hall, be advised that these trails are extensive in length, I don't see any end in sight." Mack reported. "I'll be activating the Private Eye, over."

Dr. Ryan suspected migrating herds of herbivorous or plant eating dinosaurs and their mammalian companions developed these trails to penetrate dense rain forests in order to access more lush greenery deep inside unspoiled woodland. Some of these trails extend as long as he was able to see. There were pockets of open space alongside this trail. Mack believed that such open bays were often occupied by ambushing predators. Mack then used a remote button to open his rear storage trunk of his transporter before launching a probing device called the Private Eye.

Engineers developed this geographic probe as a cleaver method of using a set of built in video camera facing down along with other sensors to trace land formations. A rotor consisting of four strong blades rotated fast enough for a device that weighed 10 pounds or over 4.5 kilograms to lift vertically up from the storage compartment located directly behind his seat. As the Private Eye rose to higher altitudes, it emitted infrared waves in all directions. Land formations traced by the Private Eye will be transmitted to the Geographic Indicator, which would permanently store new data from the Private Eye and would be able to display a three dimensional image of every area detected. Intelligence will actively study this new data in order to learn as much of the Central Continent as possible. The transporter was also equipped with a beacon so the Private Eye probe would be guided back to the storage compartment when it returns.

Each transporter possessed a navigational system aided by the Geographic Indicator. When this aerial probe continued to ascend even higher, more valuable data was collected so Dr. Ryan would learn where these trails would lead them. All researchers preferred to wait until the Private Eye revealed a maximum amount of information before entering. As they waited for results, Dr. Ryan looked over his left shoulder and noticed a large batch of weeds rattling accompanied by squeaking and high pitched calls.

"What the hell is that?" Dr. Ryan was uncertain of what could possibly be shrouded inside this tall batch of weeds.

As they cautiously approached this batch of weeds, an unusually rapid exchange of high frequency squeaking was soon replaced by an unprecedented blast of spitting and snarling. Dr. Ryan's concern flourished as they continued to hear a disquieting expression of a possible internal scuffle. Dr. Nimbus and the others didn't know that behind these weeds was one of South America's most notorious carnivores of the Tertiary period, which began when the dinosaurs perished around 65,500,000 and extended up to roughly 2,588,000 years ago!

Dr. Ryan felt perplexed to see six mammals the size of a grizzly bear emerging from behind the batch of weeds. Each marsupial was heavily built and walked and four stocky limbs. They had wide muzzles supporting bone-crushing teeth inside their well developed jaw muscles. Their body length reached up to six feet (1.83m) long and stood up to four feet, six inches (1.4m) high at the shoulder. However, their averaged body weight was about 600 pounds or 242 kilograms. Mack noticed their massive heads, forward facing binocular vision and black fur with white markings that made them appear like giant Tasmanian devils. Their healed scars tell a tale of a brutality. Martin remembered viewing *Borhyaena* at the summit when they clashed with *Gorgonops* and witnessed a bloodshed committed by both carnivorous rivals. Dr. Martin de' la' Vega was grateful to identify this genus and take necessary precautions before the crew would be identified either as potential prey or even rival predators.

"I remember what they are…that's *Borhyaena*! Let's get the hell out of here." Dr. Martin de' la' Vega frantically said when he saw two of them approaching.

Nobody wanted to harass a possible feeding frenzy, which was why the crew dispersed from this area. An invigorating scent of fresh air replaced a repulsive stench of a decomposing carcass as they proceeded into this nearby trail. Dr. Ryan became more vigilant as tall trees casted shadows over the surface of this trail, which would be more difficult to notice danger.

"It's hard to see anything. We must be careful because some potential predators could take advantage of this circumstance. If we unavoidably separate from each other, then we all should keep a constant communiqué as each of us should move directly back to Town Hall immediately to regroup." Dr. Ryan commanded.

They continued though a one hundred foot (30.5m) wide trail. Dr. Ryan was convinced that anything could be hidden inside this dense collection of plants and trees at both sides of the trail as he heard strange oral calls. Dr. Ryan refused to take any unnecessary risks. He decided to travel at the middle of this trail to provide enough distance to notice anything emerging from either side of the trail. As they continued their course more sounds of abundant wildlife continued to reveal clues of diversity and countless activities inside the bordering forests.

"Whoa...look at this!" Dr. Martin de la Vega announced before everyone slowed down to a full stop and observed a twenty feet (6.1m) long female ground sloth leaning on the base of a bordering tree and using her enormous claws to grab a low branch.

"No modern ground sloth on Earth could grow to such an impressive size." Dr. Angela de' la' Vega was shocked.

This adult female appeared carefree. A furry, elephant sized ground sloth weighed approximately three tons (2.7 metric tons). Her gray and gold fur had six vertical black pinstripes marked on her back from the top of this female's head to her tail and walked on her knuckles similar to a gorilla.

Claws that grew up to eighteen inches (45.7cm) long enabled this phenomenal adult to grab branches and pull them down to eat leaves. The crew discovered the largest ground sloth that ever lived on Earth when they existed during the Pleistocene epoch (2,588,000 – 11,700 years ago) at Patagonia, Bolivia, and Peru appeared relaxed.

"Did you get any information yet?" Dr. Ryan asked.

"I can't believe it...it's *Megatherium*!" Dr. Martin de' la' Vega replied based upon a picture on the screen of his Identification Detective device.

Dr. Ryan and the others were amazed of how this fascinating life form didn't need speed or evasive techniques to repel attacks from most predators. *Megatherium* possessed tiny bony plates under their thick skin, which made it difficult for teeth or sharpened claws to penetrate. This male's enlarged visible claws were also used as a means of defense by swinging their forelimbs and pounding their front paws into any marauder, similar to how North American grizzly bears would tackle prey or fight rivals. Although *Megatherium* appeared docile, Dr. Ryan remembered when Dr. Netherland informed him that this goliath of all ground sloths was likely to be absolutely fearless due to their physical adaptations.

"Let's go to an open field straight ahead." Dr. Ryan wanted to move cautiously around *Megatherium*.

The giant ground sloth rotated her head and saw five exotic life forms from another place and time equivocally moving away as she carelessly indulged into more soft leaves. They traveled one mile (over 1.6km) until encountering the outskirts of an open field. Dr. Ryan and his crew entered into lush meadow with a river. Congregations of shrubs, bushels, trees and weeds decorated a pasture of green grass revealing itself to be directly located between Town Hall and the Great Plains of the Central Continent. This lush meadow would provide an ample description of what could be discovered.

"Everyone...let's move over here!" Dr. Zhu said before everyone else followed him behind a tall batch of nearby bushes at their side to avoid an approaching herd of horned dinosaurs.

Dr. Angela de' la' Vega pointed her Identification Detective to a frill behind the head of one of a 10 member herd. *Centrosaurus*, once known as *Monoclonius* possessed an impressive horn over three feet (1m) long mounted on this male's snout, which curved forward past his beak. *Centrosaurus* developed impressive jaws and maneuvered their heads rapidly due to a horizontal balance of their skulls by their vertebrae. Two shorter horns emerging above his eyebrow was a common reason why *Centrosaurus* of Alberta and Montana, appeared somewhat like a rhinoceros. Reaching twenty feet (6.1m) in length, their average height reached eleven feet (3.36m) at their hips. Their red neck frills consisted of thick and durable skin and were bonded with spikes.

The Late Cretaceous or from around 99,600,000 – 65,500,000 years ago was a time this genus of honed dinosaurs migrated in large herds searching for finer pastures and waterholes. A mild cross breeze blew toward the crew's faces. Drs. Nimbus and Ryan realized that their odor would not be detected, which was a likely reason why all ten herd members continued to migrate past the batch of tall bushes and never acquired any interest of what was hiding at the other side. Vibrant groaning eventually simmered down as the last dinosaur departed the field and entered the trail. Dr. Ryan wanted to be sure they've left and checked for any other animal within the vicinity before leaving.

Once everyone emerged from the batch, Dr. Zhu discovered a group of impressive herbivores known as brontotheres, which stood eight feet or 2.5 meters high at the shoulder and measured approximately 16 feet (4.9m) long. The Sioux people of North America referred them as the 'thunder beast' originating from a legend of brontotheres walking across the skies that inspired thunderstorms. These giant mammals were almost the size and weight of a mature elephant.

Their enormous size and full physique made it possible for this genus called *Brontotherium* to resemble a colossal rhinoceros. Instead of long, pointed horns, they possessed a thick "Y" shaped horn made of an osseous organ that was covered by a thick skin or membrane similar to ossicones that insulate horns of a giraffe. This "Y" shaped horn mounted on their snout rose above their foreheads and could exceed the height of their shoulders. No one possessed any desire to antagonize *Brontotherium* since it appeared that all six males were coming into season and occasionally engaged into mock duels with each other for the upcoming season.

"Who would ever think that we would see *Brontotherium* living in the wild?" Dr. Angela de' la' Vega felt estranged, but joyful as she continued to observe such an unprecedented spectacle.

"What's wrong with those two males at the river's edge?" Dr. Nimbus noticed their horn lowered into a jousting position while focusing their growing attention toward the river.

A gentle ripple revealed a covert presence submerged underwater that swam past two agitated males at the shore while the other four stayed away from the river. A heavily plated herbivore emerged out of the water at the other side of the river. A dense plated hide made them appear formidable. Shades of black across gray leathery skin along with an elaborate tone of pink that covered this female's abdomen was noticeable once this female walked along the shore while water cascaded off her hide. Her skin appeared similar to a rhinoceros's.

All six beautifully built brontotheres eventually rekindled into another drink at the rivers edge. Brontotheres were formerly known as titanotheres. The best action to take was to avoid the river. Dr. Zhu decided to use his Identification Detective device and pointed it to what manifested from the river. He soon realized that he identified what appeared and behaved like an amphibious hornless rhinoceros-like mammal that existed from the Late Eocene up to the Early Miocene epoch at North America and Asia.

"What emerged from the river was identified as *Metamynodon*."

"This genus is closely related to modern rhinos, but existed for at least 20 million years." Dr. Zhu estimated this species lifespan ranged from approximately 37,200,000 – 15,970,000 years ago as a male *Metamynodon* emerged from the river and followed her.

Fossils of *Metamynodon* discovered at the banks of rivers indicated that this species pursued an aquatic lifestyle similar to a modern hippopotamus. *Metamynodon* possessed four toes at their front feet instead of three with the larger middle toe like a living rhinoceros. Dr. Ryan recognized their broad heads, short necks, massive bodies along with short limbs and broad feet. Dr. Nimbus was impressed by his or her 13 foot (4m) length and their three ton (2.7 metric tons) anatomy. The male and female *Metamynodon* continued their amphibious courtship.

Since *Metamynodon* has been discovered, paleontologists speculated that this genus was one of the first ancient mammals of the Amynodontidae family to live among the riverbanks and engage into a semiaquatic livelihood. What simply made these emphatic amphibians more unique were their enlarged canine teeth accompanied by prehensile lips and well developed jaw muscles. As carnivorous as they appeared, their teeth pattern was more suitable for a rough diet such as roots, tubers and possibly barks of bushels and shrubs.

Dr. Ryan and the others maintained their forty feet (12.2m) distance from *Metamynodon* as they kept their idled Drifter units steady. Dr. Nimbus realized that both of them eventually returned into the river but were still noticeable since they floated. The crew sympathize the fact of how various individuals of any species were able to adapt unique methods of transport. Rapid movement across a river's path enabled *Metamynodon* to save energy while searching vast distances for food. Dr. de' la' Vega then noticed six giant hippopotamuses that appeared much larger than modern living hippos of Africa peeking above the surface of the river.

Their prominent eyes were positioned above their heads in order to see a clear field of view, even if they're completely submerged. They were at least seven feet (2.15m) tall at the shoulder and each one weighed at least five tons or 4.5 metric tons. A species identified as *Hippopotamus gorgops* existed at East Africa during the Pleistocene epoch or from 2,588,000 – 11,700 years ago. *H. gorgops* and modern hippos (*H. amphibious*) belong to a family of herbivores called Hippopotamidae, which came from the Greek word meaning 'river horse' referring to their semiaquatic lifestyle.

"Good God! Look at that," were words of Dr. Martin de' la' Vega's acknowledgement of enlarged canine tusks inside a male hippo's mall of a mouth.

"How's the Private Eye?" Dr. Zhu asked.

"It reached its maximum altitude." Dr. Ryan activated the Private Eye's return beacon.

"I could barely believe everything we've seen so far!" Dr. Nimbus then reviewed computer files inside the Identification Detective of various life forms discovered and classified.

"Could prehistory been like this many years ago? It's almost as though we traveled back in time toward the past." Dr. Zhu told his colleagues.

As the crew continued to observe activities along the river, Dr. Ryan found his aerial probe descending on course toward him. The Private Eye tracked this beacon to the source before it docked inside its storage compartment behind Dr. Ryan's seat before the trunk closed.

"Perfect! We should have considerable data of this entire vicinity." Dr. Ryan commented. "I could barely wait until we get back to Town Hall and view the results."

Dr. Ryan didn't want to think what was beyond his position of the open trail…he wanted to know. He suspected hundreds of square miles or kilometers of land to be detected. Mack wanted to develop a map before traveling to that particular area. His first priority was to learn the patterns of these strange but useful trails.

"Mack, look at *Brontotherium*! Their nostrils are twitching rapidly." Dr. Nimbus noticed. "As far as I could tell, they smell something discomforting!"

"It seems that they're looking over to that patch of trees and shrubs over there?" Dr. Ryan interpreted.

"Hey…I saw something move behind it." Dr. Martin de' la' Vega claimed as he saw movements at the left side of his view of this batch of trees 50 feet (15.25m) away from their location.

"Mack…I don't like this." Dr. Zhu said as he heard resonating sounds of resentment and displeasure to what ever was either inside or behind those trees and shrubs.

"I hope their not overly excited by our presence." Angela felt nervous and wanted to move away from possible danger.

"Look at them!" Dr. Zhu was impressed by three, fifteen feet (4.6m) long creodonts emerging from behind the group of trees.

"That's *Andrewsarchus*!" Dr. Nimbus said as he noticed an overt pattern of cherry red tiger stripes marked on their gold fur.

The word creodont was derived from their natural order of Creodonta, which means meat eating tooth and conducted their role as an ancient meat eater. Modern carnivores belong to a large order called Carnivora or meat eaters, which evolved beyond the colossal creodonts. *Andrewsarchus mongoliensis* evolved a head like a wolf and a body like a leopard. This name means Andrew's beast, referring to paleontologist Roy Chapman Andrews who led a 1923 expedition in Mongolia for the American Museum of Natural History where Kan Chuen Pao originally discovered a preserved skull of this stunning species.

An adventurous expedition led to an unprecedented discovery and excavation of this giant fossil skull. Scientists classified this fossil as part of the Mesonychidae family. Scholars once believed this family group was an ancestor to whales. However modern researchers like J. G. M. Thewissen theorized that a hippo-like creature in the Artiodactyla order gave rise to whales. Dr. Netherland once suggested that this creodont's closest living relative is sheep!

What's more astonishing was that, they weighed over a ton or over 900 kilograms! Their solid shoulders rose six feet (1.83m) above the ground and were able to grow up to sixteen feet (4.9m) long! They had flattened nails instead of claws, which appear similar to a rhino's as a means to carry such enormous weight. Their three feet (90cm) long heads possessed molar teeth larger than walnuts and was capable of crushing bones. *Andrewsarchus* of Mongolia may have conducted big game hunting in packs, as well as scavenging and even confiscated carrion from rival carnivores. Blood soaked muzzles indicated a serious threat to any life form within the perimeter of this enlarged meadow.

Hippopotamus gorgops and *Metamynodon* took no risk by using the river as a means for protection while *Brontotherium* decided to exert an aggressive stance by bellowing *Andrewsarchus* and stood firm near the edge of the river. Drs. Angela de' la' Vega and Fan Zhu knew such intensity could be disastrous. All six brontotheres became agitated while the male and female *Metamynodon* swam back to the far side of the river for protection.

"I could barely believe *Andrewsarchus* is not intimidated by such mounting opposition? They must be hungry!" Dr. Nimbus wondered as they approached.

"Personally, it appears that *Andrewsarchus* is actually defending a recently claimed carcass." Dr. Ryan responded as three massive predators cunningly evaluated all six relentless brontotheres intensifying their warning by taking bold steps toward their potential adversary.

Dr. Zhu felt intense. "We should record everything."

"I've been recording since we left Town Hall and I won't stop until we return." Dr. Nimbus intended to study all contents of events once they return to Town Hall. Nothing so compelling to see creodonts as tall as Arabian horses and brontotheres almost the size of elephants confront each other. Dr. Nimbus felt an infusion of wonder to witness a sincere standoff between two compelling creatures.

"No wonder *Brontotherium* acted strange?" Angela realized as all three creodonts discovered the explorers' presence.

They focused their attention to the crew while exposing their massive, blood soaked teeth. Their dense fur on their shoulders rose as a simple message to leave the area. Although *Andrewsarchus* never tasted human flesh, there's sufficient certainty that they'll adapt to this new dilemma with ease as they've done with the vast majority of life forms that existed forty million years ago or within the Eocene epoch! World renowned paleontologist Edward Drinker Cope originally developed and classified the order of creodonts in 1877, which include *Megistotherium, Sarkastodon* and *Andrewsarchus*, which were among the largest flesh eating mammals ever to walk the Earth! Dr. Ryan ordered everyone to flee, so his crew's blood would end up stained across their massive mouths.

Brontotherium appeared suspicious of crew's close proximity, which was why Dr. Ryan exercised caution as they gently moved past all six giant herbivores. *Brontotherium* brandished their humungous horn before bellowing. They used their heavily built front legs to scrape the ground as their patience dwindled. Dr. Nimbus and others veered away gently as the brontotheres warned them that it'll be curtains for anyone who'll approach too close! *Hippopotamus gorgops* remained inside the river and observed all five strangers. *Metamynodon* monitored them as well, but didn't feel threatened. Their courtship remained at the other side of the river while the diameter of the river proved to be a natural means of protection from *Andrewsarchus* and five weary strangers.

Mack and his crew stayed far away from *Brontotherium* even if their true concern was four golden giants possessing a cherry tone red stripe patterns marked from head to tail. Their distinguishing patterns made them appear as though they were engulfed in colorful flames.

"Move away from the river!" Dr. Ryan ordered the crew as he witnessed *Andrewsarchus* approach *Brontotherium*.

"Hurry Angela," Dr. Zhu whispered as he found out what it would be like to see two bull brontotheres charge in a raging fury.

"Why watch a movie if we could see this?" Dr. Nimbus asked as he observed all four of Mongolia's colossal creodonts utilize an evasive tactic to antagonize two bull brontotheres.

Besides a fine physique, *Andrewsarchus* possessed enough intelligence to dodge both mature bulls. Dr. Martin de' la' Vega noticed each individual creodont focused their attention primarily to what appeared to be the youngest and smallest of four other brontotheres near the river. *Andrewsarchus* continued to circle and harass the two larger bulls.

"It appears that they're trying to separate the smaller male from the others." Dr. Martin de' la' Vega was convinced when one of three creodonts appeared to focus his attention to a younger male.

Dr. Nimbus watched six brontotheres employ their strength, body weight, and decorative nasal ornaments as a means to successfully repel their first attack. He stared intently and wondered what would happen next when he saw three creodonts gathering after they retreated.

"That's incredible!" Dr. Ryan felt a strong vibe from each active participant of this feud!

"This could make anyone quiver." Dr. Angela de' la' Vega nerves shivered as she monitored this prolonged stalemate.

Such a social melee only intensified as a young *Andrewsarchus* abruptly lost concentration and focused his attention toward one of six hippos near the river's edge. Dr. Ryan stood up on his transporter once he heard deep vibrations resonating from the river that warned a marauding creodont to stay away from the shore. Despite this creodont's rebuttal, *Hippopotamus gorgops* responded when two adult males drifted closer to the river's edge. Both males showed their indifference as they positioned themselves near the shore of a docile river. Once the front left foot of a defiant young male *Andrewsarchus* became submerged into the river's edge Mack discovered how two massive hippos revealed their own formidable size and strength!

A once dormant and timid river spontaneously erupted when two angry 14 feet (4.27m) long occupants materialized from their subaquatic shroud to confront *Andrewsarchus*. They revealed a pair of enormous tusks once their mouths cocked wide open. Such a formidable stance intimidated Dr. Ryan as both giant hippos bit the intruder's ribcage and his left rear leg while pushing him away from the shore. He listened to nerve riddling scream of the young male *Andrewsarchus* before he attempted to his massive jaws to clamp into one of the hippos neck to fend off their initial counter attack. Thunderous footsteps at the edge of the river and constant exchange of bites between two imposing rivals didn't go unnoticed by *Brontotherium*.

"The hippos must be five times heavier than the largest creodont!" Dr. Zhu watched *Andrewsarchus* escape the hippos' brutality before limping away. The crew felt disturbed hearing this creodont's agonizing outcry.

Dr. Nimbus instantly realized a discounted reaction from the other two creodonts. He noticed this young male was ultimately ignored and rejected by his companions who were fortunate to learn the dangers lurking under the water's edge. As this young male continued to limp away, his place in this group ended when the two healthy creodonts walked away from their injured companion.

"That was a devastating blow for the young *Andrewsarchus*." Dr. Martin de' la' Vega watch the giant creodont lost and ample amount of blood.

"I don't think he'll live much longer." Dr. Nimbus felt sad and sorrow for this young male calling out for help only to remain alone as grass underneath was dyed red.

Dr. Ryan remembered seeing similar tragedies on the Discovery Channel and the National Geographic Channel "It's not much different from the Serengeti or Glacier National Park. If any pack member is injured then he or she's on their own, but other group members will remember the dangers that battered their former companion so that mistake won't be repeated."

The term natural selection is based upon Charles Darwin's theory of evolution, is a process for which hereditary traits of an organism are best adapted to their environment and would most likely survive and reproduce into an expanding population, unlike other organisms that would be eliminated. Mack was compelled to observe such a surreal situation within this megafauna, which became noticeably difficult for him to predict.

Two healthy creodonts learned from their companion's costly mistake as they saw their former comrade limping toward a vindictive group of brontotheres. Once the injured male limbed directly in front of *Brontotherium*, all six mature males ultimately greeted their unwelcome guest by employing their "Y" shaped nasal ornamentation in conjunction with their bold neck and shoulder muscles to pound the body of this battered creodont.

All five explorers listened to agony when they heard echoes of flesh and bones being hammered relentlessly by their dense nasal horns. The two remaining creodonts knew there's no valid reason to rescue their fallen sibling especially when his conspicuous outcry ultimately fell silent. Survival of the fittest includes knowing how to recognize risk and taking appropriate measures to prevent imminent disaster. *Andrewsarchus* walked back toward the batch of trees and bushes while *Hippopotamus gorgops* monitored this situation from the center of the river. *Metamynodon* remained at the other side of the river as *Brontotherium* stood firm and watched *Andrewsarchus* retreat back to the congregation of trees of shrubs where they've originated.

"Has anyone ever seen such a tumultuous trouncing?" an inquisitive Dr. Nimbus stated before the crew decided to move over to a congregation of trees directly ahead of them.

This congregation appeared like an island of trees surrounded by grass rather than water. This particular patch of up to 40 trees along with surrounding shrubs, bushes and flowering plants made each explorer use their visual enhancers to scan this area to learn if it's a vital sanctuary and to search for any shrouded danger.

"My Binoculars don't reveal any sanctuary." Dr. Nimbus tried vigorously to find anything behind or within this area.

"Heat sensors didn't show anything either." Dr. Angela de' la' Vega was searching for mammals.

"Movement monitors show no vital signs of life." Dr. Zhu supplemented before Dr. Ryan felt safe to proceed.

"Okay everyone let's be careful," was Dr. Ryan's signal to approach the wooded area with extra care.

All five explorers continued to approach the woodland. Dr. Nimbus and the others continued to search for imminent danger and were relieved not to find any threat. Once they reached the border of the woodland, Dr. Zhu noticed an opening and a clear trail that led to the center of this collection of trees and bushes.

"Mack...there's a small pocket inside!" Dr. Zhu suggested before they followed him inside.

Once they entered, everyone felt a sense of security being under the canopy of tree branches and leaves. Cooler, shaded air under this canopy was a temporary relief from warm daylight. A visual display monitor revealed how much progress was achieved to Dr. Ryan as he sat idled on his transporter. He felt optimistic to learn his team recorded the immediate area of the mainland up to the southern border of the Great Plains region. He eventually activated his Watchdog communicator around his wrist.

"Guardian, come in, over?" Dr. Ryan affirmed.

A subtle female voice responded to Dr. Ryan's message before Dr. Ryan proudly announced their latest accomplishment.

It didn't take much effort for Dr. Ryan to notice cheerful background sounds of celebration as Dr. Nimbus used his communicator to inform the Central Continent's crew at Town Hall. Both explorers continued to discuss their data collected and espoused possible strategies for additional safety and health issues. Dr. Ryan discussed environmental issues and suggested that a proactive relationship between nature and human habitation is imperative for collective survival for this planet and all of its living residents.

Dr. Ryan also discussed behavioral awareness of each known inhabitant to his colleagues who were impressed to discover that Isis's inhabitants appeared similar to Earth's prehistoric life and behaved remarkably similar to modern life forms in Africa, Asia, North America and elsewhere. Angela was happy to take clear photographs and operate the diary system in order to maintain mission records. Her husband Martin continued to monitor and classify various animals discovered.

One of Town Hall's current goals was to record as much data to the Geographic Indicator as possible and use the Clairvoyance projectors to replay vital data for Intelligence officials to examine. Dr. Ryan felt his sense of joy to see his colleagues as happy as possible, which was a stark contrast to his nightmare he experienced aboard the H.S.F.S. Guardian before they approached Jupiter. Fresh air due to this region's Mediterranean climate was an additional reason to feel a sense of optimism.

While the group discussed strategies to survive, Dr. Nimbus decided to take a break from the conversation and walked over to the edge of the patch and peeked outside. Once he viewed outside his cover of bushes, Marcus wanted to inform the others of an unprecedented panorama he saw outside the patch of plants and trees. He jumped over a log, avoided ditches and dodged trees in order to reveal his news!

"Hey…you want to see something out of this world?" Marcus said with invigoration before saying "come on!"

"What is it?" Mack wondered.

"There's a migration like you've never seen before!" Marcus claimed before the others decided to follow him to the edge of the woodland.

It wasn't much of a problem for Marcus and the others to jump over the dead log and avoid all the odd shaped stones and ditches. When they arrived at the edge, Mack peeked outside before his heart felt stiff like stone as he felt a hollow sensation underneath his skin witnessed an awe inspiring migration across this miraculous meadow!

"Whoa…that's *Mammuthus imperator*," Mack said.

"They're larger than African elephants." Angela observed.

"Their curved tusks are remarkable." Mack complimented.

Mammuthus imperator or the Imperial mammoth was among the largest mammoths that ever lived. North America was the location where the Imperial Mammoth lived a dignified lifestyle. They migrated across the continent during the Pleistocene epoch or from 2,588,000 – 11,700 years ago. What made them so impressive was the fact that they stood over 13 feet (4m) high and possessed an impressive pair of 14 feet (4.27m) long tusks.

"We only have a short distance to place the Private Eye at an appropriate site." Dr. Ryan said before the whole crew left the edge of the woodland and proceeded back to their transporters.

Once the crew returned to their transporters, each person took turns of rotating their Drifters and carefully maneuvered though this narrow trail to exit the woodland. Everyone made it outside the woodland and continued to move over lush green grass of the meadow. Gentle rays of light from an encouraging parent star Osiris was felt once the crew departed the patch and continued to approach these monumental mammoths.

Mack's intuition suddenly warned him as he noticed two of these giant mammoths focusing their attention toward all five explorers. *Mammuthus imperator* was a formidable species in Earth's past and most likely would be during Isis's present. Both giant mammoths reduced their migratory pace as they stared at the explorers. Tensions appeared to escalate as the crew approached the migrating herds. This situation appeared to worsen as they captured the attention of a third mammoth. The crew felt nervous when one of the giant mammoths released a deep vibration as a means to discourage the explorers from approaching the herd any closer.

"Mack…I don't like this at all." Marcus told him as the herd of twelve slowed down before stopping.

"We'll move past behind the herd and keep a fair distance." Mack recommended as he veered right in an attempt to pass by this formidable group.

Dr. Ryan and his crew were over 200 feet or over 60 meters away when they passed directly behind the herd. Unfortunately for him and his crew, the next heard of mammoths behind the original herd, appeared to be approximately 150 feet or less than 46 meters away from their location when they passed their migrating route.

"We must maintain a safe distance," was Dr. Nimbus's suggestion as he saw all three cautious adult females from the first herd moving aggressively toward him.

"Everyone hurry!" Dr. Ryan told the crew.

"We must accelerate!" Martin shouted out loud, as he was able to hear the thundering footsteps vibrate the ground behind him before saying "their gaining on us!"

Martin and Fan felt exceptionally nervous as their abdomen tightened. They felt a powerful presence of fourteen feet (4.27m) long tusks reaching out to them in order to topple them from their transporters. Human nerves riddled though the anatomy of all five explorers as pounding footsteps vibrated the meadow's surface! If the explorers were ever knocked off of their Drifters, they would most likely be stepped on. The Imperator Mammoth was thought to weigh up to 10 tons or 9 metric tons or more. The crew knew that their only solution to this dilemma was to out pace the giant mammoths, which were capable of running faster than any Olympic sprinter.

"It seems like their gaining on us!" Dr. Zhu noticed shadows of elongated tusks creeping behind.

"Everyone," Dr. Nimbus yelled out. "If we hide behind these shrubs then it would be more difficult for them to find us."

"Good idea! Let's move to the right side of this patch of bushes!" Dr. Ryan said as a route to escape.

"Don't look back!" Angela hoped none of her colleagues would make such a fatal mistake.

"I won't." Martin pledged.

Once they passed by this batch of tall bushes, heavy thumping resonation of Imperator Mammoth softened until all five individuals couldn't hear any more pounding footsteps. Dr. Ryan wasn't confident enough to slow down just yet. He cautiously looked into his left side view mirror only to discover this adult female lost interest in her pursuit before retreating back to her herd. Dr. Ryan was grateful for Drifter to be invented, which saved their lives several times already and they've only spend less than one day at the Central Continent. He realized it would be next to impossible to walk upon the mainland and survive. Mack felt a deep sense of gratefulness for such a handy transporter.

"We're safe! The mammoths gave up." Dr. Ryan confirmed.

"I can't believe how fast they were able to run!" Dr. Martin de' la' Vega was impressed of such unprecedented speed.

"How much longer we need to travel?" Dr. Nimbus asked.

Dr. Ryan scanned his Good Samaritan device, which indicated their target nearby. "It's directly ahead."

"There's an abandoned termite mount." Dr. Zhu pointed to their assigned target that was near a 30-foot (9.15m) tall tree.

"Perfect...its height should be safe." Dr. Ryan concluded.

Wide horizontal underpinning roots inserted into the ground reassured the foundation of a six feet (1.83m) wide stem or tree trunk. Its initial branches were only eleven feet above the ground. But they were over one foot (over 30.5cm) wide at the base of some branches. Isolation of this area would be the perfect spot to place an Undercover device on top of the termite mount. Dr. Ryan decided to climb this empty mount that stood 10 feet (3m) high. Once Dr. Ryan was able to view the top, he placed this remote sensor and fastened it to the surface so it won't topple. Dr. Ryan climbed down and returned to his transporter. The federation's first objective became a success, and will enable intelligence to monitor this entire area continuously. Migrating and local life forms could be observed both day and night and would continue to transmit recorded activities.

Dr. Ryan secured his Undercover device, which appeared strikingly similar to the Private Eye except it wasn't spherical shaped and no rotating blades were installed. This domed shaped device possessed video cameras, infrared sensory, and a host of other receptors such as microphones, a thermometer, and an ability to record nocturnal activities. All video cameras and audio receptors were fully functional. Dr. Ryan knew this location would be the best place to put his device for maximum effectiveness due to unobstructed views this mount could offer and of course, a tracing device designed to identify and trace any life form's location and movement for intelligence to monitor.

"Let's scan the area first." Dr. Ryan suggested as they used their Identification Detective device to check for some tree dwellers.

Their only finding was a genet or ferret looking mammal whose orange fur with black stripes similar in pattern to a tiger (*Panthera tigris*). All four of them were close to three feet (91.4cm) long and weighed about 15 pounds

(6.8kg) each. None of them appeared threatening, but they were intelligent and agile. They either climbed on tree branches or dug burrows underground to hide from the various predators of Isis, just like they've accomplished at Kenya, Africa during the Miocene epoch (23,030,000 – 5,332,000 years ago). The adorable genus called *Kanuites* relaxed on higher branches and enjoyed their view.

"Let's head back," was Dr. Ryan and his crew's last objective was to return to Town Hall.

As the band of explorers headed south across the meadow, various herbivores continued their migration. Dr. Nimbus realized that most of the herbivores were in groups. Dr. Angela de' la' Vega noticed various strategies each herbivore adapted to find and consume food. Fan realized that none of the plant eaters took any unnecessary risks and were capable of teaching their acquired wisdom to their offspring.

"Mack! Look at them over to the left." Dr. Nimbus noticed.

"They run much like Ostriches." Dr. Ryan was amazed to see an agile heard of twenty lightweight bipedal dinosaurs with feathers.

"I can't believe how fast they're moving! They make it look so easy." Martin replied to the splendorous sight.

"They're not carnivorous are they?" Marcus wondered.

"I don't think so because they're jaws appear soft and I don't see any exposed teeth. Although their jaws are long, they appear to have a flattened tip beak." Mack emphasized.

"Wow! Look at them go!" Angela smiled as they accelerated the speed of their transporters alongside the heard of twenty fast pacing orange and white feathered dinosaurs called *Gallimimus*.

The largest of the ostrich dinosaurs was able to move over 37 miles per hour or almost 60 kilometers per hour across the ancient plains of what's now the Gobi desert of Mongolia around 99,600,000 – 65,000,000 years ago during the Late Cretaceous. Leaves and vegetation were main portions of their diets as well as seeds and insects. Some paleontologists suspect it was possible this genus known as *Gallimimus* ate lizards and small mammals. Standing over eight feet (over 2.44m) tall and measuring 13 feet (4m) long made them capable to take any necessary evasion and maneuvering tactics to maintain a desirable distance from various carnivores such as *Tarbosaurus*, *Velociraptor* and *Tyrannosaurus rex*.

Once this group of sprinters veered closer to the explorers, it suddenly appeared that humans and dinosaurs raced alongside each other. Two groups of inhabitants of different origins and lifestyles accelerated. One group used their sleek bodies with long powerful legs. The other used their thinking capacity to develop an invention to use as a mechanism to keep up with the pace. When the race ended in a draw, dinosaurs and humans mutually separated and departed back to their own separate livelihoods.

"Marcus, look at them ahead." Dr. Ryan said, as he was amazed to see a group of gigantic kangaroos grazing just ahead of the congregation of bushes and trees.

"I remember studying them on board the starship Guardian before we reached Jupiter." Dr. Nimbus recognized this genus of marsupials as the crew approached them.

These giant kangaroos measured 10 feet (3m) long and stood approximately six feet (1.83m) tall. Distinctive features such as a short face made these grazers appear a bit like a rabbit. What's even more distinguishable was the fact that each hind leg of *Procoptodon* possessed only one long functioning toe (the fourth toe) at the end of each foot. Similar to modern kangaroos, *Procoptodon* was capable of rabid bursts of speed. They could accelerate 30 miles or 48.3 kilometers per hour for short distances in order to avoid being pounced or ambushed by predators of ancient Australia during the Pleistocene epoch that ranged from 2,588,000 – 11,700 years ago. Each of these ten-foot (3m) long giant kangaroos was able to stare directly into the eyes of a six-foot (1.83m) tall person during their normal posture.

Angela appreciated their fine fur and beautiful blend of gray and white. She also noticed fine black fur on their elongated fourth toe, their forehands and at the tip of their tails. She also was impressed by their powerful hind limbs and thick tail primarily for physical balance when they lowered their heads to consume tall grass. They used their moderate sized forelimbs to provide additional support. Similar to the modern kangaroos, *Procoptodon* actually live in feeding mobs instead of organized herds. Feeding mobs are classified as a group of animals that randomly come together mutually either for feeding or other purposes. There's no formal hierarchy and no patriarch (dominant male) or matriarch (dominant female) leads the group. With the exception of a courtship and parents tending to their young, social gathering of this particular group would break-up once a feeding session ends or if there's no need for mutual protection. Angela noticed something else when she recognized both sensitive ears of *Procoptodon* moving rapidly as well as twitching of nerves behind the their necks. Dr. Nimbus then noticed sudden changes in attitude and behavior of the giant kangaroos as they instantly spent less time consuming fine grass and more time erected in order to monitor their surroundings. Dr. Ryan focused toward their rapid breathing pattern as he suspected an event to unfold.

Dr. Ryan wondered if their own presence was a factor of such recent change of the giant kangaroos' behavior and observing them would complicate their feeding session. A soft tone of wind caressed leaves of a nearby batch of trees and bushes, as silence dominated the scene.

"Look at that!" Dr. Nimbus shouted out, as he and the others witnessed a gigantic reptile burst out of this shroud of tall bushes and trees that eluded this female's powerful presence.

Fragments of twigs and leaflets flurried outward and on to the ground as the vortex of the raging force guided them on to adjourning grass. Heavy footsteps of four feet with giant claws indicated this inhabitant to weigh approximately 3 thousand pounds or 1.35 metric tons! Dr. Ryan was concerned to see a similar phenomenon he observed during the Osiris 4 Summit at the main conference room almost nine years ago. What's more emotionally stimulating was the fact that the researchers were only twenty feet (6.1m) away from *Procoptodon* and only thirty feet (9.15m) away from the most dangerous species of lizards ever to inhabit Earth and Isis.

A gentle drift of wind and silence was accompanied by a lethal pursuit. None of the explorers ever suspect to see such a sheer size and meticulous movement. Spontaneous nature of this force vibrated nerves and jolted veins of all five explorers. Martin was amazed to notice how a sprawling lizard stood six feet (1.83m) above the ground and capable of extending their heads up to 10 feet (3m) high. He was also nervous to see the keen eyes mounted on each side of the head and to witness each one of the two-inch (over 5cm) long flesh shredding teeth were perfectly serrated. Fan noticed a snake-like curvature of this giant Komodo dragon's powerful jaw as it opened wide to attack. Capable of growing up to 26 feet (7.93m) long or more, *Megalania prisca* formulated timing and agility as essential ingredients to accomplish a goal.

"Let's get the hell out of here!" Dr. Ryan screamed, as he couldn't bear to see anymore of this particular force of nature at its worst phase.

Each researcher wasted no time to flee. The fate of all inhabitants must be the way it would be if all explorers were never present. Each researcher sworn never to interfere with normal activities of nature even if they heard thundering footsteps of a massive lizard ending a life of a giant kangaroo. Dr. Nimbus viewed other kangaroos frantically hopping away from danger. None of the explorers wanted to intervene in this situation in particular, because any typical intruder could become a meal too. The fate of the other kangaroos will continue…for now.

"We must be careful…check all perimeters!" Dr. Ryan wanted to use scopes to inspect the forest's edge from a safe distance.

Drs. Nimbus and Zhu were convinced that current conditions of the forest edge are currently safe for them to enter a grassy trail. Although no sign of danger was detected, Dr. Ryan wasn't convinced that the safety conditions at the border of a dense rain forest were safe. Additional reassurance was required for a justifiably nervous commander whose intention was to insure his colleagues' best interests of personal safety and security.

"Conditions are safe." Dr. Martin de' la' Vega stated.

"Entrance is clear." Dr. Angela de' la' Vega added.

"I see no immanent danger." Dr. Zhu agreed.

"It looks good Mack." Dr. Nimbus assured him before the crew entered a wide grassy trail that would lead them back through the forest and to the shores of the extended bay.

Dr. Ryan's caution was eventually replaced by calm as they entered the trail. This trail was the fastest route to the beach. Soon, a familiar view of tall weeds and piles of boulders at the shore confirmed their desired goal. What reassured Dr. Ryan and others of their concerns was that there were no sign of any dangerous surprise.

"Since this situation appears safe, we'll deactivate our Feral Sentry device and store it." Mack suggested before he got off his drifter unit and removed this tall device mounted behind his seat and began removing an egg shaped apparatus from the rod.

This rod was able to extend up to six feet (1.83m) long and could be manually attached to one of these oval shaped devices the size of an ostrich's egg. A faint hymn would from this oval apparatus produce nontoxic frequencies generated to repel most aggressive animals. A repugnant scent emitted is undetectable to humans and harmless to the environment. High frequencies are a prime feature of a crafty device engineer's development to protect each explorer. A storage compartment at the left side of each Drifter unit was opened. Mack and the others contracted the extendable rod. Soon after, both the rod and the oval shaped egg were placed into storage. Successful testing at the Serengeti and Savuti National Parks in Africa assured the federation that the Feral Sentry would be a valuable contribution to the overall outcome of this mission.

"Let's bring all our data to intelligence." Dr. Ryan stated as the whole crew proceeded toward the shore.

Mild vibrations of hovering over water were felt once again. Happiness escalated as they moved up the hill of an island. Up to 50 members of the Central Continent crew provided a round of applause to the five survivors of a complex environment. The crew continued to receive praise as all five explorers parked their transporters at a designated area. Everyone walked up Town Hall's ramp to the main entrance. Proceeding to the third level wasn't as exciting as approaching a hologram on the large circular table. Zooming ability was designed to simulate various altitudes. Supercomputers of the Geographic Indicator received enough data to create an accurate display of land and water formations. Even actual color of the continent's terrain reflected a miniature version of the Central Continent.

"Antonio, how's the G.I.?" Dr. Ryan asked.

"You would be amazed of what we received. It's fantastic!" Dr. Marino smiled, before he initially lead all seven researchers and Dr. Art Remington into the Clairvoyance Room where they'll study the data.

Intellectual Blessings

Nine excited individuals went upstairs before they entered a domed room with a 25 feet (7.6m) radius with a glass floor. Minute pixels throughout the entire dome and floor activated after a sealed door was closed. Air ventilation ducts opened before a single light at the center of the ceiling was turned off. After a second, the entire crew was able to witness a clear visual display of the Central Continent from approximately 250 feet or over 76 meters above the surface.

Visions of a captivating landscape bestowed the minds of a spacefaring species inside this room. As ripe tropical rain forests veiled the ground, numerous activities eluded their sight. Only trails of open grass revealed a robust habitat cloaked under a lush green canopy of trees. An occasional departure of birds and pterosaurs added grace to this promising paradise. Pockets of swamps, prairies and plains were accessible by these open trails, which made it possible for many life forms to travel the continent.

It was such a thrill when Dr. Remington used his hands to maneuver their simulated position based upon new data provided by the Clairvoyance projector. Intrigue and enthusiasm flourished while they descended toward the surface until they hovered 20 feet or over six meters above tree lines. Fresh nuts, seeds, and fruits were noticeable among a generous amount of vegetation and lush greenery. The crew could see fresh vegetation that proved to be easy for planet Isis to accommodate a vast diversity of herbivores along with new inhabitants from a foreign world.

Passion became inevitable when they heard soft sounds of active leaves waving from air streams. Trees tipped gently to each side as an untainted symphony of blue skies, white clouds, green leaves and a mild breeze caressed everyone's mind, body and soul in perfect harmony. Dr. Ryan used his Private Eye device to successfully obtain clear images of various kinds of vascular plants such as ferns and club mosses inside dense canopies of trees inside the projector room. Dozens of wide trails of grass were integrated inside dense forest below and distant cloud forests. Mack discovered the Geographic

Indicator recorded a web shaped pattern of wide open trails, which also revealed their extensive range. He then suspected these trails were part of a lattice network of open trail patterns that encompassed much of the continent itself!

The Central Continent appeared to be a haven for life to prosper despite observed dangers. Dr. Ryan learned how such abundance and easy access to food and water made it possible for a diversity of organisms to survive and prosper. Gymnosperms, amber, horsetails, algae, and fungi were plentiful as well as single celled organisms. Various kinds of seed ferns and angiosperms were repeatedly discovered. Dr. Ryan suspected thousands of different single celled organisms like protozoan cells and other multi-celled organisms to flourish. Organisms without a spinal chord known as invertebrates were also discovered.

"As much as I love the Earth, Isis is such a seducing place." Marcus told his companions.

"I'm shocked how this world could support a greater biodiversity than Earth. Mack enthusiastically responded.

"I can't tell you how deeply appalled I am since we've landed here. This world is the greatest spacefaring assignment I could ever conceive." Dr. Remington proudly revealed while Lucy and Meena entered the room.

"Lucy…Meena, join us!" Mack invited them to accompany this simulated voyage.

Lucy walked over to Mack then kneeled down and looked Mack directly in his blue eyes. "Come with us," as she extended her right hand to grip gently on Mack's left wrist before she stood back up and encouraged him to rise from the glass floor.

Meena employed a similar approach Marcus. "Let's go," was her primary phase she used to simply get Marcus on his feet.

Both gentlemen stood up before both women guided them out of the Clairvoyance projector room and made their way down to the main entrance of Town Hall. As they progressed down the ramp, Meena used her Watchdog device to call Dr. Grace. She requested him to take command of Town Hall as they announced their initial departure from the landing vessel.

"Where are we going?" Mack wondered.

"We've just made a brilliant discovery!" Meena announced.

"If it's not too far, we could view it on the G.I." Marcus responded.

"It's much more exciting to see it in person." Lucy revealed.

"What was it? What did you find?" Mack asked.

"It's a surprise!" Meena smiled.

They walked to one of their portable, outdoor aluminum sheds that stored transporters. Both Drifter units stored leisure supplies. Mack and Marcus were instructed to climb aboard and pilot their assigned Drifter while each woman navigated. Idle vibrations indicated their transporters were ready to proceed. Once the sensory systems were activated, Lucy and Meena instructed them to pursue west toward the ocean. They hovered down to the island's shore before heading out to sea.

Although both gentlemen had no clue of this discovery, they were confident they'll receive an intriguing surprise. When they arrived at the ocean, they pursued north and remained over water. Warm afternoon daylight of Osiris provided favorable dry weather conditions to seven big beautiful seabirds exposing their bright colors and fine physique. They soared overhead and observed the panorama of the sea. This species called, *Osteodontornis orri* expressed their curiosity. Their 17 feet (5.2m) wingspan exceeded the length of two of their transporters that continued to hover effortlessly above the surface of the sea. Mack detected a mild scent of saltwater while droplets from the ocean sprinkled across their faces.

Mack was exceptionally grateful that both transporters never require gasoline or chemical fuels to propel the craft forward. A sophisticated array of powerful rotors within the tubular structure receives its energy from an energy converter or transducer that converts gravity waves into electric energy to power the rotors.

"Woo…faster Mack, faster!" Lucy shouted from behind, as she allowed her hair to be dragged by their speed.

"It's further ahead sweetie." Meena told a bashful Marcus who complied with her request.

Each transporter carried a male and female passenger while traveling parallel the western shoreline of the mainland. A bright turquoise haze glowed under water as beaches reflected bright daylight from white sand. Marcus noticed streaks of cirrus clouds stretching across a blue sky before they departed the turquoise shallow sea and pursued into deeper waters. Lucy noticed a cobalt shade of blue. Lucy realized only a dense blue layer of ocean water dept impaired their ability to see coral reefs. However, sixty feet (18.3m) to their left, all four of them saw a strange spectacle emerged from under water.

"Look at that!" Mack shouted as he pointed his left index finger toward it.

"Whoa! What the heck is it?" Marcus said before this strange object descended until it was completely submerged.

"Mack, I don't like this at all." Lucy felt worried as they continued their journey before this familiar strange object reemerged and rose higher than before.

The vertical object appeared like a tall dorsal fin that rose over five feet or

1.5 meters above the surface. Marcus activated his pistol shaped Identification Detective device and pointed it toward the dorsal fin that traveled up to 40 miles or over 64 kilometers per hour! Suddenly, this fin sank under water for a second time. The screen of Marcus' device was blank except for bold red letters saying "no data," which indicated this fin was completely submerged before Marcus had a chance to successfully point his device to emit infrared and other types of rays toward it.

"Damn, I missed it." Marcus felt a bit of frustration as he was determined to find an answer to this mystery because he believed that what ever it was must be as large as a whale.

"Where did it go? I can't see it anymore." Meena said as they continued north.

"What ever it was…it's gone." Marcus responded.

"Oh well, at least we saw it with our naked eyes," Mack responded as he visually scanned the ocean.

Mack estimated this dorsal fin to grow up to five feet (1.5m) long and six feet (1.83m) tall and up to a few inches or centimeters thick. Tiny hair follicles at the rear of Mack's neck revealed how an unprecedented presence disturbed an already concerned commander. The crew felt a subtle riptide directly underneath their transporters. Dr. Ryan felt less intrigue than fear to experience such an unforeseen existence he never encountered during his lifetime on Earth.

"Hey everyone…look at them over there." Meena said as he pointed toward her left side again. Only this time, his attention focused upon a new discovery that was only thirty feet (9.15m) away from all four observers.

"From over here they look like dolphins with vertical tails." Marcus commented.

"Their jaws appear longer than a dolphin's." Meena said as Marcus pointed his Identification Detective toward a pod of marine reptiles estimated to be 11 feet, 6 inches or 3.5 meters long.

"It's *Ophthalmosaurus*," Marcus revealed.

"You're kidding?" Mack responded.

"It's official," Marcus replied as they continued moving north at a comfortable 20 miles (32.2km) per hour.

These slim shaped marine reptiles showed no difficulty of achieving the same speed with both transporters. They're strong enough to sheer through the ocean's surface as their sleek physique darted them through water just like they've done in oceans of the west coast of North America and along the shores of Europe during the Jurassic period or between 193 – 136 million years ago.

Although these marine reptiles usually would migrate further north, apparently they adapted to penetrate further south to take advantage of a large addition to their geographic range for additional food. *Ophthalmosaurus* came to the surface to breathe air. Although this genus is classified as a marine reptile, their routine behaviors including their offspring emerging tail first from their mother's womb suggest that their lifestyles were similar to a genus of dolphins also referred as *Delphinus*.

Lucy peeked over her left shoulder to notice this vertical fin they discovered earlier following all twelve adorable marine reptiles "That fin is back again!

While Marcus was determined to identify this species, nobody knew what lurked under water grew 60 feet (18.3m) long and could weight between 60 – 100 tons or between 54 – 90 metric tons. This monarch of marine life weighed as much as a locomotive! He also wasn't fully aware that they've met the most powerful and deadliest predator on Isis and in Earth's natural history.

"It's back again? I though it would be gone for good!" Meena continued to observe the tall fin, as Marcus was finally able to obtain precious data.

An image Marcus never wanted to see appeared on a miniature LCD screen of his hand held probe device. "This can't be right, no!" Marcus's verbal response prompted Mack's attention and desire to learn his latest discovery.

"What was it?" Mack yelled out as he veered over toward him.

"You won't believe it when you see it!" Marcus said before both were close to each other for him to give the identification device to his closest friend to see.

"You must be kidding me." Mack's concern grew as Lucy noticed his unfavorable response to confirmed data on Marcus's Identification Detective's screen.

"You mean to tell me that we've encountered Megatooth?" Lucy giggled in disbelief.

An older pod member suddenly veered toward his right and ended up drifting toward the researchers. This giant shark's fin instantly followed the lone *Ophthalmosaurus* and aggressively pursued its target. Lucy suddenly felt a disturbing vibe as a conspicuous fin became submerged as this subaquatic chase approached the explorers. A ghostly image of a female arch predator with her jaws cocked open overlapped the marine reptile before her massive jaws slammed shut. None of the crew members was able to see the lone marine reptile anymore. Impressive rows of 6-inch (15.2cm) long teeth along with a range of six feet (1.83m) wide and eight feet (2.5m) high of her jaws made it possible to absorb an elder marine reptile and startle the minds of all four explorers.

C. megalodon better known as Megatooth, terrorized waters all over Europe, India, Australia, New Zealand and the entire Western hemisphere during the Miocene and Pliocene epochs or from around 23,030,000 –

2,588,000 years ago. Considerable issues such as the cause(s) and time of extinction are debated by scholars, including a taxonomy dispute regarding what name to assign the genus of this macropredator. Some argue that the properly assigned genus should be called *Carcharoles megalodon* rather than *Carcharodon megalodon*.

Dr. Ryan suspected this species must be agile like Shortfin mako sharks (*Isurus oxyrinchus*) and posses a broad diet like a tiger shark (*Galeocerdo cuvier*). Despite heated debates, regarding the proper classification of their species, time and cause(s) of their extinction, scholars value their photographs of posing inside the realm of Megatooth's fossilized jaws they've studied. Scientists know this life form was capable of consuming whales and could swallow a sixteen feet (4.9m) long Great White Shark whole! Such an awesome mouth accompanied by 3000 bone crushing teeth up to the size of an adult man's hand was able to consume anything. Modern science and Dr. Ryan theorize that Megatooth was the apex predator of all extinct and extant life on Earth and most likely on Isis as well!

Although the crew was able to remain out of harm's way, one vital gift every interstellar pioneer possessed was an understanding that learning is a lifetime experience regardless of age. Mack realized his volume of lessons intensified since he arrived at this new world. What's more is that an ample amount of data collected from extant relatives and fossil configuration, he's grateful that he could gather information without casting harm on wildlife, himself and his faithful companions. He reflected historical improvements in techniques of scientific research enable them to obtain more accurate data. Mack and his crew knew how lucky they were to know modern methods and techniques of survival along with valuable aid from modern technology in comparison to our ancestors who lacked such technology. His thoughts also contemplated what life on Isis would be like if he had to live the way our ancestors lived on Earth. As they traveled ten miles or over 16 kilometers north from Town Hall, Mack thought about adapting to this new way of life like no other lifestyle in history. No other life story could reflect their situation as they gently hop over gentle waves and currents.

"How much further we have to go?" Marcus asked.

"We're almost there. We must move inland." Meena responded before they approached the shores.

"Where are we?" Mack said as they came ashore and pursued a gentle congregation of grassy hills.

"There it is, further ahead." Lucy pointed to an elevated mount of bedrock near the shore, towering the neighboring hills.

Both transporters made it easy to scale up a spiraled trail of this solid bedrock until they ascended 50 feet (15.25m) above sea level. A steep, bumpy trail wasn't a desirable place to for many animals to walk, because of its barren surface lacking plants and water. Since no herbivores were found and no sign of predators were present within the area, both women were confident of this new refuge. Not even birds inhabited this mesa. All four explorers approached the end of a winding trail.

"We could park them here and climb up to the top." Meena instructed them before activated the Feral Sentry apparatus attached to the rear of both Drifters.

All four of them climbed off and walked on a glittery surface of this massive bedrock. Both men waited while Meena and Lucy opened one of the storage compartments. Supplies of beverages were revealed as a large outdoor blanket was also removed from storage. Both ladies asked them to wait until they were ready before everything was carried up to the top of this glittery mesa.

As soon as all supplies were placed, Dr. Ryan pressed a button to pop open the rear trunk of his transporter to let his Private Eye device emerge from the storage area. Frequency receptors on the main module of this unit activated rotating blades. The unit continued to climb to higher altitudes, as both men received a verbal signal to walk up steps of natural stone carving up to a flat surface. Lucy and Meena smiled at each other as two invigorated men made it up the last few steps before gradually standing fully erect on a surprisingly smooth surface. Marcus and Mack stood straight up only to be face to face with an unobstructed panorama that captivated their thoughts. Viewing such a clear view revealed another inspiring discovery for two baffled men who held even a greater regard for this new retreat!

"Isn't this beautiful Mack?" Lucy asked as both women show off their recent, miraculous finding.

"Now I've found a new purpose in life?" Mack professed.

"Oh really...what's that?" Marcus asked.

"This!" Mack exerted happiness and gratefulness once he extended his arms out with his palms facing the sky.

As daylight reflected off Mack's jumpsuit, feelings of surprise and intrigue enabled him to calculate his appreciation of how two adventurous women made it possible to find a natural landmark that embraced all four settlers from a distant Earth trying to expand human civilization on Isis!"

Marcus felt like he'd died and ascended up to heaven. Although he missed Earth, his extensive view, among others compensated for their permanent departure from a distant world that gave them their existence! The leisurely crew appreciated such an exceptionally rare opportunity to see an unforeseen migration of herbivores moving through several long trails of grass. Heavy footsteps vibrated across the ground while verbal calls resonated across the sky as they searched to find fresh greenery and ripe vegetation to fulfill their nutritious demands. A natural wholesaler of essential nutrients provided enough necessary supplies so all herbivores could fulfill their needs. An abundance of natural vegetation is a primary reason why life flourishes on Isis as well as Earth.

Both gentlemen felt perplexed to see a mosaic of life and wonder when he witnessed a group of four legged sauropods aligned in a single formation. A genus identified as *Brachiosaurus* roamed along natural aisles of open grass trails. This integrated pattern of open grass trails also had pockets of open fields. It revealed a pattern of trails similar to a road map. These lines showed routes available for herbivores or plant eaters to select.

"Look, I see a pair of Indricotheres just over there." Marcus discovered and used the Identification Detective to identify and record a pair of 26 feet or almost eight meters long, 18 feet (5.5m) tall at the shoulder and weigh approximately 20 tons or 18 metric tons. Both browsers indulged themselves to leaves at the edge of bordering woodland. It's not a challenge for *Indricotherium* to raise their heads up to 26 feet above the ground. Other names such as *Paraceratherium* and *Baluchitherium* are also used. Known as the largest terrestrial mammal in Earth's history, this genus of giant hornless rhinoceroses are large enough to possess three different names!

"Hey look at these dwellers to our right." Meena said before Marcus noticed a heron of the strange looking four legged dinosaurs migrating to greener pastures.

The average size of each adult in this heron stood 10 feet (3m) at the shoulder as their skin sails were in conjunction to his or her vertebrae, which extended over three feet (1m) from their spine. Their tail was approximately 10 feet (3m) long while their necks were only two feet or 61centimeters shorter than their suspended tails. Dr. Nimbus noticed the skin of this species to resemble an elephant's. *Amargasaurus cazaui* gently walked across this grass trail revealing that their three feet high sail that ranged from their shoulders and ending at the tip of their tail. The closer to the end of the tail the shorter the sail rose from their vertebrae or individual spinal chord bones. Marcus noticed that the elaborate skin sail along their backs was not present on their necks. Instead, two rows of long flamboyant spikes up to four feet (1.2m) long arranged in a parallel formation were stemmed behind their heads. These spikes traveled down their durable necks and ultimately connected to the edge of their sails at the base of their shoulders. Argentina and the rest of Patagonia were home to *Amargasarus* during the Jurassic and Cretaceous periods that ranged from around 199,600,000 – 65,500,000 million years ago.

"How did you discover this location?" Mack wondered.

"Arnold and Art helped us with the Geographic Indicator and the Dove plane observed this entire hillscape including the trail." Meena responded.

"I just don't know what to say? I'm amazed by this entire view!" Marcus said, as he was able to watch more herbivores browse across one of many wide grassy trails that continued through the furthest reaches of the continent.

"I'll tell you something else; the more time I spend on Isis the more possibilities, which I previously concluded as nonsense, is possible." Mack verbally reassessed his perspective with his colleagues as he continued to witness the impossible.

"I glad that the Dove plane found this place. This is a solemn retreat." Mack became grateful as he called Town Hall to designate Dr. Derrick Grace as acting commander until he returns.

"The entire planet is a retreat." Marcus laughed.

The Dove plane Meena referred to measured three feet (91.4cm) long and possessing a wingspan matching the length of the object. Solar powered receptors on top of its wings and fuselage enabled a rapidly rotating propeller attached to the front could propel it up to 100 miles or 161 kilometers per hour. Flat wings and a total weight of 10 pounds (4.54kg), made a smooth flight possible. Video cameras and infrared receptors enabled this device to receive and transmit detailed information regarding any specific area. Recorded data was so precise; that details of either side of an American dime could be identifiable from 40,000 feet or 12,200 meters above any terrain. It's also used for search and rescue operations.

"Let's hear what's on the radio?" Lucy suggested before she turned on a portable radio receiver.

Lucy then dialed a few buttons to program this unit and transmit her request to a radio station in Town Hall. What's surprising is that the station's shock jock radio personality was actually an artificial intelligence mechanism capable of playing any song performed in human history. Every known musician, composer and artist was stored inside a vast memory hard drive. Their radio could play a different request without interference and could be programmed to play a series of up to 500 requests in a row of any type of music such as Rock and Roll, Hip-Hop, Opera, Rhythm and Blues, etc. Complex circuitry within this artificial intelligence could receive and interpret verbal requests broadcasted from anywhere on Isis and aboard the starship Guardian. Lucy chose her desired request before transmitted it across Isis's blue sky.

A soft melody caressed their audio senses while a subtle breeze brushed their face and hair. Daylight from Osiris warmed their skin as Marcus stared west to view a heard of fourteen elephant-like giants bearing unusually long tusks. They stood around 10 feet (3m) tall and their tusks extended up to 13 feet (4m) long; which were as long as their physical length. *Anancus* used their gigantic tusks to tear down vegetated branches and use their trunks to pick-up and eat plenty of soft leaves from surrounding trees.

Each individual had a small pair of ears that appeared similar to an Indian elephant's (*Elephas maximus*). Their stocky limbs were shorter in proportion to their body size than modern elephants but were able to stand 10 feet (3m) tall. Meena noticed their cushioned feet that made it possible for this species to travel across pastures and forests of Europe and Asia during the Miocene epoch or from 26 million – 7 million years ago and the Pleistocene epoch that ranged between 7 million – 2 million years ago. Their unusually long tusks extended up to 13 feet (4m) long may have been used to topple trees or break off large branches and utilized their long tusks to hold broken branches while bestowing their trunk to slide the broken branches along a smooth surface of their tusks to pack fresh leaves inside their mouths. *Anancus* was able to use their trunks to gather or congregate littered leaves. Powerful neck and shoulder muscles along with a high skull were necessary to support their elongated ornaments.

Meena suddenly saw a new group of mammoths heading south. She couldn't believe the size of all twelve of them. By average each full sized adult stood 15 feet (4.6m) tall at their shoulder and their moderately curved tusks extended up to 12 feet (3.66m) long! This herd's cautious movement across a wide grass trail enabled the Eve probe to detect *Mammuthus sungari*, which existed in Northern China around 280,000 years ago during the Middle Pleistocene and lived into the Late Pleistocene. The Songhua River Mammoth was among the largest mammoths of their kind and evolved from their smaller Siberian mammoths. Mack suspected this heard to be lead by a dominant female known as the matriarch, which would guide the heard through their migration.

"How were you able to find this place?" Mack wondered.

"Luck was one reason; however, the Dove plane helped us find and inspect this area." Meena responded.

"It's amazing how Intelligence was able to find such a place like this so fast." Mack complimented their work.

"Nina and Taina told me that it was easy to see this place from a great distance." Lucy relayed their story.

Meena smiled as she said, "I'm glad we've developed the Dove craft."

Mack was also impressed to witness an awesome view overlooking a robust array of life never seen before on Earth. As he looked off the mesa he came to a realization and asked his colleagues. "You know what?"

Mack instantly gained their attention before adding. "As long as I could remember, I always wished that I could live among dinosaurs and Ice Age mammals but I knew that it was only a pipe-dream. That was one belief I though would never be proven otherwise."

"One question that lingered in my mind was what it would be like for us to coexist with dinosaurs and Ice age mammals? Not to mention, what outcome would result if we ever interacted?" Marcus wondered.

"None of us know for sure but we're at the perfect place to find out." Mack smiled as air streams raced inside and swelled his jumpsuit."

"If our ancestors had to live in such an environment lacking physical size, strength, speed, and stamina of many prehistoric life forms only their intellectual capacity and adaptability would be necessary to learn new tactics and invent new tools in order to reimburse their physical limitations." Meena concluded.

"That's interesting! I wonder what it would be like if the Neanderthals survived beyond our ancestors? Would a civilization be established? If so what kind of society would the Neanderthal's descendents would establish? Would it be different or similar to ours?" Marcus injected to the conversation.

"If the Neanderthals had a larger brain cavity in their fossil skulls are larger than ours, then it would be likely they would be able to achieve anything including art." Lucy wondered.

"I wonder if there's a living specimen on this planet that would ultimately give rise to sentience, intelligence and social complexity to become the principal intelligence of this planet's future." Mack asked his colleagues.

"You know what's strange?" Marcus said in an attempt to capture his colleagues' attention. "I've read somewhere that a small bipedal dinosaur with a considerably large brain cavity in their fossilized skulls. Perhaps the largest brain size to body weight ratio of all dinosaurs?"

"Oh…you mean the E.Q. ratio?" Lucy responded as she meant the "Encephalization Quotient," which is a ratio of brain mass of an animal in relation to body mass.

"That's right," Marcus answered before adding. "Although there's other bipedal dinosaurs with compatible intelligence and acute senses, however one species called *Tröodon* was so intelligent that if they were never extinct by the end of the Cretaceous period or 65 million years ago, then *Tröodon* could've extinct all early all early mammals including our possible distant ancestors, which would've prevented humanity to emerge!"

"Sixty five million years is more than enough time to evolve. If creativity and a sense of community were ever conceived some time within 65 million years then civilization would start much sooner than ours did roughly forty thousand years ago at the dawn of the Aboriginals of ancient Australia." Mack suspected much added time for social development would lead to a timely advantage for scientific and technological mastery.

"So if they ever learned foraging, agriculture, and animal husbandry over thirty five or forty million years ago instead of only forty thousand years ago then such considerable extra time may propel their evolution to excel where humanity would be right now. They could ultimately become a spacefaring species like us." Marcus agreed.

"What's even more interesting is the more a society advances, then the speed of progress will accelerate more rapidly. For instance within the second half of the twentieth century, the technological curve has advanced more than it did several hundred years before," Meena told her colleagues before adding. "What originally would take twenty years for research to accomplish a breakthrough would then take only a few months."

"Many people claim what happen to us was an accident. I'm not convinced. Evolving a large and active brain along with social awareness would be the main reason why such a sentient intelligence would give rise to a functioning civil society. As best I could tell, I suspect that hominids that evolved beyond 10 million years ago have proven to be the best candidates for such an achievement." Mack presented his self proclaimed hypothesis. "However a sociotechnological balance is imperative for any intelligent species in the universe to survive including us."

"Why do you believe that?" Meena asked.

"If a civilization's social advancement outpaces technological advancement, then social consciousness would influence what would be invented and for what purpose." Mack replied as Lucy continued to listen to Mack's inspiring explanation.

Mack continued to say. "However, if the opposite is the case, then there's a considerable potential for self serving individuals to develop dangerous inventions to fulfill their own goals, which would be devastating. An enlightened society on the other hand would be interested in benefiting their society as a whole."

"Sometimes you wonder how foolproof a civilization could be. I mean how could a civilization advance without destroying themselves?" Meena verbally wondered.

"One answer I believe is the idea of why rather than how." Marcus spontaneously volunteered to answer to Meena's question before saying. "When the interests of individuals or a society overshadows the truth, common sense, reason, logic, and even the law; then that society will be doomed." Marcus proclaimed while Meena listen to a man who she admired who showed his candid ability to express a transcending discussion of such a complex subject. "Although trust is an important factor for the survival of any civilization, however, trustworthiness would make it possible for any society to survive and thrive."

Meena stared at Marcus with a sense of mystique. "What an interesting thought."

Marcus then replied. "I wonder what kind of societies does exist out there. We barely explored our galactic neighborhood. So many books, films, sitcoms and even video games show a glimpse of many possibilities, but what's the truth?"

"That's a very good question. I recently thought about the possibility of nomadic, hunter gatherer societies existing in other habitable worlds within our galaxy and beyond. I wouldn't be surprised if such a society learned how to create and interpret symbols and even developed a numeric system. Language and ingenuity would also be understood. However, as far as any technologically advanced civilizations traveling across the galaxy? I doubt it." Mack told them.

"I'll definitely say the external environment is an influential factor in regards to the particular nature of any intelligence species. Psychological development and cultural norms would influence their behaviors." Lucy explained to a relaxed group.

"I could only imagine what kind of social history would've been accomplished by living descendents of *Troödon* of the Late Cretaceous? I often wonder how far they could've progress. Could they ultimately become a spacefaring civilization like us?" Mack wondered.

"I'll definitely say that adaptability and intelligence are the most significant factors for any species to survive. Expanding worldwide is no simple task. Not to mention the fact of figuring out how do cope with a diverse range of natural challenges." Lucy stated.

"What's even more interesting is that if there were ever any confirmed findings of an intelligent extraterrestrial civilization, how would their evolutionary history compare to ours? What would their homeworld be like in comparison to Earth?" Marcus added into the conversation before all four speculators gradually looked forward into a panorama no human being ever seen before as a gentle breeze of fresh air caressed their lungs.

"I'm just wondering," Lucy joined the discussion. "What if we find intelligent hominids like our distant ancestors?"

Mack looked over to Lucy before he responded. "We must maintain a considerable distance. We can't be discovered and under no circumstances should we interfere with their livelihood."

"If we study them we could unveil important clues to our origins." Meena reasoned.

"Nobody would be more enthused to study them at close range than I would," Dr Ryan responded. "But the Chamber made it clear to all of us that we're never allowed to interfere in their affairs. Doctor Netherland has forbidden us to be discovered by any native being on Isis."

"Why did they establish this policy in the first place," Lucy wanted to know.

Dr. Ryan took a deep mellow breath to recall his conversation with the chairman of the federation. "Doctor Netherland and I discussed your question. He was mostly concerned about Isis's natives gaining access to our technology and them becoming culturally assimilated as well. He didn't want their projected destiny be altered by our intervention."

Lucy and Meena tilted their heads forward to listen evermore intently to Mack's explanation. "He didn't want us to spread our potential viruses to them and vise versa. But most of all, he stated that that our technological abilities should never be revealed to any living being on Isis because they could conceive us as deities and that's one scenario Doctor Netherland doesn't want."

"Umm...so you mean that native beings on Isis could establish a philosophical foundation on life based upon their encounter with us?" Marcus interpreted.

"Doctor Netherland thinks so and I agree," Mack responded.

"Why would you think that?" Lucy wondered.

"This habitat would most likely be a burden to their lives. Our interference would make it worse for them." Mack answered.

"I understand what you mean about this particular environment. It's tough for us despite our technology." Marcus added.

A surprisingly smooth surface of the mesa provided extra comfort for all four observers. A 50 feet (15.25m) elevation above the ground was a safe haven and a romantic retreat. An inviting view along with a Mediterranean climate would be an inspiring source for imagination and creativity. Meena thought about numerous prototypes as she stared off a cliff that provided a 360-degree view. It was easy to find a vast extension of an endless ocean that met the sky at the horizon whenever she looked west while a new idea can come from anywhere...anytime.

Dr. Ryan wanted to capture the essence of experience as he looked east into a feral fantasyland. As he viewed cotton shaped clouds drifted across a clear blue sky a transparent image of tall smoke stacks and skyscrapers manifested inside his imagination. Carbon monoxide gas and dull gray particles cloaked countless utilities, factories and mills. Transport vehicles jammed the streets before his imagination forced him to turn away and close his eyes.

"No, no, no!" Mack objected before reopening his eyes only to view a beautiful day overlooking untainted forests once again.

"Mack...you're alright buddy?" Marcus wondered.

"I'm fine now...I just visualized an ugly place. It was cloaked in air pollution and toxic waste."

"I know what you mean." Marcus clearly understood Mack's desire to preserve Isis as a living paradise.

Not many words could describe an ultimate state of being or euphoria. Perhaps...an ultimate description of what generations after generations refer to as Heaven, Utopia, Nirvana, Arcadia, Canaan, Shangri-la, Elysium, or Zion. The Promised Land is also another reference of a literal paradise experienced by four scientists who held strong regards and good will for this new world. Mack believed that teamwork accompanied by individual responsibility and goodwill toward the environment and each other would be mandatory for any beautiful place to be considered paradise. Lucy and Meena watched two grateful men staring aimlessly into the Central Continent.

*   *   *

Enthusiasm and adventure were in the minds of all at Town Hall. Dr. Derrick Grace prepared two Dove miniature airplanes to scan the terrain of the Central Continent. A third aircraft that was noticeably larger than both Dove planes was also being inspected for flight. Instead of a single propeller, the Condor plane was equipped with two propellers installed on the front of the main wings. Its power sources were similar to the Dove, but the Condor model was made for long distance travel. In this particular case, a 50 pound (15.25kg) miniature aircraft will fly over the Principal Prairies located approximately 700 miles or over 1126 kilometers away from the northwest area of the Great Plains and over one thousand miles or 1609 kilometers from Town Hall.

Dr. Grace completed his final inspection before clearing an assembled portable runway. He placed this aircraft on the flat surface of the ground. His main goal is to activate all onboard sensory equipment included video cameras and receive images of the Isis's terrain and store all of its findings inside the Geographic Indicator.

Another beautiful day was imminent as a mild beam of light from Osiris. Both Dove planes will take off and assume the tasks of the original Dove, which was used earlier to discover this retreat where Lucy and Meena revealed their retreat to two grateful men. Due to the markings and footprint patterns, one of the neighboring islands of Town Hall appeared to have been actively used by amphibians or animals that live on land and in water, while the other eight were perfect candidates for agriculture and environmentally friendly production. So far, with the exception of a newly found mesa, no safe haven within the mainland has been discovered. However, the extended bay and all eight islands should provide enough resources to satisfy all food consumption. With the exception of seafood, the crew adopted a Vegan diet such as various fruit and vegetable plants of the mainland, which must be palatable to humans.

Such a flat hilltop of this island made it easy for all three mini-aircraft to take off. Mild and steady cross breezes provided additional assurance for a successful flight. "There she goes," were the words Dr. Grace said as the Condor took off the ground.

"I could only imagine what they would discover this time?" Dr. Kepa said as she continued to watch all three planes pursue their assigned destinations.

"Derrick, does Mack want us to go to the mainland?" Dr. Alicia Nevins asked.

"Yes, but please be careful. The mainland is place to be reckoned with." Dr. Grace wanted them to be cautious.

"Umm...The telepresence projector doesn't lie," Dr. Nevins replied as she wittingly smiled and raised her eyebrows in humor.

"Huh...you could say that again." Dr. Grace agreed before Dr. Nevins initially summoned a crew to accompany her in preparing their transporters for another tour through the great continent.

It took only ten minutes for Dr. Nevins to gather Dr. Fan Zhu, Drs. Antonio Marino, Nina Ivanov, Art Remington and Malik al-Saud. It took only an additional five minutes for all six transporters to be prepared. A pure scent of fresh air ignited the crew's enthusiasm. A turquoise reflection from the bay accompanied by emerald green trees and bushes provided additional encouragement for all six adventurers to shift their gear of their individual transporters and propelled forward. Air suspension and a subtle torque of their units prompted a smooth ride. Their ambition to see this continent for themselves flourished as they approach the mainland. As they approached the shore, more precise details of branches, leaves and palms within the mainland cloaked this continent in secrecy.

"We're roughly fifty feet away from the shore of the mainland and closing in. Remember what Mack told us about the mainland. Be on full alert." Dr. Nevins advised the crew before receiving their assurance that they'll respect whatever lurks beyond their immediate view.

When Dr. Nevins received their response, she then commanded the crew to follow her to the shore of the mainland before hovering over white sand. She listened carefully for any distinguishable threat the crew could detect. Alicia also remembered the group of giant salt water crocodiles Dr. Ryan reported earlier and was determined to guard her crew vigorously in the first sight of any of them. She discovered a grass trail where they'll travel to find any open meadow.

Every crewmember realized how blessed they are to be able to explore the continent. Alicia often mocked the idea of wearing spacesuits while walking on a featureless barren wasteland like Mars. She was also grateful that Isis wasn't toxic like Venus. Her greatest blessing was being able to reconsider her most cherished beliefs. Alicia was happy to participate in a new era in scientific research, instead of examining fossils; she could witness these commendable creatures living a full life.

Dr. Nevins and her crew noticed a pair of maturing bipedal theropod dinosaurs focusing their attention toward the edge of this sheltered bay. As Dr. Nevins and her crew moved discreetly, one of two carnivorous dinosaurs noticed all six researchers approaching while the other continued to search for wandering fish drifting along the shore. Dr. Nevins noticed fine plumage and feathers, which were red and measured up to four inches or over 10 centimeters long as they stood six feet (1.83m) tall. *Deinonychus* weighed approximately 150 pounds (over 68kg). Terrible claw is the English translation of the name *Deinonychus*. Dr. Nevins remembered this genus of dinosaurs was able to stand on one leg while using their second leg to strike their prey with an elongated sickle shaped claw on their second toe of each foot that reached five inches (12.7cm) long. Their unusually large cavity inside their skulls indicated a large brain of *Deinonychus* of North America (Montana) that used their superior intelligence to survive and thrive around 110 million years ago or near the end of the Early Cretaceous.

Their keen eyesight may have bipolar binocular vision along with an enlarged brain and a well developed nervous system to focus their attention to a wandering fish's movement underwater. In this particular situation, timing was essential to wait for a perfect moment for this male to instantly insert his snout into sea water. Dr. Nevins realized that this genus was able to diversify their diets by specializing from meager fish to hunting in groups in order to tackle larger prey inland. Efforts of a defiant fish to escape continued until *Deinonychus* clamped his jaws tighter in order to penetrate his serrated teeth into a resilient fish's flesh. It soon became inevitable of this fish's fate as its head and tail no longer moved. One gift *Deinonychus* possessed was the ability to learn and adapt to finding alternative food sources by using various hunting techniques. Similar to *Utahraptor* of North America as well as *Velociraptor* of China and Mongolia, *Deinonychus* lived in well organized pacts for collective hunting and defense against larger rival predators. Their social customs may resemble a pack of African hunting dogs (*Lycaon pictus*) due to their possible social hierarchy.

"Keep you eyes on them." was Dr. Alicia Nevins's advice as one of two bipedal dinosaurs continued to evaluate their presence.

Once the other male flipped the lifeless fish into his mouth and gently swallowed the fish, he glanced over only to be surprised to see six researchers.

Dr. Nevins maintained a safe distance from two agile predators. Dr. Nevins discomfort only induced more curiosity.

It's amazing how they resemble birds." Dr. Antonio Marino said as they maintained a safe distance from *Deinonychus*.

"It's interesting how you raised that topic. If I understand it correctly bipedal theropod dinosaurs are likely to have the closest relationship to modern birds of all the dinosaurs." Dr. al-Saud persuaded before he noticed a strange ripple spreading across the water's edge.

Dr. al-Saud's suspicion blossomed when he noticed this ripple approaching the shore. Nature's might was discovered once again when the sea's surface erupted to reveal a massive head he estimated to be 6 feet, 6 inches (2m) long. Dr. Nevins felt petrified to notice a wide mouth with an elongated muzzle that was capable of opening over 8 feet (2.44m) tall and revealed perfectly positioned rows of pointed teeth over four inches or over 10 centimeters long!

Dr. Nevins continued to observe a giant male salt water crocodile known as *Deinosuchus* clamp his fearsome jaw into an unsuspecting dinosaur. A high pitched scream from an unfortunate dinosaur horrified Alicia and her crew while the other one fled the area. The giant crocodile turned left before dragging a helpless *Deinonychus* into the bay. The surviving male was able to detect danger just before the giant crocodile pounced. The lucky raptor paced by the explorers while sprinting away from a crocodile measuring at least 49 feet (15m) long and weighing seven tons (6.3 metric tons) and was capable of hunting and killing some of the largest dinosaurs. Dr. Nevins and her crew realized how unpredictable this continent could be, which was why she ordered her crew to activate their individual feral sentry apparatus attached to each transporter.

"Whoa, for heavens' sake that could have been one of us!" Dr. Remington stated as he saw a gigantic crocodile carry a lifeless corpse gently across water.

Dr. Nevins felt grateful of Dr. Ryan's previous discovery she learned before entering the mainland. If Dr. Ryan didn't share his findings with others, then *Deinosuchus* would've discovered what it would be like to consume a human being. Because of vital intelligence readily available for easy access will give Dr. Nevins and her crew greater survival prospects. Alicia originally thought Mack became paranoid about the mainland. She learned that his reports turned out to be an understatement.

"Let's head east." Dr. Nevins said before all six crewmembers moved along the shore.

Lizards, snakes, amphibians and birds dominated the landscape as they continuously traveled for approximately one mile (over 1.6km) along the shore. Once they reached the southwest corner of the bay Dr. al-Saud looked up and was shocked of what he saw. "Everyone, look up in the sky!"

"What's that?" Dr. Ivanov asked when she saw an enormous female flying reptile or pterosaur gliding above.

"I have to find out what species or genus it could be." Dr. al-Saud said as he took out his Identification Detective device and pointed it as it flew directly overhead.

"Come-on," were the words of Dr. al-Saud curiosity as he barely was able to find out what genus possessed a length of 26 feet (7.93m) and accomplished a wingspan of an extensive 39 feet or almost 12 meters wide.

Although it glided one hundred feet (30.5m) above the surface, *Quetzalcoatlus* appeared much closer to the ground due to the fact that one of the largest flying reptiles ever matched the size of a small airplane. *Quetzalcoatlus* soared over the skies of North America (Texas and Alberta), Russia, Africa (Senegal) and the Middle East, particularly Jordan during the Late Cretaceous or roughly 99,600,000 – 65,500,000 years ago. Like most pterosaurs, *Quetzalcoatlus* grew plumage on its torso and back and had a stout tail. A long fourth finger bone inside their wing was made of a skin membrane and blood vessels most likely used to receive sunlight in order to control body temperature more effectively.

As they've witnessed *Quetzalcoatlus*, which the name means feathered serpent, glide away, Dr. Nevins noticed a small crest attached to the rear of this pterosaur's head as Dr. Remington admired a long, toothless beak. Dr. Marino noticed a long flexible neck, which along with a long beak was most likely used to steer or turn during suspended flight. *Quetzalcoatlus* was named after an Aztec deity known as Quetzalcoatl when their fabulous fossils were discovered at Big Bend National Park in Texas.

"I've felt a chill through my spine when she flew over us!" Dr. al-Saud's enthusiasm grew. "Look at her go!"

"So that's *Quetzalcoatlus*?" Dr. Nevins commented before saying "I remember Dr. Netherland had pictures of them within his art collection. He was fascinated by them."

"I remember Dr. Netherland told me that this particular pterosaur weighed as much as any one of us and may have achieved a wingspan of up to 50 feet, or over 15 meters wide!" Dr. Zhu reflected his memories and shared his intrigue of a flying reptile that weighed 190 pounds or over 86 kilograms.

The crew eventually decided to pursue south to a large field that was located only one hundred feet (30.5m) away from their current position. It soon became evident that Dr. Nevins and her crew came to and understanding that this natural habitat is like no other natural habitat humanity ever explored or conceived. Air ducts penetrated nearby forests as leaves and branches continue to wave a favorable response to the warm wind. The crew continued to see activities of insects, small mammals and reptiles. All six crewmembers reached the outskirts of an open meadow.

"There's our first objective." Dr. Nevins announced when the crew ended up discovering a spectacular field with congregations of trees, shrubs and bushes.

"Wow! This place is lovely." Dr. Ivanov said as she continued to view the area.

"What's that over there? They look like warthogs?" Dr. Marino noticed both inhabitants were at least five feet (1.5m) long and possessed massive bodies and heavy heads.

Each one of this courting pair possessed enormous canine teeth that originated from the rear of their mouths and curled out and upwards to form four tusks which was used for defense against potential predators and possibly for competition during the mating season. Although one seemed to be a bit larger than the other, both stood over three feet (1m) at the shoulder. Each possessed rough brown fur with a thick black brush on their head and shoulders.

If scientists ever traveled to east Africa from the Late Pliocene to the Early Pleistocene that raged around 3,600,000 to 781,000 years ago, then they'll observe a species called *Metridiochoerus andrewsi*, which roamed across Africa's ancient savanna. Fossils show cheek teeth that extended high as an indication of an omnivorous diet. Although *Metridiochoerus* belonged to the Suidae family of pigs that evolved two toes with a reduced lateral on each foot instead of a modern pig, which have four toes and barely any lateral reduction. Like other members of the pig family *Metridiochoerus* was capable of adapting to numerous environments such as the open plains, tropical rain forests, even engage into a semiaquatic lifestyle! Not to mention that some even could have discovered existing burrows and use them for shelter or protecting their young, which was one of the main reasons why the crew recognized such a resilient inhabitant of Isis as well as prehistoric Earth.

As the crew observed *Metridiochoerus*, Dr. Remington looked over to his left side and became startled of what he witnessed. "Look at these bulls!"

"Where?" Dr. Nevins wondered before she saw three large male bulls from behind a congregation of trees and bushes, she was shocked to see that these particular bulls looked familiar.

No one could underestimate such significance of an amazing animal that grew at least ten feet (3m) long and stood at least seven feet (2.1m) at the shoulder! Closely related and appeared similar to Africa's modern buffaloes (*Syncerus caffer*) everyone was impressed to see an enormous set of horns mounted on their heads. Their horns stretched well over 10 feet (3m) across! Their formidable physique was estimated by Dr. Nevins to weigh up to 2 tons or 1.8 metric tons.

Dr. Marino pointed his Identification Detective device to one of these buffaloes to discover what species these bold bulls represent. "So this is *Pelorovis antiquus.*"

"I studied their fossils a long time ago!" Dr. Nevins revealed. "I never thought I'll ever see any of them alive!"

Pelorovis antiquus lived a flamboyant life in East Africa during most of the Pleistocene epoch until approximately 12,000 years ago. While Dr. Nevins continued to observe each specimen living his or her normal routines, she realized how lucky she felt by earning an unprecedented privilege of experiencing such a spectacular safari unlike anything she ever encountered. She remembered all of her research assignments at the Serengeti, Savuti and Kruger regions of Africa. As she observed such a spectacle she covertly wiped a tear from her hazel eyes.

Dr. Remington received a strong but subtle feeling inside his chest. He also remembered Africa and Australia and all of his expeditions across these colossal continents. A tear also managed to escape his eyes because he always desired to permanently live an adventurous life. Dr. Marino was also impressed because he wished to explore the beautiful countryside. He never though within his lifetime that he'll actually see an ancient landscape with a collection of life forms that existed within numerous time periods of Earth's history. Ever since Dr. Netherland selected him for this assignment, he continued to feel as though he received his lifetime wish. Dr. Fan Zhu had no desire to ever leave Isis under any circumstances, which was why he sympathized with Dr. Nina Ivanov and Dr. Malik al-Saud, who conceived Isis to be a soul mate for 1500 space travelers. Despite any potential challenges, none of the crewmembers felt any regret about their permanent assignment.

As the crew continued to view this ancient landscape, a herd of grazers that appear like large zebras revealed themselves as they originated from behind another batch of trees and bushes. All ten members of this herd possessed similar striped patterns to Africa's modern plains zebras *(Equus burchelli)* but were noticeably larger. Standing at least six feet (1.83m) at the shoulder, *Equus capensis*, better known as the Cape zebra gently galloped across the meadow. The giant buffaloes and warthogs eventually acknowledged and accepted the Cape zebra's presence.

The Cape zebra lived a flamboyant lifestyle in the Pleistocene epoch, (2,588,000 – 11,700 years ago) and grazed the plains of South Africa and other regions of eastern Africa. Some of Africa's most talented and dedicated scientists discovered the Cape zebra and many other impressive fossils at a remote region of mobile dunes known as Elandsfontein. Since 1960, preserved bones, fossils and early human artifacts were carefully excavated and displayed at the South African Museum where people from all over the world would view a trace Africa's past during the time when early humans traveled across the Serengeti plains and Congo basin and settled beyond the Great Rift Valley. Since then, humanity flourished worldwide and became the only species on Earth to prosper into an interstellar civilization. The crew's hearts and minds blossomed as they saw a living reflection of Earth's ancient landscape, which gave rise to humanity's existence.

Dr. Nevins noticed all three bachelor males walking toward their direction. "We should leave this place now!"

Pelorovis antiquus lowered their heads and galloped toward all six researchers aggressively prompting the crew to flee; only to be relentlessly pursued by three powerful males. They struggled to escape a threshold of three antagonized bachelor bull buffaloes as Dr. al-Saud heard thundering footsteps and hollow bellowing from a group of what's reputed to be the most powerful buffaloes to exist in Earth's history. Dr. Marino's spine felt stiff when he sympathized with Dr. al-Saud's fears once he felt a presence of elongated horns from behind.

"They're gaining on us! We have to accelerate!" Dr. Marino shouted out whey they crossed the field.

Dr. Nevins knew her transporter would be her only solution to maintain a safe distance despite their tenacity. Side view mirrors installed on both sides of each transporter's handlebar would be their safest method to find out that all three males eventually lost interest in chasing them and decided to return to their original location where they could graze once again.

"The bulls disengaged!" Dr. al-Saud informed everyone.

Once the crew received Malik's reassurance, everyone gathered at the other side of the field, where they knew danger was no longer present. Alicia was relieved to see both gentlemen alive and well. "Malik! Antonio! Are you alright?"

"We're fine, thank goodness." Dr. Marino responded.

"Whew! Did you see that? I never saw bulls look and behave like that anywhere." Dr. al-Saud commented.

"I have more good news." Alicia informed her colleagues as she held her Good Samaritan device. "According to this data, there's a trail that runs parallel to the eastern shore of the sheltered bay and another trail that leads west until it reached the shore itself. All we have to do is take this trail directly ahead."

Dr. Nevins led her crew across the meadow until they've reached an entrance of a trial of grass up to 150 feet or over 45 meters wide. Once they entered this trail, trees and bushes bordered and towered both sides of the open trail that led them to the bay. Dr. Nevins and the others detected birds and small mammals randomly crossing the trail while they approached their desired junction, where they could take another trail that would lead them to the southern shore of the bay. They were only one hundred feet (30.5m) away from their desired intersection when Dr. Marino noticed a gigantic land beaver gently crawling out from bordering woodland at the left side of the grassy trail.

"Look at the size of that!"

"This place is full of surprises." Dr. al-Saud responded as he pointed his Identification Detective to what species lived during the Pleistocene epoch or from 2,588,000 – 11,700 years ago at North America, particularly Canada.

Castoroides canadensis generally appeared similar to North American beavers but didn't build dams to modify their habitat like their modern counterparts. However, living beavers don't grow as large as a grizzly bear and no beaver existing today could possibly weigh 1000 pounds or 454 kilograms! The crew noticed this male's nose rapidly twitching his elongated whiskers.

"Be careful." Dr. Zhu noticed this male focused his attention to all six strange visitors. "I can't forget what Dr. Netherland told me about *Castoroides*."

"Me either." Dr. al-Saud added. "I remember seeing modern beavers successfully defend themselves against a mountain lion.

"I remember seeing one fend off a young grizzly bear." Dr. Art Remington revealed.

"You're kidding?" Dr. Nina Ivanov asked.

"Not this time. When I saw it happen at Alberta, I was completely taken by surprise."

Dr. Zhu didn't want to provoke such a giant beaver, which would most likely be vigilant against any potential rival. This male's keen black eyes continued to study all six researchers as he crawled slowly toward them. Dr. Zhu remembered another species of giant beavers known as *Castoroides ohioensis*, which coexisted at the same time period in the United States of America, particularly Ohio. He suddenly realized yet another problem.

Another mammal emerged from the same woodland area where *Castoroides* originated. While this giant brown beaver hissed his firm warning to stay away, this other mammal appeared to crawl quietly behind the giant beaver. Dr. Marino pointed his I.D. device to find a suitable identity of such a cunning carnivore that resembled a giant wolverine with brown fur with a wide beige stripe that circled around this male's back and hips. Dr. Marino discovered a genus that's a member of the mustelid family that consists of badgers, otters, weasels and wolverines.

"Whoa, I've never seen a wolverine with such intensity." A worried Dr. Ivanov complimented a male predator employing a stealthy method of attack by remaining silent.

Matching the size of a large male black bear (*Ursus americanus*) *Megalictis* was persistent in regards to hunting their prey at North America during the Early Miocene that would be approximately 23,030,000 – 15,970,00 years ago. Dr. Nevins's knowledge of modern wolverines and beavers convinced her that this pending interaction would not be a pleasant to say the least!

The crew activated their retro turbines to propel the craft in reverse. *Megalictis* pounced on top of *Castoroides* and bit behind his neck. All six crewmembers were startled to see *Castoroides* roll his body over before viciously gnawing *Megalictis* at his shoulder. Dr. Nevins wanted to establish a greater distance from a formidable clash between two well regarded life forms of Earth and Isis. Loud cries, growling, hissing and snarling disturbed a quiet landscape. Small lizards and mammals within this vicinity fled the area once pin sharp canines of *Megalictis* and dense incisors of *Castoroides* penetrated each other's fur. Nearby birds flew away from a bitter rivalry on Isis that consisted of a long history of horror and hate!

"Hold you position!" Dr. Nevins told the others as just before *Castoroides* managed to break free before fleeing into nearby woodland at the left side of the trail before *Megalictis* pursued the giant beaver inside.

Once they entered the left side of the trail, all six crewmembers moved across the trail to the right side. Dr. Nevins wanted to move cautiously until they've reached their desired intersection. Once they turned left all six researchers were able to see the sheltered bay and Town Hall as they faced west before moving straight ahead. Everyone instinctively looked in both directions to find any sign of the giant beaver or the massive wolverine.

"There's *Castoroides* again!" Dr. Ivanov recognized the same brown beaver straight ahead, although this male appeared tired as his shoulders bled, there were no signs of any life threatening injuries.

"We must pass by him slowly at a safe distance." Dr. Nevins warned the group as they drifted over the right side of the grassy trail as *Castoroides* continued to stare at the crew from his position at the other side of the trail.

While the crew maintained a safe distance from the giant beaver, Dr. Marino felt his transporter jolt from behind. When he turned around his heart vibrated his chest when he discovered a ferocious carnivore attempting to tackle his Drifter unit.

"Oh no!" was all Dr. Marino said before *Megalictis* reappeared once again, with bloodstains on his shoulders and back.

This persistent predator used his powerful jaw in an attempt to clamp into Dr. Marino's left ankle. Dr. Marino shouted out "flee everyone, flee" as he tried to pull away from a tormenting grip of *Megalictis*. Dr. Marino heard a brief sound of torn fabric as he continued to struggle free. As soon as he broke loose from the prehistoric wolverine, Dr. Marino raced away from a blood thirsty male determined to catch him.

Dr. Marino then heard a heavy impact once *Castoroides* collided into the left ribcage of *Megalictis* and felt distressed to hear a blood letting brawl elevate as he desperately darted away toward the shore. As Antonio looked into one of his side view mirrors, he saw both rivals rollover into a gutter that bordered the woodland. All Dr. Marino wanted to do was follow his colleagues back across the shore and into the sheltered bay. Dr. Nevins wasted no time to use her Watchdog device to contact Town Hall's medical team to attend to Dr. Marino's infliction on his left leg.

"Medics...we're approaching the shore!

Further relief was imminent once all six crewmembers reached the shore of a flat island at the middle of the shore where Town Hall stood along with medical doctors and paramedics awaiting their arrival. Once Dr. Nevins and her crew stopped near the bottom of the ramp, she jumped off her transporter and ran over to Dr. Marino to help him off.

"Antonio! Are you injured?" Dr. Nevins asked.

"Believe it or not, I'm fine but my jumpsuit is torn to shreds."

"We need to examine any direct contact you received." Dr. al-Saud suggested before his wife Ada examined his left leg to diagnose his injury.

"Thank God your skin wasn't penetrated but you still need antibiotics to prevent any transmitted disease." Dr. Ada al-Saud advised.

A Night of Tranquility

By the late afternoon, Mack was still intrigued to observe his unexpected view as Lucy lied on a knitted blanket. Marcus and Meena continued their intimate conversation as Osiris luminosity began to fade casting shadows of tall trees reflecting their height across shaded grass. Mack knew that Osiris will soon set behind distant mountains as Lucy stared into the sky. Mack reflected his time on Earth as his comfort for this new world flourished. Viewing the landscape of a foreign world while the ocean breeze blew across his face made it possible for him to learn how the Central Continent would never be boring and even when he ages, he'll always have fun.

Marcus thought about such an impact Dr. Netherland made when he originally discovered Isis. Some originally dismissed Isis as a gaseous planet deprived of life and habitability. But Dr. Netherland wanted to know for certain by sending the Adam and Eve probes that ultimately revealed the truth about this discovery. Marcus understood have Dr. Netherland ever lost interest pursuing planet Isis and its habitability, then he would've ended up standing on an airless canyon on a cold and dusty day on Mars. He recalled his experience with Dr. Netherland's lectures, which he told his audience to ensure bias would never interfere with their thinking and to maintain an intricate balance between faith and skepticism. Dr. Netherland also concluded that faith doesn't mean gullibility and skepticism never meant closed mindedness.

A mellow breeze comforted the entire crew as Osiris maintained a gentle glow. Mack continued to observe migrations of mammoths, buffalos and sauropod dinosaurs such as *Diplodocus* and *Brachiosaurus*. He felt ever more appalled, but grateful for their discoveries. Mack felt forever indebted to Dr. Netherland's determination to search and find the truth including this awe inspiring Earth analog planet that's full of surprises and suspense.

Mack remembered his first class trip to the American Museum of Natural History in New York City when he was in the fourth grade. He also recalled watching scientific expeditions he saw on the Discovery Channel, the National Geographic Channel, Animal Planet and The Learning Channel. The crew love to watch such programs as well as viewing other topics presented on A&E and The History Channel.

Mack continued to capture a steady cross breeze that migrated across the nearby ocean. Lucy was lying on her back before she opened her eyes and lifted her head.

"Mack."

"What?"

"It'll be dusk soon. Shouldn't we return to Town Hall?"

"Umm…you're right, we'll pack up."

Lucy called Marcus and Meena before gathering their belongings and folding their blanket. Once the area was cleared, Meena and Lucy hiked down a slope before they placed all items into storage compartments of both transporters. They activated both vehicles before they carefully winded down a slope at one side of the mesa until arriving at sea level.

Lucy and Meena felt cautious of reentering the ocean due to their clear memory of what they saw earlier. *C. megalodon*, also known as Megatooth inflicted their emotional discomfort as both women remembered their close encounter with the whale sized shark that attacked *Ophthalmosaurus* directly beneath them. Meena felt that she or one of her closest colleagues could've been swallowed whole by the meticulous Megatooth.

"Mack, I'm nervous," Lucy expressed her feelings as she sat behind him with her arms tightly wrapped around his torso.

Although Mack felt safe, he sympathized with Lucy's feelings because he knew that if he ever lost her, than he would not be able to forgive himself for being responsible for such a tragedy.

"Don't worry I'll monitor this entire parameter."

"What if Megatooth returns?" Lucy showed her concern.

"Our transporters could out maneuver the whale sized shark." Mack assured her.

Mild ocean currents vibrated the crew's transporters as they continued their course over cobalt blue water. Marcus and Mack took their companion's concerns to heart as they actively looked toward all directions for any sign of danger including any tall fin. As attentive both gentlemen were in regards to detecting possible danger there was no sign of *C. megalodon* anywhere.

Relief finally arrived when all four colleagues finally reached the extended bay. Shallow debt, a steady outflow of water into the ocean and a group of barrier reefs that bordered the bay and ocean would complicate Megatooth's efforts to enter the sheltered bay. What's most important is there's not enough food sheltered in the bay to support a giant shark for long. Megatooth's diet consisted primarily of whales.

Mack noticed an erection of a conductive tower station located at one of ten islands that was furthest from Town Hall. This station that was over one mile (over 1.6km) away was almost completed. Standing 200 feet (61m) high, this tall rod was harnessed with support beams along with a deep foundation. Gentle waters inside the bay reassured the crew from Megatooth.

The right side of Lucy's head rested on Mack's left shoulder as her gesture of relief when they soared over land before moving up a small hill to reach Town Hall. Meena shared a similar gesture, as she also felt relaxed once they made it to shore. Both Drifters were brought in front of the ramp where all four occupants climbed off before they gave both vehicles to two associates, who brought both units into the main entrance to store them into an assigned storage hangar.

"Thank goodness we didn't see Megatooth again." Meena mentioned, as she felt grateful to be back safely.

Dr. Ryan noticed Dr. al-Saud walking down the ramp along with Dr. Tracy Marino and her husband Antonio, who wore a bandage around his left leg under his knee. "What happened?"

"*Megalictis* nipped on my leg. It was a close call. But I'm fine." Antonio displayed no evidence of limping.

"You've encountered *Megalictis*?" Dr. Nimbus asked.

"Yes, we also encountered *Castoroides* as well." Antonio told Marcus and the others. "You should have seen it! Both of them engaged into a ferocious fight."

"What else did you encounter?" Dr. Ryan wondered.

"Believe it or not, we saw *Deinonychus* and *Quetzalcoatlus*."

"We saw *Indricotherium*, *Anancus*, *Amargasaurus* and the Songhua River Mammoth." Dr. Ryan responded.

"You saw all of them in one area?" Tracy asked with intrigue.

"Oh yes. We even saw a migration of sauropods such as *Diplodocus* and *Brachiosaurus*."

"Really," Dr. al-Saud responded. "We saw *Metridiochoerus*, *Pelorovis*, and the Cape zebra."

Dr. Rosalila expressed. "I wished we saw the Cape zebra instead of Megatooth."

"Huh…you can't be serious? You encountered Megatooth?" Antonio was shocked to hear the news.

"I wonder what we'll see next…Pegasus?" Marcus replied before the others laughed.

As they continued their conversation, Dr. Ryan's Watchdog device vibrated his wrist before all four expandable prongs stretched out from all four corners before a holographic display showed Dr. Darryl Hollis. Dr. Hollis was a member of the Chamber along with Karl Gruber and Donald Netherland. Both his parents were distinguished professors at Spelman and Morehouse Colleges at Atlanta. His parent's mentorship enabled him to discover his true passion for space exploration. Because of his passion, he along with Dr. Jordan Tyrell was among the youngest crewmembers to have traveled to Mars, with Dr. Netherland. Dr. Hollis called from the Starship Guardian and waited patiently for Mack's reply.

Once Dr. Ryan saw his display, he noticed a surprised facial expression, which was rare in part of Dr. Hollis. "Darryl, is everything okay up there?"

"Everything's fine. We've just discovered something shocking north of the Artic circle of Isis. I'll transmit the data."

Once Dr. Hollis's transmission was complete, all four prongs contracted in length until his wristwatch device was deactivated. Mack and the others proceeded up the ramp. Once they reached the main level, they took one of two stairwells to walk two flights upstairs until they were at level five. It didn't take much time to walk down a corridor to enter a domed shaped room with a glass floor.

Once everyone entered the Clairvoyance room, a center light inserted into the top area of the dome activated before Marcus closed the entrance door. As soon as everyone sat at the middle of the floor, Dr. Ryan verbally called out for the center light to turn off before saying "display new data."

Once his command was received, all seven observers were cloaked in darkness for two seconds before the simulator placed them at a northern taiga where a mist of ice covered pale grass in recess to prepare for a long winter ahead.

"Whoa, this can't be!" Dr. Ryan was oblivious to see a migration of familiar looking mammoths heading south.

"What did I.D. reveal?" Dr. Nimbus referred to the Identification Detective as he stared at their tusks that curved upwards and back and appeared to extend over eight feet or 2.44 meters long if they were straight.

Dr. Ryan studied their thick black fur used to insulate them against the frigid cold of an Artic winter and to absorb as much of the sun's rays as possible. "So that's how *Mammuthus primigenius* appeared."

"The Woolly mammoth?" Marcus interpreted.

"I thought I'll never see the Woolly mammoth alive." Dr. Antonio Marino was shock to see such a spectacle.

Their bold physical shape impressed Dr. Tracy Marino. She also noticed that each mammoth had only one enlarged hump on top of their heads instead of two smaller humps like modern elephants. Standing up to ten feet (3m) tall at the shoulder Tracy was impressed by their brawny bodies.

Dr. al-Saud focused his attention to their reduced humps behind their heads, which covered most of their upper shoulders. These inflatable humps were strategically important in order survive harsh winters. During the warmer seasons, the Woolly mammoth will consume an enormous amount of conifers, birches and other plants of the northern flora. Similar to how camels store much of their consumed water as a means to survive despite extreme drought. Food reserves will prevent the Woolly mammoth from suffering seasonal famine.

An enormous body size of *Mammuthus primigenius* made it possible to contain their body heat. These prehistoric legends are known and revered worldwide as the telepresence projector revealed their primeval paths across northern steppes just like they've done at Alaska and Siberia during the Late Pleistocene. Only an exceptional few at Wrangel Island in the Artic Ocean lasted into the Holocene epoch (11,700 years ago – present) until around 6000 years ago. Prehistoric cave paintings in France and Spain traced an intriguing lifestyle of these famous mammoths that continue to be a household name in modern times. Although *Mammuthus primigenius* can't be found alive on Earth, all seven researchers inside the Clairvoyance room understand how that the Woolly mammoth lives on to inspire humanity as seven crew members watched this herd continue their long migration.

Dr. Hollis is a veteran sensory specialist who has sent two probes to Isis. One was assigned to the northern tip of the Central Continent, which was above 90 degrees latitude north. The other probe was successfully situated at the southern tip of the Western Continent, which is only 200 miles or almost 322 kilometers from the South Pole. These probes were specifically designed to withstand the most extreme climatic conditions. They will be assigned to monitor all four seasons of both regions. Infrared sensory, video, audio, and other receptors will detect natural activities and record all this information so Intelligence officials at the starship Guardian and in established Town Halls could examine the data.

As all seven observers inside the Clairvoyance room watched the last Woolly mammoth migrate south on the taiga while scientific findings and analysis continue to progress. As they watched *Mammuthus primigenius* fulfill their hunger, the Central Continent crew met their previous missionary expectations as the entire bay and some of the central western region of the mainland has been identified along with all of its mystique and magic.

Marcus wanted to view the latest update of a species list, which displays their actual size, appearance and other valuable information. Stored data within the Soul Mate database would provide extensive information if a life form has any resemblance to either prehistoric or extant animals on Earth. Besides DNA and skeletal formation, this database contains various photos and footages of every plant and animal ever studied.

Marcus suspected a host of new data will be sent to Earth. Radio signals from the orbiting starship will be sent directly to Earth. He understood it would take three years to their message to reach humanity on Earth. "Mack."

"Yes."

"What's the latest update of the taxonomy chart?" The rest of the observers inside the Clairvoyance room shared Marcus's desire to view a holographic sample image of each life form discovered and their exact characteristics.

"Species list," was Dr. Ryan's verbal call before the northern steppe scene disappeared and the entire dome above the floor showed a sapphire blue background, while the floor displayed a flat emerald green surface.

Marcus and Antonio were both excited to be present before a clear moving hologram of a beaver that grows as large as a grizzly bear. Although this beaver wasn't authentic, it was a strange sight for those who never saw *Castoroides* before. Antonio knew exactly what they were capable of when this bold beaver ransacked *Megalictis* soon after he escaped the giant wolverine's grip.

A clear realistic four dimensional holographic projection that records length, width, depth, and time; made this simulation of *Castoroides* look as though a bear sized beaver was actually inside the Clairvoyance room with all seven observers. Added authenticity was noticed as the crew heard thumping footsteps and an occasional grunt. Even twitching of a large nose, whiskers and a faint scent of a giant beaver reflected the wild into Town Hall, similar to what this device done inside the conference room at the federation's headquarters during the Osiris 4 Summit. The crew appreciated the fact that any undesirable stimuli such as extreme temperatures, repulsive odors, and any other form of potential nuisance could be removed by verbal commands.

"Huh...that's what I saw." Dr. Antonio Marino confirmed as an image of *Castoroides* walking calmly around the room.

Dr. Marino established a strong foundation of respect for Isis's habitat including *Megalictis*.

Although he encountered a risky situation Dr. Marino was fascinated by Isis's biodiversity, which was why he was still willing to embark on such a risky adventure despite what happened earlier. "You have *Megalictis*?"

"We should." Mack answered before a simulated, bear sized wolverine suddenly appeared from the right side of this dome shaped room as the simulated *Castoroides* continued to randomly walk around the room.

Antonio observed familiar body shape and fur characteristics of the world's largest and most powerful mustelid to exist on Earth. His wife Tracy recognized pin sharp, bear size claws, which appeared gray, mixed with a white chalky shade. Dr. Nimbus was impressed by the prehistoric wolverine's fluffy tail, while Dr. al-Saud acknowledged his bold physical shape. After Antonio noticed his claws, he looked over to Tracy "You should have seen *Megalictis* in action. He shifted my transporter. I was surprised how strong this ancient wolverine was."

"Honey, you could have been killed."

"I know. That one moved faster that I ever expected."

Tracy placed her left arm around his back and rested her hand on his left shoulder. "Tell me about the conflict between both of them?"

"Once my jumpsuit was torn, I managed to break free just before *Castoroides* collided into *Megalictis*. Before I knew it, both of them relentlessly fought each other as they rolled down a gutter bordering the woods."

"That's strange." Tracy reacted. "Beavers are commonly defensive. I never observed such aggressive behavior."

"A wolverine is so persistent in regards to hunting, that counter-aggression might be necessary. Antonio explained. "In this case *Castoroides* could have actually defended a nearby den. Who knows, his den may have his mate or even offspring."

Mack then requested related information before two tabloids appeared on the floor next to each other as they overlapped the emerald green floor. Both measured two feet (61cm) wide and three feet (91.4cm) long. Both tabloids were brown, accompanied by yellow imprints of available information. A set of scroll bar arrows was at the right side of each tabloid so by pressing either one to scroll up or down for additional information. Each digital tabloid revealed facts regarding every species observed. For example one tabloid revealed important facts about *Castoroides* and the other showed valuable information regarding *Megalictis*.

Holograms of both species randomly walked, observed and emitted verbal calls. Antonio was certain that a blood spilling brawl would result if these two life forms were ever placed inside this room. Dr. Ryan verbally requested the projector to save both samples of *Megalictis* and *Castoriodes* before he said, "*Quetzalcoatlus*."

Seconds later, a giant distant pterosaur appeared before gently gliding toward their direction. Dr. al-Saud focused his attention to the flying reptile's appearance as this aerial splendor of the sky approached. "This simulation showed exactly how our pterosaur appeared."

Each observer gently leaned their heads back as *Quetzalcoatlus* approached their position. Dr. Ryan and the others leaned over after the feathered serpent for which this species name means, reached its simulated location and hovered vertically in front of all seven observers. Gently flapped wings and a pivoting head added a live action image of the flying reptile. As this simulated pterosaur showed its fine physique, a new tabloid replaced the other two and showed all known facts and figures of one of the largest and most spectacular flying life forms on Earth and Isis.

Dr. al-Saud felt a minor reminiscence of his earlier expedition. "When we saw *Quetzalcoatlus* glide above us, my heart felt stiff."

Once everyone read the digital tabloid on the floor, the crew viewed the flying pterosaur one last time before Dr. Ryan provided another verbal command, "Save."

He verbally requested *Pelorovis* before a live action hologram of a giant buffalo appeared from the right side of the Clairvoyance room. Dr. Malik al-Saud confirmed their general appearance. He knew this simulated version of an enormous buffalo was much safer than his recent experience with three bachelor bulls. As this holographic image of a buffalo walked gracefully to the left side of the room, His wife Tracy was intrigued to learn that such a specimen was discovered only a few miles or kilometers away from her present location.

A faint smirk was Dr. al-Saud's expression as he saw *Pelorovis antiquus* grazing on the emerald green floor just like they saw on the mainland and similar to how these bulls consumed ancient Africa's grass. Their modern relatives in Africa, such as the Cape buffalo (*Syncerus caffer*) continue to graze the African Savanna as their prehistoric ancestors did millions of years ago.

"When *Pelorovis* charged us, I though we were in a heap of trouble." Malik explained. "I never saw anything like it."

"The group of males we saw looked just like Africa's bachelor bull buffaloes that randomly chase lions and hyenas." Antonio remarked. "But they were much larger than any I saw in Africa, their horns were massive."

Dr. Ryan decided to add the Cape Zebra (*Equus capensis*) and *Metridiochoerus* into their simulation as *Pelorovis antiquus* continued to walk around the Clairvoyance room. All three holograms of Earth's former inhabitants impressed all six researchers as they reflected how it may've been living among a dynasty of life and evolution before the earliest humans emerged.

Dr. Ryan instructed for all current displays supplied by the Soul Mate to be saved. Soon after, all three simulations of Africa's ancient inhabitants vanished from their view. Dr. Tracy Marino asked Lucy about their encounters. "How did the Songhua River Mammoth appear?"

"I'll show you." Lucy replied.

Once Lucy verbally commanded for *Mammuthus sungari* to appear, everyone witnessed a hologram of a colossal mammoth standing 16 feet

(4m) tall with midsized ears and a pair of thick, curved tusks. This hologram appeared to walk gently across the room. Abdullah, Antonio and Tracy remained silent as they examine what's among the largest mammoths in existence, which lived from the Middle Miocene to the Late Pleistocene or from approximately 15,970,000 to 11,700 years ago. Spectators were appalled to view this hologram of this monumental mammoth.

Dr. Ryan knew the word species means a group of plants or animals with similar characteristics and are genetically related. Each specific species is able to produce offspring, but cannot reproduce with any other species. He knew a genus is a group of two or more different species that have common characteristics and have no close physical resemblance of any other species.

A family group of animals or plants consists of similar genera, which is plural for genus, share a common ancestor. For example a lion, tiger, leopard and cheetah all are part of the feline family or cat family. A group of families which scientists classified in many ways similar and correlate to each other consists of an order similar to how gorillas, monkeys, baboons, gibbons and humans are part of a single order called primates.

Various orders linked together by a basic common feature are under a single class. For example, all life forms that could maintain a self regulating body temperature internally, instead of relying on external temperature to maintain body heat and suckle their young are members of the mammalian class or mammals. Other known animal classes such as reptilians or reptiles and aves that consist of birds, all make up a phylum. All plant classes combined consist of a division.

All phyla, which are plural for phylum, consist of the animal kingdom while all divisions consist of the plant kingdom. Scientists also combined both kingdoms along with the fungi kingdom and the protist kingdom into a domain. The Archaea, Bacteria and Eukarya domains consist of every living organism on Earth and based upon the Three-domain system introduced by Professor Carl Richard Woese in 1990. Professor Woese's Phylogenetic Tree of Life separates and distinguishes all three domains, which are the highest taxonomic rank of organisms.

Once Lucy told Tracy about *Anancus*, she then requested for *Indricotherium*, meaning giraffe rhinoceros, appeared after *Anancus* vanished. The largest known mammal ever to live on land appeared before a stunned crew studying its physiology and reading information about a slow moving monument of flesh and blood. A gray colored hornless rhinoceros standing 18 feet (5.5m) at the shoulder could extract leaves that are suspended up to 26 feet or almost eight meters above the ground.

Scientists are convinced that smaller and more agile browsers would follow this mammal until leaves fall to the ground for easy picking for many smaller browsers that would never gain access to these leaves by any other means. Mack knew it would be necessary for smaller browsers to be quick in order to prevent being accidentally kicked or stepped on. Paleontologists also believe that birds often land on *Indricotherium* so they could extract parasites and other insects off their back and neck. The 'giraffe rhinoceros' was large enough to subconsciously be a provider for many other smaller life forms.

Once everyone viewed *Indricotherium* and read all of its related information, Marcus and the others decided to clear the giraffe rhinoceros's image before the words "Clairvoyance projector off" was said by Marcus before a sapphire blue ski and an emerald ground became white again. A solitary source of light inserted at the middle of the dome made it possible for everyone to walk over to the entrance.

"It's hard to believe that all living specimens exist in one planet!" Antonio concluded after he viewed all of the data.

"It's even a greater miracle that we're here to examine such a biodiversity. I'm glad we didn't settle on Mars. It would have been a boring assignment compared to this." Dr. Ryan agreed to Antonio's comment.

Lucy listened to their conversation before she added. "What's more is that it feels almost like a natural resort. This is the only living museum of prehistoric organisms."

"I appreciate the fact that we could study life that resembles Earth's prehistoric fauna instead of fossils." Antonio said.

Malik sympathize with Antonio as everyone walked down one of two stairwells until they reached the main level of Town Hall. Malik soon felt relieved as they approached the main exit to walk down the ramp. Peace of mind settled into all seven researchers as they noticed Osiris setting down into the western horizon. Additional comfort was felt as they recognized a gradual change in reflective shades of colors such as pink, orange and purple on the surface of various cirrus and stratus clouds.

Once everyone reached the lower end of the ramp, Marcus was able to hear soft resonations from numerous chimes installed on a suspended wire that were horizontally installed on top of two vertical poles. This chime set varied in size and style. A mild cross breeze soothed their souls as soft ringing resonated through the air. Barely able to hear verbal calls from life forms at the mainland, nearby sounds of acoustic guitars, a mandolin, a lyre and a heart warming rhythm of Caribbean steel drums.

Mack indulged into this harmonic sensation as he and the others approached a large circular campfire. They sat six feet (1.83m) away from exterior cobblestones that enclosed a pile of old logs emitting a coalescing scent of burning wood as flames stretched up to five feet (1.5m) tall. Marcus recognized a faint collection of distant stars manifesting from a previous navy blue shroud of an afternoon sky. While Lucy noticed daylight from Osiris rescinding, Meena felt temperatures decline until her Watchdog device indicated a comfortable temperature of 68 degrees Fahrenheit and almost 20 degrees Celsius or Centigrade.

Antonio and his wife Tracy rested next to each other next to the campfire and stared at an early evening sky. Alicia and her husband Harold sat besides each other near the fire as they wrapped their arms around their shoulders. Malik decided to participate in playing an acoustic guitar as his wife Ada listened to his enchanting sounds. Arnold Weinstein used a long twig to burn marshmallows along with his wife Esther. Viktor and Nina Ivanov burn their own marshmallows along with Claude Moreau and his fiancée Zarina Ansari.

Haru Nakamura, Taina Kepa, Julia Grace, Doris Remington, Fan and Ying Zhu commonly shared laughter, while Art Remington and Derrick Grace smoked traditional cigars. Everyone enjoyed a fine rhythm from Caribbean steel drums played by Martin de' la' Vega as his wife Angela played one of two mandolins. Low humidity added more pleasure to an enchanted crowd as twilight converted into a crisp and clear night.

Some lights inside Town Hall were either dimmed or turned off, which gave everyone an easy opportunity to see plenty of stars up in the sky. Not much visual effort was needed to notice how some stars appeared much closer than others. Yet some seemed considerably farther away than most. Faint tints of blue and orange distinguished some of many visible stars. As Mack lied on grass and stared into the sky, Lucy called for his attention. "Mack, let's go to the shore."

Mack listened to her words before he stood up and took her request into consideration. "I'll be at the shore if you need me."

Lucy and Mack held hands as they departed the campfire. Music was still heard as the couple approached the shore's edge. Although a pleasurable scent of burning wood was no longer present, a gentle halo of a distant campfire reflected off the exterior of Town Hall. Mack inhaled cool air along with a mild salty scent of the bay water's surface while soft waves merged with white sand at the outskirts of their settled island. Lucy stared through an evening mist to capture a distorted image of the mainland. Shrouds of tree lines and distant foothills captivated her conviction of the Central Continent's elusive significance before she felt comfortable to speak her mind to a close friend.

"Mack…I'm glad we selected this continent instead of the Eastern and Western Continents." Lucy informed him.

"Me too, all the best data we've received originated here. The other two continents appeared odd or even strange." Mack claimed with confidence."

Lucy knew Mack was energized to be assigned to this desirable location. "Mack, I was thinking about what Alicia told me earlier."

"What did she tell you?" Mack wondered.

"There's so much activity going on out there. Malik was nearly stampeded by *Pelorovis* and Antonio narrowly escaped being bitten by *Megalictis*. Personally I think your obsession with planet Isis could place you in considerable danger."

Mack thought about his nightmare aboard the Starship Guardian and connected his experience with Lucy's message. "I understand your concerns but this is the only place of its kind anywhere."

"That's exactly why we must take additional precaution. We barely have any experience whatsoever. What's more is that all animals on this planet are well adapted for this environment. I mean millions of years of evolution in the wild. We don't have much experience in the wild, not to mention that we're from an urbanized environment." Suddenly both of them heard distant howls and deep moaning coming from the mainland.

An echoed resonation from the mainland supplemented her ever growing concern for Mack's safety. Lucy then looked over toward the mainland while Mack looked down toward the ground and thought about Lucy's concerns as howling calls pierced through an early evening sky. Mack bit lightly on his lower lip and considered the fact that he must balance his blind ambition with common sense before he focused his attention to the mainland with a new perspective.

"Lucy." She then turned around to listen. "I don't intend to take your advice for granted. I just want to get the most out of Isis. Heck...we're lucky to be assigned here in the first place."

"All it takes is one mistake out there!" Lucy simultaneously pointed her index finger at the mainland. "Even the wisest animals in the mainland make mistakes. Nature wouldn't be anymore forgiving to us than any other life form out there."

"I'm not underestimating any potential challenges we may encounter. Doctor Netherland and the Chamber provided us with ample information we need to survive. We've learn so much about dinosaurs and other prehistoric animals."

"Although we analyzed their fossils with careful scrutiny and compared them to all living relatives. We never encountered them alive. All I'm saying is that despite centuries of fossil excavation and examination, there's much more to discover. I don't want you to learn a harsh lesson that ended your life."

"Lucy, we're learning at an incredible rate like nothing we ever experienced! However, let me reassure you that I'll encourage every safety precaution and take considerable measures to insure my safety and the security of the crew."

"I know you mean well. Before we departed Earth, each and every single one of us signed a formal release of exempting any liability against the federation whatsoever. We professed full responsibility for our actions. I know that you've been an explorer for a long time now and you've never rejected accountability. That's one of many reasons why I admire you. I just don't want to hear any news that you're not returning alive."

Mack felt a tight knot inside his chest as he thought about the consequences to the crew if he ever died. His deep seated desire to explore the Central Continent and its indigenous population of life could make him vulnerable to danger. He thought about how his perfect life could disappear forever, without warning if he's not careful. Mack was reminded of another reason why Lucy was selected for this assignment. An additional source of awareness and wisdom beyond his own made it possible for him to survive, so he could continue to send messages of their triumph to Earth. Mack continued to think about Lucy's advice of imminent risks as he continued to monitor a vibrant mainland cloaked in darkness. Lucy looked over to him as he was thinking about his choices and waited patiently for his verbal response.

"I'll be careful."

Once Lucy heard his acknowledgement, she then took out a green object from one of her pockets. "I want you to have this."

There was enough surrounding light to recognize that this object was a polished spherical stone that measured about two inches or over five centimeters across. Along with a smooth surface, Mack noticed this solid object appeared to have a gentle mixture of green and white. "It's gorgeous! Where did you get this?"

"I had this with me for a long time. It's made of pure jade."

"I keep objects like this with me for traditional and cultural good luck. It symbolizes my wish for you to be safe and secure."

Mack looked at this quaint object and felt a sense of how much he was appreciated. Not only was the object unique and beautiful, it represented someone's unbridled support. As he viewed an enchanting green object he visualized Lucy's face and recognized her unconditional care. After he observed this jade sphere, he then looked over to her as she awaited his reply.

Mack felt a strong, but subtle force penetrating his body as her dark brown eyes persisted to stare at him before he responded. "I hope you won't think that I don't appreciate everything you've done."

Lucy remained silent before Mack said, "I'm thinking about when you took us on top of the mesa earlier. Because of your surprise, I was convinced that there's no better place to be than right here."

I know you're the best person for this role. I still remember when the federation discovered Isis. All you and Marcus talked about was this planet. Every time you've talked about it you appeared weightless." Lucy revealed.

"I never though such a discovery would ever be accomplished in our lifetime." Mack admitted.

"Ever since we were aboard the starship, I tried numerous times to get your attention. Although I was frustrated, I knew you were ready to travel three light years to this new world."

Mack then, lowered his head forward in disbelief because he focused too much personal attention towards new data inside the Clairvoyance room instead of her. "I'm sorry for my failure to communicate."

Mack raised his head and stared at Lucy. "I remember when I received news back in January 17th 2033. I traveled on a lunar rover to collect some samples on the moon and observed the lunar sky. I received official news that changed my life."

"I was at headquarters when Meena told me everything before our discovery was released to the public," Lucy revealed her experience. "Tell me more?"

"I drove the rover as fast as I could to the lunar station. Once I entered the main corridor, Marcus was riveted as he told me more news. Seconds later, we received a transmission from headquarters for us to attend the summit. While we headed for Earth, Dr. Netherland assured us that this new discovery will be the federation's primary goal."

"So once Dr. Netherland called, you felt as though this was the best discovery ever?"

"Absolutely, Marcus and I were destined to travel to Mars to terraform its atmosphere. But once Isis was found, I didn't want to travel to Mars anymore. I wanted to come here." Mack said.

"I remember how you felt when you viewed the telepresence projector during the summit." Lucy recalled.

"It's impossible to forget. Once I saw a violent clash between *Gorgonops* and *Borhyaena*, I knew Mars would be out of my life and Isis will become my dream come true." Mack concluded.

Lucy felt startled by his remark. She then looked keenly at Mack before she asked, "all of your dreams?"

"Oh...umm...no, what I meant was this world was the best career decision I ever made."

"Do you have any other dream?" Lucy asked.

"Yes, I do." Mack then approached Lucy and embraced her passionately before he placed his right cheek on her right dimple. Lucy calmly placed her chin on his right shoulder before he took an initiative to mildly move her black hair up and back behind her shoulders. Lucy eventually twitched when she heard a mild squeak as Mack pressed his warm lips gently against her ear.

He continued to hold his new spherical jade emblem inside his right hand as he used both arms to embrace her. "For a long time I've always had strong feelings for you. You're the most amazing woman I've ever met! I'm so happy that you came with us to this new world. Although I love this world, Isis wouldn't be the same if you didn't come along with us. I never had any feelings for any woman like I have for you."

When he finished revealing his secret to her, he noticed her ear rise from its position, which indicated that she was smiling. Mack felt more affection from her response before he relinquished his embrace so he could look into her eyes. Lucy expressed a mild giggle when she noticed Mack's watery blue eyes and reddish dimples on both cheeks.

"Oh Mack," She laughed.

"Yes?"

"I don't remember you being as shy as you are now."

He suddenly felt short of breath as he initially stuttered. Once he regained his poise, he decided to tell her "Lucy...umm...I wish to tell you that I love you and I wish to establish a meaningful relationship with you."

Mack suddenly felt a sharp increase of emitting body heat racing out his pores. His stomach tightened as Lucy continued to stare into his eyes. Lucy's eyebrows rose in unison with Mack's body temperature before he felt his knees weakening while hair follicles at the rear of his neck stood almost upright. Despite a hollow sensation inside his heart along with sweaty palms and legs, Mack commended his courage of revealing the truth to Lucy.

"Oh Mack, I love you too."

Lucy then placed both of her arms around his torso until her hands touched each other behind his back. Mack felt her lower biceps press against his ribs. Mack placed his arms on her shoulders then held on to both of his elbows behind her shoulders. Lucy rested the right side of her head on his left shoulder and felt a warm presence on her cheek before separating.

Lucy then looked up into the nighttime sky. "Which star out there is our sun, which we often refer to as Sol?"

Mack studied the sky before he recalled exactly where it's located. "The sun's right there."

"How are you able to know where it is?"

"Intelligence produced a three dimensional model of the Milky Way galaxy. They showed me their latest edition." Mack explained as they focused their attention to a point of light.

"You want to join others at the campfire?" Mack asked.

"Sure."

Once she agreed, they proceeded toward the campfire. Mack and Lucy held hands as they approaching the others who notice their bonding relationship. As they walked over to the fire, Meena then placed her right arm around Marcus's shoulders. Although Marcus felt modest, he was optimistic about their relationship when she placed her chin on his left shoulder.

"Mack! Old chum!" Marcus greeted him.

Everyone surrounding the campfire greeted and encouraged them to sit and join in on the fun. Music and marshmallows accompanied by an enchanting flame made everyone feel at home in a foreign world. Long time friends and acquaintances felt satisfied of what they've learned about Isis as well as themselves. Marcus felt euphoric to overcome his modesty for Meena, as she was relieved that she could finally connect to him. Mack's heart no longer beats rapidly in fear whenever he approaches Lucy, whether it's for professional or social purposes.

Mack thought of his former social block being burned away permanently as he used a twig to hold a marshmallow above the fire. Mack realized how 12 hours made an enormous difference in his life. Not only did he learn more about life in the Central Continent, he also witness the Wooly mammoth migrate across the open taiga. Meena and Lucy also took him on top of a bedrock mount along with Marcus. Both ladies suggested calling this mesa Grace Stone; because of such impeccable views it offered and it's where he overcame his social struggle on top of this enchanting elevation. Mack sympathize its significance because he was finally able to connect to the woman he admired.

Acoustic guitars, mandolins and Caribbean steel drums continued to entertain a delightful crowd. While Mack lied flat on his back, he was able to look directly up and noticed congregations of moths hovering around nearby portable outdoor spotlights. He would see bats fly in front of each spotlight so they could capture moths and gnats. Mack remembered that many species of bats use a unique sensory projection known as echolocation. Instead of vision, bats, like dolphins and some whales would constantly emit a high frequency. He suspected these vibrations would trace and reflect their signals back to the source, so a three dimensional image would estimate distance and movement similar to how it's performed by modern radar systems. Mack saw a mature female bat aim precisely toward a moth's position before she captured the moth during flight.

Marcus began to stare at the stars and reflect his life's history, while Meena lied next to him. He thought about his childhood years in Los Angeles while she looked at fragments and debris burning up as they entered Isis's atmosphere commonly referred as shooting stars. Marcus remembered joining the United States Navy before he toured most of the Pacific. He thought about when NASA accepted him and when he first met Mack Ryan. As he continued working for NASA, he was invited along with Dr. Ryan to a lecture about long distance space travel hosted by Dr. Donald Netherland. Since he attended Dr. Netherland's lecture, his life changed dramatically and once the Humane Space Federation was founded in October 12th 2019, he was formerly initiated as a permanent member along with Dr. Ryan and everyone else sitting around the campfire.

Some of the most significant impacts Marcus ever experienced was when he intercepted an asteroid and when a suspicious planet was originally discovered. Both of them studied the data vigorously and suspected this newly discovered planet was like no other world they've ever seen. Because of its unique characteristics, Dr. Netherland testified to the General Assembly of the United Nations where he provided enough evidence to convince all member nations to advocate their legislature or parliaments to appropriate funds in order to conduct further research by developing the Adam & Eve probes. Because of what both probes revealed, additional financial support from member nations made it possible for Marcus to stare into an alien sky!

A similar procedure was achieved when an invading asteroid threatened Earth. Governments of each nation wasted no time to provide financial support that made it possible to save the world from a known global killer capable of disrupting basic social systems and services. Such a disaster would impede every normal aspect of human civilization. Governments, private organizations and the Humane Space Federation all collaborated to save the world from a global mass extinction and propelled humanity into a promising future.

The campfire began to rescind when Marcus looked over to see Mack lying on his back. While Marcus stared at him, he realized so much has happened between them and they accompanied each other during the most intriguing events in their lives. As Meena showed him her caring attention by feeding him more hot marshmallows, Marcus clearly understood that his longtime friend and colleague made more of a difference in his life than anyone else except his parents and immediate relatives.

Martin de' la' Vega held both steel drum sticks as he stretched his arms up before he yawned. "I'm getting tired."

"So am I." Malik said after he stopped playing his guitar to clear his watery eyes.

Most of who congregated around the campfire stood up and walked away before proceeding up the ramp. When Mack raised his head off the ground, he noticed Dr. Harold Nevins approaching with a bucket of salt water from the bay. Once he reached the outer cobblestones, Marcus, Mack and others moved away before Harold gently poured the bucket into the radiating wood.

A once faint residual orange glow converted into charcoaled remains that released steam and gray smoke into the air. Saltwater vaporized while heat emitting from decomposing wood ceased. Once the smoke cleared, Harold checked for any areas he could've missed before he acknowledged the fire was extinguished. The empty bucket dangled from Harold's right hand as everyone walked up the ramp to the main deck.

"Where do you want to explore tomorrow?" Mack wondered.

"We could go to the Great Plains?" Martin responded.

"What about the Principal Prairies?" Marcus suggested.

Lucy and Meena observed what they said to each other. As Mack held a spherical jade artifact in his shirt pocket, he knew that she would not appreciate him taking unnecessary risks. Despite an evening of relaxation, Mack remembered Lucy's concerns "For now...I think it's too far to travel ourselves. We'll send one of our Condor planes to scan that area."

When an elevator arrived, everyone walked inside and continued to discuss what would be done tomorrow. Meena and Lucy listened but kept silent. Marcus seemed a bit surprised by Mack's conservative approach in regards to exploring the mainland. Although his interest and desire to observe the mainland never declined, he didn't want his blind ambition to interfere with his common sense.

Once the elevator reached the upper crew deck on level #15, everyone walked out to proceed to their living quarters. Dr. Martin and Angela de' la' Vega entered their living suite. Meena kissed Marcus on the cheek before she proceeded into her quarters. A bashful Marcus then said "good night" to everyone before he went inside. Lucy and Mack then hugged each other one last time. Lucy walked into her suite while Mack looked on. When she closed her door, Mack then proceeded into his room.

He turned on one of his lamps using a light switch next to the front door and closed his door after he entered. Mack untied his boots before removing his jumpsuit before he took a brief shower, brushed and flossed his teeth. After he was dressed up into his pajamas, he inserted his hand into his chest pocket of his jumpsuit and removed a particular jade sphere given to him by someone special. Once he placed his jumpsuit into a hamper, he then lied on his bed and held this hand crafted item as he stared at it until he fell asleep. Since sensory projections inside his living quarters detected his low metabolism, the lamp was programmed to automatically turn off as a means to save energy. Mack slept through the night with his precious gift wrapped inside of his right hand.

NATURAL WONDERS

A colossus of distant stars in the sky faded once Osiris peeked over the eastern horizon. An atmospheric transition continued as a navy blue sky concealed distant points of light. One of these distant stars that disappeared into a clear morning sky would be remembered as the sun often known as Sol, which was known as the body or eye of Ra in ancient Egypt and Apollo in classical Greece. The crew would experience a gentle morning for the first time on another planet. As compatible to how a day would begin on Earth, the crew would experience a new day like no other as the parent star Osiris elevates above Isis's eastern horizon.

A cherry red glow of a parent star in the sky transformed itself as the sun's twin rose higher above the horizon. A tangerine glow illuminated the eastern sky while 250 crewmembers serving the Central Continent gently rolled over in the beds as daylight painted distant cirrus clouds pink and purple. An inviting cross breeze prompted pterosaurs and seagulls to awaken early and become the first in flight for the day. An elliptical shaped lander, which became the principal colony, possessed reinforced windows that invited subtle gold rays from a spectral luminosity type G2 main sequence yellow dwarf star, which reflected off the walls of the crew's living quarters.

A changing magnitude of Osiris continued to penetrate a tinted window of one bedroom where a reposed occupant shifted his sleeping position so he could remove his comforter. His right hand covered his eyes to remedy morning brightness. Officially the first morning on another planet is a reason why Dr. Ryan awakened before he proceeded to take a shower. Another of his favorite jumpsuits was removed from his closet. A navy blue jumpsuit made him appear thin. After he put on his socks and jump boots, a voice from his intercom activated.

"Doctor Ryan, come in please? Doctor Ryan?"

"This is Doctor Ryan, over."

"They're waiting for you at the main deck."

"Splendid! Tell them I'll meet them soon."

Dr. Ryan gathered all essential items before departing his living quarters. He pursued through a corridor before approaching set of four elevators and pressed a call button. Eventually one of elevators arrived at level 14 when a pair of sliding doors separated. Dr. Ryan entered the elevator and proceeded down toward the third level. Once he arrived, Mack was aware of a spacious area with ceilings that were 12 feet (3.66m) high. Dr. Ryan then passed by a wide doorway to enter another large room where he met everyone. Walking over to a collection of parked transporters with the bottom half of this prototype inserted into the floor. Engineering made it possible to store these valuable transporters without harming the receptors and emitters. Dr. Ryan was delighted to see Drs. Martin and Angela de' la' Vega along with Drs. Nimbus and Weinstein.

"Good morning Mack!" Marcus said with invigoration.

"Good morning everyone, I haven't had such a peaceful night's sleep for a long time."

"Mack, I have good news!" Arnold announced as his voice faintly echoed across a transporter hangar. "Our electrical conductor tests are complete."

"Great! I was quite worried about lightening striking Town Hall. At least the tower will prevent this from happening."

Mack was grateful the National Aeronautics and Space Administration, the European Space Agency and various other space agencies erected similar structures near launch pads and gantries as a means to prevent their spacecrafts and booster rockets from being struck by lightening. He remembered one structure at the Kennedy Space Center at Cape Canaveral, in Florida saved hundreds of lives and billions of dollars worth of valuable equipment by employing such a clever preventive technique. Mack advocated for a similar protection for all four landers before departing Earth.

"The Geographic Indicator provided us a clear route on the mainland." Arnold handed out a flat crystal screen devices.

Arnold handed out more of these six-inch (15.24cm) wide devices with a four inch (10cm), flat LCD screen. All five portable Geographic Indicator screens received an image from the main unit inside Town Hall. A device that's two inches (over 5cm) thick and five inches (12.7cm) long equipped with elastic straps to wrap this device around anyone's forearm for easy access.

"My best advice is to proceed up the original path, then move east...here." Arnold suggested as a red arrow pointed right.

"There are more alternative trails if we travel in that direction."

This red arrow was artificially added to the image as a guide from a device Arnold referred to as the Good Samaritan and was originally made as an electronic map. The object was then customized to detect and understand a person's physical condition my monitoring heartbeats, blood pressure, body temperature and much more. All anyone had to do is press one of his or her fingers on the LCD screen and then it will decode a person's physical condition and transmit all vital information to Town Hall. Engineering added another feature to serve as a beacon, so if anyone sustains injury, then the feature will activate a signal to reveal their location from the Geographic Indicator inside Town Hall. A search and rescue team will be dispatched to rescue the troubled individual from further danger.

"The only question I wish to ask everyone is that we would be subjected to considerable survival risk. Anyone who wishes to withdraw for any reason whatsoever, it would be understandable?" Dr. Ryan affirmed to the others.

"Where ever you go, I'm right by your side!" Arnold pledged.

"My husband and I are with you!" Angela concluded.

"You know me long enough to understand what my answer would be, let's head for the mainland!" Marcus responded before all five researchers prepared their transporter by activating the main power switch. Soon after each prototype became activated, they gradually rose from its inserted position.

All five Drifters rose from their recessed platforms and were driven out of the storage bay. Dr. Ryan managed to guide his transporter out. Martin and Angela's were amazed how easy it was to push their prototypes out of the storage basin. Marcus was also surprised to know that an object that physically weighs over one 1000 pounds or about 454 kilograms, felt as light as a sheet of paper. While guiding his transporter to the main entrance, he though about how much social progress and technological advancement was achieved in only a couple of decades. Mack recalled merely thinking of colonizing another planet 20 years ago was considered overworked imagination or even ridiculous.

Dr. Ryan called via his Watchdog device around his wrist to inform Dr. Derrick Grace to assume temporary command of Town Hall and directed Dr. Esther Weinstein to initiate a foraging, agricultural and fishing project called Cornucopia. Fresh fruits, vegetables and nuts would be searched for and ultimately identified. Once a discovery is made than this new information will be available in the Geographic Indicator, which would illustrate its location before a qualified crew of foragers and agriculturists will be dispatched to the area. Men and women will use the shores of the island, for nets and traps and use assembled boats and fishing equipment to catch local fish. Larger motorized boats will search the ocean for fish. A portable fish production facility will be perfectly suitable in order to preserve fresh fish and other seafood.

Dr. Ryan then spoke to Dr. Grace to initiate the Cottage Industry which is irrigation, utilities, land surveying, energy production and light construction.

An environmental friendly blacksmith is under construction. The Dove plane used an infrared scanner to find essential minerals underground for surface mining. Water supply is readily available thanks to a water desalination plant to remove the salt from bay water and send the filtered water into a purification processor. A similar process is done with a far greater scale in Middle Eastern nations such as Saudi Arabia, Kuwait and the United Arab Emirates.

Aqua-Spring could purify water from any condition. Any potentially toxic waste will no longer be a threat. Human manure will be placed inside containers to be used as fertilizer for crops to harvest. Trees that have been naturally knocked down or fallen from their foundation will be searched for and identified by naturalists and lumber specialists and use these dead trees for timber. Trees that are occupied by birds or small animals would never be in danger and reforestation is required. Mack didn't notice any visible sign of these giant saltwater crocodiles while the crew approached the mainland. Mack scanned the area intensely to prevent any surprise ambush from *Deinosuchus*.

"This way," Mack persuaded them to pursue east through a wide grass trail penetrating a forest.

"Oh look at these impressive land birds!" Angela said when she and the others saw a courtship of two huge flightless birds standing up to eight feet or almost 2.5 meters tall.

Although the small wings of this genus were never used for flight, *Gastornis* also known as *Diatryma* were boldly build and possessed a massive head and their thighs were as thick as adult human's torso! Dr. Nimbus estimated each of them to weigh approximately 350 pounds or 159 kilograms. Their beautiful red and white plumage made it easy to notice their yellow, leathery shin, feet and toes. Their large, black beaks made their skulls match the size of an adult horse's head. No odor was noticeable and they revealed no sign of blood stains or wounds. These big beautiful land birds were identified as a sheer spectacle of Europe, particularly England, France and Belgium as well as in Wyoming, New Mexico and New Jersey during the early Eocene that ranged from approximately 55,800,000 – 48,600,000 years ago in Earth's natural history.

"They're walking toward us." Martin said and the two brawny land birds appeared cautious as they studied all five researchers.

"Are they carnivorous?" Angela asked.

"Primarily, but they're also able to consume tussocks and occasionally scavenge too." Mack replied.

"I know they're capable of hunting." Marcus claimed.

"Well...we shouldn't be their next goal." Mack added before they decided to travel northwest on a wide grassy trail.

Gastornis weren't interested in five researchers monitoring their affair. However, the giant land birds noticed an unforeseen hovering behavior of each of the transporters. This couple continued their courtship as the explorers departed the area. As they traveled, the crew discovered more small mammals, reptiles and other vertebrae inside the forest and was lucky enough to detect many types of animals that appear like birds and insects.

Marcus recognized a group of migrates roaming across a junction straight ahead. Each armored plant eater was more concerned with finding food instead focusing their attention to five researchers since these majestic dinosaurs were up to thirty feet long as they were during the Jurassic period (193 – 136 million yeas ago) in Colorado, Oklahoma, Utah and Wyoming! Both rows of flat bony plates were wide. The largest ones were at their hips and at the base of their tails, which expanded over two feet six inches or 76 centimeters tall. Dr. Ryan suspected their bony plates mounted on their backs were used for defense, as well as regulating body temperature. He thought about another possibility due to the noticeable flow of blood through their vessels, which was likely used to lure potential candidates during their mating season. Mack estimated their four long curved spikes at the end of each tail were over three feet or one meter long.

One of the larger herbivores appeared agitated. This elephant sized dinosaur weight over two tons or over 1.8 metric tons. An uncomfortable male moved aggressively toward the crew. A deep goggling verbal call indicated an unmistakable warning to all new comers to stay away as the others crossed the intersection. Marcus noticed that his bony plates did not appear to be directly connected to his spinal chord as this huge male gently swung his heavy tail side to side with relative ease.

"They seem to be agile." Mack observed.

Martin and Angela noticed both rows of broad bony plates swelling and turning red due to a rapid acceleration of blood flow through his plates. This impressive display within a short time should send a subliminal message to any potential threat including five observers who waited for this entourage to end. Mack was amazed of how an enlarged cavity inside a hip vertebra of this genus called *Stegosaurus* was considered to be a second brain of the dinosaur. This alleged second brain was most likely used to skillfully control their spiked tails. Mack remembered another theory that suggested this huge cavity was a storage place for glycogen producing glands to be used as an additional influx of energy in time of serious or life threatening situations. Once this brave male was convinced that he wasn't in any real danger, he eventually rejoined the migration.

"Okay everyone follow me." Dr. Ryan directed his crew before they continued their journey.

"Wow, did you see that? *Stegosaurus* had such an elaborate transition of their plates and skin." Dr. Martin de' la' Vega observed as they continued in a northwesterly direction using a typical grassy trail littered with footprints of diverse life forms.

"He wasted no time to protect his herring. I wouldn't be surprised if dinosaurs were caring parents." Dr. Nimbus realized.

"I was surprised of how agile they were! They appeared in great physical shape." Mack realized as they moved on. Everyone noticed another intersection directly ahead. Because of their recent encounter, the crew approached this next junction with caution.

"What's that thumping noise?" Marcus emphasized.

"It's coming from our right side." Martin emphasized before they noticed small birds and mammals racing out from the area where these thumping patterns originated.

"Good God!" Mack stuttered as he saw small trees tip over at the right side of the trail about 20 feet or over six meters ahead of the crew's position before he viewed a gigantic mature male gorilla.

The only small physical features were his canines and incisors. His jaw appeared shorter than a modern African gorilla in proportion to his handsome head. He ate roots, tubers, and low vegetation just like the same species done in China, India and Pakistan during the Late Miocene epoch and up to the Early Pleistocene epoch for which would be around 11,608,000 – 781,000 years ago. Small mammals and reptiles were most likely part of this male's diet as well.

Dr. Nimbus continued to monitor and record this latest discovery while Dr. Weinstein pointed his Identification Detective to this beautiful bachelor walking on his knuckles across the wide grass trail. His fine black fur contributed to his bold appearance and his body scent was barely detectable.

"You won't believe this, but my device reads *Gigantopithecus blacki*! He's a legend!" Arnold was startled to view the most impressive primate in Earth's history.

"Look at the size of him!" Angela commented.

"I like his leathery face, ears, and extremities." Arnold revealed before *Gigantopithecus* looked over his left shoulder.

"Mack." Marcus requested.

"Yes?"

"It wouldn't be wise to antagonize a male gorilla standing at least ten feet (3m) high that possess the strength of twenty five of the strongest men in the world combined." Marcus wondered.

"I hope it wouldn't be the case with this male."

This huge male wasn't in his best mood. Despite a normally mild mannered primate suspected to maintain a low profile, *Gigantopithecus blacki* was never anyone's fool, especially when he stood on his hind legs and measured over 13 feet or almost four meters tall. It was easy to hear echoes of this male's heavy hands slapping his clouted chest warned the crew to stay away. This male successfully delivered his message to all six explorers before he remained motionless as a method of standing firm. Mack was impressed with such intelligence of a perplexing primate.

If this male's original message wasn't convincing to a potential threat, then his next message would be more intense. This bachelor male then used his two forelimbs to grab a small tree and pulled this tree off the ground! Without warning, the mature male *Gigantopithecus* then used his right forearm to toss this broken tree toward them as his final gesture for them to leave the area. The largest and one of the most mysterious primates of Earth's past and Isis's habitation gently approach the explorers before seeing all five of them dart away from the area. He then took the broken tree and began eating its exposed roots. *Gigantopithecus* was able to find food and fend off his potential nuisance simultaneously. Mack was impressed of this primate's wise response during an encounter with five strangers.

"Whew…that was close. "Angela was able to say while they continued back toward the first intersection where they originally met *Stegosaurus*. Fortunately for the explorers, *Stegosaurus* migrated far from where their original encounter occurred and the next intersection was clear.

"Everyone, the next cross section is open, let's use that path." Dr. Ryan informed everyone as he watched *Stegosaurus* migrate further away from their position.

Everyone assigned himself or herself a portion of a 360-degree view. Careful scrutiny of any possible danger was mandatory to fulfill their compound desire to stay alive! Small mammals, reptiles and birds were found everywhere. An abundant habitat of insects, centipedes, spiders and other jointed legged animals known as arthropods populated a resourceful landscape of the Central Continent.

Without any considerable population of small vertebrae, insects and microorganisms, life in the Great Plains, Grand Steppes and Principal Prairies would be bleak or even absent! Mack realized this continent's megafauna established an extensive food chain that must remain intact. Even birds and pterosaurs that extract and eat tormenting parasites from vulnerable skin of large herbivores fulfill their hunger, cure skin irritation and prevent infections.

"I'll inspect this intersection straight ahead." Dr. Ryan announced before he accelerated ahead to the middle of the grassy crossroad.

"I hope he would be alright." Dr. Weinstein said before he noticed him waving his right arm as a signal to follow him making a right turn and head northwest to their destination.

This 60 feet (18.3m) wide trail was surprisingly smooth to ride on. Bright green grass appeared recently grown, which veiled old foot prints of animals that used this trail in the past. As they proceeded, all of them noticed a frightening looking feline emerge from bordering woodland at the right side of the trail directly ahead.

This male was known for his short tail and a ten feet (3m) long physique. Although he was a similar size in length than an adult male tiger, he weighed twice as much! Despite his thick muscular body, he was best known for his massive upper fangs that were six inches (15.24m) in length! All museums would refer this giant with gold fur as the Sabre-tooth cat; while the Identification Detective Dr. Nimbus held referred this species as *Smilodon californicus* of California. Knife tooth feline of California is the meaning of this species that populated North and South America during the Pleistocene epoch or from 2,588,000 – 11,700 years ago. Their legendary tales of big game hunting and confronting rival predators are revealed by their fossil formations at the Rancho La Brea tar pits in Los Angeles, California!

Dr. Ryan and his companions were intelligent enough to maintain their distance and to activate their Feral Sentry device just in case. Fascination and fear were common among the scientific staff. All five of them detected a harsh odor of a decomposing carcass emitting from where the Sabre-tooth cat emerged. The rare sense of ease was felt among the crew due to the fact that *Smilodon californicus* appeared relaxed with bloodstains riddled across his mouth, which indicated that the most important part of his day was accomplished and was no longer concerned with hunger!

Mack felt an obligation to flee when this purring prince suddenly looked over his left shoulder and poised as he initially discovered five surprised strangers looking back at him. "Please be sure your deflectors are operable."

Deflectors are another word for a device known as Feral Sentry, which was designed to protect the crew without casting harm to any of Isis's inhabitants in the wild. The Sabre-tooth cat had a desire to display his own form of acknowledgement by raising his thick fur on top of his shoulder and neck. An intimidating sound of this massive male's snarl and a strong grip of his heavy paws gripped the surface. Dr. Ryan ordered the crew to back away cautiously once this male walked toward the explorers. Mack recalled Lucy's concern as this accomplished hunter with a physique similar to a bear, anticipate a stand off.

An advanced education and keen survival skills wasn't necessary to interpret a simple message of bitter disapproval of the explorers' presence. A bloodstained facial expression of *Smilodon* californicus accompanied with loud groans and an aggressive stance reveal another clue. This male had something to protect, and would be dammed if he would ever let anything steal his carcass! He deliberately hid his prized kill inside the forest to prevent rival predators from discovering it. *Smilodon* had no desire to abandon his kill against any natural adversary including what the crew noticed moving inside the forest that bordered the opposite side of the grassy trail. Dr. Nimbus recognized that *Smilodon* possessed incredibly wide paws as this Sabre-tooth cat initially pursued what emerged from the other side of the trail.

"Look over there!" Dr. Angela de' la' Vega, emphasized as she pointed her finger to another carnivorous mammal, which emerged from the bordering woodland.

This meat eating marsupial grew orange and brown fur and generally abbreviated orange mane around his, neck, shoulders and at the tip of his tail. His stout face also made this strange feline appear like a carnivorous wombat. All five explorers realized this particular encounter would be disastrous at best!

This male marsupial grew enlarged incisors from his front upper and lower jaws like a rodent. Although his incisors appeared deadly, this marsupial evolved meat shredding blades at the rear of his jaws that worked like scissors to slice flesh with efficiency. The Identification Detective helped Dr. Nimbus learn how this trimmed marsupial hunted giant kangaroos and other mammals in ancient Australia during the Pliocene epoch (5,322,000 – 2,588,000 years ago) and throughout the Pleistocene epoch (2,588,000 – 11,700 years ago).

Native Aboriginals of ancient Australia knew very much about a genus called *Thylacoleo*, which is also known as the Marsupial lion. Marcus read how *Thylacoleo* terrorized their villages, preyed upon their livestock and even killed people. Ancient texts and paintings depict a discomforting history of a disturbing relationship between humans and the Marsupial lions! Dr. Ryan and the others could only feel sympathy for the Aboriginal people's experience when they noticed the hissing expression emitting from *Thylacoleo* as he displayed his three-inch upper and lower central incisors to fend off the Sabre-tooth feline.

"Everyone evade," Dr. Ryan calmly told everyone just before both competing carnivores clashed!

Dr. Nimbus noticed the Marsupial lion's warning only provoked *Smilodon* to attack. Drs. Martin and Angela de' la' Vega couldn't bear to watch such a ravaging rivalry. The Sabre-tooth cat used his six-inch (15.24cm) upper canines and powerful neck muscles to stab the Marsupial lion, which in turn employed his enlarged incisors to gnaw his rival. Both mammals expressed their hostilities by as they continued to use their claws and teeth to maul their rival. Mack couldn't believe such resilience in this fight after a series of exchanging blows. Marcus was sure both predators could be seriously injured. However, to his dismay the Marsupial lion's managed to escape. Although they were separated, tensions escalated once the invading *Thylacoleo* ran across the open trail and proceeded into the woods where the hidden carcass was located.

Under no circumstances would *Smilodon* ever give up a hard earned carcass to absolutely any other life form. So in typical prehistoric fashion, he darted into the woods and pursued *Thylacoleo* inside. Arnold understood there's never any incident where two or more species of carnivores ever share carrion peacefully. Angela conceived this clash to be dreadful as she heard distinguishing sounds of an intense brawl inside a once peaceful shroud of bushes and trees.

"I hope none of them would be hurt!" Angela said.

Arnold was shocked to hear intensive sounds from a flamboyant fight inside the woodland. Marcus and Mack couldn't believe such persistence as they though about anything could go wrong and may result to a serious injury to each other and could directly affect the crew's safety.

"There they go!" Marcus told everyone while he pointed toward *Thylacoleo* racing out of the woods and directly across the open grass trail. Their highest concern now was the idea that the marsupial lion was only 20 feet away when he reappeared. Before the intruder made it halfway across the trail, the Sabre-tooth cat then emerged from the woodland and proceeded to chase the faster intruder across the open trail and into the woods where *Thylacoleo* was discovered.

"Let's get the hell out of here!" Mack shouted before they continued to follow the trail based upon accurate navigational directions from their Good Samaritan devices.

High pitched hissing and thundering roars continue to dominate sounds of this forest. Mack found an opportunity to move ahead while both rivals were preoccupied with their stalemate. Their rage continued as all five of them continued forward until they couldn't hear anymore debauchery. The trail continued to lead them to a large, open grass field. This field grew only a few congregations of trees, but it was the size of four soccer fields. Although this wasn't the Great Plains, this open field appeared to be served as a rest stop for browsers and grazers.

"Everyone look! That's *Moropus elatus!*" Dr. Weinstein mentioned after his Identification Detective gadget revealed the identity of a group of three browsers with a head like a horse.

Each individual grew gigantic claws on their front feet and smaller ones at their two rear legs. Their limbs didn't evolve any sprinting ability like horses, but were sturdy and powerful. Their necks sloped diagonally up from the shoulders, as their backs slanted down toward their crouched rear legs. Each browser stood up to eight feet (2.44m) at the shoulder! Their faces appeared like a hybrid between a horse and a modern tapir. Their front limbs appeared long, while their calf exceeded the length of their flanks. Although they lacked subtle manes on the top of their necks and at the end of their tails, each individual grew up to ten feet (3m) long and possessed a dazzling array of fine fur. An extended neck made *Moropus elatus* resemble a horse and giraffe. All three browsers indulged into bright soft leaves suitable for their low crowned teeth. Dr. Ryan remembered Dr. Netherland's lecture where they were informed that the name of this species actually means sloth foot or slow foot due to their massive front claws and learned that horses were most likely to be their closest living relatives.

"They must weigh almost a ton or so?" Mack wondered, as he was impressed by their bold appearance that weighs over 900 kilograms.

"That seems to be the case." Dr. Weinstein responded.

"Feast your eyes on them over there." Dr. Nimbus mentioned as he discovered an unusual, but gorgeous looking forest dwellers originating from the left side of the open grassy field.

"Check to see if that's a mastodon or not?" Mack requested.

Marcus pointed his Identification Detective to one of the group of three forest dwellers. "Guess what? I.D. says, *Mammut americanum*, better known as the American mastodon."

"My goodness, I remember Doctor Netherland made a miniature model of one of them! They're ten feet or three meters at the shoulder. They weigh almost five tons and were extinct around ten thousand years ago!" Arnold informed everyone.

"Doctor Netherland talked about his models of dinosaurs and ice age mammals. I couldn't believe how much he knew about Earth's prehistoric life. I was astonished." Mack admitted as they continuously observed these living legends.

The American mastodon dwelled the forests of the Western hemisphere from the Late Pliocene to the Late Pleistocene epoch, which ranged from 3,600,000 – 11,700 years ago. Mainly populated in Alaska, New York, and Missouri, their fossils were found as far south as Florida! Their enormous neck and shoulder muscles mounted far above the head and back made it possible to maneuver their long heads and a long wooly trunk. Their powerful limbs were in excellent physical condition. Mack, Martin and Marcus couldn't take their eyes off of such beautifully developed tusks that gently curved upwards and outwards, which exceeded eight feet (2.5m) long. They eventually spread out the open field and continued to indulge into to fresh leaves and bushes.

"Whoa…take a look at what's coming out of the forest's edge!" Arnold couldn't believe what he discovered.

"They're huge! They must be Brontotheres or Titanotheres?" Martin informed everyone as this group of monumental herbivores entered the open field.

"I'm impressed by the arrangement of their nasal ornamentation." Arnold responded as they continue to view this new spectacle.

"If I'm not mistaken, they appear like *Brontops*," Mack said as he felt convinced of their gigantic size and rugged characteristics of two bulky brontotheres.

"Mack…I don't believe it! You're right. It is *Brontops*!"

Marcus confirmed Mack's suspicion.

Marcus was impressed when he received a reference of a North American giant whose shoulder was eight feet (2.5m) above the ground! Four tons of brawn and beauty was their usual looks from the end of the Eocene epoch or roughly 34 million years ago. *Brontops robustus* easily exceeded 13 feet (4m) in length and weighed at least four tons or 3.6 metric tons.

Brontops possessed a dense rhinoceros-like skin similar to their cousin *Brontotherium*. The stem of the "Y" shaped nasal horn was short and broad. A pair of thick horns rose from both sides of their stems that held two swollen spherical knobs at the end of their nasal horns. Both of these knobs stretched up to two feet (61cm) above the snout!

"How do you thick all three species will react to each other's presence?" Angela wondered with concern.

"Well…all three life forms are browsers. Natural food supply is abundant and all three species share a common interest to survive. I thick they should tolerate each other." Arnold responded.

"I think that if any predator shows up than there might be a form of mutual protection. Personally, I wouldn't rule that out." Marcus concluded.

All five explorers continue to use the Identification Detective to identify various types of insects and small vertebrae or animals that have a spinal chord. The small agile inhabitants paced past and maneuvered under the migrating herbivores standing tall and moving freely across the Central Continent.

The mastodons (*Mammut americanum*) brontotheres (*Brontops robustus*) and chalicotheres (*Moropus elatus*) formally acknowledged each other's presence before a mutual truce was established. Sometimes tensions could mount when maturing males are in season, which may cause a commotion. But the grand majority of any physical conflict among herbivores would be from potential bulls of the same species clashing for dominance so they could attract mates and reproduce. All five explorers couldn't believe such civil behavior of all three species.

Each individual assumed their own responsibility to scan for potential danger while the other herds browsed. Both will take turns over and over again. Suspicion from each explorer aroused when these brawny browsers became tense. Dr. Ryan and his colleagues knew each life form could sense potential danger much better than humans can, which was why all five researchers learned to monitor their reactions as additional means for protection.

"Angela there's something in those woods!" Dr. Weinstein became concerned of possible danger lurking nearby.

"Good heavens, no! Take cover!" Mack cried out when noticeable sinister looking shapes began to reveal themselves from shrouded woodland bordering the field.

"These hyenas are huge!" Arnold said, as he couldn't believe he was observing lion sized hyenas showing their stern body language revealing their intention to kill.

Exceeding eight feet (2.44m) long *Percrocuta giganteus* was estimated to weigh over 400 pounds or over 181 kilograms and was also known to possess jaws that were powerful enough to penetrate through the bones of elephants! An entire crew of five instantly made sure they stayed clear out of the way of this clan of giant spotted hyenas. Nobody was able to believe the largest ones were able to stand on all four legs and elevate their heads high enough to match the height of the average adult.

Moropus used their snouts to sound off a natural alarm to warn companions of imminent danger. Their considerable height and heavy limbs provided them with enough assurance to place their front limbs on the ground. Each of their individual claws grew larger than a person's fingers and could possibly employ a multitude of defense techniques depending upon if any attack is from behind or directly ahead. Frontal defense would be used primarily by their enlarged claws on the front limbs by swinging similar to bears or their rear defense includes kicking their rear legs out similar to horses.

All seven clan members raced out of the bushes and pursued *Moropus* before gathering into a circular formation. *Moropus* huddled into a circular formation and faced out enabling them to swing or thrust their enlarged claws against this species of giant hyenas, which terrorized China during the Miocene epoch that ranged from around 23,030,000 – 5,332,000 years ago. Mack couldn't believe how fast *Moropus* was able to thrust. Marcus knew all too well, that a powerful impact by such enormous claws of *Moropus* could be curtains for these pursuing carnivores!

A loud disquieting laugh and deep howling emitted from *Percrocuta* was used to psychologically and emotionally traumatize their intended prey. One of the female chalicotheres used her from claws to pound and rear legs to scrape the ground and kick dirt to distract the menacing marauders in order to hinder their concentration. Dr. Ryan felt sympathy for *Moropus* as they resist their life and death challenge.

Arnold noticed two of the first attackers temporarily withdrew so they could reclaim their energy. He realized tactics are common among carnivores whether conducting long distance endurance, quick sprints, ambushes along with bobbing and weaving. Many predators on Earth and Isis adapted to living in social groups such as packs, clans or prides for a simple fact that such defiant herbivores were powerful, brave and travel in large herds of their own. If danger's immanent then various species of migrating herbivores would unite often in the face of adversity for mutual protection. Additional challenges also originate from skillful solitary predators that travel alone and are powerful enough to solely confiscate carrion from an entire group of rival predators.

Their stalemate continued until all three subsequent attackers withdrew from the stalemate as the original two pursuing clam members reengaged. One of the seven giant hyenas was a bit smaller than the others and more curious. This inquisitive youngster approached one of three agitated mastodons that dissuaded this young male's desire to evaluate the herd. Two of the three mastodons swayed their massive tusks as their persuasion that startled the youngster to move away, not knowing that he was approaching one of two brontotheres, which shared no hospitality of this predator's presence as well. Mack's heartbeat intensified when he saw the right knob at the end of this male brontothere's nasal horn crash into the left rib cage of the young predator. *Brontops* showed one reason why the family name Brontothere means thunder beast as the whole crew heard a violent impact of his giant knob merging into this prehistoric hyena's ribs!

Angela was horrified to see a maturing youngster soar twelve feet (3.66m) horizontally across the open field. Marcus and Martin saw the young hyena airborne until the crew witnessed this unfortunate *Percrocuta* collided into one of two sharp ends of the American mastodon's thick tusks.

"Ooh, that must hurt!" Arnold commented as a loud scream from a devastating injury vibrated across the open field and proceeded into the bordering woodlands.

A vocal blast of pain suspended an intense stalemate between predator and prey. A mauled body of a battered youngster then fell from this tusk and slammed on the ground. To each researcher's amazement a resilient *Percrocuta* surprisingly staggered back on his feet but struggled to walk across the grassy trail.

"Oh, that's terrible!" Angela could barely see such carnage when she saw six sharp eyed predators surround and tackle *Moropus* that mistakenly walked away from his huddle when the ancient hyena screamed.

Two surviving chalicotheres moved away, but continued to defend themselves relentlessly to prevent a similar fate of their colleague. Strange as it seemed, the other clan members was more concerned of consuming their prey as quickly as possible than assisting their injured clan member. The young male *Percrocuta* didn't appear coherent because he was noticeably swaggering and what's worse, instead of joining with his peers, he stumbled toward the two remaining chalicotheres.

"Good heavens…this doesn't look good." Mack said as he realized this event will continue to unfold with even more pending disaster.

One of the two middle-aged males that exceeded one ton or 900 kilograms acquired considerable experience in dealing with a diverse array of hunters. Exceeding the size of a Clydesdale, an antagonistic male suddenly timed this situation perfectly in order to wait for his precise moment to strike!

He pressed his front limbs on the ground before he cocked his right rear leg forward. Marcus, Martin and Mack knew all too well what would happen when a brutalized predator staggered behind an awaiting male *Moropus*. His dense muscles, strong spinal chord along with the agility of his limb joints were possible to thrust his rear foot back. Arnold lost his desire to observe this giant hyena's imminent fate.

"I can't look." Angela also shared her lack of desire to watch as she used her right hand to cover her dark brown eyes.

Suddenly, a thunderous impact of the right rear foot of *Moropus* sent an influx of tragedy and horror into the crew's consciousness. The male's leg remained stretched out as everyone observed a lifeless body of a predator that weighed 300 pounds or slightly over 136 kilograms tumble across the open meadow. Arnold and Angela only wished they were able to cover their ears while the others could feel a faint cramp on their ribs as a subconscious means to empathize a tragic outcome of a fallen youngster whose life was cut short.

Dr. Ryan's activated his communicator before four miniature antennas expanded to activate a holographic video display.

"Town Hall, come in please?" Dr. Ryan requested over his Watchdog device.

"*This is Town Hall, over.*" A familiar face and voice of Dr. Derrick Grace responded.

"Connect me to the video room." Mack requested before another familiar face appeared and answered over his communications device.

"Meena, were you able to receive our transmission?" Dr. Ryan wondered.

"*Yes…we couldn't believe what just happened!*"

"Who else saw it?" Mack was eager to know.

"*Viktor, Art, Taina, Nina and Lucy saw it too.*" Meena revealed.

"Has anyone else view it?" Mack wondered.

"Fan and Ying are currently reviewing the video along with Harold, Alicia and Nina."

"Great! Please inform Haru, André and Zarina about what we saw so they could view it too." Dr. Ryan instructed her.

"Sure! I'll dispatch them." Dr. Singh assured him before their transmission ended.

"Mack! Look at that," were the words of Dr. Nimbus as he discovered a group of twelve frightening mammals moving alongside the forest's edge from the left side.

"This can't be true!" Dr. Ryan commented as he and the rest of the crew were shocked to see a group of what appeared to be gigantic rats or hutias approaching the group of prehistoric hyenas consuming their kill.

Dr. Nimbus was nervous to point his Identification Detective to one of the twelve giant rodents ranging in size from a large capybara to a grizzly bear! Their keen black eyes focused upon all of the surviving hyenas. Each of these giant rodents grew four toes on each foot. Martin and Angela recognized these species to be *Amblyrhiza inundata*, which were giant fossil blunt toothed rodents that lived in Anguilla and other parts of the Caribbean around 125,000 years ago or near the beginning of the Late Pleistocene.

Angela monitored these giant rodents and noticed they also resemble a fearsome and gigantic version of an extant species of rodents known as *Elasmodontomys obliquus* of Puerto Rico. Angela remembered one of Dr. Netherland's lectures revealing the fact that Anguilla, Saba, St. Barts and St. Martin were all one single island during the last ice age when water levels were shallow. She also recalled during the year 1868, a manufacturing firm known as Henry Waters & Brothers of Philadelphia, Pennsylvania received a strange shipment from Anguilla. Since Henry Waters noticed it was a fossil, he brought it to world-renowned paleontologist Edward Drinker Cope. After careful examination of these fossils and excavation sites where these fossils were found, he came to a remarkable conclusion that a land bridge once connected this region to South America but was submerged under water during a flood when polar caps melted at the end of the last ice age.

They boldly displayed their pair of blunt incisors planted in their upper and lower jaw. Low frequencies of noticeable squeaky calls from these giant rodents were intended to make *Percrocuta* leave so they could claim the carcass for themselves. Modern scientists suspect *Amblyrhiza* was able to adapt to a similar broad diet to modern hutias such as vegetation, carrion and even insects.

"I just thought of something." Mack revealed.

"What's that?" Marcus asked.

"Heavens forbid, but if they could carry and transmit fatal diseases such as Bubonic plague. Wouldn't they possess some form of infectious bacteria?"

Once Dr. Ryan made his speculation, the others cringed at such a disastrous possibility. Although Angela was curious to find answers to such a question, she knew it would be futile to pursue such a dangerous quest once this stalemate intensified. A concerned crew couldn't believe such rebuttal in part of *Percrocuta*. Dr. Ryan and others noticed this rivalry erupted when all six massive spotted hyenas charged the giant rats. The crew noticed *Amblyhiza* utilizing their adaptive intelligence and collective teamwork to repel their initial attack.

Four of twelve ancient rodents exposed their powerful incisors before gnawing the rear end of two giant hyenas. Their heated stalemate was superseded by a full scale ferocious confrontation. The other eight giant rodents behaved cautiously as they maneuvered to confuse the giant hyenas. As aggressive all twelve invading rodents appeared, avoiding the terrible grip of well developed bone crushing jaws of *Percrocuta* was the invading rodents' arch concern as they continued to move swiftly around their dangerous rivals. Deep squeak and hissing signals annoyed and ultimately provoked *Percrocuta giganteus* to respond more aggressively to ensure their hard earned catch remains in their sole possession.

"Whoa…did you see that?" Mack asked his crew.

"I'm recording everything." Arnold replied.

Dr. Weinstein observed and recorded this full scale clash as a giant adult male rodent lashed forward and gnawed an adult male hyena at his right shoulder, resulting in an open wound. Once *Amblyrhiza* attempted his second strike, two other giant spotted hyenas retaliated by attacking their menacing rival. Dr. Nimbus realized a downward spiral of vigilance and violence as two other giant rodents pursued both retaliating hyenas.

Such an escalating feud alarmed *Brontops* and the American mastodon to disperse this area as *Percrocuta* and *Amblyrhiza* continued with their cunning clash. The crew noticed three giant hyenas and rodents revealing their conspicuous injuries with blood soaked fur and dysfunctional limbs. *Moropus* decided to walk rapidly away from this tragedy and headed toward an entrance of a bordering trail that lead them out of the open field and led them to a safe haven from the mist of chaos and calamity.

One of the female invading rodents attempted to separate herself from her dispute by running over to the carcass to feed a rumbling stomach. One of the giant hyenas didn't appreciate her acquisition to a free meal. So the female hyena pounced on top of *Amblyrhiza* indulging the carcass. Dr. Ryan continued to be convinced that this dispute will not diffuse soon as he saw a giant female rodent struggling to free herself from a tormenting female *Percrocuta* aggressively biting her spinal chord behind her shoulder.

Once she was able to free herself from such aggravation, *Amblyrhiza* decided to unleash her own rage in revenge for her wound by gnawing a persistent perpetrator when her incisors scraped the female hyena on her left rear leg. Squeaking disquieting howls of a battered female *Percrocuta* alarmed other members of the clan of giant hyenas to relentlessly attack the vengeful rodent. Two clan members organized a successful timely attack on another rodent. As both clan members assaulted an adult male, his companions joined in and launched a counter attack on both hyenas before a battered male rodent rejoined the attack.

"Everybody back...everybody back!" Mack warned his colleagues.

Drs. Nimbus and Ryan continued to learn that Isis possessed such an impressive, but dangerous diversity of life! Any noticeable hierarchal relationship among various carnivorous life forms was too difficult to decipher because none of these life forms were ever observed before. Mack even suspected this habitat was too diverse and competitive for a stable hierarchal relationship to be established over long periods of time.

"I could barely look at this anymore!" Marcus admitted before others agreed with him and decided to move on.

Each explorer occasionally looked back to reassure their own safety. Although this fight raged on, Mack finally felt at ease as they dispersed this sickening scene. "I never saw anything like that before...whew!"

"This place makes me a bit nervous." Arnold agreed.

"We must be extremely careful for now on. Everything happened almost instantly." Angela advised her colleagues before Mack turned his head to Angela in agreement as though she said exactly what he wanted to say.

Mack then pressed a button located directly in front of him near the center of his handlebars. His rear truck hatched open automatically before launching the Private Eye device into the sky. A continuous ascent proved a successful takeoff. He used a voice activated report log within his Good Samaritan device and verbally described this particular area. His latest translations will be recorded into an electronic codex compartment of the Good Samaritan for future reference information. This device would also transmit verbal logs over to Intelligence at Town Hall so no valuable data would be lost if the device was ever destroyed or misplaced. Intelligence actively monitors the local area for any activity that hasn't been discovered.

Distant echoes of battle over a carcass resonated across the open sky. Dr. Ryan was satisfied by what was discovered so far before he decided to return to Town Hall. "Let's return to Town Hall."

Rays of light from Osiris eventually tanned Dr. Ryan's face. A cobalt blue sky accompanied by various types of white clouds provided a visual meditation necessary to remedy his intense encounter. Mild cross breezes reinforced emotional calm while all five explorers continued their course. Marcus never though he'll ever witness such a struggle to survive! Arnold felt quite shaken of his experience but knew deep inside that this was like no other natural habitat he ever visited. Despite his caution, Arnold felt proud to explore Isis and examined some of the most dynamic plant and animal life anywhere that were just like Earth's prehistoric life.

Angela felt worried but with her husbands support and her natural desire to explore the wild, she expressed gratitude for her participation and would cherish her experiences. Martin clearly understood his wife's concerns but shared her enthusiasm to explore this extrasolar Earth analog. Mack felt estranged of seeing such an interaction he just witnessed but understood there were no other megafauna like this remotely as he's seated on his transporter before focusing his attention to an open trail heading west.

Since Mack noticed this empty and quiet trail to be safe, he decided to inform the others to meet him at the shore. "I want to see the data we send over to Intelligence when we return."

"Sounds great," Martin agreed as they continued to pursue this trail until they reached an open area of the shore that bordered the end of the forest.

Once they arrived at the shore, Mack wanted to check the area for any signs of *Gastornis* or *Deinosuchus*. Once he noticed both species were absent from his sight. He led his crew into the bay and moved rapidly over water until they reached the shore of Town Hall Island. As all five explorers saw a cheerful group of colleagues waiting for their arrival, Dr. Ryan thought about his entire experience at the Central Continent as he stopped next to a cheerful group of colleagues.

"What a wilderness!" Mack told everyone as their workday ended and an inviting evening encouraged rest and relaxation.

ANOMALIES IN THE AIR

Emerging from Town Hall was Dr. Ryan first goal for this new morning. A mild sleepy rainfall ceased as moist clouds dissipated. A burst of fresh air psychologically elevated his morning fatigue. He remembered the first time he went to a sleep away camp for two weeks in Pennsylvania during his adolescence. Such memories inspired him to travel to the countryside more often. He also reflected his appreciation of nature as multicolored clouds reflected Osiris's rays from the eastern horizon!

Mack feels energetic to experience another morning on a different planet. He was happy to learn that the Eastern Continent Crew finally made their landing. They were fortunate enough to secure themselves on top of a steep hill. This crew of 250 crew members will use their Feral Sentry devices to provide any necessary protection for both the crew and Isis's inhabitants. They will use the Feral Sentry to produce a matching scent of various predators to scare off any unwanted intrusions. A morning mist stimulated Mack's senses once he walked down the ramp and stood outside Town Hall. His new day began once he noticed Lucy, Marcus and Meena walking down the ramp before approaching him.

"Good morning." Mack said before everyone replied by wishing him the same.

"This time it's strictly voluntary, I can't expect for anyone to volunteer except me." Mack announced as he anticipated proposing today's new objectives.

"Where should we travel?" Marcus wondered.

"The outskirts of the Great Plains would be challenging. If we reach this location, we should discover an entire habitat."

"Whoa...we should find more life there than anywhere else. I like the idea." Marcus replied.

"Marcus, don't do it!" Meena objected to Marcus's reply to volunteer.

"Mack, we can't deny what we saw yesterday. It's risky out there." Lucy supported Meena's objection.

"We'll bring the Feral Sentry with us." Mack replied.

"Mack we talked about this remember? You know how easy it is to die in the mainland?" Lucy emphasized.

"Lucy…I understand…besides, this is the best assignment we ever had. We're selected to explore this entire world. Heck, we're lucky to even find Isis and at the same time acquire an exceptional insight of Earth's past! There's just no way I'm letting this once in a lifetime opportunity pass me by." Mack explained to both women just before Marcus tilted his head forward as his gesture of his willingness to pursue this challenging expedition with his trusted colleague.

A disappointed expression of Meena's eyes didn't go unnoticed by Marcus before he said. "Mack's right. It's a miracle we've traveled three light years and survived, that's why I'm going."

"Let me tell you something! First of all, you must travel a considerable distance just to reach the outskirts of the Great Plains. Second, anything could be encountered between here and your desired destination, not to mention when you'll arrive, who knows what could happen then? Meena firmly stated as she pressed her right index finger on Marcus's sternum and stared at him.

"Ladies, we have a technological advantage, our transporters outpaced any form of danger we've encountered. We can repel imminent danger using the Feral Sentry and the Good Samaritan device contributes to our survival skills by identifying our location and we also have our Watchdogs to communicate." Mack said.

"One question you should ask yourselves is that have you discovered everything…umm? We only discovered less than one percent of Isis's terrain. We barely know what's left?" Lucy emphasized before silence succeeded their heated debate.

As Mack thought about their concerns, he looked east to view the mainland. As he admired his panorama, something else caught his attention. Marcus looked over and noticed Mack staring into the sky as he showed a puzzled expression of bewilderment.

"What was that?" Mack became baffled and had difficulty acknowledging what he just saw.

Both women spoke to each other trying to find a way to prevent both men from pursuing their next goal. Meena and Lucy knew that a loss of their colleagues would psychologically devastate them and could distract their ability to fulfill this mission's demands.

"Mack...what's the matter?" Marcus asked as he visually scanned the mainland.

Due to Mack's estrangement, Marcus then wondered. "Hey Mack, what did you see?"

"It was a bizarre meteorite! You should've seen it. It was the strangest thing I ever saw!"

Mack appeared surprised.

As both men discussed Mack's claim, both women overheard their discreet conversation. Meena and Lucy looked at each other in suspicion of Mack covertly trying to devise a reasonable ploy to pursue the mainland.

"What's strange about this meteorite?" Meena smirked.

"You won't believe this, it was spherical in shape and it had a bright, reflective surface similar to a mirror! Its speed declined when it approached the surface without any tail of debris. It generally appeared like a large silver sphere." Mack revealed.

"Umm...A silvery ball defying gravity...huh?" Lucy whispered to Meena as they chuckled a bit of laughter in response of such a claim they overheard.

Lucy and Meena couldn't help but giggle to Mack's testimony and looked over to the mainland with skepticism after they initially heard his strange description of a descending object from the sky. Both women thought and agreed that this could be a likely tactic to come up with an excuse to pursue the mainland, which was why they continued to discuss a solution to convince them to take more precautions as they also watched for any sign of them attempting to leave the island.

"Mack, are you sure?" Marcus said when he accidentally glanced over Mack's right shoulder.

"What the..." Estrangement and fear disturbed Marcus as he looked over to the mainland and observed another silver sphere that matched Mack's description.

Mack felt even more intense when he realized this object was visually similar to the first one he saw. He noticed Marcus viewing this phenomenon as it descended behind a row of tress near the shore of the mainland. Marcus froze and kept silent while Mack attempted to contemplate what both objects were.

"What was that?" Marcus stuttered.

"I don't know! But it's exactly the same object I saw just before. You see how it decreased its speed of descent as it approached the surface?" Mack confirmed.

"I didn't hear any impact, but I know what I saw!" Both ladies felt irritated to listen to Dr. Nimbus's affirmation.

"We have to investigate!" Mack's suggestion to Marcus prompted both ladies to respond.

"We're not letting you go to the mainland!" Meena said as the both women promptly walked over to them.

"So where did you see these so-called objects?" Lucy asked.

"Directly behind the first row of trees ahead, there was no sound of any physical impact at all!" Mack informed both women before all four of them continued to look ahead.

"Mack…I'm in no mood for games." Lucy rebuffed both men's claim as a hoax.

"I wish it was a game because I'm baffled." Mack responded.

Before Marcus could say a word, Meena reacted, "Marcus, don't even think about it! You should've planned much harder if you thought you could possibly fool us."

Neither one of these ladies ever witnessed a meteorite that appeared remotely like any of these strange entities both men described. None of them ever witnessed any meteorite that decreased its speed while approaching the ground. Physical movements of this unprecedented phenomenon they claimed to witness, doesn't comply with any currently known, natural laws of physics that's agreed among all science institutions worldwide.

Both women observed the sky before their heartbeat accelerated as they witnessed two more large silvery spheres they estimated to measure up to 50 feet (15.25m) across, plunge toward the surface and saw them reduce their speed of descent as both objects approached the ground.

"Mack! We have to investigate what we saw." Lucy said as both men looked at each other and felt considerably different regarding their desire to explore the mainland.

"We can't wait…we have to go." Meena added her emphasis to resolve this matter.

"Maybe we should take extra precautions? The mainland is a dangerous place." Marcus expressed his sudden loss of interest to pursue the Central Continent.

"I wouldn't argue over additional precautions. But I have a terrible feeling about this." Mack stressed as they initially walked up to the top of the ramp that lead to the main entrance of Town Hall.

"What bad feeling you're talking about?" Marcus wondered.

"These objects were no natural phenomenon I know."

All four individuals wasted little time race over to the storage bay where each individual transporter is parked. Meena felt a cushioned surface as they darted across the room and approached a group of parked Drifters inserted two feet or 61 centimeters into the floor. This room's soft surface ensured all transporter units would be parked safely.

"Mack do you think it could be technological in nature?" Marcus asked.

"We could speculate as much as we wish, however, let the evidence guide us to an educated conclusion." Mack emphasized as they unharnessed their all terrain transporters and activated four units.

"Whatever they are safety is supreme. Be certain your equipment is ready." Mack commanded. "We must beware of known hazards such as radiation and biocontamination."

Everyone proceeded down the ramp to investigate this strange phenomenon that mystified their minds and riddled their nerves. The most unprecedented event since the discovery of Isis would soon be confronted once they'll travel to that particular area of the mainland! The courage of all four researchers was accompanied by fear of the unknown. Dr. Ryan eventually guided his companions over to the shores of the island while Marcus focused his attention toward the sky over the mainland for any additional apparitions of these entities.

"What ever they were landed behind that row of trees, we should be able to find out what they were." Marcus argued.

"You're probably right...by then we should know for sure what we saw." Lucy felt a sense of relief.

The crew managed to handle mild vibrations as when they traveled over the extended bay. Thanks to identifiable natural landmarks he selected, Marcus was able to estimate where all four spheres landed. His main concern was to pinpoint the exact spot. Mack never heard any sound of impact after it lowered itself behind the first row of trees and in front of a range of foothills further away. Due to their clear visual detail and shadow angle all four explorers were convinced they were approximately one thousand feet (305m) away from where these objects landed!

"Just be careful as we approach the mainland. I didn't forget about the giant crocodiles we encountered earlier" Mack insisted his crew as they approach the mainland.

When they reached the shore, Mack kept a watchful eye on a group of giant crocodiles resting on the beach. They laid carelessly on the sand absorbing daylight entering their enlarged scales on their back and tails. Dr. Ryan thought about any possible age and appetite of *Deinosuchus*. If these giant saltwater crocodiles possessed enough similar genes to modern crocodiles, then they would most likely be able to abstain from feeding for up two years and the largest *Deinosuchus* could easily live through their second century!

Terrible crocodile fits the meaning of all six crocodilians deliberately holding their mouths open to help regulate their body temperature more efficiently. Solar energy from Osiris would generate their warming process before reaching their ideal body temperature, which would be approximately 89 degrees Fahrenheit or just over 31 degrees Celsius. As cautious Mack felt in regards to all six sunbathers at the beach, he acknowledged them being part of an order known as crocodilians, which existed for an estimated 250 million years of Earth's evolutionary history based upon modern paleontology. Mack and his compatriots developed enough common sense to know that they wouldn't exist for 250 seconds if they came too close to these cunning crocodilians. It was intriguing to see them appear and behave similar to the Estuarine crocodile (*Crocodylus porosus*) of the Pacific Ocean, Asia and Australia but weighed at least seven tons or 6.3 metric tons!

"This is the best path." Dr. Nimbus pointed to the same trail they traveled through yesterday.

"Does everyone agree about these object's description?" Meena wanted a reassurance from her colleagues.

"I remember it clearly! They appeared almost like a shiny silver ball. I estimate it could be approximately fifty feet wide. They made no sound at all!" Mack said.

"That's exactly how saw it! Since I didn't hear any sound of an impact at all, I'm presuming that it stopped before hitting the ground! There's no meteorite anywhere that behaves in such a matter." Marcus explained.

"I agree to what everyone said so far. I never saw anything like it ever before." Lucy said to the others as they continued their present course straight ahead.

"That's exactly how I saw it too." Meena agreed.

They fell directly behind the row of trees directly ahead! I remember it clearly. According to this screen, there is open grassland behind it." Mack said as he was referring to data displayed on the Good Samaritan's screen.

Dr. Ryan didn't hesitate to call the orbital starship to report strange, silver spheres in the sky. "Guardian, come-in please!" Dr. Ryan continuously requested, by using his Watchdog device around his wrist. Thinking about such a strange aerial phenomenon he experienced only activated his feelings of mounting unease.

Various scenarios of this object's possible identity manifested inside a concerned person's mind who's contacting the flagship, "Come in please! Starship Guardian! Come in please!"

Dr. Ryan established contact with Dr. Karl Gruber aboard the orbiting interstellar starship. Dr. Gruber listened to Dr. Ryan's testimony of what he just witnessed. Once Dr. Ryan told his story, Dr. Gruber then informed him of their recent finding.

"Mack, we've recently traced what appeared to be a group of fragments penetrating the atmosphere."

"Those weren't fragments." Dr. Ryan emphasized.

"That's strange, because we traced them entering a region further west from your position. Dr. Gruber revealed.

"How far?"

"They were originally approaching the Western Continent."

"Contact Doctor Tyrell and find out if he detected anything unusual." Dr. Ryan ended his communiqué open with Dr. Gruber.

"There should be a visible sign of severe physical damage to trees and even the terrain." Dr. Singh estimated.

"There's the junction." Dr. Ryan pinpointed the precise location.

"Just be careful!" Lucy warned as Dr. Ryan cautiously steered toward the intersection. The crew focused their attention to a nervous Dr. Ryan inspecting the immediate area where all four objects allegedly landed. All three of them continued to stare at Dr. Ryan's reaction.

"It's safe," Mack expressed his remarks with a considerable amount of confusion.

"Mack! What is it?" Marcus wondered as he saw Dr. Ryan checking his Good Samaritan device as they approached him.

"This doesn't make any sense whatsoever!" Mack said while the crew showed sympathy for Mack's reaction when they observed a pristine grass trail with no craters bordering forest trees standing tall and intact on both sides of this empty trail.

"Hey...I trust Art and Viktor's judgment. This is exactly where they landed. One of the two emergent trees is right here, and the other is over there." Dr. Nimbus confirmed.

"I'm convinced they landed right here! I'll launch the Private Eye and we should be able to detect craters or damaged trees." Dr. Ryan said as he launched this device from the rear trunk space of his transporter. As it climbed to higher altitudes, all four researchers dialed their own pass codes on their assigned Good Samaritan device to show live video from the Private Eye that ascended above 1,000 or above 305 meters high. As the aerial device continued to ascent to higher altitudes, Lucy's heart rate accelerated as she discovered a ferocious male theropod dinosaur focusing keenly in her direction as he quietly approached from behind.

This male's evolved large arms and a sleek physique that weighed between 1 – 2 tons or 0.9 – 1.8 metric tons. His 15 feet (4.6m) tall bulk of muscular mass made it possible to be among the fiercest hunters of the Late Jurassic period and the Early Cretaceous period, which ranged from 145,500,00 – 99,600,000 years ago and is most likely to be the apex predator of the Mesozoic era that ranged around 251,000,000 – 65,500,000 years ago. This dinosaur also scavenged and was capable of confiscating carrion from rival predators. Besides displaying his candidacy during the mating season, an enlarged ridge above each eye acted as a shade against sun glare. Both eyes appeared to be mounted sideways, but faced forward in order to see all four explorers directly ahead. Lucy knew that time was more precious than finding craters. She visually recognized the official species of this adult bipedal dinosaur evaluating all four researchers as a potentially scrumptious solution for his demanding diet!

"Everyone flee!" Lucy shouted as soon as the male bipedal dinosaur paced toward them.

The explorers' priority changed instantly to escaping an uncompromising pursuit of a dangerous dinosaur in pursuit. This experienced male took quiet steps and maintained a steady posture while employing a stealthy hunting technique. *Allosaurus* accelerated along the bordering trees to close in his distance as discreetly as possible. *Allosaurus* successfully avoided pits during his hunting attempt.

Dr. Ryan volunteered to approach a junction directly ahead. Once he reached the area, the crew saw another adult *Allosaurus* race out of the left side of the junction to pounce Dr. Ryan.

"Mack!" Dr. Nimbus cried out as the second *Allosaurus* cleverly used a pouncing technique similar to African lions.

As the crew witnessed this larger female chase Dr. Ryan down the trail Lucy's Watchdog device activated by her troubled commander. "*The left and right turns are clear; take either one of them while I'll lure both of them away from the junction.*"

"Mack!" Lucy cried out as she made a sharp right turn before the pursuing male dinosaur decided to follow the larger female pursuing Dr. Ryan.

Once the others raced over to the center of an open field where they'll have a wide range of view, Marcus looked into his Good Samaritan device to track his friend's position by observing a blue dot moving rapidly down an electronically mapped trail. "I have Mack's position."

All four explorers were aware that their flexible necks and stiff tails were two collaborative anatomic tools of balance, as a fine plumage of follicles covered their skin. The anatomy of *Allosaurus* consists of a brain similar in shape to a crocodile's, however their stamina, speed and rapid growth were more akin to modern birds. Dr. Nimbus thought about how an indiscriminate feeding habit of *Allosaurus* along with such agility would likely be the most dangerous biological and physiological combination of any predator to evolve!

Two adult dinosaurs continued their carnivorous crusade after Dr. Ryan while Marcus watched events unfold on his screen. "Come on Mack, hang in there."

"I hope he's alright?" Lucy cried.

"As long as the blue indicator is moving within this display, he should be fine." Dr. Nimbus assured his colleagues.

Meena looked in all directions for any signs of additional danger within the field when Lucy used her communicator to contact Dr. Ryan. "Mack come – in please, Mack!"

A brief period of silence prompted Marcus to call Mack with his Watchdog device. "Mack come – in, Mack!"

"Mack here, I've just evaded both pursuers and heading toward your position." The crew eventually noticed Mack race out of an adjacent trail before approaching them.

"Damn it Mack, you had me scared to death." Lucy's feelings of experiencing a near disaster prompted him to respond.

"I'm sorry for what happened. I was racing along the shore and one of those giant crocodiles lurked out of nowhere and nearly clamped its jaws into my rear trunk. So the first dinosaur that was chasing me practically saved my life by accidentally colliding with the crocodile." Dr. Ryan's skin was covered with body moisture along with a rapidly beating heart. Dr. Ryan then removed his Good Samaritan device from his left fore arm and studied a geographic map on the crystal screen.

"Come – on! I can't believe this." Dr. Nimbus and the others noticed Dr. Ryan displaying unforeseen frustration.

"Mack, what is it?" Dr. Rosalila wondered.

"Nobody's going to believe this, but there's no sign of craters or even scars in the woodland. Everything is as clear as though nothing ever hit the surface at all!" Dr. Ryan revealed to the others before they took their navigational devices and thoroughly evaluated information displayed on their screen.

"Are you sure it's not the equipment?" Dr. Rosalila questioned Dr. Ryan in regards to their unexpected result.

Dr. Ryan took her question into consideration by calling Town Hall over his watch like device and told Dr. Grace to perform an inspection, which is a confirmation procedure to ensure all computers and electronic devices are online and functioning. This procedure could detect dead, rechargeable batteries. Electronic circuits built inside the Soul Mate, the Geographic Indicator, and other components inside Town Hall. Dr. Grace assured him that all circuitry would be probed and tested to ensure full functional ability that lasted only a moment before Dr. Grace returned to confirm excellent conditions of the hand held Good Samaritan device as well as the Private Eye.

"Mack, our tests prove our devices are fully functional and ready." The image of Dr. Grace personally confirmed.

"Thanks Derrick, over and out." Dr. Ryan said, as he was more surprised to see a wider space of terrain coverage and still an impressive altitude of 6000 feet or 1830 meters and still no trace of any impact or terrain damage of any kind.

"There's nothing's wrong. Our equipment is fully operable." Dr. Ryan confirmed as he directed the Private Eye to search for his transporter unit and dock back into the rear storage compartment directly behind his passenger seat.

"This is outlandish…we all know what we saw. But we have no proof of anything." Dr. Nimbus felt frustrated.

"The best strategy is to search for any other one of these objects and use the I.D. to interpret any biological or technological properties. At least we'll know the nature of these entities." Dr. Ryan suggested using the Identification Detective.

The entire crew proceeded to search for this new phenomenon until they reached another intersection where three independent paths met. Dr. Ryan didn't want the crew to separate by taking different trails, so he preferred for everyone to take the trail that led to another junction, where he then took extra precaution as he approached the intersection while the others waited for his response.

"We can't deny what we saw." Dr. Rosalila concluded. "They landed within this vicinity.

"Since there's no crater no damaged trees we have no choice but to face the music." Marcus concluded.

"What music are you referring to?" Lucy asked.

"All four of these entities never touched the ground at all."

Lucy remained quiet as she heard Marcus's hypothesis of a possible anomaly of identity of these entities.

"Mack gave us the signal." Meena announced before they approached him at the intersection, while Mack continued to scan the area for any possible danger.

All four congregated at the junction's center. As much as the crew wished to unravel the mystery of all four objects that raced toward the ground, none of them felt comfortable about this encounter. The Private Eye managed to locate Dr. Ryan's Drifter before his rear trunk opened for the aerial device employ its build-in laser guidance apparatus and its horizontal set of four rotating blades to dock into the rear compartment. As soon as the Private eye landed inside it was fastened into place while all four rotor blades declined its speed of rotation until it eventually ceased. Dr. Ryan pressed a close button in order to close the compartment lid automatically.

"Mack, the Private Eye didn't show any evidence of an impact at all." Marcus confirmed.

"This doesn't make any sense." Mack admitted.

"Look at them overhead!" Meena screamed out and pointed diagonally up.

"Look…there's another one!" Mack responded with bewilderment.

"These aren't meteorites partner! They have no resemblance to anything normal!" Marcus nervously said as he continued to share Mack's mounting fear.

"What we're dealing with appears technological in nature!" Meena evaluated.

Mack didn't anticipate her remarks. Lucy suspected something very strange about such an unusual appearance and unpredictable physical behavior. The crew shared Meena's suspicion but never suspected to see anything like this and the only technology available on Isis would be of human origin. They continued their descent toward the shore. When the object descended 300 feet or over 91 meters above the bay's surface, the crew watched it veer right and proceed toward a different direction. The object's rate of descent ended before it glided carelessly across the bay.

"I have a bad feeling with them." Marcus reluctantly expressed his discomfort.

"To be honest with everyone, I'm more afraid of this than any living inhabitant we've encountered on Isis." Mack admitted.

Dr. Ryan dispatched Town Hall to summon a second team of explorers to meet them at the island. All four of them proceeded back as they prepared their story of a phenomenon they don't understand. Dr. Ryan was ever increasingly concerned for an imminent prospect that these entities were non indigenous of Isis due to its inexplicable behavior and strange appearance. He wondered how such an entity could originate on Isis due to natural selection.

"The shore's straight ahead!" Meena told everyone as she pointed in the same direction.

"Watch out for *Deinosuchus*!" Marcus warned.

The others adhered to Marcus's warning when one of the six giant crocodiles lifted her head and focus her attention to all five strangers she and her giant companions increasingly recognized. Lucy was convinced *Deinosuchus* acknowledged their existence. Mack felt a bit reassured once they reached shallow waters of the extended bay. A second group of explorers were ready to respond. Despite sufficient reassurance Mack and others received from seeing their fellow explorers on the island, Mack's tensions mounted when he looked over his left shoulder and saw another disturbing sight.

"There they are again!" Dr. Ryan shouted out when he witnessed three more of these silver spherical devices located 500 feet or over 152 meters south, from the island and hovered at the outer bay before drifting west toward the ocean.

"I don't like this at all!" Lucy admitted as she reluctantly observed three spheres following each other until they moved north alongside the shore of the ocean.

"No meteorite ever seen behaved like this. This is like nothing I know. All we see is a clear reflective, metallic surface. Meena's right, they must have technological properties, my only question is who or what made them?" Dr. Rosalila concluded.

"It's moving much too slow for them to be dragged down by the planet's gravity. Look…it's still moving perfectly horizontal. We're facing an anomaly!" Marcus said with conviction before they proceeded to the settlement island. Once they reached the shore, they rushed up the hill and continued on until they met Harold, Fan, and others outside Town Hall.

"Mack, what was that?" Dr. Fan Zhu wondered.

"I tried three times and couldn't get any reading!" Dr. Harold Nevins told everyone as he was holding his Identification Detective device in his right hand.

Lucy and Meena testified what they saw to their colleagues while Mack attempted to interpret something he never studied or even witnessed. He can't even recall any experiments dealing with something of this nature. Mack's abdominal continued to twitch while tensions within his muscles hardened. Shortness of breath and sweat were in unison as he realized that he's facing an unprecedented situation.

"I thought I'll never say this in my lifetime, we're witnessing UFOs." Mack nervously admitted to the others before he decided not to waste any time to activate his Watchdog device and made an emergency call to the orbiting flagship.

"Look!" Lucy shouted out as she initially felt disturbed due to such unpredictable whit in part of this mysterious phenomenon.

Lucy frantically pointed her right index finger before the others suddenly felt a severe sense of instability when one of those large reflecting spheres rose slowly above a tree line until it became visible to their naked eyes. Meena eventually used her two hands to vertically cover her opened mouth because these objects did not behave according to known natural laws of physics. Lucy and Meena took a covert step back as Mack saw a second sphere rising above the same tree line until it match similar altitude of the first hovering object that was 200 feet or 61 meters away from each other and 100 feet or over 30 meters above the highest point of the visible tree line. Both were estimated to be approximately a mile or over 1.6 kilometers north from the island they were located.

"Guardian, come in Guardian!" Mack spoke over his wristwatch before Harold took a few steps back and Marcus froze as he saw these two strange entities hovering motionless.

"*Guardian here,*" Dr. Gruber replied.

"We're encountering a bizarre situation! We're facing an anomaly! We're facing an anomaly!" Mack announced over his communicator.

"*What happened? What did you see?*" Dr. Gruber asked.

Mack provided ample detail of silver spheres with a smooth surface while two of them remained hovering above the tree lines. It was difficult for him to describe such objects while a third slowly rose above the tree lines and aligned itself exactly in the same altitude as the other two and remained two hundred feet away from the second hovering object. By the time Dr. Ryan completed his description, a fourth object rose and hovered next to the third object. Since all four entities developed a perfectly aligned horizontal formation, an idea of four intelligently guided objects was inspired due to the fact that all four spherical objects demonstrated a proven ability to judge physical distances in order to assemble this organized formation.

"*I hope these objects are not technological devices.*" Dr. Gruber nervously said.

"Why?" Mack wondered.

"*What if these devices were created by an intelligent civilization whose purpose is to claim this planet as a colony?*"

"Well, as far as I'm concerned, we arrived here first! So they have to get used to our presence or they could leave planet Isis permanently." Mack affirmed over his communicator.

"*But what if this planet was originally part of their interstellar territory all along, even long before we discovered Isis?*"

Mack then paused for a moment and stared at four hovering UFOs stationed above the distant tree lines. "Although these four objects remain still, I don't see any sign of their objection of our presence. It appears that these things could be studying Town Hall but they don't seem aggressive or hostile."

"*We checked the surface of Isis thoroughly and found no sign of any urban or industrialized activities whatsoever. Since that's the case Planet Isis is not their home world.*" Dr. Gruber claimed.

"Our main priorities are to continue our regular mission schedule and to find out exactly what these entities really are before making any premature conclusion." Dr. Ryan suggested before their transmission was completed.

"Mack, what do you think they are?" Dr. Fan Zhu asked.

"We know that they're not normal."

"Whoa…there they go!" Dr. Zhu said.

Once all four spheres simultaneously raced up in a parallel formation through the sky, Lucy and Meena ran from their position and frantically paced up the metal ramp until they entered Town Hall's main entrance. Fan and Martin took a few steps back while Marcus couldn't move from his position. Mack shared Marcus's intensity as all four objects maintained their physical formation as they penetrated clouds.

"Mack! I don't like this at all! These devices could be programmed to show us what they could do." Marcus stuttered.

"The question is why? What's the purpose of their demonstration? Could it be a subliminal message? " Mack asked.

Martin and Fan slowly approached Marcus and Mack before Martin wondered. "What's next?"

"We'll continue with the cottage industry and cornucopia operations for now. Meanwhile we'll wait until we see another one of these entities and study them further. I would also advise caution as we study them." Dr. Ryan concluded as Harold nervously took a few steps forward and rejoined the others in complete shock of what he saw.

"I just had a strange thought in mind," Harold announced.

"What is it," Marcus replied.

"What if…what if," Harold chuckled before saying "What if they were an intelligent civilization of sentient beings like ourselves who's exploring this planet just like us?"

"That's what Karl suggested to me earlier." Mack said.

"We have to be very careful. This is the most sensitive situation we've ever encountered." Harold mentioned as a recommendation for a diplomatic solution if Karl is correct about the origins of these strange spheres.

"All we know besides their physical appearance and behavior is that all four of them flew unconventionally with no visible propulsion system." Marcus observed.

"That's it!" Mack injected into the conversation. "We'll use the Dove planes and the Condor craft. We'll also use the Private Eye from each transporter so we could study these objects without accidentally provoking any aggression."

Harold, Fan and Marcus all smiled due to Mack's cautious idea. Martin was especially pleased by such a careful approach Mack emphasized and appreciated it verbally. "I like it. I'll send the Dove and Condor into flight immediately."

"We also need to conduct a town watch in order to monitor any activity in the sky. All observations would be sent to Intelligence for analysis." Mack proposed.

"Would we return to the mainland?" Marcus wondered.

"Once we discuss this issue with intelligence then we'll return to the mainland and resume our scheduled studies. However, if we encounter these objects again, then we have to conduct a Town Hall meeting." Mack concluded.

SIGNS FROM ABOVE

"Mack, are you alright?" Marcus asked.

"Where are they?" Mack continued to scan the entire bay area for any visual sign of these spheres he saw an hour ago.

"Whatever they were, they're gone."

"I've been feeling very tense lately." Mack said.

"I don't like this anymore than you do...I'm scared too. Think about this, at least they're not malevolent."

"True...but I just didn't like their magic trick at the mainland. What were they trying to prove?" Mack emphasized.

"They proved to be peaceful."

Mack paused and took a deep breath once he heard his friend's answer to his question before he continued to survey a clear blue sky. He lowered his head before turning around to face his friend. "I apologize for being uptight. I have no ample clue what they were. This type of mystery is undesirable."

"I have no clue what they were either, nor does the rest of the crew." Marcus advised.

"I personally suspect these objects are self aware. What if they developed a self defense mechanism?" Mack wondered.

"I wouldn't be surprised if all of these spheres actually developed group awareness. These objects would share behavioral traits similar to packs, bands, prides or clans. These reflective spheres could even operate as an organized team." Marcus presented his hypothesis.

Mack thought intensely of what he was told. "If they are a collective intelligence like you described, then I wonder how smart each individual sphere could be and how effective could operate as a group. We should treat them like a sentient group of intelligent entities, which may have desires and even preferences."

"We must study these objects as often as we can. Knowledge is the only solution to any challenge like this." Marcus replied.

"I'll study them and I'll learn everything." Mack pledged.

Marcus placed his left hand on top of Mack's right shoulder as a means to agree and compliment his suggestion. "I don't think we have anything to worry about."

"Well...I guess I'm overreacting." Mack laughed.

"What's our objective for today?"

"I think we should continue our normal research schedule by exploring the southern shore of the bay and beyond to the open field." Mack suggested.

"You mean where Alicia and her crew explored?"

"Sure, why not?"

"Good, I hope to see *Megalictis* and *Castoroides*."

Mack activated his Watchdog device and requested two Drifters to be delivered to their location. Once a request was made, Marcus noticed Drs. Fan Zhu and Martin de' la' Vega approaching them. Dr. Zhu was curious of their intentions before he asked, "Mack! Marcus! What's our assignment?"

"We plan to explore the field beyond the southern shore."

"Oh you mean where Antonio and Alicia were?"

"Yes, you want to come along?" Marcus asked.

"Of course," was Fan's response before Dr. Ryan requested two more Drifter units to be dispatched.

Neither Martin nor Fan wanted to initiate any discussions regarding any silver sphere from the sky. Both were convinced that their earlier discussion was sufficient and were confident in Mack's decision regarding handling such an unusual affair. Both were less concerned with any possible unidentified flying object or UFO than adventuring into the charismatic Central Continent!

While all four individuals continued to discuss their next assignment, Marcus noticed four associates gliding down the steel ramp. Each associate steered a transporter over to Dr. Ryan and his colleagues near the shore. Mack subconsciously viewed above the tree lines at the mainland's shore. His occasional search resulted in finding nothing unusual.

"Here are four units you requested." One associate said once all four Drifters arrived, they conducted an initial inspection of their assigned unit.

"Thanks." Dr. Ryan replied.

Once all four associates relinquished their transporters Mack inspected and tested his transporter along with his colleagues. Mack covertly monitored the sky while discussing further details of their next goal. Dr. Ryan activated his communicator before assigning temporary command to Dr. Derrick Grace before all four resilient researchers departed Town Hall Island.

A familiar jolt and sway was felt while they crossed the bay. As they approached the mainland another flock of giant seagulls flew overhead and continued their desired course. This species known as *Osteodontornis orri* glided down until all three of them were only three feet or one meter above the bay's surface. Suddenly one of them dipped their bony toothed beak into the water. In less than a second, the crew noticed something caught between the jawbones of this bird's elaborate beak. Similar to a modern albatross, this female then flipped a dead fish into her mouth and consumed it during flight. Her two other companions that appeared physically smaller continued to glide toward the mainland before Marcus watched both maturing males dip their beaks into the bay before capturing a fish and a small squid.

As the explorers approached of the mainland, it appeared obvious to all four crewmembers that something was wrong. Mack noticed something near the beach. It appeared to be submerged but was visible from their position. Dr. Ryan continued to monitor whatever it could be underwater.

"Where did it go?" Dr. Nimbus wondered.

"What ever it was it sank completely." Dr. Ryan witnessed as mild ripples slowly dissolved.

"The shore's not much farther." Dr. Nimbus was ahead.

"We'll steer left and head south." Mack said as Marcus looked back and noticed something rapidly moving to them.

"Hey...There's something moving behind us!"

Once they heard Dr. Nimbus's frantic scream, the crew accelerated without looking back. Dr. Nimbus was ever more suspicious of this strange current raging from under water. As they traveled faster, Marcus noticed this disturbing sound intensify. Once they arrived at the shore all four explorers raced across a beach. The crew started to hear heavy thumps of stocky limbs pounding on white sand.

Nerve fibers riddled each crewmember heard a sizzling hiss as this enormous male amphibian cocking his jaws wide open and revealing a white leathery interior. Long pointed teeth would have been used to engulf unwary prey in this male's mouth. Once this giant crocodile came to a sudden stop, he closed his mouth before he reluctantly crawled back to the shore. Dr. Ryan received an opportunity to look into one of two side view mirrors and saw this giant salt water crocodile retreating.

"Gentlemen, *Deinosuchus* returned to the water!"

"Have you ever seen such agility for an enormous crocodile?" Dr. Martin de' la' Vega wondered.

"No extant crocodile in Earth could terrorize us like what we just saw." Dr. Fan Zhu was convinced of such unprecedented danger from a colossal crocodilian.

"I think we should use an alternative shore when we leave the mainland. They're much too dangerous." Dr. Ryan suggested.

All four explorers proceeded south. They eventually traveled over grass beyond the beach. As they continued to the southeastern part of the extended bay, Dr. Nimbus wanted to know the precise location of a meadow. "How far is this open field?"

"It's about 2000 feet. All we have to do is travel through this trail straight ahead." Dr. Ryan confirmed 610 meters to travel.

As they drifted through a grassy trail, Dr. Zhu saw something strange inside bordering woodland at the left side of the trail. Although this life form didn't appear threatening, it seemed rather bizarre because of its unprecedented appearance.

"Gentlemen…take a look at this."

"What is that?" Mack wondered as Marcus looked on.

Dr. de' la' Vega smiled before he chucked in a minor laughter because he remembered the identity of what looks like a giant armadillo. "That's species is *Doedicurus clavicaudatus!*"

The other three men looked over with a bit of surprise and encouraged Martin to tell them more about this mysterious mortal. "*Doedicurus* lived in the southern portion of South America or Patagonia during the Pleistocene epoch Adults average thirteen feet long and their armored plated shell over their back could rise about five feet high."

"You're kidding? That's about the size of a small automobile." Dr. Nimbus responded.

"Half this animal's length is their tail and you see that club at the end covered with spikes known as a mace?" Dr. de' la' Vega explained. "They used them to fend of potential predators such as *Borhyaena* and other carnivorous marsupials.

"That's amazing! What else you know?" Dr. Ryan wondered.

"They're from the family Glyptodontidae. They're an ancient relative of modern armadillos but are much larger and well armed. Their defense tactics is unique as well. If a predator tries to tackle them, not only would their hard shell casting would be impossible to penetrate, but they'll be able to judge the attacker's position and swing their club at precisely their location."

"The perpetrator could be killed?" Dr. Zhu asked.

"Not exactly, you see they would not want to accidentally crack their own armor so they'll just try to swing soft enough to prevent any self inflicted damage, but hard enough to stun the attacker."

"Then what?" Dr. Zhu wondered.

"Once their attacker is stunned, *Doedicurus* will then sway their body around and swing hard horizontally. This technique would disable the aggressor, as they would swing far away from their shell and that's when they'll apply their full force." Dr. Zhu was impressed by what Dr. de' la' Vega told him as he watched this maturing male stroll across the trail.

"As heavy as this male's mace appears, it's amazing how he could control it with such ease." Dr. Ryan noticed.

"You know something?" Dr. Nimbus realized.

"What?" Dr. Martin de' la' Vega wondered.

"This is a similar self defense strategy of certain dinosaurs such as *Ankylosaurus* of North America and *Saichania* of Mongolia would use in the face of danger." Dr. Nimbus realized.

The crew noticed *Doedicurus* standing directly into their way as this adult male stood at the middle of the trail. Mack didn't want to place himself nor his crew into unnecessary danger and decided to remain stationed for a moment until the armored Glyptodont moved on. Marcus noticed *Doedicurus* grazing on fresh grass on this trail. As they patiently waited, Dr. Ryan began to hear cackling sounds originating from a neighboring forest that bordered the right side of this grassy trail.

"Shhh...listen. Do you hear that?"

"What is it?" Dr. Nimbus wondered as they heard crushing twigs and weeds.

"What ever it is, it seems that it's coming from over there." Dr. Ryan claimed.

"Everyone, take a look at that?" Marcus wondered as he saw a heavily built brown mammal with four stout legs with large toes.

"I'll use my I.D. and find out exactly the true identity of this particular life form." Martin mentioned before pointing his Identification Detective device.

Once a usual match making process was complete, Martin was surprised of the initial results. "Has anyone ever heard of a genus called *Kvabebihyrax?*"

A moment of silence was necessary in order for Mack to remember Dr. Netherland's lecture and a painting he collected illustrating an ancient hyrax that lived during the Late Pliocene, which would be around 3,600,000 – 2,588,000 years ago. This particular hyrax the crew discovered grew over five feet or over 1.5 meters long and lived in Europe particularly the Caucasus.

"I remember Doctor Netherland told me about *Kvabebihyrax* a longtime ago. He mentioned that there were different types of ancient hyraxes that adapted a few niches." Dr. Ryan revealed. "He reminded us that all hyraxes are closely related to elephants and sea cows."

Each crewmember noticed how this life form that was identified as *Kvabebihyrax* displayed a waddling gait as it walked flat footed similar to a brown bear. It had four toes at both front legs and three larger sized toes at both rear legs. Although no tail was seen, such a profound presence possessed a heavy body that appeared to resemble a small hippopotamus. *Kvabebihyrax* had an abbreviated snout, small ears and black eyes mounted high on this

221

male's skull. Such a facial arrangement prompted Mack and the others that this ancient hyrax may have burrowed or even swam in lakes or rivers.

The most notable feature was this female's dental arrangement.

This female had a pair of massive incisors on both of her jaws. The upper incisors were separated and appeared like enlarged canines. What's more remarkable was she possessed four lower inner incisors that pointed diagonally up. Marcus thought that these teeth could have either dug up roots or scraped bark off of a tree, while using larger teeth at her upper jaw for chiseling. Whenever this female closed her mouth, her lower near horizontal teeth would fit perfectly between her two massive upper incisors. Marcus and the others believed that such a rare dental arrangement could have been an efficient instrument to scrape for food.

"Both of them look impressive!" Dr. Ryan was amazed.

Doedicurus and *Kvabebihyrax* noticed each other's presence. *Doedicurus* seemed a bit nervous but wasn't threatened. *Kvabebihyrax* kept a reasonable distance because *Doedicurus* initially wagged his tail slowly as a means to feel more secure. However, both herbivores sense of security were suddenly suspended when they noticed two gigantic predatory land birds elusively walking along the forest edge at the left side.

"Whoa...I didn't even recognize them over there." Dr. Nimbus was startled to witnessed two land birds that revealed how their species appeared at Patagonia during the Middle and Late Miocene or approximately 15,970,000 – 5,332,000 years ago.

Martin suspected these tall land birds often settled into habitats lacking rival predators on Earth. They evolved into greater size because there wasn't any need to hide from dangerous carnivores. He was confident that's how they became apex predators themselves on Earth. Mack noticed these calculating carnivorous land birds evolved a fine muscular physique accompanied by their impressive agility, which was suitable for hunting.

Once Martin received official confirmation from his Identification Detective device, a species called *Phorusrhacos longissimus* was able to stand 8 feet (2.5m) tall. Although they evolved unusually small wings, both grew large feathered heads and curved beaks designed to hunt and scavenge carrion. Mack was impressed by their strong orange feet, lower legs and black talons while Fan recognized their white head and neck along with a blue feathered torso with black stripes from their throats to their tails, while both thighs were covered with white plumage.

Any prehistoric predator including *Phorusrhacos* adapted to an organized, concerted effort to remain hidden until it's too late. Both land birds kept their heads low and walked along the forest's edge in an attempt to blend in with bordering bushes, shrubs and tall plants. It was obvious to Martin and the others that neither one of the giant land birds didn't want to be discovered by two feeding herbivores. Predators employing this technique would judge according to what direction their prey would be facing. These land birds monitored the direction of the wind and preferred the wind to blow in their direction so their body scent would not be detected. Marcus interpreted *Doedicurus* and *Kvabebihyrax* accepted each other once both species took turns eating grass and tall weeds while the other observed the area for any possible danger, both of these male land birds remained quiet and patient.

Mack and his crew remained motionless. All four adventurers respected the rules of the wild and decided to remain idled and quiet. As they covertly observed this pivotal circumstance *Kvabebihyrax* noticed four hovering transporters and began to stare at each occupant. Mack felt uneasy due to such unpredictable behavior of this ancient hyrax and he didn't want to distract this female's attention from the immediate area.

One of two land birds raced out from his elusive position and attempted to tackle *Doedicurus* by circling around the glyptodont in order to confuse their intended prey. The giant land bird waited patiently for the rear of this male's neck to be exposed. The tall land bird's pursuit of *Doedicurus* caused *Kvabebihyrax* to shift her attention away from four observers and refocus toward this struggle. Marcus felt stunned to see such a bold land bird attack an armored glyptodont.

Martin continued to observe *Phorusrhacos* attempting to bite the rear of this male's neck. Martin witnessed his mace attached to his tail cocked to his right side before it swung into the perpetrator's left leg, causing this young male land bird to lose balance and collapsed on his left side. Fan saw an experienced male retaliate by rotating his body before an intense swing crashed into the land bird's right rib cage. Everyone instantly saw *Phorusrhacos* become engulfed in pain before the crew noticed a compound fracture of several rigs. *Doedicurus* instantly fled down the grassy trail in the opposite direction of where Dr. Ryan and his colleagues were located.

"I just felt a sting through my ribs." Marcus uttered as he heard an echo of impact that forced *Phorusrhacos* to frantically scream out as he quivered on the ground.

Fan noticed *Kvabebihyrax* displaying her dental arrangement as a warning to an injured land bird as she cautiously walked backward before sprinting away in the opposite direction. Mack continued to monitor the surviving male *Phorusrhacos* he thought was most likely a sibling that made no attempts to pursue the fleeing *Doedicurus*.

It was soon evident that after *Kvabebihyrax* reentered the neighboring woods this fallen male kicked his feet up repeatedly until both legs folded gently and became motionless. Silence replaced relentless outcries of pain and anguish. Both of his keen eyes gradually closed for the last time after his body rolled over on his right side.

"I feel sorry for the land bird." Dr. Fan Zhu shared.

"What a terrible way to go." Dr. Ryan monitored a once vibrant youngster as he passed by a lifeless corpse and monitored the other surviving land bird staring back at them from his elusive position.

As they were far ahead Marcus looked back and saw the other giant land bird emerge from hiding before approaching his fallen sibling. Once he sensed his brother deceased, the surviving sibling decided to walk away and learn from such a terrible experience. Similar to what happened to many young predators on Earth and Isis. Dr. Ryan understood that Isis and Earth were not safe places for predators to make mistakes, which could result in death.

While the crew continued to approach the open field, Dr. Ryan thought about how two sibling land birds were born and raised until they encountered *Doedicurus*. He thought about them receiving food from their parents after hatching and reflected their adolescence of learning how to hunt and scavenge carrion. Emptiness voided Dr. Ryan's chest as he thought about the fact that a once long history of two brothers abruptly ended once a surviving *Phorusrhacos* walked away from his long time sibling, who'll never experience fatherhood.

It was obvious to Dr. Ryan that there's never a safe time or phase during any creature's life. Some perish before birth when the egg that contains new life is eaten. Other life forms of advanced age become exhausted and outclassed by younger competitors. However, some manage to survive and reproduce. Although the majority would suffer a similar fate of a deceased *Phorusrhacos*, there would be others who'll avoid danger and teach their offspring proven methods of survival that would propel their species to evolve for millions or even billions of years!

An expanse of grass straight ahead proved to be the edge of the Southern bay field. Open grass and comforting cross breezes gently penetrated erected trees and flickered leaves once four ambitious individuals entered an inviting meadow. A sea of green grass engulfed islands of small trees and shrubs. Mack noticed Marcus staring into a congregation of shrubs.

"Marcus…Marcus, what is it?"

"There's something behind those shrubs."

"Which one?" Mack asked.

"The second group from our position." Marcus answered.

"The wide batch?" Mack suspected.

"Yes! I saw something move behind it. I'll keep my eyes on the batch."

Mack knew that Marcus's judgment was as authentic as Isis's air quality. He scanned the area until he was surprised to see a group of some of the largest early reptiles emerge from another batch. Mack's Identification Detective device confirmed that this particular group of four life forms was similar to what existed in South Africa's legendary Karoo Basin, as well as east Africa and Eastern Europe over 251 million years ago near the end of the Permian period and the beginning of the Triassic period.

"What are they? They look weird." Fan tried to decipher their identity.

"Based upon this, they're known as *Pareiasaurus*." Mack responded as he held his I.D. device in his right hand.

All four legs of *Pareiasaurus* stood more upright than a typical crocodile or lizard, which was why each stood around five feet or 1.5 meters tall. Elusive bony plates lodged into their thick gray and black skin protected their backs while heavy legs supported their massive bodies. *Pareiasaurus* grew up to 8 feet (2.44m) long and was likely to weigh at least one ton (908 kg). Although each had a small tail, their skulls were dense and riddled with spikes and lumps. This ancient herbivore's teeth were designed to consume rough plants such as ferns and cycads. One of these four early reptiles appeared older.

Marcus continued to stare at the distant batch of plants and trees with growing suspicion. Fan and Martin continued to observe all four Permian pioneers while Mack checked the entire area for any potential threat. *Pareiasaurus* migrated diligently across a quiet field. Marcus became instantly surprised once he detected three strange but ferocious looking protomammals racing out from behind the small batch of shrubs and charged relentlessly toward the old male that lagged behind the other herbivores.

"It's *Gorgonops longifrons!*"

Mack could barely believe to see one of the most dangerous apex predators that ever existed before the dinosaurs. All three powerful Permian predators stood more upright than a lizard and matched a similar stance to their intended prey. It was easy for Martin to notice their fine muscular physique while Marcus recognized a sleek dynamics of their bodies that showed an agile ability to chase any potential prey. Reaching a length of up to ten feet (3m) long, their massive heads were estimated to be up to 30 inches (76cm) long that possessed pin-sharp, flesh shredding teeth. Their heads appeared to look like a monitor lizard, because they didn't evolve any upright ears and their forward facing eyes were mounted on the sides of their skull. Mack noticed a fine thin set of minute scales, which made them appear like a hybrid between a lion and a giant monitor lizard with a short heavy tail.

Two relentless attackers used their four-inch (10cm) upper canines and three-inch (7.6cm) long lower canines to bite the old male's rear legs to prevent him from fleeing. The third one clamped her powerful jaws into the victim's throat as a means to penetrate his heavy skin and crush his esophagus to cut off oxygen. All three younger pareiasaurs fled the area while this struggle continued. Each *Gorgonops* took every preventive measure to prevent *Pareiasaurus* to escape and insured that this giant won't fall on top of them because they could become permanently crippled. Mack felt surprised to see three persistent gorgons attempting to tackle giant pareiasaur. Fan was startled to see *Pareiasaurus* willfully fighting back.

Pareiasaurus resisted all three attackers until a lack of oxygen, loss of blood and physical exhaustion caused a senior citizen of the wild to relinquish longevity and a robust history as this bold male tilted over to his right side before four observers heard a vibrant echo of impacting flesh on a clear grassy meadow.

The name gorgon originated from a Greek monster myth known as Gorgona who was able to transform humans into stone just by looking at their dreaded appearance could only reinforce such horror by viewing a frenzied feeding when two gorgons that originally held both legs of *Pareiasaurus* initially disembowel the abdominal area while the third continued to maintain her merciless grip of this unfortunate male's throat. Fan was surprised how resilient *Pareiasaurus* was despite his advanced age. He continued to kick and shake until his energy wore off and caused his limbs to become immobile. Fan couldn't decide which was more horrible, the legend of Medusa or the gorgons he's observing.

Marcus and Mack thought about such a question ever since seeing them clash with *Borhyaena* during the Osiris 4 Summit. As soon as the larger female was sure her role was fulfilled, she snarled at the other two males as a means to claim her share of their difficult food source. Once this larger female claimed her share both males eventually joined in on this feast. Their black and gray shade on their hairy scales on their heads, neck and shoulders were entrenched with blood.

Martin thought he'd seen it all until he saw another group of two rival predators of the Permian period approaching three accomplished hunters. "Whoa...look at them!"

Their skulls were at least 18 inches (45.7cm) long and evolved massive upper and lower jaws. Mack noticed these protomammals appeared much like their counterparts but were heavier. One of two male gorgons warned the others that *Inostrancevia alexandri* was tempted to join in on the feast. So, both notorious apex predators of the Permian period decided to settle their dispute in typical feral fashion.

Blood dripped down from a deliberately displayed set of teeth as a gesture from three protective gorgons to diplomatically warn both marauders to move away. However, matching the size of a large tiger, *Inostrancevia* opened their massive mouths in response and growled as a gesture against their rivals. The name *Inostrancevia alexandri* was originated by Professor Dr.

Vladimir Prokorovitch Amalitzky of the Paleontological Institute of the Russian Academy of Sciences to honor A. Inostrantzev, a Russian geologist. Dr. Netherland knew very much about how fierce this specimen was during the Late Permian or from 260 – 251 million years ago at the Dvina River, Arkhanglsk region of Northern Russia. Mack remembered their conversation regarding such an imposing Saber-tooth gorgon could weigh well over 500 pounds or over 227 kilograms and have an ability to sprint and even swim!

Marcus knew all too well that this situation would explode like dynamite once *Gorgonops* initially charged *Inostrancevia*. Forbidding sounds of this bloodletting brawl forced the crew to abandon their current position. As they fled, they could still hear echoes of torment and tyranny from both groups of ancient protomammals desperately attempting to tear each other apart.

As they watched from a further distance, Mack witnessed one *Gorgonops* chasing *Inostrancevia* away before another came from behind and bit the pursuer in his right rear leg. "That must hurt. That mouth opened just like how a hippo would yawn!"

Such a fierce inflicting strike made *Gorgonops* fall allowing his attacker to bit him on the stomach as his back lied on grass. Mack learned how much of a stout fighter this particular individual was when he made a stunning counterattack by using his right front claw to grab *Inostrancevia* by the left side of his neck before curling upright to bite his right side. Fan saw two other invading protomammals or reptiles that posses mammal features such as fur and nocturnal hunting, tackle another defending gorgon before one bit her on the ribs and the other clamped on her left rear leg as she lied on her back. What amazed him most was the female's ability to shake both of them off before getting back on her feet.

"This is insane!" Fan concluded as an angry female *Gorgonops* savagely retaliated by tackling one of her attackers and bit this male *Inostrancevia* mercilessly at his abdomen while the other fled the immediate area to avoid further danger.

Complete *Gorgonops* fossils were considerable difficult to discover in the Karoo Basin, South Africa where many strange species of the Permian period existed from 280 – 225 million years ago. However, on November 17th 1998, scientists discovered the first complete fossil skeleton that appeared to be a member of Gorgonopsidae family resting on top of a high plateau at Karoo region. Roger Smith curator of geology at the South African Museum and Peter Ward, professor of geological sciences at the University of Washington at Washington State led a five-person team to unearth an exceptional fossil that revealed such an awe-inspiring ability of these ancient protomammals.

As Dr. Martin de' la' Vega heard sounds of a ravaging war resonate across a peaceful meadow, each crewmember, especially Martin suddenly learned how a bitter faunal rivalry on Isis revealed a trace of Earth's brutality during its ancient history! "Did you ever see anything like that? What a screwed up way to live!"

"One thing's for sure, I'm glad our ancestors didn't have to co-exist with such dangerous life forms we've encountered so far. If we did, then the possibilities of early humans surviving an environment like this would be low." Mack agreed.

When Marcus looked back he noticed *Gorgonops* bobbing and weaving while *Inostrancevia* shifted and rotated their standing position in order to prevent being attacked from behind. Members of both fighting factions suffered obvious scars and punctures on their limbs, shoulders and backs. Both groups of contenders applied considerable effort to regain their breath to recover as much energy as possible before their rival recuperates. Neither group of predators showed any intention to retreat as they prepared for another clash.

"This is worse than seeing lions and hyenas fight in Savuti, or Tsavo! I never saw such a brawl from rival predators." Marcus claimed as both species clashed once again.

Marcus remember Savuti being located at the central northern area of Botswana, west of Chobe National Park. He also reflected how Tsavo National Park of southeast Kenya is divided in half by the Athi River; one side of this river is Tsavo National Park West while the other is Tsavo National Park East. Marcus watched *Inostrancevia* temporarily retreat before *Gorgonops* decided to conduct a fanatical feeding frenzy in order to consume as much carrion as possible so when *Inostrancevia* returns then they'll consume enough food to either fight again or flee if they're appetites are fulfilled. Lions judge similar situations when their pride successfully defends their kill against spotted hyenas or rival lion prides in Africa.

Dr. Netherland lectured Mack, Marcus and the others regarding group or pact behavior of various species. For example, a clan is a close knit group with a common ancestor that don't mate nor socialize with any other individual of the same species outside their common origins. All clans of hyenas are disciplined by a dominant or Alpha female known as the matriarch. The only time outsiders of the same species ever communicate is during feuds. Prides usually identify a group of lions ruled by an Alpha male (the patriarch) leads his group and dominates the mating process. Packs are commonly referred to canines such as wolves and dogs, which up to two or even three generations would comply within a strict hierarchy regarding each individual's role and privilege. Packs are lead by a dominant male and female.

"Let's leave this place." Dr. Ryan shouted.

"Our devices recorded and confirmed their identities I'm certain that

Town Hall will be impressed by what we encountered." Marcus felt relieved to flee the area.

"I never though I'll see such a ferocious fight." Dr. Zhu added as they continued their present course.

The crew carefully checked all directions for signs of potential danger; Martin placed his right palms across the rear of his neck before squeezing it then tilting his head back with his eyes closed before opening his eyes again. "Look!"

A disturbing chill raced vertically through their spines as all four researchers witnessed a single reflective sphere from the east gently gliding 200 feet or 61 meters above. What was more disturbing is when they detected this sphere it was losing altitude as it headed west. This object was gliding diagonally down toward the ground. Marcus thought what ever it was would likely crash at the western area of this large meadow next to bordering woodland.

"I think it will crash near those woods."

Muscles tightened as it reduced speed. Absolutely no sound or odor was detected when it passed above of the crew. Sounds of crickets, macaws and toucans were not difficult to hear as this object made a sudden stop before hovering fifty feet (15.25m) away from the forest's edge and a similar height above clear grass. What made the crew even more nervous was once this sphere with a diameter of 50 feet or over 15 meters emitted a steady green inverted V shaped beam of light from the bottom of this object, but produced no sound.

"What is it doing?" Dr. Nimbus barley was able to say as this steady beam lasted for about ten seconds.

Dr. Ryan inconspicuously took out his pistol shaped device and carefully pointed it to this hovering object. He quietly pressed the trigger button before a matchmaking process initiated. He displayed a modest response as he saw a black background on the screen with bold red block letters that said 'no data' before making more covert attempts to point his Identification Detective device to this strange object that spontaneously emitted a red, inverted V shaped beam of light onto the ground.

"Mack. What are you doing?" Dr. Nimbus quietly asked.

"There's no reference at all." Mack responded.

"If we're not careful then there may be no reference to our own existence anymore." Marcus warned.

"Even the surface material of this thing is strange." Mack said.

"What do you mean?" Dr. Nimbus wondered.

"I'm getting no response from my I.D. device."

"Mack…you're kidding?"

"I made repeated attempts but no data was revealed."

Dr. Zhu then whispered to the others to confirm his previous attempts to identify this particular entity. "When you returned earlier after viewing these objects for the first time, I tried numerous times to find a reference from the Soul Mate, but my I.D. device only read no data. I couldn't even identify the composition of its outer surface."

Dr. de' la' Vega didn't want to say a word while he used his left hand to cover his droopy mouth. Dr. Nimbus didn't feel comfortable with their testimony. "Guys, are you're sure?"

"Unfortunately yes." Dr. Ryan reluctantly admitted.

"This can't be right." Dr. Nimbus concluded as this second steady tracer beam lasted for ten seconds before it abruptly stopped.

As four explorers talked about their recent finding, their discussion was interrupted when they heard an obviously deep and loud belch originating from within this object's interior. Body sweat began to form beads from their pores while nervousness acquired temporary control of their emotions.

"What the hell that noise means?" Dr. Nimbus nervously wondered as he anticipated fleeing to area.

"I don't know but I think we should leave this vicinity at once." Dr. Ryan concluded before all four explorers instantly rotated their Drifter unit 180 degrees and accelerated in the other direction.

Nobody desired to look back to see how this object would respond to four explorers darting away with hovering transporters. Dr. Ryan and the others detected a large congregation of trees, shrubs and bushes located at the middle of the meadow as a perfect place to hide. "Gentlemen, let's hide here."

Once all four hid behind this island of trees and tall plants, Mack climbed off of his Drifter unit and proceeded over to where he could see through leaves and branches to find out if this object followed them. Marcus and the others surveyed the area for any signs of danger including both species of predatory Permian protomammals they saw earlier.

"I don't see anything but a clear meadow. What ever it was somehow disappeared." Dr. Ryan interpreted as he continued to search for this strange sphere shaped enigma from the sky.

"Mack, are you sure?" Dr. Nimbus asked.

"I'm positive! It's gone."

He walked slowly back to his Drifter before he climbed back on. Drs. Zhu and de' la' Vega continued to look in all directions but found nothing. Dr. Nimbus felt it was his duty to tell his colleagues of what he noticed about certain behavioral traits he recognized in regards to this mystery.

"One thing I recognized was that when you pointed your tracking device toward this object, it seemed to respond to various wave lengths it emitted."

"That is strange." Dr. Ryan replied. "Taking that fact into consideration, what ever it was, must be capable of detecting various stimuli and respond to it."

"Personally I'm convinced it has sentience as well as intelligence not only could it detect and respond, it could possibly think?" Dr. Zhu regarded to this object's abilities.

"We have no choice but to acknowledge that this thing could posses a self awareness mechanism." Dr. de' la' Vega concluded.

"What's even worse is that my I.D. couldn't find a match with the Soul Mate databank, which means that this is a true anomaly." Mack confirmed that his Identification Detective device couldn't even identify what they saw before they remained silent.

Dr. Nimbus remembered another failed attempt of a colleague to identify this object before he revealed it to the others. "I also remember Harold telling me that he pointed his device toward these things several times but proved futile."

"I think we shouldn't use or I.D. devices to identify these UFOs anymore." Dr. Ryan suggested before they pursued south.

All four of them moved slowly but looked carefully in all directions. Dr. Ryan often looked up while Dr. Zhu continued to search for wildlife. As they moved south Fan noticed something looking out of an open crevice at the forest's edge.

"There's something looking at us from the edge of the forest."

"We better be careful, what is that?" Marcus wondered as he saw a rodent's head that was estimated to be just over one foot or over 30.5 centimeters long with bulging jaw muscles on both sides of its mature male's face.

Martin noticed certain physical similarities of a giant capybara that could burrow underground. Once this massive rodent climbed out of a ditch, all four spectators were shocked to see such a living specimen that grew at least seven feet (2m) long and possessed a physique like a hairy hippopotamus. A short tail and powerful limbs helped Martin remember reading about an ancient rodent that was a member of the Pacarana family which was referred to as burrowing dinomyids or terrible mice of South America during the Late Miocene to Early Pliocene or from around 11,608,000 – 3,600,000 years ago. Martin knew that this particular life form looked and behaved just like a massive capybara and evolved to be among the largest rodents that ever lived in Earth's history. While the other explorers were impressed to see such an imposing presence, Martin activated his I.D. device before eventually seeing a picture of a ringleader of rodents known as *Telicomys*!

This powerful male's black fur with a gray tint patterned across his back illustrated a visual form of his current status of his group. His deep hissing provided additional clues as two other giant brown rodents peeked out from other crevices nearby. Martin suspected all three rhinoceros sized rodents, would most likely stand their ground and even attack if necessary. *Telicomys* showed no anticipation of retreat as all three males emitted a strange barking pattern toward the explorers. Fan only suspected that females and their young were most likely alerted and more maturing males could be mobilized to assert this situation.

Mack instantly learned how intelligent and socially active an ancient rodent species could be on prehistoric Earth and modern Isis. "Whoa...don't move any further ahead."

"They appear well organized." Marcus observed while all three males walked toward the explorers as other members of this group peeked out behind. "Let's move away slowly and quietly."

When all four adventurers made their wise decision to flee, the three males charged them for a short distance before they abruptly stopped before growling toward the sky. Mack peeked into his side view mirror and noticed all three pursuing males rapidly returning into their burrows. Mixed emotions riddled Mack's mind. He was grateful that *Telicomys* no longer wanted to pursue them, but was irritated to see a clear reflective silvery sphere hovering fifty feet (15.25m) directly above their position and realized that *Telicomys* fled from the spheres.

Mack twisted his waist and pivoted his shoulders toward his right side only to see this mysterious suspended object drift across the southern border of the meadow and continued to drift horizontally above the forest's upper tree lines. "Damn, I just saw it again!"

"Where did it go?" Marcus turned around in response to Mack's verbal reaction.

"It drifted over the southern woods."

Fan and Martin felt more nervous than their recent encounter with *Telicomys*. None of the explorers were able to identify these objects as they done with many life forms discovered. Mack suggested that someone must view the sky at all times while the others would monitor the immediate area for danger. Mack suspected that these spheres could out maneuver any modern plane or helicopter and he learned that such a phenomenon could attain an impressive air speed. Dr. Ryan dismissed the notion that these entities are living creatures of Isis's natural habitat and was evermore convinced that these objects must be technological in nature. Mack felt estranged to witness these objects behave unlike any known technology made on Earth.

"This is unreal." Dr. Nimbus remarked.

"We'll head south." Mack suggested.

"Mack, what's that near the woods?" Fan asked.

As Mack focused his attention to the area, Marcus recognized dog-like faces of these primates walking on all four legs across the open meadow. Their shaggy fur and flexible tail enabled four explorers to view them as a giant version of the Gelada baboon of Africa (*Theropithecus gelada*) that grew to match the size of a dominant male silverback gorilla!

"Wait a minute! This can't be!" Marcus replied after he pointed his Identification Detective to one of six massive males standing in front of twelve females holding their offspring under their stomachs. "Mack...I think we should flee."

"Why?"

"They're skeletal structure is similar to *Theropithecus brumpti* that lived at and around the Omo River in Ethiopia."

"You're kidding?" Mack was surprised.

"I remember Doctor Netherland told us that this species existed throughout the Late Pliocene." Marcus continued to describe how a group of Africa's bodacious baboons were able to climb trees and maneuver on piles boulders, logs and even termite mounts in Africa from around 3,600,000 – 2,588,000 years ago.

Mack noticed the males were massive and yet very colorful almost similar to a modern mandrill (*Mandrillus sphinx*) and most likely employed their facial and body décor to display their excellent health to potential mates. Despite their impressive size, he suspected they evolved a sleek physique under their thick layers of fur. Mack suspected this group of monkeys lived in harems, where a dominant male guides a group of females similar to modern baboons. He also suspected these baboons have evolved an advanced degree of social awareness and intelligence.

"Everybody flee!" Mack realized why Marcus advised everyone to retreat once he noticed each female darting into the woods with their offspring while six adult males charged vigorously toward him.

Marcus fled immediately before Martin and Fan departed. Mack needed to rotate his hovering craft before he would be able to accelerate forward. Once he initially moved ahead, he detected a loud bark from one of the pursuing males before he heard something scratch the rear of his transporter. Mack noticed his craft decelerate in speed once his transporter tilted back. He instantly turned his head and looked behind his seated position. Mack discovered a determined adult male attempting to maintain a steady balance on top of his rear trunk. This large male instantly flipped his upper lip up to expose his pink gums and sharp teeth.

Mack knew if this persistent male *Theropithecus* ever achieves balance then he would be in serious jeopardy. Mack instantly accelerated and made a sharp left turn so he could tip this male off balance. Mack's muscles twitched once he felt a stiff palm of this male's giant right hand grasp his right shoulder!

Mack instinctually leaned his body toward the right side of his Drifter unit and shifted his steering handlebars to make a sharp right turn before he no longer felt this threatening grip.

Slipping claws scraped the rear trunk when the giant baboon slipped off the rear of Mack's transporter. Mack heard a soft impact of four limbs landing on grass while accelerating at top speed. Additional relief was felt when he looked into one of two side view mirrors and noticed all six males retreating rapidly toward the bordering forest. He remembered that most species of baboons live in large groups of twenty individuals or more. Modern gelada baboons live the most complex social life of all baboons that could comprise of up to 700 individuals. Females are devout mothers while males that grow twice as large, would vigorously defend their group. If danger ever occurs then females would flee with their offspring while males would fight or attack. Mack was finally able to meet his colleagues once again. Mack thought about Dr. Marino's near encounter with a giant wolverine known as *Megalictis* and began to Lucy's concern of his safety in the mainland. He acknowledged his own near fatal incident, which he feared Lucy will discover.

"Did you see that? I was nearly ransacked by them."

"That was so close." Dr. Zhu replied with concern.

"Because of their sheer size, I felt like a child sitting next to them." Dr. Ryan added before he regained his full confidence of his safety and security.

Nobody was able to recognize any presence of life at the meadow except a large mammal walking out from behind a batch of trees and bushes. Marcus instantly noticed two rough horns, which grew stout branches covered with an outer layer of skin known as ossicones. He also saw a small pair of conical stubs emerge from on top of this male's head above each eye that was also cover with ossicones. Fan realized that a sloped neck made this adult appear like a massive okapi with horns that could stand at least seven feet or over two meters at the shoulder!

When Mack pointed his I.D. device and received data, he was surprised to see a life form similar to *Sivatherium* walking calmly across the field. After a near encounter with *Telicomys* and *Theropithecus*, Mack had no desires to neither antagonize nor provoke any aggressive response from this adult male. Their impressive fossils were discovered in northern India, particularly at the sub-Himalayas and were also found in Libya. *Sivatherium* existed from the Early Pliocene to the Late Pleistocene or from around 5,332,000 – 11,700 years ago. Both continents of Africa and Asia received sequential vibrations of patterned footsteps from a paramount plant eater roaming vast distances across rugged terrains. The name *Sivatherium* is derived from Shiva's Beast. Shiva also spelled as Siva, which is a principal Hindu deity.

"Let's be more careful this time." Mack smirked before maintaining a safe distance as they crossed in front of *Sivatherium*.

A sense of earning a break was greatly appreciated when this adult male maintained a peaceful posture by only staring at all four explorers. Martin and Fan didn't want to look back while Marcus didn't make a sound. Mack decided it would be best to employ peripheral vision as they moved away from this handsome herbivore that remained indifferent.

Although *Sivatherium* indulged into soft leaves, all four explorers continued applying their strategy of not provoking any unwanted response. Dr. Ryan then informed his crew. "We only have a short distance to reach a trail heading west."

Dr. Nimbus looked into the left side view mirror and noticed the giant herbivore strolling south. "Wonderful, he's moving away. I think we're safe."

Dr. Ryan slowly rotated his head left so he could verify Marcus's claim. Once he saw this magnificent male disperse, he instantly felt a sense of relief. "I'm glad that's over."

No danger was in sight as all four explorers headed south inside a wide trail where Alicia, Antonio and others traveled before. The crew scanned the area and found no sign of *Megalictis* or *Castoroides*. Actively looking at both sides of this trail, lizards, small mammals and birds reassured the crew of a calm and quiet landscape until they no longer heard anymore exchange of peaceful calls once they were one hundred yards (91.5m) before the next junction.

"Why's everything so quiet all of a sudden?" Marcus asked.

"Where did everything go?" Mack concurred, as he couldn't sense any living organism anywhere.

Fan and Martin continued to listen and visually search for any signs of activity. However, the crew heard intimidating sounds of belching and groaning accompanied by a deep pitch of air streaming through hollow passage tubes. As they approached the junction, additional sounds of clamps and crushing objects were detected by the crew.

Fan realized the origins of these unorthodox noises. "What ever it is must be originating from the right side of the junction straight ahead."

"What could it be?" Marcus wondered about such repulsive crushing and growling he detected.

Mack knew it was his duty to tell his companions to remain in place as he investigated what's behind the trees. Marcus insisted for him to be cautious.

All three individuals watched Mack drift over to this nearby junction where he would most likely find out what's causing such repulsive noise. He decided to move gently and quietly in order to remain undetected by whatever could be at the other side. Mack felt grateful for such a quiet transporter as he continued to approach the edge of the junction. Once he arrived near the end of this trail, he decided to move closer to trees that that bordered the trail.

"What is he doing?" Martin wondered as Mack rotated his transport unit until the front portion of his unit faced toward their direction.

"I think he learned his lesson with the giant baboons." Marcus suspected as he watched Mack climb off his transporter before he quietly walked over to the junction along bordering trees.

Neither one of three spectators wanted to shout out to him because they fear what ever is behind those trees would hear them as well and place their commander and colleague at severe risk. All three faithful friends waited patiently for his response once he peeked over the corner of dense woods that cloaked the source of these disturbing sounds. Once he established a direct sight of what caused such disturbing noise, his anatomical posture suddenly lost physical bearing, only his right arm frantically waved forward indicating an unmistakable sign of retreat due to a visually disturbing revelation.

Dr. Ryan's main concern was to remain elusive as he suspected that this source was able to detect his presence. He rapidly returned to his assigned transporter before accelerating relentlessly. Dr. Ryan's response was all that's needed to inspire others to follow.

"Let's get the heck out of here!" Dr. Ryan screamed out before deep impact vibrations of sequential footsteps along with a more rapid groaning."

"What was it?" Dr. Martin de' la' Vega asked.

Crewmembers heard bushes and trees tipping over, which caused Marcus to look back as he paced away. He was able to decipher an enormous skull, which were appeared heavy and possessed bone crushing teeth that matched the size of bananas. Two forward facing eyes appeared bird-like but the pupils and iris seemed identical to a salt water crocodile.

He noticed that this organism evolved tiny arms that couldn't even touch one another, but were compensated by two bulky legs capable of carrying up to eight tons or 7.2 metric tons of titanic terror. It was easy to notice how a massive, stiff tail was used to balance such a behemoth of a body that stood almost horizontal instead of an upright position. Both legs were unique because the thighbones were longer than the shins, which was adapted for long distance walking instead of sprinting. Although this particular life form didn't run, its considerable size enabled only a few steps to travel an impressive distance. Tiny arms and slow movement indicated this creature is an acute scavenger. However, once Mack noticed a bright red head and neck along with short spikes pattered along this female's back he realized this carnivore was noticeably capable of defending what he suspected to be a carcass laid out at the other side of the junction.

Her torso, legs and tail revealed a coordinated blend of short, black and brown individual hairs grown from her pink and gray skin. Mack and Marcus recognized shapes of her huge muscles swelling as they're being used as well as a pattern of veins and arteries revealing a complex circulatory system whenever tensions arise. The crew learned that *Tyrannosaurus rex* could utilize their horrific physical appearance along with their enormous size and an impressive amplification of verbal calls to inflict fundamental fear into any accomplished predator willing to defend their carcass, even if an efficient group of organized hunters attempt to defend it collectively. Any large *Tyrannosaurus rex* would confiscate carrion from more efficient hunters and would kill anything that dared to challenge this natural born bully's formal supremacy.

Dr. Ryan remembered Professor Robert T. Bakker, Ph.D. of the University of Colorado who's an adjunct curator of the University Museum and paleontologist John "Jack" R. Horner, Curator of the Museum of the Rockies in Colorado used their forensic investigative techniques to envision a new insightful perspective of dinosaurs' lifestyle and how their physical anatomy were comparable to modern life on Earth.

Dr. Ryan brought a copy of Professor Bakker's best selling book The Dinosaurs Heresies; New Theories Unlocking the Mystery of the Dinosaurs and Their Extinction™ with him to planet Isis. It revealed a startling new theory based upon many years of careful reexamination of past theories. Mack realized that his dedication and paleontological skills revealed a new perspective of the world of dinosaurs including *Tyrannosaurs rex*. Professor Bakker revealed how dinosaurs were much more intelligent and physically agile than older popular belief of dinosaurs being dimwitted, docile cold blooded life forms barely able to meet their basic demands of simple survival!

Dr. Ryan also reflected Paleontologist Jack Horner, who conducted extensive research at Hell's Creek, Montana to unravel the mysteries of the world's most recognized meat eating life form ever. Ever since Mack watched Valley of the T-Rex™, Walking with Dinosaurs™ and When Dinosaurs Roamed America™ on the Discovery Channel when he was a kid, he established a passion to explore a habitat like Isis. Jack Horner revealed startling clues of how this massive meat eating monster scavenged more like a modern vulture and confiscated carrion from smaller hunters similar to how lion prides would seize prey from wild dogs and hyenas.

Dr. Ryan recalled Dr. Netherland praising such brave pioneering scientists and anatomical engineers. Because of inspiring intellects who present their discoveries on the Discovery, the National Geographic networks Dr. Ryan developed a more accurate understanding of Isis's ecology, which would become an important contribution to this mission's success.

For the crew, it was difficult to stare at a horrendous looking creature with sticky saliva that could stretch from her upper to lower jaws, especially along her rear teeth. Her fluid saliva overlapped her jaw frame before dripping to the ground. Marcus recognized this watery saliva on the ground as a possible scent marking technique to claim and expand her territory and warn any possible intruders to stay away!

After her fourth step she then turned the corner and followed the crew's trail. She emitted a powerful and violent roar of rage accompanied by warm air flaring from deep within her interior. Once all four researchers were able to smell her warm breath, Mack and the others nearly became ill by smelling such a foul rotten malodor, which was barely tolerable by those who were most resilient to such a sickly stench.

"I can't take it anymore I'm going to vomit!" Dr. Martin de' la' Vega affirmed of his displeasure.

"Hang in there!" Dr. Ryan replied. "Once we get to the field the *T. rex* will turn away."

"I know we could out pace her! We'll be safe before you know it!" Dr. Nimbus reassured his colleagues.

Dr. Ryan knew this particular life form that's compatible to *Tyrannosaurus rex*, which means tyrant lizard, would be persistent in this chase. He also knew this female was capable of scaring away the most persistent rivals including other marauders of the same species. One reason is because this particular carnivore must be exceptionally hungry and was lucky enough to find such a welcoming feast. Another may have been that she's experienced rare resilience from more efficient hunters in order to confiscate this particular feast.

As patterns of footsteps began to recede, concern of the crew about a massive *Tyrannosaurus rex* was suddenly rescinded by what they saw directly ahead of them. Fear and tension mounted within their nerves as they saw an undesirable sight of a silvery sphere in the sky. This time, this object transformed its appearance that inflicted more fear and intimidation than ever!

"Mack! What the heck's going on?" Marcus screamed out when a once peaceful looking silvery reflective sphere instantly transform into a menacing black ball that the crew through it was an unnerving gesture of waging war!

"This doesn't look good at all!" Mack frightfully concluded as it approached their direction but was estimated to be 20 feet or over 6 meters above the ground.

Fan and Martin were petrified of how this dark black surface didn't reflect any light at all. Instead it appeared to be absorbing light, making it look somewhat like a visual black hole in the sky. All four crewmembers heard a rumbling vibration they've heard earlier. Only this time it was louder and emitted a deeper tone.

"Gentlemen, it's not pursuing us!" Mack shouted out. "It appears to be going after the *T. rex* behind us!"

Each individual jumped off their transporter once this strange object drifted 20 feet or over six meters above their heads as a passive response to prevent any physical contact with such an anomaly despite the object being too far above the ground to touch it by any means. Dr. Ryan's new concern since he avoided the object was to catch up to his unoccupied moving transport vehicle and prevent it from moving any further ahead from their position. As all four of them chased their slow moving idled units, none of them anticipated such an intense thundering outburst that riddled their nerves and vibrated their eardrums. The crew felt an aerial shockwave that caused them to fall.

Once Dr. Nimbus turned over, he noticed a once black surface transformed into a residual fireball with a molted surface that shifted in various directions. Deep shades of red, orange and strips of black made it appear like the sun's photosphere. Dr. Ryan noticed a glowing halo around the outer surface of this object, which appeared like the sun's corona. The crew heard another thunderous roar emitting from this object, which became louder than ever before. Dr. Ryan was surprised that no nearby trees ignited into flames.

"We have to catch up to our transporters." Mack suggested before running over to regain control of their assigned units.

After they got back on, it seemed that the fiery sphere and the *Tyrannosaurus rex* were gradually moving further away. Mack watched this object force the giant meat eater to move back until it reached the original trail where Mack discovered the giant dinosaur. Martin watched this strange object successfully intimidate the *T. rex* to back away. Once an estranged dinosaur retreated before it turned into the junction, it rapidly walked over to the carcass before clamping her powerful jaws into exposed meat before dragging it away from a persistent sphere, which calmly followed the agitated dinosaur.

When Fan scanned the junction after this tumultuous standoff occurred he noticed another sphere approaching them. Only this time its surface emitted a blue halo of light and showed a friendly expression of encouragement by emitting a subtle whistle similar to sparrows. "What the..."

Once Dr. Ryan's attention initially focused to Dr. Zhu's discovery, he felt even more disturbed even though this second sphere of similar size appeared to persuade the crew to follow it out of the area. "I think it wants us to move ahead."

"How could you be sure?" Dr. Nimbus wondered.

"It's moving toward us, and the other object clearly turned the corner after the *T. rex*, it wants us to pursue this trail straight ahead." Dr. Ryan answered.

"Come on, do you think that these things are trying to protect us?" Dr. Nimbus wondered.

"I think so, how else would you explain the fact that the first object forced the *T. rex* away from us?" Dr. Ryan argued.

"Personally, I can't think of any other reason for the first object to repel the dinosaur." Martin injected into their discussion. "Even though I don't have a clue why it would try to guard us, however, we should this fact for granted."

"I'll go first and remain ahead." Dr. Ryan assured the crew before everyone agreed to follow him.

Once everyone proceeded ahead, this beautiful blue display and whistling expression of peace and tranquility continued to gently persuade them to continue their course. When they arrived at the adjoining trail, Mack looked over to his right and noticed the first sphere hovering approximately one hundred and fifty feet (45.75m) away from their position. A faint but deep belching and growling from the first object, which turned black once again, injected more antagonism into *Tyrannosaurus rex*.

Mack was appalled to witness this visual black hole moving further away from their position while it continued to confront this carnivore further away from where all four explorers were positioned. Loud outcries from a resentful *Tyrannosaurus rex* never impose any intimidation nor harm to the dark sphere that continued to push the dinosaur further away.

"Let's get out of this area at once!" Mack affirmed before they darted ahead.

Each crewmember discovered why this *Tyrannosaurus rex* was so vigilant when they departed the area. It didn't require keen eyesight to witness a dead bipedal theropod dinosaur lying motionless on the grass. Mack noticed a pattern of diamond shaped spots printed on this male's down feathers. They ranged from his head to his tail and were most visible over his spine, while his stomach and throat was white. A light structural frame with short thighs and long shins also had large arms to grasp prey unlike the *T. rex*. Deep puncture marks of tyrannosaur teeth alignment were inevitable. He observed this 15 feet (4.5m) long male *Utahraptor* that became an unfortunate member of a group of skilled hunters, which were most likely the suspects responsible for the death of an animal that is now a mangled carcass. Despite sequential puncture marks across this predator's ribs, available evidence indicate that this sharp eyed cunning killer that lived 125 million years ago or within the Early Cretaceous, be able to grow 20 feet or over 6 meters long. *Utahraptor's* biology and physiology is generally synonymous to *Velociraptor* and *Deinonychus*.

However, Utah's plunderer commonly known as *Utahraptor* grew larger and was heavier than any of the raptors of the Mesozoic era that ranged from

225 – 65 million years ago. Once Dr. Ryan scanned the area for any possible danger, he felt it would be safe to pursue this trail to the end. He took no risks by ordering his crew to move full speed ahead. The crew was no longer concerned with their safety while they crossed the bay and reaching a safe haven.

While an excited group waited for their arrival, Dr. Ryan and his colleagues fear was replaced with joy and fulfillment when they traveled over green grass. Dr. Ryan remained puzzled of why these sentient spheres would intend to protect and guide the crew to safety. Mack's greatest concern is how to establish a formal communiqué or even a diplomatic relationship to the source that manifested these objects into physical reality, which he's barely able to accept. When the crew approached Town Hall, Mack thought about how such a mystery could be unsettling, discomforting and even disturbing. However, he arrived at his conclusion that denial never solved any known problem and that a persistent, unbiased and relentless investigation to unravel the truth of these spheres is the only solution.

Ancient Island

Lucy's stood on Town Hall Island and her dark brown eyes stared east into a sheltered bay to watch four explorers travel swiftly over the surface of the bay. She didn't recognize what happened to all four explorers returning until she noticed a dismal facial expression from Mack. She also discovered Fan's dismay as well as Martin's puzzled expression. She also recognized Marcus feeling unusually nervous.

Even when all four gentlemen boarded the island, none of them showed any signs of relief. Additional bafflement struck Lucy when all four of them passed by her without any form of acknowledgment whatsoever. "Mack! Mack!"

Lucy decided to inquire about their strange behavior by walking over to where they've stopped. Meena walked over to meet and escort Lucy to meet the returning crew. "Lucy, are you alright?"

"Not really, something must have happened to the crew."

While both women approached, all four men remained hovering on their transport units. Lucy remembered a robust Ryan who would rapidly climb off and either race up the front ramp or talk to anyone nearby. This time he staggered off and subconsciously stumbled away. Meena suddenly sympathized with Lucy once Marcus and the others slowly climbed off their units before walking aimlessly away. She also noticed all four Drifters were left unattended, without transporting them into storage bay or calling for an associate to park them.

Lucy activated her watchdog device to call four associates to steer all four unattended transport units into the hanger as she diligently watch Mack and three others walk over to a secluded area before sitting on the ground. As soon as four associates arrived to gain custody of all four unattended transport units, both women walked over to them to find out what caused each explorer to be in such a state of shock.

"Lucy, what do you intend to say to them?"

"I just want to find out what's wrong."

Lucy's quest for answers flourished as she approached them and failed to hear any verbal exchange of their experience. Both women noticed Mack focusing his attention to green grass while Marcus stared at the bay.

Meena shared her concerns as she failed to hear any talk about troubleshooting, exchange of ideas, or bragging about resolving potential challenges. She only saw four lamented individuals who appeared shocked or disturbed. Although none of the returning explorers appeared to suffer any physical injury, Lucy's suspected they're experiencing some form of stress. Their most challenging moment arrived when both women stood in front of them.

"Mack?" Lucy requested his attention.

Dr. Ryan sat on the grass with both feet rested flat on the ground. His knees pointed up, which enabled his elbows to rest on them. He eventually raised his head until he looked at her directly. She maintained her patience while Mack appeared dismal.

"What happened?" she wondered. "Why are you acting so strange all of a sudden?"

Marcus, Fan and Martin all silently looked over to Mack in order to find out what he'll say in response. "Strange?"

"Yes…strange?" Lucy added.

Mack lifted his eyebrows in response to her question. He used more time to speak than normal and Lucy noticed him stutter before he was able to complete his explanation.

"We're facing a very serious problem." Mack told her.

Lucy looked over to Meena wondering why Mack would make such a claim. Lucy then wanted to know more about what's troubling the crew. "What do you mean a serious problem?"

Mack appeared to feel a bit annoyed by her inquisitive demands, but he decided to reveal his story. "We were at a wide trail where Alicia and her crew surveyed earlier."

"Yes," Lucy encouraged Mack to explain further.

"Then…based upon our I.D. device, we saw a *Tyrannosaurus rex* eating carrion."

"You saw a *T. rex*?" Lucy responded.

"It wasn't the *T. rex* that concerned us."

Once Mack made his remark, both women wanted to know what possibly could frighten four explorers more intensely then a meat eating mongrel of the Mesozoic era. Lucy suspected Mack would never lie or create any hoaxes. "What did?"

"It was one of those damn objects."

"What do you mean? What happened?" Lucy cried.

Mack paused for a few seconds to regain his personal and professional stance and took his time to explain their recent encounter. "We have our data recorded. Since we encountered *Telicomys*, we grew suspicious of the nature of these things. It seemed to be sort of..."

"Sort of what?" Lucy wanted him to continue.

"It seemed to be watching out for us or trying to protect us."

Once Marcus revealed his observation, Meena had difficulty believing his claim. "Marcus, are you sure?"

Marcus looked over to Meena without any sign of humor; however he showed determination and unbridled support for Mack for he too believed that these objects provided protection. "Meena, he's not lying! We had a massive female *Tyrannosaurus rex* that killed an adult *Utahraptor* and was willing to sink her teeth into us. Suddenly from nowhere, one of these UFOs raced down toward it before it turned black and didn't reflect any light whatsoever."

"Turned black?" Meena asked. "You mean that it was like a black hole in the sky?"

"Exactly," Marcus responded. "It was one of the most frightening objects I ever saw in my life."

Lucy looked over to Fan before he raised his head and noticed her concern. "Fan, what did you encounter on the mainland?" Fan instantly provided his testimony by repeating everything Marcus and Mack told them.

"It appeared to follow us. I remember when we saw *Telicomys* at the edge of the meadow we could've been attacked but suddenly all three powerful males darted back into their burrows and crevices for no apparent reason until we noticed one of those spheres hovered over us as we fled the area."

"What happened with the *T. rex*?" Lucy asked.

"It was consuming carrion that was confiscated from a pack of raptors. Once this female detected us, she mistook us as a group of rival predators attempting to harass her, so she engaged into a short distance chase." Fan explained. "Once that happened I saw a reflective silvery sphere convert into a black one. What's strange was that no reflection of daylight emitted from the sphere; instead it appeared to have been absorbed.

Meena looked over to Martin who was still a bit shaken. She used her right hand to brace his left shoulder. Once he felt her hand, he then looked up and signaled his gratitude as he instantly felt personal relief. Immediately after, Martin stood up and looked back toward the Central Continent with added courage and confidence.

Mack continued to explain how it suddenly transformed itself into a mock molted surface that emitted a halo of light. He also discussed how despite the dinosaur's efforts to repel the object, it became even more aggressive toward the dinosaur. He revealed how it forced the *T. rex* around a corner into another junction before it continued to push the giant female further back.

Once the master of marauders was repelled, Mack told everyone that another sphere appeared and encouraged them to move ahead by turning blue and chirping like a sparrow. Lucy and the other women were shocked to hear such a story from four distinguished gentlemen who continued to feel a bit of shock of how their lives were saved from an unknown phenomenon. Mack also addressed the fact that he made numerous attempts to use his Identification Detective device to access any information regarding the composition of these objects…but failed.

Lucy had no idea such an event could ever take place. Angela felt nervous because she was convinced that a sentient intelligence that's compatible or even more advanced than humanity's interacted with the crew. Ying thought how early ancestors of human history could develop an impression of sympathetic gods or angels rescuing humans in dire need. Mack reflected the times he rebuffed stories, legends and folklore that reveal early humans encountering such an inexplicable phenomenon. Lucy and Meena were shocked of such physical abilities beyond their scientific explanation and behaved as a benevolent guardian by protecting the explorers from extreme danger.

Meena was impressed of such physical ability and ingenuity. She suspected that such unprecedented abilities in part of these strange entities could only pose limited possible scenarios of their true origins. Although she wasn't convinced that it could be an indigenous, biological inhabitant of Isis; Meena clearly understood these objects were produced by exceptionally talented creators. She suspected that these objects could be developed where scientific applications could match or even surpass known human technological ability.

Lucy decided that since these objects appeared friendly, she desired to emphasize this fact. "Mack, maybe we have to come to a realization that whatever they are, at least these things behaved benevolently. They weren't obligated to save anyone from an irritated *Tyrannosaurus rex*. Not to mention, it never attempted any harm to you. Our best choice is to accept this coexistence!"

"Coexistence?" Mack wondered.

"Yes," Lucy answered. "We could learn a lot from them and if these objects are from a society other than ours then it's our duty as federation members to pursue diplomatic relations."

Meena supplemented Lucy's suggestion. "Gentlemen, we can't deny the facts. These objects appear to possess a rational intelligence. Maybe we're experiencing a new phase of human history. Not only being an interstellar civilization, but we could possibly be in contact with an unknown society?"

Mack raised his eyebrows and bit his upper lip softly. He then took a deep covert breath before he responded. "Whew...I never though I'll ever be involved with a mission remotely like this. But someone has to command it and it will be me."

Mack rose from his sitting position on the ground as a gesture of him willing to fulfill his role within humanity and the universe. Marcus then stood up and was equally determined to handle such challenges. Fan also stood up and decided he will accept this task like none he's ever experienced. An injection of energy and relief struck Martin as he felt reassurance from his close colleagues.

Mack's communicator activated once he regained confidence. The device vibrated before four prongs extended out before a hologram of Dr. Daryl Hollis from the orbital starship that ultimately became a space station of planet Isis. *"Doctor Ryan, come-in please, Doctor Ryan."*

"This is Doctor Ryan."

"I received some intriguing data from the central region of the Western Continent."

"Who discovered this data?"

"Doctor Tyrell's team discovered a chain of islands located alongside the equatorial region west of the Western Continent However, there's one large island that contained strange data. Doctor Tyrell suggested that this area reflects how the Earth and even Isis appeared during their earliest stages of life."

"Interesting," Mack felt intrigued.

"What's more intriguing is what we found on this island. "Doctor Hollis revealed before he continued. "If you go to the Clairvoyance room, I'll transmit this data called Ancient Island."

"Ancient Island?"

"Yes...this name is perfect for this location Doctor Tyrell utilized the latest edition of the Diver submarine model to obtain this data." Dr. Hollis explained.

"We'll pursue upstairs. Thanks again." Mack replied.

"My pleasure, I'll talk to you soon." Dr. Hollis responded before Mack's communicator deactivated.

"Everyone, guess what?" Mack announced. "Dr. Hollis informed me that a brilliant discovery has been made at the Western Continent. He told me of the latest findings is included in this new data sent to the Clairvoyance room.

"Great!" Lucy became excited. "We made some discoveries ourselves.

After we view the Western Continent, we'll show what the Dove and Condor planes revealed.

All six scientists and engineers used a stairwell and walked up two flights until they reached level five. Their desired location wasn't far and not much time passed by once they entered a domed room. After everyone entered, the door was closed and each individual sat near the center.

"Everybody ready?" Mack asked.

Once he received encouragement, he then requested for the system to activate before he asked for "Ancient Island."

A usual process of a ceiling light deactivating before a clear image of a barren shore appeared before their view. Enclosed of an audio and visual illusion of a place where a collection of accretionary structures that appeared like rough stones that stood above the water's surface. Marcus remembered such sentiment formations erected by microorganisms. Although these structures rose up to three feet or almost one meter high and were one foot or over 30 centimeters wide this collection of modern stromatolites reveal an insight of the earliest forms of life on Earth and most likely on Isis. As he continued to study this strange shore, Marcus realized these structures were a reason why life forms on Earth emerged including humans.

"If I understand it correctly, these sediments contain some of the most fundamental life forms on this planet and reflect how life on Earth began." Marcus claimed.

Mack realized. "Oh yeah...I remember Dr. Netherland's lecture about these sediments. Isn't it true that bacteria assemble these mounts so they would be able to climb higher and closer to the water's surface so they could receive more sunlight?"

"Definitely!" Marcus supplemented. "The sole reason would be to be able to receive a greater amount of nutrients from the sun. The more sunlight both life forms received, the more nutrients and better opportunities to reproduce and they'll ultimately produce oxygen. Early life forms didn't even need oxygen; they actually produced it for the first time in Earth's natural history."

Fan and Martin noticed pools of hot springs and mud pots at the shore of a volcanic island. Steam subtly rose from an extremely hot surface of water that seemed though the cracks of Isis's crust. Water would descent down for miles until an evaporating force of magma beneath the surface forces it back up. Fumaroles or thermo underwater vents emit vaporized water from deep underground. All such ventilation of Earth and Isis's surface enables to prevent more violent eruptions from active volcanoes and provide an ideal environment for thermophilic bacteria, which thrives in extreme environments such as water as hot as 185 degrees Fahrenheit or 85 degrees

Celsius. Although it appeared fruitless, everyone knew that places such as Ancient Island became an ideal environment for life to emerge.

"Mack couldn't believe such a setting similar to some areas in Yellowstone National Park in Wyoming. "What we're viewing is a trace of how it all began on Isis as well as Earth."

Lucy wrapped her arms around his upper back and rested her left hand on his shoulder and pressed her cheek against his shoulder. "That's why we're all here."

Fan acknowledged such enormous significance of life forms such as blue-green algae or bacteria produced oxygen for animal plankton to emerge, which ultimately inhabited the entire Earth. "It's amazing how life forms could thrive in an environment that would be deadly to us."

Martin looked over to Fan and agreed. "What's even more fascinating is that there are many other kinds of bacteria that could survive various other types of harsh environments."

"Tell me more?" Fan requested.

"Have anyone ever heard of psychrophile bacteria?"

Meena joined into their discussion with her knowledge of such intriguing life. "I have, these bacteria enjoy an extremely cold environment such as the Arctic and Antarctic circles and thrive in near frozen water."

"You're kidding me?" Fan felt surprised.

"I was shocked to find out myself," Meena confirmed.

"Believe it or not, modern stromatolites, like their ancient counterparts, currently rise slowly above warm shallow waters of the Sea of Cortez in Mexico and elsewhere." Martin stated.

"Wow, as far as I know, all such bacteria are part of group called Archaebacteria, which is capable of surviving the worst environments imaginable, it most likely conduct an important role for the Carbon and Nitrogen cycle of Earth and Isis." Mack revealed fascinating information of such dynamic abilities of ancient life. He knew that without such vital microscopic life, it would be impossible for any complex life to exist on Earth and Isis including humans.

Suddenly, a new scene viewed by a mini-submarine known as Diver searching underwater. A variety of early sea plants were common. However, when a pink and white vertebrate swam across their view, each spectator was captivated. Mack noticed a pair of antennae mounted on top of its head like a snail. Marcus recognized a vertebrae pattern from head to tail. The others recognized this life form to be exactly what one was like during the Middle Cambrian or approximately half a billion years ago at Burgess Shale inside British Columbia, Canada.

American paleontologist Charles Doolittle Walcott discovered this fossil preserve site as he crossed a ridge between Mount Field and Mount Wapta. Once he noticed a fossilized pattern on hard shale, he instantly recognized its paramount significance to science. Similar to how all eight spectators noticed how important this species known as *Pikaia gracilens* is to all vertebrae. All life that has a spinal chord exist because of *Pikaia* or a closely related relative of this species gave rise to all living things that evolved a spinal chord!

As this mild mannered life form swam away from their view, Mack realized that if this specimen and others like it ever became extinct then the Earth would ultimately be predominated by invertebrates such as arthropods on land and mollusks in water. He also realized humans would never emerge and possibly an emergence of an alternate sentient intelligence to give rise to a collective civilization of insectoid beings. Mack appreciated his understanding that no extant species anywhere in the universe is in command of evolution and there's no predetermined disposition for any species in existence.

"Eve number three," Lucy suddenly called out.

Once she made her announcement, the underwater scene tuned off and casted the crew in temporary darkness before viewing a stunning array of steppes.

Oak and maple trees accompanied by some patches of pine trees indicated that a northern environment. A cool breeze of lowering temperatures was sympathized by all. Insects randomly flew across their view of sporadic trees and bushes randomly placed on top of tall grass. A temperature gage within a floor plate revealed a scene at 60 degrees Fahrenheit or over 15 degrees Celsius, which showed early signs of autumn.

Mammals that appeared like squirrels and chipmunks collected walnuts and kernels to bury or hide for future consumption during the winter when food supplies are scarce. Birds flexed their wings and cleared feathers of debris as their final preparation before they engage into a long flight across the entire Central Continent to migrate south before colder weather would settle for months.

As they viewed such a timid tale of winter coming, it was apparent that everyone noticed something moving behind a batch of bushes. All they could notice was a gorgeous array of black, gray and white fur patterned along a bulky physique. Lucy was able to detect pair of sapphire blue eyes within a canine shaped head. Marcus was able to notice a puffy black and white tail standing upright as an expression of excitement.

"Whoa...It's beautiful!" Lucy stated as a heavily built wolf walked out from behind a tall batch of bushes.

Mack noticed two more wolves emerge from behind the same batch. "Wow! Look at them! They all look superb."

Three more handsome individuals manifested to form a group of six. Two appeared to be a dominant couple consisting of a socially dominant male and female. The others appeared younger. Although they mostly resemble wolves, Mack was curious to find out what particular species all six canine creatures resembled.

Mack requested an information tabloid to appear on the floor, which were brown and displayed yellow inscriptions. Since all Eve probes were equipped to identify life forms, Mack instantly realized that they were looking at a pack of Dire wolves known as *Canis dirus* that lived in North and South America throughout Earth's last Ice Age or the Pleistocene epoch that ranged from 2,588,000 – 11,700 years ago.

Marcus reflected his childhood years in Los Angeles when his parents took him and his siblings to the Rancho La Brea tar pits to see fossils of the Dire wolf. Natural oil deposits in ancient California dried up to become death traps where large herbivores such as the ground sloth and woolly mammoth would accidentally fall into a tar pit and would die from famine or exhaustion. Some predators would take advantage by tackling easy prey trapped inside these pits, only to face a similar fate.

Every animal caught into this trap eventually sank under the tar pools before resurfacing many years later. Museum curators and staff members would recover perfectly preserved remains for assembly and study. Marcus remembered witnessing ancient specimens emerge during his family visit at the tar pits where he originally learned about the Dire wolf and many other Tertiary era mammals. Since his parents took him to see various exhibits, Marcus developed a curiosity for science. During his grammar school years, his teachers also took his class to Rancho La Brea and other places where he discovered more specimens, which reinforced his passion for exploration.

It became evident that all six members of this pack will disperse once they rested and regained their energy. Once the dominant male stood on his feet, the other five members of this pack followed suit before all six individuals continued to survey the area. Marcus continued to reflect his childhood memories while reading a printed tabloid that revealed these wolves grew at least five feet or over 1.5 meters long. He also read various differences between the Dire Wolf and the extant Grey Wolf (*Canis lupus*) of North America. Both species coexisted for roughly 100,000 years.

Who wants to view Eve number four? It should be at the center of the Central Continent." Mack asked.

Once Dr. Ryan received an encouraging response, he then verbally requested "Eve number four" before a new image appeared that propelled them into a realistic but eerie collection of lifeless trees and embittered grass. Mack realized this region to be fruitless and exceptionally tense as he observed a group of mammoths approaching cautiously. While Mack studied the heard, the crew was interrupted by a spontaneous manifestation of two powerful looking predators from behind their projected view.

"Whoa! I didn't even notice them?" Marcus shifted around as a subconscious gesture of being taken by surprise.

All six spectators shared Marcus's feelings as they heard belching vibrations originating from both predators. Marcus noticed that although they had short stocky legs, both creodonts were able to stand six feet (1.83m) at the shoulder and use their necks to raise their heads over seven feet or over 2.1meters above the ground. Mack noticed a species called *Sarkastodon mongoliensis* grew at least 10 feet or (3m) long and weigh at least one ton or roughly 908 kilograms.

While Fan read another tabloid illustrated on the floor, he also realized that this particular species were part of the Oxyaenid family. Meena noticed enlarged claws at end of both front limbs as she initially became annoyed by such a deep goggle from both predators watching the heard approach.

Marcus continued to monitor both carnivores as they displayed their enormous teeth. They appeared fierce due to their black fur around their legs and underside and longer gray fur on top of their heads, back and tail. From stored data he read and seeing such a surreal sight, Marcus conceived *Sarkastodon* to appear like a gigantic ratel (*Mellivora capensis*) of Africa and Asia.

"Everyone, these mammoths are identified as *Mammuthus trogontherii* of England and Germany around one million years ago or during the Middle Pleistocene." Martin revealed.

"You mean the Steppe mammoth?" Mack asked.

"Yes, they appear much larger than the Woolly mammoth we watched earlier." Meena was propelled to watch an image of a monumental mammoth with momentum.

An accompanying old male carried a pair of elongated tusks that curved horizontally forward until both tips horizontally criss-crossed directly in front of the bottom of his foreboding face extended almost 17 feet (5.2m) long. As he led this group closer Mack realized that he was able to stand at least 15 feet (4.5m) tall before he lowered his head and aimed his elongated ornamentation toward the two intruders.

"This doesn't appear encouraging." Lucy acknowledged as both creodonts demonstrated their defiance when the male raised his long bushy tail and rattled its black and gray fur in defiance to the giant male mammoth's warning.

Once this old bull male mammoth realized his message was in rebuttal, his short tempter and mutual intolerance of both giant predators provoked him to charge against the defiant male creodont. Dr. Ryan was startled, but

impressed to see a 10 ton or a 9 metric ton male mammoth move with agility as his testosterone level surged. As he charged toward the male *Sarkastodon*, the creodont displayed his massive teeth before he positioned himself to attack the charging male *Mammuthus trogontherii* that positioned his enormous tusks just before they connected to the male creodont's upper chest and lower neck.

Fan and Martin were amazed to see how two carefully aimed tusks could lift the one ton predator off the ground and tossed the giant male 10 feet or 3 meters from his original position. Meena recognized the female creodont to be more vigilant than previously expected when she attacked the giant mammoth by biting the adult bull under his abdomen between at the mammoth's left side. The crew felt exacerbated to hear a powerful instantaneous scream from the male mammoth before his pain subsided by his relentless range. Lucy felt intimidated to watch a mammoth's xenophobic zeal as he launched a counter attack against a tenacious truant.

The Steppe mammoth maneuvered until he was able to position his curved tusks under the rebellious female creodont's chest. Spectacular strength was shown when everyone inside the domed room witnessed *Sarkastodon* airborne until the female landed on her right side. She instantly stood back on her feet once again.

"I'm surprised the female isn't injured." Martin realized as this tough female creodont retreated as her larger male companion resented what he saw by racing over to the Steppe mammoth in order to bite him on his front right limb.

Once his teeth penetrated the mammoth's limb, the male mammoth instantly activated his inherited aggressive drive to swing his trunk and jab his tusk against the monstrous marauder of ancient Mongolia. Lucy felt nauseous to see a giant male carnivore be kicked persistently by an avenging mammoth. Fan and Marcus though the male *Sarkastodon* would incur serious injury especially when two female mammoths joined this standoff to reinforce the herd's efforts to repel the gigantic predators. Mack was impressed to learn to discover a carnivorous mammal that grew larger than an adult Black rhinoceros (*Diceros bicornis*) with a body shaped like a wolverine and fur patterns like a ratel. Lucy reinforced her imminent concerns for Mack's safety by holding a firm grip around his arm as both creodonts retreated by bobbling backwards, rattling their bushy tails as they growled and grumbled.

Mack's Watchdog device activated once again. This time it was Dr. Derrick Grace. *"Doctor Ryan, come-in please."*

"This is Dr. Ryan."

"We have two of those flying objects hovering near the western shore of this bay."

252

"For how long?"

"*They just arrived.*"

"Prepare a transport unit right away." Mack ordered. "I'm on my way down."

"What happened?" Lucy asked.

"We have two of those objects at the eastern edge of the bay."

Once Mack revealed what Dr. Grace told him, Lucy then provided her verbal command to deactivate the Clairvoyance projector before everyone followed him down two flights of stairs to reach the main deck. Two technicians prepared a transport unit for Mack before he climbed on.

"Wait! I'm coming with you too." Marcus said before he requested a unit for himself.

"If both of you are investigating then I should inquire about these objects as well." Meena then requested her unit before Lucy said the same to both technicians.

Soon after, three other units were prepared as Mack waited. Once all three individuals inspected each unit, Mack received their reassurance before all four proceeded down the ramp. It became inevitable for all four explorers to see two spherical objects hovering parallel next to each other at the same altitude.

Once they reached the shore of their inhabited island, Mack advised his colleagues to stay behind him, as they'll approach with caution. Dr. Ryan reduced speed as they closed in on their distance. So far no abrupt response occurred in part of the both hovering spheres. The last thing Dr. Ryan wanted to do was to provoke a conflict, especially when Town Hall was nearby and could possibly be attacked as an added consequence. While the crew monitored both spheres, nobody was able to hear any sound emitting from either one of these objects.

Once they were positioned 250 feet (76.25m) away from both objects. Dr. Ryan decided to decelerate. Dr. Nimbus drifted slowly over to Dr. Ryan's left side.

"Mack."

"What?"

"These objects appear to be studying *Deinosuchus*."

"If so, then they could be surveying this entire planet." Once Dr. Ryan made his remarks, both objects drifted over the mainland and proceeded to move further east.

Dr. Ryan told his colleagues; "Let's follow them quietly and look out for *Deinosuchus*."

Dr. Ryan kept a keen eye towards both objects while Dr. Nimbus monitored surrounding water as an assurance that no giant crocodile would make any attempts to ambush the crew. Dr. Singh and Dr. Rosalila drifted behind two curious men. Once they arrived at the mainland, Dr. Ryan noticed one object followed the other inside a grassy trail.

"They entered this trail." Mack pursued this trail while the others followed him.

Once Dr. Ryan arrived at the trail's entrance, he was no longer able to see any of the objects. "Damn it…they're gone."

"We could take this trail that leads to an opening. Maybe we could find them there." Marcus suggested before they entered the trail and headed east.

"Okay, I'll look for the flying objects while everyone else should look for any danger." Mack suggested as they continued.

Scattered trees and bushes along with an open field would be their likely destination. This particular area wasn't covered completely by elevating trees or a canopy of branches and leaves. All four explorers were aware of a partly cloudy sky during a warm afternoon. They also monitored trees, bushes, shrubs and tall grass, which occupied less than one quarter of this area's terrain. While Mack continued to search for strange entities, Meena discovered a ferocious creature that appeared like a warthog, feasting on a disfigured carcass that appeared dead for over a day.

She felt uneasy by this male scavenger's crocodile shaped muzzle attached to two large bony knobs that swelled under each eye. She believed each knob consisted of a port that connects their upper jaw muscles. "What the hell is that?"

Once Marcus focused his attention to her discovery, he instantly recognized that this adult male appeared much like a prehistoric member of the Entelodont family, which is a distant relative of wild pigs. However, this particular individual grew as large as a full grown cow with elevated shoulders, a powerful neck and dark shaggy bristles on top of his head, neck and shoulders. Although this male's fur appeared gray, Marcus noticed a striped pattern of black laced across his back and legs. He also noticed a large pair of ears constantly shifting as a method to detect intruders.

Lucy felt surprised to discover how capable this male scavenger was when he tore flesh and used his rear molars to crush bones. She estimated this adult male to weigh at least 500 pounds or 225 kilograms! Since Mack continued to search for metallic spheres, Lucy felt it was her obligation to inform him. "Mack, look at that over there."

Mack recognized this genus to be *Archaeotherium* that means ancient beast, which evolved a physique similar to a buffalo rather than a modern pig. Since Dr. Netherland's lectures, he knew such an affirmed existence could eat virtually anything from roots to rotten meat. "Let's move away very carefully."

As the crew attempted to evade the area, *Archaeotherium* detected the crew before his dark eyes monitored their movement. Since this male was hungry, he became more vigilant to defend this hard to find carrion. His shaggy bristles suddenly rose several inches or centimeters and stood firm as his shoulders swelled. All four of his feet braced, while both ears faced forward at their direction and moved in accordance to the crew's movement across his view. As each explorer took every precaution to prevent an accidental provocation, *Archaeotherium* spontaneously shifted his attention toward his left side when another fierce entelodont approached.

This intruder possessed a similar physique but was beige instead of gray with random, odd shaped black markings. This formidable foe grew ten feet (3m) long, which was almost two feet or nearly 60 centimeters longer than *Archaeotherium* and stood almost six feet or nearly two meters at the shoulder! Although this other male's bony knobs were similar than his counterpart, he possessed a noticeably thicker and heavier muzzle. Instead of bristles, it appeared that such an imposing intruder possessed a mane around his neck shoulders, which individual hairs were either black or gold that showed off a mixed tinge of both colors.

He belonged to the same family group as *Archaeotherium* and both males evolved two toes on each foot similar to bulls. It took more time for Dr. Ryan to accept his visual fact than identifying this invader as *Dinohyus hollandi* also named *Daeodon*. This male revealed a set of heavy teeth capable of an omnivorous diet from roots to rotten meat. Mack remembered his nightmare as he saw *Dinohyus* enter the open pasture before making his first attempt to attack *Archaeotherium*.

"Mack, are they carnivorous?" Lucy observed.

"As carnivorous both of them could be, neither species are active hunters." Mack informed his colleagues.

"You're kidding?" Meena replied.

"*Archaeotherium* and *Dinohyus* are both omnivores and they'll eat almost anything they could find just like wild boars."

Once Meena heard Mack's revelation, she noticed *Dinohyus* open his powerful jaws before emitting a gutting sound. The larger intruder bit *Archaeotherium* at his left loin. "Huh…they don't look much like simple minded scavengers to me."

Swift action in part of *Archaeotherium* saved his rear leg from being seriously wounded. The original occupant of the carrion fled from *Dinohyus*. While the crew continued to be cautious, Marcus noticed the larger marauder engage into a feeding frenzy by gobbling up the carcass as relentlessly as any animal could. Suddenly and without warning the original smaller scavenger clamped his powerful jaws into the right rear leg of his rival.

Lucy and Meena felt disturbed by a low frequency squeak as the larger male suspended his feverish feast and focused his attention to the source of his agitation. Lucy was shocked to see such a bitter relationship between two species of the same family of Entelodonts. She acknowledged how such a daunting circumstance of scarcity could bring out the worst of any life form on Isis as well as Earth. Once *Archaeotherium* lost his grip, *Dinohyus* used every bit of energy to ignore his wound when he chased his attacker.

Rapid echoes of even toed feet thumping on grass proved that both were as agile as cattle as this chase continued. Elongated bristled hair of both prehistoric omnivores raced back as they paced across scattered woodland. What troubled the crew was that patches of tress and bushes blocked their full view of this intense standoff. The crew's concern flourished once they noticed *Archaeotherium* running toward them while *Dinohyus* pursued his rival from behind.

"They're heading straight for us." Mack shouted out once he realized that the crew must disperse or be run over by two massive entelodonts. A steady breeze cloaked the crew's faces as all four of them accelerated. Everyone heard snarling and heavy patterned footsteps that intensified in volume as both inhabitants became dangerously close to the explorers.

"Hurry, they're gaining on us!" Lucy was positioned at the rear of the convoy, urged everyone to accelerate when she heard feverish panting from behind her right side.

"This way!" was Mack's reply as he noticed an open field where they could sprint ahead of a neighboring batch of trees.

All four explorers veered right before passing a batch of bushes. Once she looked at her right shoulder, she saw *Archaeotherium* and *Dinohyus* were far behind and were too busy fighting each other to pay any attention to a group of fleeing scientists. Tensions eased as frightful sounds of snarling and guttering dissipated. Lucy felt a welcome relief as she's no longer threatened by this relentless chase.

"I'm gland we've escaped." Lucy couldn't be anymore happier to avoid being caught in the middle of a conspicuous clash that could've placed her in jeopardy.

Lucy's lips tightened and her eyebrows sank as she thought about what she told Mack during their first evening on planet Isis. She didn't forget about how easy it was to be injured or even killed without any warning. Lucy reflected each discovery that could've been responsible for their tragedy. When the crew arrived at a junction they pursued the path directly ahead. This trail eventually led them to a wide panorama of a meadow; the crew felt relief to enter a docile area until Mack noticed something massive emerge from a trail at the other side of the meadow.

What a sight to behold when a heard of sauropods migrated into the open field. Dr. Ryan felt compelled to see a walking mountain of mass standing up to five stories tall gently walking over to a group of trees. Elongated necks mounted diagonally up in reminiscent to a giraffe while a stiff horizontal tail maintained their physical balance. Their thick leathery hides were dark gray and were imprinted with a recognizable pattern of stripes. Both migratory giants' front legs were longer than their rear.

Dr. Nimbus suspected this living specimen resembled a familiar legend that traveled exceptionally long distances required to fulfill a vast appetite. The word sauropod actually means lizard foot in Greek because of fossil formations of their feet. However, steady support of such massive bodies required a spongy insulation under their heels and toes, similar to what make it possible for modern African elephants (*Loxodonta africana*) to roam across the open plains of the savannah without physical stress. Marcus identified both gigantic sauropods as *Brachiosaurus*, which were among the largest life forms ever to walk on land.

"I thought I'll never see them alive," Dr. Lucy Rosalila expressed while both towering giants devoured leaves from each tree of a large congregation.

"What do you know about *Brachiosaurus?*" Lucy asked.

"During the Late Jurassic, *Brachiosaurus* roamed across North America and Africa. Would you believe that adults could grow up to 75 feet long and over 40 feet tall?" Dr. Ryan estimated they were over 23 meters long and over 12 meters tall.

"Judging what I'm seeing, it's not difficult to agree. Besides, older adults could weigh up to ninety tons!" Dr. Ryan knew that 81 metric tons was needed to emit a deep toned howl as they continued to move across scattered woodland.

Once the giant male sauropod sent his message across vast distances, both of them scented their desired destination when they heard a response signal from other distant sauropods. As this migration continued, each researcher noticed their necks waddle back and forth in conjunction to each step. The crew observed their tails moved in unison to their necks to counter balance their entire physique and prevent the weight of the head and neck to tip them over.

Meena suddenly felt discomfort as her back became stiff. Although she was amazed to see *Brachiosaurus*, an unexpected intuition called for concern as hair from her neck erected and pores rapidly released body heat. She subconsciously looked into her left side view mirror that reflected a justifiable reason why she experienced such unprecedented tension.

Shock ravaged her nerves once she saw two completely black eyes looking back! Both eyes showed a cold expression along with a massive head that measured at least three feet (1m) long that grew enlarged canines. Only a head that could reach two feet (60.1cm) wide evolved a formidable jaw along with a wide muzzle. Standing almost six feet (1.83m) at the shoulder and weighing at least a ton (908kg). This male creodont's black fur added more intimidation to an already shaken scientist.

"Everybody flee!"

Dr. Singh leaned forward as anticipation for her body to jolt back as she twisted the right handle similar to how a contender would start a motorcycle race. However, this particular race would include a specific outcome of whether she would live or die.

Her companions were faithful to her call and complied with her warning. Her colleagues were grateful of Meena's acute senses and her desire to contribute to their collective survival. Such selfless qualities reflected similar characteristics of all 1500 astronauts and cosmonauts who've settled on this new world. As they continued to flee, Dr. Nimbus looked over to his right shoulder before he noticed sets of grooved nails similar to a rhinoceros. He ran on short but powerful legs necessary to support his massive 13 feet (4m) long physique!

"Hurry," was Dr. Ryan's verbal response to what resembled his nightmare of when he saw a similar looking compulsive killer with a set of massive white teeth. "Everyone, stay at my right side! I'll try to repel him as long as possible."

"Mack what the hell you're doing?" Dr. Nimbus shouted.

"I'll distract him so you could flee...hurry!"

"Mack, don't do anything dumb." Dr. Nimbus warned.

"I'll maintain a steady distance while identifying it."

Dr. Ryan was physically positioned to this carnivore's right side, which gave him an opportunity to verify his suspicion by pointing his Identification Detective device toward this persistent giant. Once a match was made, Dr. Ryan didn't like the outcome of what his device identified.

Dr. Ryan gasped as he read *Megistotherium osteothlastes* on the screen along with an image and details of what terrorized Libya and Egypt during the Miocene epoch (23,023,000 – 5,332,000 years ago) by hunting some of the largest herbivores including mastodons and most likely confiscated carrion from other smaller, more efficient hunters. *Megistotherium* was formerly named by Dr. Robert J. G. Savage in 1973 after he found and classified fossils of this behemoth of a beast! Dr. Ryan instantly viewed his nightmare to be an insightful warning of possible scenarios he could encounter along with his faithful constituents.

"Keep moving ahead, while I'll distract it." Mack commanded before he raced diagonally across the creodont's line of sight.

Meena thought about what made it possible for her to discover this creodont before being ambushed from behind. She thought about her intuition or her subconscious or perhaps a divine intervention. She even thought about extrasensory perception or even cosmic consciousness. Whatever the source or combination of sources, Meena discovered it took more than talent and skills to ensure success as well as survival. All four transporters also made it possible to out pace *Megistotherium* as everyone looked into their side view mirrors to find out that they were far ahead of what could've ended Meena's life.

"I'm grateful we escaped." Dr. Ryan felt reassurance.

The further away they separated from *Megistotherium*, the closer they approached both sauropods walking approximately three miles or over 4.8 kilometers per hour. As they approached these dinosaurs with caution, everyone felt hollow as they were near this courtship of towering giants whose shoulders stood over 20 feet or over 6.1 meters above the ground! Modern paleontologists suspect that *Brachiosaurus* didn't run but could only walk. Since all an adult needed was their enormous size to discourage and fend off any potential attack from predators, there was no need for an ability to sprint away from trouble. Another reason was because these massive herbivores were armed with thick hides, which would be difficult for predators to penetrate their teeth and claws into their hides that could cause any sufficient injury. Layers of tough flesh that protected their precious veins and arteries were an additional benefit for them. Members of this group were able to kick or even step on any intruder.

Faint thumping vibrations were noticeable once four explorers were positioned near this pair of dinosaurs that could raise their necks as high as a five story building! Dr. Rosalila recognized a disrupted pattern of heavy breathing for which she suspected that one of the sauropods detected them by scent. As she looked up, the female was looking down to them but was not alarmed. However Lucy remained nervous.

"Mack! Let's move away. One of them is staring at us."

Once Dr. Ryan noticed the male *Brachiosaurus* monitoring their movement, he told the crew not to interfere in their courtship, which was why he led his colleagues away form the sauropods. As they steered further away from this group, nobody had any difficulty hearing low pitched howls from two sauropods. Such a reverberating sound felt as though it resonated across the entire region. As threatening it sounded, Dr. Singh looked back before she noticed that the courtship continued and neither one of the sauropods maintained any interest in four fast moving strangers they never encountered before.

"Sounds like the gods are calling out." Dr. Singh commented as they continued to pursue their direction.

As they moved on, the crew noticed a group of duck billed dinosaurs grazing directly ahead. These life forms appeared to have a single short erected snout mounted on top of their heads that pointed toward the rear. Each member of this group grew two large rear legs and two smaller front limbs. With the exception of walking, their two front limbs appeared to serve an additional purpose of achieving balance during feeding. Their color and pattern were gorgeous as each one showed off their yellow base that was covered by large white spots over their head, back, legs and stiff tail. The white crest mounted at the rear of their heads displayed a thin black stripe on each side. What's most interesting is a noticeable notch on his backbones directly behind each male's shoulders. Such notches were naturally designed to place or rest the tip of their crest so their necks could form an 'S' shape pose in order to improve their dynamics when they sprinted on their two rear legs.

Dr. Singh and Dr. Rosalila noticed females possessing shorter crests than their male counterparts. Since all crests were hollow, various frequencies could be produced depending upon gender and age. Sonic identification of each individual was possible. So when a member of a group emits a call, others would easily identify a trusted companion.

Reaching a full length of 33 feet (10m) or more, the hips of *Parasaurolophus* rose higher than their shoulders as a result of their longer and more powerful rear legs. Such a sleek physique was necessary for this species to survive during the Late Cretaceous period or roughly 99,600,000 – 65,500,000 years ago within North America, particularly in Alberta (Canada), New Mexico and Utah. Their front shoulders at the base of their necks rose only 10 feet (3m) high, causing their spine to slope upwards to the top of their hips, which rose to an astonishing 16 feet (4.9m) above the ground. Although full grown adults could weigh up to 5 tons or 4.5 metric tons, Mack and Marcus were impressed or even startled to see this group behave with such agility that resembled a plains zebra (*Equus burchelli*) when various members conducted mock chases as a means to condition each other for the mating season and for fleeing from any potential predators.

Another group of duckbilled dinosaurs with hallow crests commonly referred as Hadrosaurs, followed *Parasaurolophus*. This group grew just as large and weighed the same. Body structure and physical ability were similar to the first group discovered. Their only differences was that this group had an emerald green base color, which was cloaked in orange that was covered with black spots along their head, neck, back and tails. Most notably, instead of a long hollow crest, this group evolved a dome shaped sail mounted on top of their heads. Their sail rose from the front and curved down to the rear and rose at least one foot (30.5cm) at the center. Dr. Ryan's Identification Detective device revealed a genus called *Corythosaurus*, which lived a similar livelihood in Alberta and Montana during the same time period as *Parasaurolophus*.

"These dinosaurs are amazing!" Marcus told his companions.

"What makes both species so special?" Meena wondered.

"Because both species of duckbilled dinosaurs had rows of cheek teeth in their upper and lower jaws that grew to replace old teeth throughout their lifetime and their adaptive snout was used for snatching various plants." Marcus answered.

Meena then wondered; "Were they able to eat flowering plants that appeared during the Late Cretaceous period?"

"Of course," Marcus responded. "That's the main reason why Hadrosaurs spread throughout most of the world, while other herbivores such as sauropods were limited to ferns, horsetails and conifers."

Meena was impressed by Marcus's knowledge before he continued to explain. "Their agility and strength in numbers made it difficult for predators to catch them. They employed a similar strategy to how zebras would flee from lions and spotted hyenas in Africa." Dr. Singh then realized that both species of Hadrosaurs were covered by what appeared to be sophisticated scales.

Once Marcus finished his explanation, Mack noticed both species monitoring them with curiosity and suspicion. "I think it's a good idea to move on," before they continued north to prevent being stampeded.

It took less than one minute before encountering another large herbivore searching for food. Instead of grass, this hornless rhinoceros indulged into leaves from trees and bushes located throughout the field. Dr. Nimbus recognized how this powerfully built browser grew up to 13 feet (4m) long and stood 7 feet (2.15m) at the shoulder! Dr. Ryan realized that although no defense enamel mounted on this male's nose, he was surprised how agile and quick this gray thick armored skinned hornless browser could be. His limbs were longer and much more durable than today's Black Rhinoceros (*Diceros bicornis*) of Africa that made this colossal creature maneuver almost as fast as a large horse.

Dr. Ryan had no intention of being run over by such a spectacle so he covertly used his I.D. device to find out what life form could match this profound presence. As soon as he received official results, Dr. Ryan reflected a distant memory of Dr. Netherland's personal discussion of a North American hulk living a secured life during the Miocene and Pliocene epoch or somewhere from about 23,030,000 to roughly 2,588,000 million years ago.

"Whoa…you won't believe this!" Dr. Ryan said. "The genus of this male hornless rhinoceros is identified as *Aphelops*!"

"No way, you're kidding me?" Dr. Rosalila responded.

"I used the I.D. device twice and received the same results."

"Mack, he's walking toward us." Dr. Nimbus interrupted while the snout of *Aphelops* twitched rapidly to signal his detection of four strange visitors he never encountered.

Since he had a bulky, erectable neck, he was able to raise his head up to approximately 9 feet (2.7m) above the ground for better surveillance of what he detected. Despite the fact that *Aphelops* weighed at least two tons or 1.8 metric tons, the crew was impressed how fast he was able to run as he galloped when the crew headed west. This chase only lasted for less than a minute. Luckily for the crew, it appeared that this giant male was more curious than furious.

"Whew…that was so close." Dr. Ryan showed no desire of taking any chances to slow down.

"I'm surprised how easy it was for *Aphelops* to move." Dr. Nimbus observed.

Dr. Singh noticed such biological ingenuity. She was impressed how despite a lack of defense mechanisms such as horns or hooves, *Aphelops* used both his massive body size, a brawny physique and impressive speed would make it extremely difficult for predators to tackle them. Both Hadrosaurs such as *Corythosaurus* and *Parasaurolophus* employed a similar combination of defense techniques for survival.

"I could only imagine what outcome could have been if we had to hike without our transporters?" Meena wondered.

As they continued to move west, Dr. Singh and Dr. Rosalila adored two groups of mild mannered sprinters grazing and monitoring their immediate area. Although it was noticeable that each group differed in regards to horn ornamentation and arrangement, both species had two functioning toes with a third that were so significantly reduced that it didn't touch the ground at all and both species grew up to six feet or (1.83m) long.

Their backs and shoulders reached over four feet (over 1.2m) tall and were capable of raising their heads high enough to kiss an adult person standing six feet tall, which Meena and Lucy would mind receiving from such adorable creatures. The first group possessed two long straight horns by which each horn enabled a spiral twisted formation that appeared like a traditional candlestick that ended with a bi-tip fork. Because of such an arrangement, Lucy perceived each horn to be two entwined horns into one but was distinguishable until they separated at the tip.

The second group had a more decorative ornamentation arrangement. It had two different pairs of horns that totaled up to four independent horns rising above their heads. The smaller pair of short, broad forked horns rose behind their eyes, while a pair of straight, long and narrow horns rose from the rear of their skulls.

Based upon data proved by the Identification Detective in conjunction with the Soul Mate databank, confirmed data identified the first group to be similar to one species that lived in North America particularly in Nevada during the Late Miocene, which would be between 11,608,000 – 5,332,000 years ago. The second group was soon revealed to be identical to what existed during the Middle Pleistocene or approximately 781,000 – 126,000 years ago in the Nebraska plains. Males of both groups possessed longer horns than females.

"The first genus over to the right is *Ilingoceros* and the second genus over to the left is *Hayoceros* of North America." Dr. Nimbus informed everyone.

"They're so adorable." Dr. Singh adored them.

"Their bright base marked with spots makes them appear like fawns." Dr. Rosalila added.

"I heard about both species of the Antilocapridae family." Dr. Ryan remembered. "They could easily sprint fifty five or sixty miles per hour and leap over twenty five feet!"

"They could sprint like White tailed deer?" Dr. Rosalila asked.

"Certainly," Dr. Ryan confirmed.

When the explorers cautiously approached both groups, adult males suddenly alerted their herds by rapidly wagging their tails and emitted a short, high pitched call to flee before both groups rapidly dispersed away with stunning speed. It took only a few seconds for each individual to end up over one hundred yards or over 91 meters away from his or her original distance. Once both groups were satisfied with their safe distance from four unknown observers, they started grazing once again while some members continued to monitor them.

Dr. Nimbus noticed something interesting. Although North America's pronghorns (*Antilocapra americana*) are living relatives of both species, *Ilingoceros* and *Hayoceros* possessed agility and employed survival tactics similar to a modern Thomson's gazelle (*Eudorcas thomsonii*) of Eastern Africa. He visually recognized how they'll spring away if a stalker comes too close, but for larger, slower moving predators, the Thomson's gazelle would actually follow their potential enemies but maintain a safe distance as a means to spy upon their intentions.

Additional precaution is used by sleeping as little as an hour a day during the warmest part of the day as a means to save energy from a depriving heat and because through experience, the Thomson's gazelle knows that most predators prefer not to waste precious energy or they'll dehydrate from a basking midday sun. Such innovative tactics would most likely be part of this collective creature to survive under the harshest circumstances. What's more is that since their horns stand vertically, both species were able to sprint inside scattered woodland where most pursuing predators would find it burdensome to chase prey.

"We shouldn't be too persistent in pursuing them." Mack suggested before the others agreed to monitor both species from a desired distance.

While viewing *Ilingoceros* and *Hayoceros* Lucy looked into the other direction before she abruptly screamed, which caught her colleagues' attention. "Mack! Look behind us!"

Two silvery spherical objects hovered above the ground that appeared to be monitoring their research disturbed Dr. Ryan and the others. Both objects were suspended only 20 feet or over 6 meters above the ground as they established a parallel formation only 400 feet or 122 meters from their location. Dr. Ryan suspected these objects monitoring their research activities. What discomforted him even more was the fact that such a phenomenon was capable of a stealthy approach.

Both objects suddenly hovered away from the crew before it glided diagonally up and east from their original position. Everyone observed both objects maintaining a perfect parallel formation as they darted away. Since Dr. Ryan felt violated because he was be watched, he decided to pursue them. "Come-on! Let's follow them."

Each one braced as they accelerating east. Dr. Rosalila felt concerned of Dr. Ryan's determination to chase these two silver spheres that could possibly endanger him and the crew. "Mack! Why are you doing this?"

"How dare they monitor us?" Mack cried out.

"Don't you know you could be killed?" Lucy warned him.

"I'll report it to Town Hall."

Dr. Ryan then used his Watchdog device and called Town Hall to report their latest incident. Once all four apparatuses extended into position, a holographic display of Dr. Derrick Grace appeared. "Derrick! We caught two objects monitoring us!"

"*Where did they go?*" Dr. Grace asked.

"They moved east and we're going after them."

"*Could you still see them?*"

"Barely!"

"*I'll notify the starship.*"

"Better yet, I'll contact the starship myself and relay my position." Dr. Ryan suggested before communications ended.

Dr. Ryan then reactivated his device once again and called for the starship Guardian to respond. "Guardian, come in please."

Dr. Karl Gruber appeared before Dr. Ryan informed him of this latest incident. "Karl, we have two of these objects monitoring us at our location. We're currently pursuing them."

"*Mack! I have something very important to tell you!*"

"What is it?"

"*The Planetary Indicator just detected your position!*" Dr. Gruber told him. "*There's a strange disturbance just ahead.*"

"How far?" Mack wondered.

"*Do you see a large batch of trees and bushes directly ahead?*"

"Yes! It's roughly half a mile away!"

"*There's something at the other side!*" Dr. Gruber revealed.

"Could you tell what it is?"

"*We don't have the slightest idea. We never saw anything like it. Let me add that it's no carcass of any kind.*"

"I'll investigate! We should keep our frequencies open," was the last words Dr. Ryan said before he focused his attention to his three colleagues.

"Everyone, listen up! Doctor Gruber just informed me there's something at the other side of this batch of trees and bushes straight ahead."

Dr. Nimbus wondered about the recent discovery. "Who told you about this?"

"Dr. Gruber."

Both women listened carefully for what Dr. Ryan will say next. "He told me that the Planetary Indicator detected some type of disturbance."

"I suggest we should veer right and maintain a safe distance until we find out exactly what type of disturbance we're dealing with." Dr. Nimbus advised before Dr. Ryan led them around a peculiar batch, where they noticed tumbled trees and broken branches.

PREVENTIVE DIPLOMACY

Dr. Ryan felt more intense as he was able to see bright beige of cellulose interior of damaged trees. Dr. Nimbus recognized scattered topsoil, as well as some unveiled roots of plants and trees that didn't survive this incident. As they veered left, concern became a principal emotion due to the fact that no detectable evidence of any animal causing this mess.

Drs. Singh and Rosalila monitored the immediate area for any sign of wild activity. Both of them were surprised that with the exception of all four explorers, no other life form had enough curiosity to approach this area including birds. The whole crew reluctantly noticed a smooth reflective silver surface buried under twigs and branches. What ever it was broke into pieces. Dr. Ryan realized that it wasn't a carcass of any animal as he suspected of scented burning silicon.

"Mack! What do you think this is?" Dr. Nimbus wondered.

"It looks as though it was some kind of shell." Dr. Ryan shared his initial analysis.

"Mack, you should find out if there's any form of toxic contamination present before we approach because it smells awful." Dr. Rosalila recommended before removed a small device from his waistband.

A vulgar sulfuric scent from this wreak annoyed Dr. Ryan as he used his Good Samaritan device to detect any form of poisonous gases due to such a hideous stench. Wind randomly carried this nauseous odor over to a displeased group waiting for Dr. Ryan to carefully analyze any threat. The smell was so harsh from their distance, Drs Rosalila and Singh decided to face in opposite direction of the wind's origin.

Once his probing was done, Dr. Ryan was intrigued by the final results. "Everyone, believe it or not, there's no trace of any known form of toxic fumes.

"Mack...you're sure?" Dr. Rosalila wondered.

"There's no sign of any form of disease or toxins. I think we should approach this object and find out what it is."

"I'll escort you." Dr. Nimbus showed he was just as determined to inspect the disaster site.

Both women thought about whether to accompany them to the craft but decided to watch the area for any signs of wildlife anywhere. Mack felt suspicious because the Central Continent is rarely quiet. Both women continued to scan the area and monitored their colleagues inspecting the wreckage. Based upon Mack's surprised expression Dr. Rosalila suspected he made a remarkable discovery. "Mack! What is it?"

"You won't believe this, but this object is one of these strange spheres we saw all day."

Both women raced over before climbing off their transporters and walking over to them. "Are you sure?"

Mack inspected a piece of an outer layer of what appeared to be the outer hull. Dr. Ryan estimated this shell to be 10 feet (3m) thick. He then peeked inside this massive hull and saw a black interior with endless strands of gold geometric patterns. Lucy refused to touch the silver surface, which appeared like metal but felt like plastic according to Dr. Ryan.

As Dr. Rosalila felt unsettled of what he showed, Dr. Nimbus chuckled at such an ordeal and Dr. Singh noticed. "What's so funny?"

"I'm sorry, but this situation reminds me of the story of Roswell." Marcus admitted.

"Huh…that's the last thing I want to think about." Mack responded to Marcus's statement.

During the 4th of July, Independence Day weekend in 1947 at Roswell, New Mexico, a rancher by the name of W.W. "Mack" Brazel heard a thunderous explosion during a rainy evening. When he woke up the next day, he rode his horse along with a neighbor's son to inspect his sheep and his ranch's terrain. As he surveyed his estate, he discovered strange debris on the ground.

After collecting as many pieces as possible, he took them to his co-witness's parents Floyd and Loretta Proctor. All four residents of Roswell tested these materials by attempting to cut an aluminum foil-like sheet with scissors and knives but with no success. Also none of the 'I' shaped beams couldn't be bent nor broken by any conventional means they've attempted. The Proctors suggested that he should take these samples to Sheriff George Wilcox.

Since none of these materials Sheriff Wilcox inspected was ever experienced during his lifetime, he immediately contacted Major Jessie Marcel of the 509th Bombardment Group of the Roswell Army Air Force. Major Marcel was appalled by such resistance to pressure as he made numerous attempts to cut holes into the strange foil and couldn't even bend the strange 'I' beams, which he also noticed strange hieroglyphics, which was never seen printed inside any conventional air frame.

On July 8ᵗʰ a press release informed the world that a strange flying disk has crashed and was recovered by the Roswell Army Air Force (RAAF) only to be permanently rescinded on July 9ᵗʰ when the Army Air Force stated it was only a sophisticated weather balloon and not a flying disk. Dr. Netherland conducted several lectures regarding UFO origins. The most subjective cases were speculated to be a time machine from humanity's distant future or an interstellar spacecraft from a technologically advanced extraterrestrial civilization. World renowned science fiction writer and inventor of the communications satellite Dr. Author C. Clarke once stated: "Any sufficiently advanced technology is indistinguishable from magic."

"We should be careful!" Dr. Rosalila advised. "What if another one of these spheres appear to survey the damage? I wouldn't be surprised if these entities perceive us to be responsible.

"We only arrived at the scene." Dr. Ryan responded.

"Yes...but these other objects would think we shot it down." Once she made her point, Dr. Ryan decided to move away from the wreckage.

"What is that over there?" Dr. Singh asked.

Dr. Singh noticed four strange looking life forms emerge from behind the wreckage. Each one of them walked on two legs and evolved relatively large arms. Standing over three feet (1m) tall, each one grew a sleek tail aided by a flexible neck, enabling this bipedal creature to hunt with impressive efficiency. Dr. Nimbus discovered their flexible necks and high hips. Dr. Rosalila recognized white fringes and red feathers with black stripes covering their entire bodies, except their toes and muzzle.

Although their eyes mounted on each side of their heads, both eyes faced forward and appeared to have a bifocal visual ability and likely to possess nocturnal vision. Once Dr. Nimbus used his Identification Detective device, he was shocked to learn about how paleontologists claimed these theropod dinosaurs evolved the highest E.Q. of all dinosaurs. The Encephalization Quotient is a ratio of an animal's brain size in relation to their body mass. Paleontologists and zoologists employ this scale to determine how intelligent any life form could be by studying brain cavities inside a fossilized skull and analyzing the rest of their fossilized physique to determine their body mass. They conclude that the larger the brain cavity and the lighter the physique, then the higher E.Q. rating of any life form.

"Marcus, what's your reading?" Dr. Ryan requested.

"Based upon my reading, this genus is called *Troödon*."

"No way! Are you sure?" Dr. Singh wondered.

"This genus existed during the Late Cretaceous period in North America such as Alberta and Montana." Marcus replied.

Dr. Rosalila remembered Dr. Netherland telling her how this particular species could have threatened the extinction of all ancestral mammals of that time period on Earth. "I remember, Dr. Netherland telling me that if *Troödon* survived the K-T Boundary, their descendents could've prevented mammals to flourish. Their acute intelligence would permit this species to ultimately evolve into a sentient species like *Homo sapiens*.

"So *Troödon's* evolutionary descendents could've given rise to an alternate civilization instead of ours." Dr. Ryan asked.

"Yes, *Troödon* means wounding tooth in Greek, which could have evolved and perfected over time without any competition from early mammals and our early ancestral hominids would've never been able to emerge. Any descendent of *Troödon* would find a niche of superior intelligence and eventually establish a culture over a long period of time." Dr. Nimbus evaluated.

"I remember when Dr. Netherland told me that paleontologist Dale Russell suggested such a theory in the early 1980s of how a dinosauroid being instead of a human being would've emerged if the most intelligent bipedal dinosaurs survived the KT boundary." Dr. Nimbus recalled.

The KT boundary is time borders between the end of the Cretaceous period and the beginning of the Tertiary period, which is roughly 65 million years ago. Both periods were divided due to a large asteroid collided into Earth before the dinosaurs perished. Modern paleontologists such as Dr. Jack Horner suggest that birds could be modern descendents of bipedal dinosaurs. Dr. Nimbus reflected these theories before wondering about a possibility that these UFOs could be made by such intelligent life.

"I was just thinking." Marcus injected.

"What?" Meena asked.

"What if we're competing with an alien civilization that is similar to what I've talked about earlier at Gracestone?"

"You mean the dinosauroid beings?" Lucy wondered.

"Exactly...there could be another habitable planet besides Isis that could be the dinosauroid beings' homeworld."

Dr. Ryan though about Marcus's speculation. Although he didn't accept this idea in its entirety, Mack realized it requires considerable intelligence to design and produce such an object.

"I'll say that since these devices appear to be technological in nature, if they're not made on Earth, then they must be made some place else. We should view the creators of these objects as a sovereign sentience of rational beings. I suggest we engage into preventive diplomacy with them." Mack suggested before Lucy saw two metallic spheres approaching them.

"I see two of these UFOs straight ahead!" Dr. Rosalila revealed her concern to her colleagues' attention before everyone dispersed the area.

All four curious dinosaurs fled the area as well. Dr. Singh saw them dart away and sprint toward a distant group of bushes located west from the crash side. All four researchers frantically moved from this area, before viewing two silver spheres cautiously approach their fallen companion. Dr. Ryan and his crew traveled 300 feet (91.5m) south to hide behind a batch of trees directly ahead so both entities wouldn't notice the crew. Once they hid behind a dense batch of trees and bushes, Dr. Ryan peeked out to monitor how two surviving objects would respond to such a tragedy.

"Mack, what's going on?" Dr. Nimbus whispered.

"Both of them appear to be morning."

Dr. Nimbus hopped off his transport unit and walked over to see for himself. "I don't like this."

Both women showed no enthusiasm to view this situation, much less monitor their behavior or programmed emotion. Dr. Rosalila learned that a complex intelligence was able to decipher the difference between life and death based upon their evaluation of these resonating outcries.

Dr. Rosalila heard sounds of strains she perceived as a verbal expression of remorse for a fallen colleague. "Mack, we have to report this to Town Hall."

"Just one moment." Mack responded.

"I think we've seen enough!" Dr. Singh affirmed.

Both gentlemen continued their observation before Dr. Rosalila threatened to depart. "Mack, if you don't come with us, then we'll leave on our own."

Dr. Nimbus suddenly intervened. "Ladies, please! We'll leave soon."

"Now!" Dr. Singh affirmed that prompted both gentlemen's attention.

Dr. Nimbus felt agitated by her imposing demand to leave the area. "Meena, why are you so uptight?"

"We have no desire to be detected...that's why!"

"Marcus, she's right." Dr. Rosalila supported her concerns. "If those things ever discover us here then they'll suspect that that we're responsible for this incident."

Dr. Ryan noticed both hovering spheres emitting a rumbling vibration before they turned black. Due to a previous confrontation with the mighty *Tyrannosaurus rex*, Mack realized their argument consisted of considerable substance and merit. He verbally agreed to disperse before telling his friends of a bitter visual transformation of both devices.

Thunder resonated across the entire vicinity that provided another reason why Dr. Ryan and his crew must disperse. Dr. Nimbus reframed from his original argument as he rapidly returned to his transport unit. The most obvious direction for all four explorers to pursue would be south at full speed!

Dr. Ryan peeked back and saw another spherical object hovering behind them. This one displayed a familiar molted surface that emitted gold rays Mack perceived it to be a possible signal to its two companions at the wreckage because once he heard a rumbling vibration from the third object; he noticed both hovering black objects racing toward his direction.

"We have to leave...pronto!" Mack commanded before they dispersed the area.

"There's a trail...hurry!" Dr. Nimbus shouted before racing away toward a charted trail penetrating a bordering forest.

Trees standing on both sides of this trail provided shelter for four frightened individuals desperately trying to evade. Drs. Ryan and Nimbus scanned the sky for any sign of being pursued by these spheres before stopping at an intersection.

"I think we lost them." Dr. Ryan said at the intersection before a powerful red laser beam instantly struck the ground 20 feet of over six meters ahead of an already nervous crew.

The initial blast startled the crew while grass and topsoil erupted before being splattered across the trail. Mack realized one of two available trails was blocked by the laser beam. He saw no choice but to pursue the right trail.

"This way!" Dr. Ryan shouted out as a suggestion to move right, which eventually veered south toward the extended bay.

Darting through this alternate trail became their focus of escaping a possible wrath from the unknown. Birds, small reptiles and mammals evaded the immediate area. Both men eventually regretted how their curiosity overshadowed their common sense despite two women persuading them to leave. After moving one thousand feet or 305 meters, all four crew members were able to travel to the end of this trail.

"Mack! There's Town Hall straight ahead." Dr. Rosalilia expressed her worries that three intelligent, but possibly vengeful entities would discover their home base and most likely launch a lethal attack against the giant lander.

Dr. Ryan and the others adhered to her concerns and decided to hide inside a forest that bordered the edge of the bay as a strategy to evade these objects. Dr. Ryan noticed a pocket of open space inside the forest so they could hide all four transporters and its occupants. Once they entered, they used leaves twigs and bushes to hide all four units before taking cover inside a deep ditch.

Mack employed considerable caution when he peeked over the edge of the ditch to see if they were being pursued. He pierced through open space between two bushes so he could covertly find out where any of three objects could possibly be. Muscular tension and unstable nerves was the result when he noticed trees of the same forest he took shelter inside reflect off a silvery surface of a low gliding craft originating from his right side directly ahead. Hair follicles at the rear of Mack's neck stood tall as he monitored this object sway directly past his fixed position. Mack wasn't able to notice any vibration on his wrist before all four antennas of his Watchdog device expanded.

"*Dr. Ryan...come in please.*"

Once Dr. Derrick Grace made initial contact, Mack's device emitted a high pitch verbal sound causing this UFO to abruptly stop before it rapidly moved right to position itself directly in front of Dr. Ryan's elusive hiding spot once again. All he could do was say, "mute" before his device was no longer able to make any more sounds and placed his right index finger against his lips in order to give Dr. Grace a visual hand signal to remain quiet in order to prevent any further mischief.

Barely any time passed by when he ducked under the surface of this large ditch. Dr. Nimbus folded his two hands near his forehead and faintly prayed, while Dr. Singh reflected her devotion to the Trimurti. Dr. Rosalila settled into deep atonement of the universe as she wrapped both hands around a jade artifact she then pressed it toward her chest. As soon as this device emitted a flat horizontal funnel shaped green beam that flickered through the woods, Dr. Ryan reached into his pocket and took out a jade sphere given to him and placed it between both hands. He pressed his thumbs against his chest before closing his eyes.

An illuminated beam's triangular shape expanded and contracted numerous times in pulsation before it disappeared. Dr. Ryan decided to wait an extra moment until he felt it was safe to peek above ground. He peeked over the edge of the ditch and no longer saw any more reflection of himself and the surrounding woodland. Once he saw nothing but opened trail and bordering woodland directly across, Dr. Ryan was convinced that the strange craft was gone.

Mack slid back down into this protective ditch with a colorful jade spherical artifact wrapped in his right hand. Film of sweat gleamed as daylight reflected off his face and hands. Topsoil stained their jumpsuits as they remained in hiding. Mack then stated "low volume" before he verbally responded to Dr. Grace's initial contact.

"*Dr. Ryan, I have some bizarre news to tell you.*"

"You have some bizarre news? You should have been with us." Dr. Ryan replied.

"*That's what I want to tell you.*"

"Huh...what do you mean?"

"*We know that you've discovered the wreckage, however we encountered something more unusual.*"

Dr. Ryan paused before he asked. "What could possibly be stranger than our recent encounter?"

"*As strange as this may seem, we just received enormous data into our Geographic Indicator from an unknown origin.*"

Dr. Ryan grimaced as he rolled his eyes. He applied sarcasm when he asked. "Well…we all should thank the crew operating the Planetary Indicator for their valiant effort?"

"*The Planetary Indicator is currently surveying the Eastern Continent and hasn't contributed to this surge of data we received. We evaluated the information for errors and found the new data to be accurate. Be advised, it wasn't any of your equipment that produced this data. We received it elsewhere.*"

"Where did you get this data from?" Dr. Ryan's sarcasm replenished.

"*Fifteen minutes ago one of these objects was positioned close to Town Hall and remained in position.*"

"What happened then?"

"*We didn't detect any hostility in part of the object. However, once this object hovered next to Town Hall, we suddenly received this geographic data of the entire Central Continent.*"

"What happened after that?"

"It rapidly ascended into the sky and disappeared."

"Are you sure this didn't come from the orbiting ship operating the Planetary Indicator?" Mack wondered.

"*Originally we though that was the case, but Doctor Gruber informed me the Planetary Indicator was scanning the Eastern Continent.*" Dr. Grace answered.

"We'll evaluate the data as soon as possible." Mack concluded before their communications ended.

"Mack, what happened?" Dr. Nimbus asked as he wiped dirt particles off his jumpsuit.

"We have to go to the Geographic Indicator room and evaluate new data, which was allegedly supplied by one of these reflective spheres that hovered next to Town Hall earlier."

Dr. Singh felt unsettled by Mack's news. "You mean these objects know the location of Town Hall?"

"This whole idea could be very risky for us." Dr. Rosalila suggested. "We could be subjected to their surveillance."

"We must return to Town Hall," was the last words Dr. Ryan said before reemerging from the ditch, brushing off of their dirty jumpsuits and maneuvering their transporters out of the open pocket inside the woodland.

*   *   *

Intelligence agents and researchers continued to evaluate fresh data given to an unknown source. One operative was a veteran of analyzing data for authenticity and validity. Originally born in Istanbul, Dr. Ozdem Yilmaz main passion is to unravel the mysteries of many ancient ruins and artifacts. Dr. Yilmaz traveled to many exotic locales in Egypt, Iraq, Mexico and Guatemala. He also pursued to study one theory of how the Giza Necropolis, which stands on the Giza Plateau, was erected over 12,500 years ago by an unprecedented sentient intelligence, which weren't indigenous of Earth.

Standing six feet (1.83m) tall with an olive complexion and black hair, Dr. Yilmaz maintained a slim physique along with a passion for topography. During his exploration, he teamed up with the world's finest navigators including his current wife from Kazakhstan, Dr. Natasha Aliyev. She possessed similar supreme skills of pinpointing accurate locations and current geographic conditions of Isis's terrain as well as Earth's. When this new data arrived, both were skeptical of its legitimacy but after numerous tests both were convinced it's authenticity.

Since then, this matter was discussed with Dr. Weinstein along with Dr. Nevins and many others at Intelligence's main research center on level six of Town Hall. As they continued to discuss this matter further, Dr. Ryan and his three colleagues entered the research center along with Dr. Nina Ivanov.

"Mack! I'm glad you're here!" Dr. Yilmaz showed enthusiasm for the crew's arrival.

"Ozdem! How you've been?"

"Fine...I'm fascinated by the data we received. Let's go into the main display room and I'll show you all the details. I also wanted to show you something else first."

"What is it?" Mack asked.

"The Condor craft showed us this relatively strange region we viewed earlier today." Dr. Yilmaz revealed before he activated a large flat screen.

"What the heck happened?" Dr. Ryan said when he saw a panorama of dead trees and scattered corpses.

What was formerly green grass transformed into pale brown as spectators witnessed scattered bones and fragments. Hardly any leaves managed to survive as the last resilient leaves lost their grip of their branches before a timid breeze glided them to their final resting places on the ground.

"What you're viewing is a region located at the middle of the Central Continent. It lies perfectly between the southern region of the Grand Steppes, the Northern region of the Great Plains and the eastern region of the Principal Prairies." Dr. Weinstein informed the group.

Dr. Ryan reluctantly watched a few remaining dinosaurs and Tertiary era mammals struggling to migrate or even stand fully erect. "Good heavens, this looks like the bowel of hell."

"It's intriguing how you said that phrase, Ozdem and I studied this region and decided to call it Hell's Den."

Dr. Nimbus and Dr. Ryan lifted their eyebrows as they looked at each other in conformity. "Umm…well, based upon what we're viewing the name fits rather well."

Once Dr. Ryan agreed to this suitable name to assign this region, Dr. Yilmaz informed them that all images Eve number four showed originated from that particular area. Such traumatizing data from Eve number four revealed a sustainable hint of various inhabitants struggling to survive in a region that contradicted their will to survive. Mack's lower jaw dropped when he saw a wide mesa that appeared similar to what he envisioned in his dream before the Spaceship Guardian approached Jupiter.

"Do you have a geographic map of Dr. Netherland showed us at the summit?" Dr. Ryan asked.

"Yes…I have it here." Dr. Weinstein said before activating a neighboring monitor before displaying Isis's terrain.

Once everyone found their suitable view of the map Dr. Arnold Weinstein used his right index finger to draw an imaginary circle around the center of the central continent, which was located northwest of the Great Plains, also south of the Grand Steppes and east of the Principal Prairies. Dr. Ryan looked back over to the video data provided by the Condor craft and felt tense as he saw a large lake near the giant mesa before he noticed a distant river.

"You won't believe this but I had a perplexing dream of landing on top of a mesa that looked just like what I'm viewing now." Dr. Ryan s revealed his secret.

"You're kidding?" Dr. Nimbus chuckled.

"No…It happened before we approached Jupiter." Mack told everyone. "We landed on top of the mesa and traveled down a winding hill before we approached a lake similar to this."

"What happened?" Lucy wanted to know.

"I called it the Bull's Eye region because it was at the center of this continent. I remember everything, even the river. Huh…the Bull's Eye region; I should've called it the Black Eye region." Dr. Ryan continued to reveal devastating incidents of his dream as everyone stared at Hell's Den. Mack became evermore tense when he saw a silver sphere appear from the left side of the LCD screen.

"Hey…what's that thing doing?" Mack showed his concern while this object descended toward a carcass before emitting a green inverted V-shaped beam that enveloped the dead animal.

Once this flickering beam ended, the crew detected 12 more of these objects appearing from their left side of view before each one descending toward other carrion before conducting a similar process that puzzled Dr. Ryan. "You know what...we must go to the Geographic Indicator projector room to find out exactly what we're dealing with...let's go!"

Dr. Yilmaz then guided four explorers into a large room similar to the Clairvoyance telepresence projector room but the image from this holographic projection would not involve time or duration. Dr. Nevins, Weinstein, and Ivanov followed them into the room. Instead of a completely empty room, this one was equipped with maneuverable reclining chairs aided by built-in side trays to place loose items such as utensils or small devices including pens. All seven researchers positioned their seats into a single line formation across to face one side of the holographic view dome. This entire scene was motionless while a joystick attached to Dr. Yilmaz's seat could simulate any viewer's movement from a first person's viewpoint. Dr. Yilmaz then requested "lights off" before he requested a scene called wreckage.

A timeless image of trees and grass dominated this simulated landscape. Dr. Yilmaz used a small joystick to travel in any direction possible, he was also able to zoom in or out as well as rotate 360 degrees. Within seconds he could change his aerial view to viewing on ground level. As he maneuver adjusted his simulated position, Dr. Nimbus recognized that this was the exact location where the crew discovered the wreckage earlier.

Dr. Singh's eyes widened and covered her mouth with her right hand as she noticed a congregation of bushes, weeds and trees where they were. "That's where we hid in the open plains from two UFOs that turned black when they discovered the wreckage.

"You're sure?" Dr. Ivanov asked.

"That's it...the wreckage should be approximately three hundred feet directly ahead if you pursue north."

Dr. Yilmaz used his controls to move to that location. After traveling 300 feet (91.5m) north, everyone saw a hologram of another group of weeds bushes and trees. However, this batch of trees was shredded while bushes were flattened. All four crewmembers who explored this area confirmed the location and details of the wreckage. Metallic pieces were noticeable almost everywhere the searched. The largest piece lied pocketed inside an opened arch of trees and plants while other debris were scattered all over an immediate area.

Spectators were able to hear a mild ringing sensation inside their ears, as they remained silent. Dr. Yilmaz decided to adjust their view outside this congregation by maneuvering toward this batch where the main component of the wreckage was located. A live action quality graphics that's frozen in time was all in Dr. Yilmaz's control thanks to a joystick in held.

Focus was a common activity as he guided his view closer to the main component of this fallen craft. Once they stood a few feet away from it, Dr. Ryan recognized the hull, which he estimated to have been 10 feet (3m) thick. This massive reflective silvery outer surface along with a black interior covered with of intertwined geographic patterns of gold lines and strips he suspected to be nanocircuitry and quantum CPUs. The most intriguing section was discovered when everyone detected daylight reflecting off a large broken container at the center of its interior.

"What the heck is that?" Dr. Nimbus was intrigued to see an image of pink liquid oozing out through cracks around the bottom of this elliptical shaped container.

"This inner capsule appeared to possess a noticeably thick shell to protect what's ever inside." Dr. Weinstein confirmed as he focused his attention to this centerpiece's dimensions.

Dr. Ryan's heart nearly stopped as daylight enabled him to discover what he never suspected would be inside this container. "It looks like a gigantic brain!"

Once Dr. Weinstein and Dr. Yilmaz heard Dr. Ryan's remarks, they decided to activate a tracing mechanism to reveal the shape of this unprecedented core. Spectators suspect they're viewing the central control unit of an aerial craft capable of exploring Isis and transmitting data to Town Hall. Once the structure of this unit was traced, it became highlighted so observers would be able to study a complete diagram of what's inside.

Mack's disturbance haunted him even more as this diagram revealed an enormous cerebral hemisphere, which appeared to have fulfilled a principal role in this object's self awareness and behavior. What complicated matters for the worse is that despite this organ to extend four feet (1.2m) wide, Dr. Ryan observed swelled gyri tissues, which were thin and entwined into a complex pattern that was separated by minute grooves or fissures.

Dr. Weinstein recalled viewing diagrams of various brain organs. "I remember Dr. Netherland compared several holograms of various cerebral patterns of several animals and a human adult."

Everyone else listened as he continued. "A dog's brain pattern had a small cerebral hemisphere with large patterns of gyri tissues separated by fissures. A human's brain grew a considerably larger cerebral hemisphere with a more complex pattern of gyri tissues and grooves. But a killer whale's brain possessed the largest cerebral hemisphere with the most complex pattern of gyri tissues and fissures and their brain were more than double in size than an average person's brain."

Dr. Weinstein paused before he concluded. "You know as well as I, that killer whales are among the most widespread mammal on Earth if this is a brain possessing an active intelligence including emotions; then what we're observing is an intellectual capacity far superior then what we ever experienced."

Dr. Ryan realized. "If such advanced technology aided and collaborated with this brain, then these objects could be a cyborg with unprecedented abilities of interstellar travel. I have no idea who or even what created this craft."

"With a brain like this and its surrounding mechanisms, I wouldn't be surprised if it could conduct a form of levitation by manipulating gravity waves and magnetic waves causing it to achieve such movements?" Dr. Rosalila thought as this strange biological phenomenon continued to be examined.

"I never viewed circuitry of such complexity. It was so advanced I would consider it nano-technology and I couldn't find any power source within the craft." Dr. Singh described cell sized central processing unit (C.P.U.) and electronic components with a similar capacity to a personal computer or P.C.

"Maybe its power source could be the forces of nature or even various frequencies received by the craft?" Dr. Nevins described how infrared, light, X-rays and other wavelengths that are abundant everywhere in the universe.

"You mean that it could be interchangeable to receive many sources of energy even if other viable sources aren't available?" Dr. Nimbus conceived. "In other words, if daylight isn't available then it could adjust itself to receive radio waves as a substitute in order to adapt to changing conditions?"

"That's what could possibly explain how these objects could travel vast distances without energy depletion. I suspect none of these objects would ever be subjected to fuel shortages or dead batteries." Dr. Ryan acknowledged.

"What concerns me most is how they're able to judge distances by forming aerial formations and possessed a form of morning when they discovered the wreckage!" Dr. Nimbus realized.

"That's not good." Dr. Ivanov mumbled.

"What do you mean?" Dr. Ryan showed concern as he saw her facing down.

Dr. Ivanov looked over to him. "If these objects are sentient, then I wonder if these UFOs possess a form of personality complex."

A moment's silence passed by before Dr. Rosalila testified. "One of them fired a powerful laser into the ground near us."

"Where?" Dr. Yilmaz asked as he adjusted his controls.

"Go through this trail and follow it until you see an intersection." Dr. Rosalila guided him to steer until there was a trace of any ditch, where they could see burned grass and charred topsoil.

"The beam impact forced us to steer right." She added.

"What's strange is that at first these objects demonstrated its ability to hover and maneuver then it tried to protect you from the *T. rex* and other inhabitants, despite firing a powerful weapon, it appears that it deliberately missed you. It either fired a warning shot or it prevented you from entering that trail."

"Hopefully...but you should've seen all three of them at the open field. They didn't appear too hospitable." Dr. Rosalila stated.

"Maybe they tried to monitor you." Dr. Yilmaz speculated.

"Why it shot a laser at the junction?" Lucy wondered.

"Let's find out." Dr. Yilmaz responded before he entered the left trail and travelled until he noticed a pocket of grass inside the woodland at the right side of the trail. Once he rotated his control to face this particular open pocket, the entire crew was shocked to stand directly in front of two gigantic creodonts that stood six feet (1.83m) at the shoulder and extended at least 10 feet (3m) long or more with out their thick bushy tails.

These particular creodonts were heavily built with short powerful legs. Dr. Ryan noticed that this species were part of a family called oxyaenids or oxyaena. Each had dense skin, thick fur, and bold teeth. A built-in Identification Detective device inside this room identified this genus as *Sarkastodon* of Mongolia during the Late Eocene or around 37,200,000 – 33,900,000 years ago. They had black underbellies along with a fizzled white and gray layer along the top of their heads back and tail. With dense fur and a thick skin enabled these giant creodonts appear to resemble a gigantic Ratel or African honey badger.

"Look at the size of their claws. We could've been ambushed by them! These objects actually saved our lives instead of trying to end it!" Dr. Rosalila arrived at her conclusion.

"What about when we hid inside the bordering forest." Dr. Ryan wasn't convinced of these entities' benevolence.

Dr. Singh recalled her description of a flickering green beam penetrating through the forest that sheltered the crew as they hid inside a ditch. "One observation I made was this green beam appeared mild. There we're no markings on any tree barks when we left. It appeared to be used as a search mechanism to find us."

"Maybe...but why was it trying to pursue us in the first place?" Dr. Ryan questioned this particular incident.

"Since they rescued us from a *Tyrannosaurus rex* and other dangerous encounters with *Telicomys* and *Sarkastodon*, I'm convinced that they're benevolent. If they were hostile, then they would've never intervened when you were in trouble with all three different animals. You would have been left to fate." Dr. Yilmaz observed.

Drs. Ryan and Nimbus remained silent as they thought about the fact that each encounter actually benefited the crew. Marcus considered the fact that at any time, each one of these strange and curious spheres had an easy chance to attack each explorer without warning. He came to a conclusion that since these objects were unquestionably capable of such hostilities and numerous opportunities to attack or ambush the crew thought it was a benevolent decision in part of this phenomenon's intention not to harm the explorers.

Taking these facts as evidence of such benevolent behavior, Dr. Yilmaz's findings and Dr. Singh's explanation were ultimately taken into consideration. Dr. Ryan recognized one more important fact; he realized how important it is to keep an opened mind for various opinions and reasoning in order to realize important arguments, which he could've overlooked. Have it not been for their opened minds then both veterans of science would've made grave decisions based upon prejudice and ultimately cause further mischief.

Drs. Ryan and Nimbus were grateful for Dr. Yilmaz's persistence in finding elusive clues. As they continued to view such immense size and monumental power of *Sarkastodon*, Dr. Ryan felt reassured that there will always be someone within his crew who'll have an answer to any question.

Dr. Yilmaz decided to end his visual presentation. "I'm very impressed by such an altruistic orientation in part of these objects. If they are from an alien world, then we should engage into some form of progressive dialogue."

Dr. Ryan loved the idea. "We should extent an olive branch of our organization and negotiate a peaceful and progressive coexistence. I'm convinced that an enormous brain at the center in collaboration with such advanced technology could maintain contact with their creators."

"How do you plan to execute such a task?" Dr. Singh asked.

"I'll have search for them. I'll use a beacon device to attract these spheres to me. Then what I'll do is attempt to communicate with these devices to see how they'll respond."

"Mack this could be very risky." Dr. Rosalila objected because of such a grave risk Dr. Ryan is willing to take. "What if you're conceived as deceptive?"

"The rewards clearly outweigh the risks."

"How?" Dr. Rosalila wondered.

"Once these objects understand our intentions, then they'll respond accordingly. As soon as a diplomatic channel is established, then a communiqué will commence."

"Mack! This could be very dangerous!" She concluded and made her objection known among her peers.

"Dr. Weinstein could call his most qualified operatives then we'll contact engineering to meet inside the main conference room to discuss the best possible details." After Dr. Ryan's suggestion, Dr. Weinstein immediately activated his watchdog device to contact, Dr. Marino and Dr. Taina Kepa to meet them inside the conference room. Dr. Nimbus called Dr. Claude Moreau who joined with Dr. Art Remington.

Dr. Nimbus suggested that both individuals attend this meeting and discuss details of how to safely approach a sensitive situation such as this. Dr. Rosalila reluctantly contacted Dr. Malik Abdullah al-Saud and suggested him to participate in this meeting before he enthusiastically recommended his wife Ada and his key personnel such as Dr. Doris Remington, Dr. Tracy Marino and Dr. Julia Grace.

Dr. Ryan called Dr. Martin de' la' Vega and his wife Angela while Dr. Yilmaz used his watchdog device to contact his wife Natasha before he contacted Dr. Derrick Grace and asked for his help at this meeting. Dr. Grace told him that he'll attend. Dr. Singh contacted Dr. Ying Zhu and her husband Fan before she spoke to Drs. Haru Nakamura and Zarina Ansari so they could attend this meeting. Once all calls were made, Dr. Yilmaz guided everyone into the main hallway before entering a stairwell that brought them one level down.

When he reached level five, he met with his wife Natasha who stood five feet, four inches (1.6m) tall with a light physical shape who kept her brown hair in a bun behind her head. Her hazel eyes are keen that made it possible to unravel geographic mysteries inspired by her passion for paleontology and archaeology. She willfully guided them into a large domed room equipped with an oval shaped conference table along with plenty of cushioned velvet seats. Only one white illuminating light at the top center of the dome lit up the entire room.

Dr. Ryan sat in the middle of this elongated table. Dr. Nimbus sat at this right side while Dr. Rosalila sat at Dr. Ryan's left side. Dr. Singh sat next to Dr. Nimbus. Dr. Arnold Weinstein arrived with his wife Esther while Drs. Derrick and Julia Grace sat next to each other directly across the table from Drs. Ryan and Rosalila. Within moments, Dr. al-Saud arrived with all key medical personnel before finding their seats. Viktor Ivanov showed up along with Drs. Nakamura, Ansari and Remington. Once they took their seats, the rest of the invited participants entered.

Drs. Fan and Ying Zhu arrived along with Martin and Angela de' la' Vega while Dr. Tracy Marino came to sit next to her husband. Dr. Alicia Nevins, who was contacted by her husband Harold, entered the conference room along with Dr. Claude Moreau who ended up sitting next to Dr. Zarina Ansari. Once all 28 scientists, engineers, explorers and Chamber officials were seated, Dr. Ryan initiated this formal meeting with his testimony of near encounters with strange entities.

"In all of my experience, I never encountered such an unprecedented set of circumstances. Their propulsion ability was never duplicated by any craft I ever witnessed. We're dealing with an exceptional technology." Dr. Ryan professed.

"I agree," Dr. Nimbus presented his views. "Since no intake valve or exhaust system was detected, I've noticed no moving parts and none of these objects made any sound when they traveled except when the object pierced through this planet's atmosphere."

After Dr. Nimbus's evaluation, Dr. Arnold Weinstein decided to reveal a hologram of this spacecraft's interior to other participants. He then, called for "lights-off" before requesting a built-in Clairvoyance telepresence projector to illustrate a four dimensional hologram of what he conceived as a giant brain hovering directly above the conference table.

"Huh?" was a principal verbal response along with raised eyebrows and hands covering up cocked opened mouths. "As you can see, this brain reaches seven feet in length and stands up to four feet high." Dr. Weinstein told a shocked group of spectators.

Dr. Moreau analyzed this data to his astonishment. "Does anyone think this spacecraft could be controlled and managed by an enormous brain?"

"I'm certain that this organ does control this craft, however, I'm not entirely convinced that it assembled anything because of a lack of appendages such as arms and legs. I'm inductively theorizing that such an organ could be a sophisticated centerpiece of an artificially sentient intelligence." Dr. Weinstein explained.

"You mean to say that this brain could be artificially developed inside of a test tube?" Dr. Ansari asked.

"Yes, we know of no being that would evolve a brain such as this." Dr. Weinstein suggested. "If it is a being then their skulls would have to be enlarged, which could complicate natural pregnancy. The average extraterrestrial being must stand at least 60 feet or over 18 meters tall.

"It could be possible that a living intelligence could develop artificial organs including a brain. However, unlike any other organ, the brain is the most difficult organ to duplicate because it must undergo an intense learning process, which could take decades. What's more is that this organ we're viewing must adapt to the surrounding technology that's contained inside the craft." Dr. Antonio Marino contributed his theory.

"I wonder with a brain this large would be able to conduct telepathy, or perhaps even levitation. It could communicate telepathically between other spheres and even the place of origin." Dr. Nina Ivanov told about how thought most likely won't have any physical mass but instead achieves superposition, which subatomic particles could be present in two or more locations at the same time. She described the nature of mental telepathy from this brain into the minds of intelligent beings or other giant brains inside other spheres rather than sending radio waves that could take years to arrive at an intended target and could be subjected to gravitational influence from numerous celestial bodies.

"I wonder what level of sentience this intelligence would achieve. Would such intelligence understand dark matter or energy much better than us? What level of conceptual abilities do they possess? Would they understand our concept of the multiverse? What level of understanding they have of the afterlife?" Dr. Weinstein wondered.

Dr. Ryan felt a bit nervous due to such intense cognitive competition from an unknown intelligence whose intention has been elusive, despite the crew's optimistic attitude toward the spheres. "I'll contact the Starship Guardian."

Dr. Ryan activated his Watchdog device and called the orbiting flagship Guardian before Dr. Gruber responded. Once they connected Dr. Ryan then described the interior of a wrecked spacecraft before he suggested quantum abilities of transmitting telepathic messages back to its source. Dr. Gruber also noted how telepathic messages could instantly be transmitted to any receiver located anywhere. Dr. Ryan desired to know the amount of time required to activate the Mercury One interstellar communicator to notify Earth of their latest discoveries. Dr. Gruber told him it would take approximately one hour for both planets to position Mercury One's sending and receiving units before sending a pattern of teletransported light before the receiver on Earth would receive decipher and translate this message.

Dr. Ryan then told Dr. Gruber which strategy the Central Continent crew will pursue. Dr. Ryan suspected the homeworld these objects originated from would likely have learned what their objects discovered on planet Isis. Dr. Ryan felt that the Chamber would be the most suitable recipients of their recent encounter and knew they'll treat this matter maturely in relating to the general public. Dr. Ryan also told Dr. Gruber to send his message over to Dr. Jordan Tyrell, who commands the Western Continent crew. Once communications ended Dr. Ryan reengaged into their discussion.

"I just wonder how the federation will respond." Dr. Harold Nevins felt nervous because he wondered if the federation would take an aggressive stance because of such an intellectual ability of anyone or anything that created such mysterious technology.

"How are you going to engage into contact with these spheres?" Dr. Art Remington asked.

"So far I'm the only person obligated to take this risk. I'll carry a Good Samaritan device in order to trace my location. If I should be killed by one of these objects, then my orders are for Dr. Marcus Nimbus to assume command and he'll succeed me to take appropriate measures." Dr. Ryan announced to this panel.

"What's your plan?" Dr. Esther Weinstein was concerned about such a grave risk Dr. Ryan is willing to assume.

"Lately these entities appear to develop an interest of our presence." Dr. Ryan observed. "I'll return to the meadow or the scattered woodland so I could be detected from above. Once they recognize me then I could provide an organized series of signals to attract them.

"What if you're tricked or trapped by their lure and subjected to an inescapable attack?" Dr. Rosalila felt that such an encounter could turn sour.

"Since we noticed no signs of planetary competition from their civilization, I suspect they would be cooperative." Dr. Arnold Weinstein emphasized to Dr. Rosalila.

Dr. Ryan arrived at a new perspective in term of relating to this elusive intelligence. "They have to realize that we're here to stay and we must understand that these devices and their respective civilization are here to stay as well. We must establish a peaceful coexistence with them."

Engineers could install video cameras into our transport unit and another either on my shoulder or I could use a Clever Cap device to record all the events." Dr. Ryan explained. "You'll be able to view live events. If any form of malevolence occurs then you'll know to suspend Town Hall and lift off this bay and return to the flagship."

Dr. Ryan paused for a few seconds before the panel agreed to his tactical strategy before he asked. "Anyone wants to accompany me may volunteer by rising you're right hand. Whoever declines then you'll be assigned to your respective workstations."

Dr. Ryan eventually heard a mild ringing sensation inside both ears as all 28 panelists thought about numerous consequences of his endeavor to resolve this mystery and achieve diplomacy. Soft whispers echoed inside a domed conference room as he patiently waited for their response. Dr. Ryan knew if nobody volunteered he'd decide to go by himself, so if danger occurs then he'll be the only casualty.

Moments later, exchange of whispers ended before everyone refocused their attention to Dr. Ryan. Panelists thought about Dr. Ryan's offer, while he remained calm and quiet as he anticipated their response. While he waited, other members of the panel shifted their attention to Dr. Nimbus who slowly raised his right hand indicating his willingness to share such uncertainty with a man who he trusted even with his life.

"I'll accompany you Doctor Ryan!"

After Dr. Nimbus's decision, other panelists looked at each other to anticipate their response. Raised eyebrows resulted in a surprise when two more individuals raised their right hands in support of Dr. Ryan.

"This has to be settled once and for all!" Dr. Fan Zhu stated as he held his right hand high along with his wife Ying who also agreed to volunteer. "We have nothing to fear."

Dr. Alicia Nevins listened to Dr. Zhu's statement that inspired her to raise her right hand. "I can't think of any better alternative. We can't live here in fear, especially if we're three light years away from Earth."

Once she agreed, two more hands rose in acceptance to an ultimate challenge, which could determine the direction of such a historic mission. Panelists recognized the risks being assumed by a happily married couple that agreed to risk everything in order to overcome their greatest challenge yet.

"My wife and I agree to be with you during this event." Dr. Martin de' la' Vega spoke on behalf of his wife Dr. Angela de' la' Vega before one more individual raised his hand.

"Well…since you agreed to go, it would be necessary for a medical doctor to accompany you." Dr. Malik Abdullah al-Saud knew it was imperative to volunteer.

"Great, seven volunteers altogether including me would be sufficient. I can't expect anyone else to escort me. I rather minimize this risk as much as possible." Dr. Ryan was pleased until he noticed an entire group of panelists raising their hands.

"Mack, although it would be burdensome for the rest of us to accompany you, however each and every single one of us is behind you all the way. We will monitor every activity and take all measures to ensure your safety." Dr. Arnold Weinstein affirmed.

Although Drs. Rosalila and Singh supported their initiative, however they mounting concern for seven volunteers became immanent. They knew if a conflict was provoked then all seven volunteers would be vulnerable to attack and wouldn't have any means to escape these UFOs. Dr. Rosalila unconsciously bit her lower lip as a gesture of her concerns, while Dr. Singh expressed her fears when her eyes became moist. Droplets of tears fell off her face once she blinked. Unfortunately for them, since they didn't want to spoil anyone's confidence, both of them decided not to reveal their true feelings and remained silent.

"We'll prepare this encounter by activating seven Drifters equipped with video cameras and we'll all wear the Clever Cap devices as an additional observational measure. I recommend that we keep our Watchdog device on standby to keep in touch." Dr. Ryan instructed the panel before everyone stood up and initially left the conference room.

Dr. Ryan read a tabloid that revealed how the topic of UFOs and space travel accompanied human civilization since our emergence well over 40,000 years ago. From cave paintings in Lascaux, France to medieval biblical art depicting aeronautical crafts revealed clues of a possible experience with strange devices that were once interpreted as angels or even gods. One of the most distinguished Ufologist in modern times known as Stanton T. Friedman, a nuclear physicist who attended the University of Chicago in from 1953 – 1956 along with legendary astronomer Dr. Carl Sagan as his classmate during his later years. He worked to design and develop nuclear generating and propulsion projects for General Electric, General Motors, Westinghouse and others for 14 years and routinely gained open access to the most advanced and most secretive technology known to humans.

Mr. Friedman argues that since these objects were witnessed by thousands of people worldwide throughout human history proved that if these objects weren't made here on Earth, than they were made some place else. Although UFO skeptics such as Dr. Sagan reasonably argues that since no applicable theory of such abilities of these objects could be deciphered and implemented then such a phenomenon must remain subjective or it should be considered a hoax. Mr. Friedman contends that it would be nonsense to deny such abilities just because we didn't know how they worked.

Dr. Ryan listened to recorded lectures by both brilliant scientists and other profound scholars including Dr. Johannes von Buttlar and the grand wizard of science fiction stories known as Dr. Isaac Asimov. Dr. Buttlar argues that there're over 200 billion stars in the Milky Way Galaxy alone and that most of these stars have planets orbiting around them. He also points to the fact that since most of these stars are older than the sun, then any intelligent civilization would have considerably more time to evolve to the point of producing and operating these objects. Isaac Asimov, Carl Sagan, Johannes von Buttlar and Stanton T. Friedman believe that humanity is scientifically and technologically capable of unraveling the most elusive mysteries and would one day transcend society across vast distances of outer space.

Once this conference ended, every individual returned to their workplaces to prepare seven brave volunteers to engage into the most sufficient task ever experienced. Dr. Art Remington and Dr. Haru Nakamura both took a stairwell down one level to their labs so they could activate seven Clever Cap devices. Dr. Ying Zhu along with Dr. Viktor Ivanov and Dr. Zarina Ansari pursued to the main level so they could install their video equipment on each Drifter unit before preparing them outside the main entrance. Dr. Arnold Weinstein ordered his intelligence staff to activate all audio and video reception modules to they could trace all activities and actively monitor this event. While Dr. al-Saud was leaving the conference room, he directed his medical staff to prepare the hospital emergency room at level 10.

All seven volunteers exchanged their ideas while Drs. Rosalila and Singh listened covertly. While all seven volunteers preparing for their departure reaffirmed their confidence, while both ladies whispered their concerns and pending ordeal they'd anticipate when seven volunteers depart the island. Although they wanted to share the volunteers' enthusiasm, unfortunately their mounting fear for their safety complicated their efforts.

"Well, this is it!" Dr. Nimbus proved to be ready when they used another stairwell to arrive at the main entrance.

Engineers tested seven transport units equipped with a compact device of video cameras with installed microphones placed to the front of each transporter. While seven volunteers approached the main entrance Dr. Art Remington, Dr. Ying Zhu and a few associates carried seven individual Clever Cap monitoring devices before issuing them to all volunteers.

"Here you are." Dr. Remington said to Drs. Ryan and Nimbus as he provided them with a helmet that appeared to resemble a construction laborer's hardhat that was equipped with a miniature video camera and microphone. Such a design made it easier to record audio and video data. Interior padding along with an adjustable chinstrap provided additional comfort while recording this event.

Intelligence will receive all data transmissions from each helmet and transmit them into a set of assigned monitors and speakers. Activities would be recorded at Town Hall rather than from inside these helmets, so recorded data won't be lost if a helmet ever became destroyed. Once each volunteer installed their headgear, they communicated to Intelligence via their Watchdog device to confirm their persistent communiqué.

Their rubber soles touched the metal ramp as all seven volunteers exited the lander and contemplated their outcome. Once Dr. Ryan walked on blades of green grass, Dr. Rosalila walked over to accompany him. "Mack, do you have the artifact?"

"Of course...I have it here." He then took it out of his left shirt pocket and showed it to her.

"Good...place it in here." She then opened a flap that covered the opening of his right pocked at his chest and placed it inside before she closed the flat and sealed it closed so this ancient relic she provided would protect the man willing to risk his life to unravel the truth of this mystery.

"Dr. Ryan, each Drifter unit is tested and ready." Dr. Nakamura confirmed before all seven volunteers formed into a circular huddle along with Dr. Singh and Dr. Rosalila.

Dr. Remington joined into this huddle with Drs. Nakamura, Zhu, al-Saud and Nevins. Hands connected to create a fully connected circle of scientists and engineers. Their heads bowed toward the center of this human circle in complete silence. Since this procedure was commonplace within the federation's customs whenever a challenging mission becomes immanent, the entire area fell silent once everyone within this congregation engaged into prayer, meditation and desired hope for a safe return for all seven volunteers. Their plural silence of unity and faith ended when their heads rose before they reopened their eyes. A tight grip of hands loosened before separating the perimeter of this collective huddle.

Dr. Fan Zhu was the first to climb aboard his transport unit after his wife Ying kissed him on his cheek. Dr. Alicia Nevins received a kiss from her husband Harold before she boarded her unit. Both of the de' la' Vega's hugged each other and exchanged an elongated kiss before they attended to their units. Dr. al-Saud reassured his wife Ada of him coming back while he embraced her and her concerns.

As Dr. al-Saud tested his assigned Drifter, Dr. Singh provided her support to Dr. Nimbus. "Marcus, I just want you to know that although I'm worried about you, I will always be faithful."

"I always believed in you too," was Dr. Nimbus's response before he kissed her on her left cheek and proceeded to his unit.

Dr. Ryan comforted Dr. Rosalila by hugging and kissing her in compliance to his willingness to return. He placed his left hand over his right chest pocket to feel an artifact of good luck and protection to reassure her that he will not perish. As Dr. Rosalila watched her beloved companion board his transporter, Dr. Nakamura noticed a 50 foot (15.25m) wide reflective silver sphere racing down toward the surface of the bay between Town Hall and the eastern shore of the extended bay.

"There it is!"

Additional personnel ran down this steel ramp to capture an unobstructed view at an object that forever changed the lives of the crew. None of the witnesses anticipated this aerial entity to perform a fascinating feat before it decreased its speed of descent until it stopped to remain motionless. Not much time passed by when all seven volunteers viewed the object hovering directly ahead. Dr. Ryan and his co-volunteers stared at this entity while the others felt nervous by such a bewildering presence, which hovered 30 feet or over 9 meters above the bay's surface.

"Follow me," was Dr. Ryan's initial command as he gently approached this stationary object with extreme caution.

Dr. Ryan suggested traveling five miles or over 8 kilometers per hour when this sphere gently drifted left toward to the northern shore. Dr. Ryan guided his crew north and passively followed the UFO. He chose not to accelerate because he had no desire to show any form of aggression.

As seven cautious individuals followed this craft to the northeastern shore of the extended bay, Dr. Rosalila struggled with anxiety until a woman's hand rested on her right shoulder. "Lucy, I know how you feel."

Lucy felt reassured once she heard this woman's sympathy. "Meena, I hope they'll be safe."

"I'm worried too. I just want them to return." Meena replied.

Lucy was worried as both of them saw them follow this object inside a wide grassy trail bordered by forests. "There they go."

"Why don't we go up to Intelligence so we could monitor what's going on?" Dr. Singh suggested.

"Sure, why not? I rather know what's going on instead of standing here."

Both women walked up this steel ramp along with Dr. Remington and the others. Since they witnessed initial contact with a UFO, everyone either took an elevator or a stairwell up to Level 6, where Intelligence monitored current activities. They diligently ran up three levels of stairs until Meena opened a stairwell exit door of their desired deck.

*   *   *

"Town Hall, this is Dr. Ryan. We're following it through this trail. There's no sign of any wildlife anywhere. Keep in contact with Dr. Gruber of our current position." Dr. Grace stood next to Dr. Weinstein within an enclosure of a portable holographic screen receiving the latest news.

"*It appears that you're traveling northeast from the shore. Within two hundred feet, you should enter a meadow slightly smaller then the first one you discovered.*" Dr. Weinstein informed them as he received confirmation from Dr. Harold Nevins, who navigated the crew through the open trails while all seven volunteers follow this craft into what they believed, would be a meeting place.

Columns of trees and bushes stood tall on both sides of a trail wide enough for this mysterious object to travel through and visually block the crew's sight of their destination ahead. Without any foresight, this hovering device instantly raised its altitude and revealed an open meadow.

"I think it's leading us to this open field." Dr. Nimbus suspected as they approached the meadow.

Dr. Alicia Nevins felt suspicious about being exposed to an open field without protection of a dense forest. "I wonder what will happen next?"

"Arnold, this data that you've received from this object must be accurate. I see an open field. We're entering it now." Dr. Ryan reported via his communications device around his wrist.

"Based upon our new data, you should be inside the meadow and there should be stone outcroppings directly ahead of you. They only rise approximately two feet above the surface. Could you see it?" Dr. Weinstein decided to test this data's authenticity so if there's any discrepancy, then he would suspect a malicious intention in part of the object.

"Yes! There appear to be two that's almost submerged but I could see them. They appear exactly like what you've described." Dr. Ryan confirmed the validity of fresh data stored inside the Geographic Indicator.

*   *   *

Meanwhile at the Intelligence center inside Town Hall, Dr. Weinstein felt surprised. "There's absolutely no flaw in this data's accuracy."

"What about the two boulders?" Dr. Marino, who monitored these activities, viewed these kopjes near the entrance of the meadow at his assigned Geographic Indicator.

"Mack just confirmed them." Dr. Weinstein revealed.

Dr. Marino initiated a discussion with Dr. Harold Nevins. "Whew…I don't know what to make of this whole scenario. So far there's no evidence of any intention to mislead all seven volunteers. I think there might be some form of communiqué being established." Dr. Marino said.

"I hope so. The real question is what are their intentions? Since their exposed from their aerial view, the crew's completely at their mercy." Dr. Nevins responded.

"Indeed, but at least this potential meeting point isn't far from Town Hall. I'm glad this object isn't guiding them to any distant place that would be too dangerous." Dr. Marino concluded.

Once Dr. Marino explained his analysis Dr. Nevins realized that a close distance along with a comfortable setting of a large meadow would be an ideal place to meet. Both men realized each volunteer were well accommodated by this mysterious craft that provided the best of both worlds of open space and a short distance from Town Hall.

*   *   *

After passing both inserted boulders, all seven explorers continued north until they've reached this field's center. Once they're positioned at the center of the meadow, Dr. Ryan detected numerous trails the crew could use as an escape route in case of any trouble. The crew remained idled while the sphere hovered 300 feet or over 91 meters ahead of their location.

"It appears to be descending." Dr. Ryan testified to Intelligence.

Dr. Weinstein continued to observe a row of monitors viewing this event as it unfolded. *"Mack! Be careful! Maintain your distance and monitor this object. Stay calm and maintain your distance!"*

"I wonder what its trying to do?" Dr. Nimbus wondered.

"I have no idea. Just be subtle." Dr. Ryan responded.

The crew noticed this object began to change its surface appearance. A once reflective silvery surface of the craft transformed into a black surface that revealed many faintly points of light scattered across. Judging from a noticeable variation of each individual point of light, it appeared to be stars in a simulated sky based upon Dr. Ryan's interpretation.

"If I understand this correctly, it looks like we're looking at outer space?" Dr. Ryan noticed a familiar pattern of stars congregated into a constellation. Within this constellation, one of these faint stars appeared to be pulsating. Judging from his memory he realized which star was distinguished from the others "This highlighted star is where the sun is located!"

"Mack! What the heck you mean?" Dr. Weinstein asked.

"I remember this particular pattern of stars! The single pulsating star is where our sun is located on the star map."

"One moment! I'll confirm this!"

*   *   *

Dr. Weinstein wasted no time to verify Dr. Ryan's claim. "Nina! Transmit a copy of our star map and it's coordinates into my computer so I could match both images. Be sure it's presented from this planet's angle."

Dr. Weinstein them zoomed one of the camera's lens until this image of space that covered the entire view of his monitor. Once he received a clear view of this constellation, he waited for the exact timing when this series of variable illumination of what resembled the sun was at its brightest point. He pressed a button that caused this monitor's image to freeze. He then used a computer mouse next to the keyboard to conduct a match making process by comparing data from Dr. Ryan's video camera built inside his Clever Cap device and from the Flagship's latest images of Isis's orbital view and calculated positions of numerous distant stars and their respective constellations.

Dr. Weinstein's monitor showed his original diagram from Dr. Ryan become visually overlapped by an image of Earth's constellation and the sun's precise location supplied by Dr. Ivanov. "Oh mother of pearl!"

"What?" Dr. Ivanov asked.

"Both diagrams show a perfect match!" Dr. Weinstein confirmed.

Dr. Nevins and Dr. Marino instantly became suspicious of such similarity of both images. They remembered when one of these objects inserted new data into the Geographic Indicator. Dr. Nevins walked over to Dr. Weinstein. "Antonio and I think that this could be fabricated. Since this object injected new data into our system, it could have copied our information."

"Possibly, but how did it know about our origins."

Dr. Nevins paused for a moment as he developed two scenarios of how it received such accurate data and why it revealed this information to the crew. "I only have two possible scenarios."

"What?" Dr. Weinstein asked.

"First, either I think that this device may have recorded our data from the Soul Mate system or these UFOs may have visited Earth at some time in the past and explored our solar system."

"One way to find out is to trace all activities of records transactions conducted since we left Earth." Dr. Weinstein suggested using a chronological activities recorder within the Soul Mate's system in order to verity if any data has been extracted or even copied.

Dr. Nevins paced to Dr. Marino before both specialists probed a long history of technical transactions. Although it seemed to be a tedious task, it only took about 30 seconds to confirm that no duplication of any data was ever transferred. However, the Soul Mate did confirm its recent reception of new data from an unknown source. Beads of sweat emerged from Dr. Nevins's face as he walked over to inform Dr. Weinstein.

"Our data was never duplicated...ever."

"You're sure?"

"I'm positive. We specifically checked for any data extracted or copied. But there's no record whatsoever." Dr. Nevins added.

Dr. Weinstein took a deep breath. "We must be dealing with an advanced civilization that's aware of our settlement here and knows the location of our homeworld as well."

"If that's a fact," Dr. Nevins thought. "Then they could have been monitoring our society's history for a long time?"

"Perhaps, but we must investigate further." Dr. Weinstein advised his colleagues before relaying this news to Dr. Ryan.

*　　*　　*

"I just wonder how this thing knew about birthplace of our species." Dr. Ryan wasn't enthused with the latest news.

Dr. Nimbus noticed how nervous he was when Dr. Weinstein confirmed his initial suspicion. "Mack, what are the results?"

"What we're seeing is Earth's constellation and that distinguishable star is where a star named Sol is positioned."

"You mean to say that these objects know where our sun is located?" Dr. al-Saud became nervous because he never suspected this device was capable of revealing such accuracy.

Dr. Zhu recognized a gradual development of a humanoid shaped image he conceived to be a silhouette of a being forming at its surface overlapping the background of the universe. "Whoa...look at that!"

Although this image appeared hazy, nobody experienced any difficulty recognizing what appeared to be a head, torso, and arms while both legs remained covered by nebulas. Dr. Ryan moved closer to the object as it remained stationary. Dr. Nimbus reluctantly followed before the others eventually moved ahead.

Hands along with five fingers emerged from a shroud of haze at the end of each arm. Facial features continued to develop in conjunction to Dr. Nimbus's recognition of it appearing hominid as the entire crew remained approximately 30 feet (9.15m) away from an artistic sphere. Dr. Ryan realized this figure continued to develop ample details as it transformed from its two dimensional appearance into a three dimensional image of what the field crew interpreted as a healthy male of an advanced age.

Dr. Nimbus continued communications with Intelligence. "It appears to be drafting an image of a human being."

A vivid detail of a male figure with white hair, wearing a white blazer and trousers startled everyone especially Drs. Nimbus and Ryan who were physically closest to the object. Rows of metals were attached to this man's chest along with robust silver ensigns attached to both shoulders. Once a light skin tone was finally revealed, the entire crew became compelled.

"*Dr. Ryan, Dr. Ryan,*" this manifested figure's voice echoed.

Dr. Ryan's eyes widened as he sobbed. "Dr. Netherland?"

"*Don't fear me.*" This image pronounced.

Tears watered Dr. Ryan's eyes, as he was shocked to be viewing a clear image of his mentor. However, the others maintained their distance as Dr. Ryan suddenly left his transporter before he walked over to the object holding a clear image of a man that inspired him to become commander of a historic mission to this new world.

Transparent light exhibited a subtle aura around his upper body as clouds of developing stars overlapped his legs and waist, a background of stars and their constellations portrayed a peaceful image of a supreme mentor to all witnesses present as well as observing this event from Town Hall. Dr. Nimbus climbed off his transporter before sneaking over to his colleague.

"Mack, what are you doing?" He placed his right hand on Dr. Ryan's right shoulder in an attempt to pull Mack away.

As Marcus tried to pull him away, this image focused his attention to Dr. Nimbus. *"Don't fear me Doctor Nimbus."*

"Huh?" All Dr. Nimbus was startled to be recognized by this image of their mentor.

Dr. al-Saud pinpointed his Clever Cap to broadcast this event as Dr. Netherland's voice echoed softly. He noticed a calm and slow movement in part of Dr. Netherland as a halo of light corresponded to his gradual movement. Dr. Nimbus continued to stare into this unpredictable manifestation as it generated discomfort to five other pioneers who kept a measurable distance behind two curious men.

Dr. Ryan continued to observe his mentor's image while Dr. Nimbus watched his entrusted friend sob over his meeting with a simulated image of Dr. Netherland. Dr. Ryan wished his mentor would've accompanied the entire crew to Isis before this image told him that he must remain on Earth to lead the federation and guide humanity into this new age of discovery. Dr. Nimbus's heartbeat pounded his chest as he felt that this object employed a psychological lure for Dr. Ryan to approach the object.

"Mack, for crying out loud...move away!" Dr. Nimbus cried.

"Mack, you have nothing to fear...it's me."

"Is it really you?" Dr. Ryan expressed his hopes.

"The time has come." Dr. Netherland announced. *"A hidden revelation will unravel the mysteries of your encounters."*

"What is it? What is it?" Mack cried.

Dr. Nimbus was less concerned with Dr. Netherland's message than assuring Dr. Ryan's safety. "Mack, you could be killed!"

Other voices of concerned colleagues shouted out their concerns for Dr. Ryan to move away from an object's lure as it presented a convincing display of a benevolent figure. This incarnation continued to present Dr. Ryan a message assuring mission success and his rightful position of commander.

"Mack, I promise you this mission's triumph under your command. You will lead a global community on Isis!" Dr. Ryan became perplexed by such a claim from a transparent figure inside the circumference of a UFO.

Shock gripped Dr. Ryan's right forearm as a solid physical grip clamped onto his wrist. Once he turned his head over his right shoulder, Dr. Nimbus stood nervously determined before he made an original attempt to pull him away. "Come on!" he said as he continued pulling him away from this strange craft.

An apparent feeling of disappointment was expressed by a puzzled facial expression of Dr. Netherland as he watched both men stumble away before climbing back on to their transport units. Dr. Netherland's image began to dissolve as it provided a final message.

"You'll no longer be shrouded in mystery!"

Details of metals attached to his chest faded along with his silver buttons and emblems. Facial features declined as his hands and fingers lost their details. A once precise manifestation of the chairman of the Humane Space Federation dissolved into a misty shroud before it eventually evaporated. A display of distant stars remained as all signs of Dr. Netherland vanished. All seven volunteers reported this picturesque of space beginning to fade until a reflective silvery surface reappeared.

"The object's rising." Dr. Martin de' la' Vega noticed.

"Look at it go!" Dr. Zhu was impressed of ever increasing speed of vertical ascension into the sky.

"Damn it Mack, what the hell were you thinking?" Dr. Nimbus expressed his outrage.

"Revelation...I think there's some truth to what the image of Dr. Netherland told us." Dr. Ryan explained while five other spectators rushed over to him.

"Mack, what do you mean?" Dr. Angela de' la' Vega wondered.

"First it was telling me not to be afraid. Then it said that a revelation would resolve and unravel all the mysteries of these entities regarding their origin and intentions. The image of Doctor Netherland assured me of this mission's success. Then it mentioned that we'll no longer be shrouded in mystery."

"Are you saying that there're possible answers in regards to this phenomenon?" Dr. Nimbus wondered.

"I'm convinced that they're from Earth and not from any other extraterrestrial source." Dr. Ryan revealed his suspicion.

"I don't know if you're correct, that gigantic brain inside its capsule provided no resemblance of humans." Dr. Nimbus showed doubt of his colleague's latest theory.

"But an accurate display of Dr. Netherland and the words he used. Not to mention such a compatible behavior. These devices could be the latest prototype of artificial sentient intelligence designed for interstellar travel and exploration." Dr. Ryan continued to explain his reasoning for his latest belief.

"But often they appeared to be conducting their own research," Dr. Alicia Nevins injected into this conversation. "It seemed to me that each craft were autonomous from our control. If they don't report to us, then they must be autonomous or work on behalf of someone else."

A transmitted message of Dr. Weinstein interrupted their debate. *"Dr.*

Ryan, come in please? I have an urgent message from Dr. Hollis! Do you want me to patch you through?"

"Yes!" Dr. Ryan authorized before a holographic image of Dr. Hollis appeared on his wrist watch.

"Dr. Ryan! Dr. Gruber and I just received a decoded message."

"What decoded message?"

"We have a decoded message from the federation."

"What does it say?" Dr. Ryan wondered.

"We need you, Dr. Nimbus and Dr. Grace to access a disk that's been stored inside the vault room. It claims that the official identity of these UFOs would be revealed. All three of you must leave Isis and return to the flagship."

"You can send one of the shuttle transporters to us." Dr. Ryan suspected a few of these flight craft would be an ideal means to be transported to the orbiting flagship.

"All ten transporters are ready and online." Dr. Hollis said.

"Send one down to pick us up." Dr. Ryan responded.

"I'll contact Dr. Grace so he could be ready." Dr. Hollis then ended their communication before Dr. Ryan reestablished communications with Intelligence.

"What does this disk contain?" Dr. Nimbus interfered.

"I suspect it contains the answers we've been searching for. I suspect that everything we need to know is contained within these disks. Both of us must return to the Starship Guardian along with Dr. Grace." Dr. Ryan was convinced that such a cryptic message would make a positive impact to this mission.

Dr. Rosalila suspected this message could be a pivotal factor of this mission's outcome. "Mack, what do you think this message would reveal?"

"I don't know." Dr. Ryan answered. "But we must return to Town Hall."

The crew departed this mild mannered meadow before heading back to Town Hall. Everyone remained silent and thought about what could possibly be revealed in regards to the unknown. Lizards and small mammals climbed trees and ran across a trail of grass while birds flew above their line of sight. Open space of grass adjacent to sand of the shore encouraged this entourage to cross the beach and hover over the depth of the extended bay until all seven volunteers successfully arrived at Town Hall Island.

HYMN OF HOPE

Dr. Grace stood outside waiting for Dr. Ryan and his co-volunteers to arrive. "Mack! Marcus! I just received a message from Doctor Hollis!"

"Doctor Hollis told us. We'll have to wait for one of our shuttle transporters to take us back to the flagship." Dr. Ryan told everyone as he climbed off his transport unit.

"*Doctor Nimbus, come in please,*" An image of Dr. Hollis initialed contact.

"Dr. Nimbus here."

"*A shuttle craft should reach your destination within a minute. I instructed both pilots to land at an island next to Town Hall.*"

"Instruct them to land on an island directly north of Town Hall. There's only one large island, you can't miss it." Dr. Nimbus instructed Dr. Hollis to inform both pilots of his suggestion.

A short time passed before spectators recognized a familiar sleek craft descending from the sky aiming to land on an island lacking trees and bushes similar to Town Hall Island. Both pilots carefully positioned the shuttle craft over this island's center for a safe vertical landing. Since each person destined to board this flight weren't required to bring any additional items, all three individuals would depart to this northern island located almost 400 feet or 122 meters from the edge of Town Hall Island.

Dr. Alicia Nevins offered Dr. Grace a ride on her transporter to cross over bay water and take him to this neighboring island. Dr. Singh persuaded Dr. Nimbus to sit behind her, so she'll transport him over there as well. Dr. Ryan saw both pilots emerge from the bottom of the shuttle before they waved over to Town Hall. Mack's left hand felt warmth and compassion from a warm palm with embracing fingers.

"I'll transport you over there." Lucy gently guided him over to her surface transporter.

Mack sat behind her before she propelled ahead. He felt reassured when he wrapped his arms around her waist. Lucy felt snuggled in Mack's arms as she held the handlebars and steered her transporter over to the neighboring island.

"Hold on," Lucy demonstrated her preference before reaching the island's shoreline.

Light pressure was the result of scaling up a low hill leading them to two signaling pilots standing ahead of a versatile transporter capable of air and space travel. Dr. Singh decelerated until she stopped near both pilots. "Well, this is it."

Others arrived as Dr. Nimbus and Dr. Singh both climbed off. He looked over to the shuttle transporter as she clamped his shoulder from behind. "Marcus."

"Yes?"

She then leaned over to him before extending her arms to find their way around his shoulders before both her hands met behind his back. "You might be gone for a while. I'll be waiting for your return."

Lucy watched both of them as she approached the shuttle craft. Thinking of a complicated task ahead, and Dr. Ryan's possible long absence, she wanted to assure of her impeccable connection she achieved in duration of their mission. Lucy gently reduced her speed until they became idle for Mack to gently climb off. Lucy hopped off before she walked alongside him.

"Mack!" Lucy captured his attention by enthusiastically embracing him. "I hope you won't be gone for long. Let's go to Gracestone when you come back."

"Great! I'll tell Marcus and Meena." Mack looked over to both of them giving Lucy an early sign of him informing them of a future endeavor.

Lucy however, had different plans in mind, which was why she prevented him to speak to them by grabbing his arm as he walked over to them. "We'll go alone."

"Sounds...great." Mack stuttered before they embraced and kissed for one last time before he led Drs. Nimbus, Grace and both pilots inside the Transcend shuttle transporter.

Dr. Arnold Weinstein will command the Central Continent's Town Hall until they return. Dr. Ryan provided verbal instructions via his Watchdog device to Dr. Weinstein while finding a seat. This shuttle craft was equipped with a pair of cushioned seats on both sides of a single aisle. Both pilots paced through the aisle to enter the cockpit room directly ahead. Once all harnesses were fastened, Dr. Ryan sat directly across the aisle from Dr. Nimbus while Dr. Grace sat ahead of Dr. Nimbus.

Gentle gravitational pressure shared among this crew became an initial sign of a vertical takeoff. Mild power generation intensified as they suddenly became pressed against the back of their seats. Dr. Ryan then leaned over to Drs. Nimbus and Grace. "Since it's the three of us, I'm speculating that there's something written on that disk inside safe number three."

"Safe, number three?" Dr. Nimbus wondered. "That's interesting because only the three of us could open that vault."

"I haven't been at that part of the ship for years." Dr. Grace barely remembers this vault room where they prepared their first directive of this mission, which could play a pivotal role for a conclusive outcome of this historical exploration.

"You know what I think?" Dr. Ryan asked. "I think it contains answers of what those UFOs are and how to deal with them."

"Suppose if a top secret affair took place, which the federation established initial contact with an extraterrestrial civilization." Dr. Nimbus reflected his suspicion.

"I don't know." Dr. Ryan wasn't sure about such a theory.

"I would love to find out how a giant brain could be created or organized?" Dr. Nimbus hoped to find an explanation regarding these objects' origins as well as their role. Mack's desire is to review the information on this disk so all of his questions and concerns would be answered.

"It may be artificial?" Dr. Grace explained.

"It could've been cloned before it was genetically engineered?" Dr. Nimbus provided his thoughts.

"What brain was it modified from?" Dr. Ryan wondered life form could possibly possess such a brain.

"An intelligent mammal such as a killer whale," Dr. Grace proposed.

"Who ever made this craft must possess extensive knowledge of medical science." Dr. Ryan hypothesized. "How such a brain could be assembled with individual neurons?"

"All I know is that there's no known person or animal that evolved a brain like that." Dr. Grace concluded. "I wouldn't be surprised if it was artificially assembled."

*　　*　　*

Meanwhile at Town Hall, Dr. Rosalila walked over to the Clairvoyance telepresence projector room alone. She opened the entrance door to an empty domed room with a single white light at the center of the dome illuminating the room. Once her left foot led her inside, a voice cried out for her attention.

"Lucy, wait." A female's voice called out.

"Meena."

"I was looking all over for you."

"I thought about visiting this room since Mack departed." Lucy shared her latest ambition.

"Umm…you were never so enthused about this room?"

"Ever since Mack showed and explained the Great Plains and the Grand Steppes, my passion for this simulator grew. You want to join me?" Lucy explained.

"Well…Marcus was never quiet whenever he sat inside this room. However, over time it became appealing to me." Meena agreed before they entered. After closing the entrance door, both sat directly at the middle of this empty room with a glass floor. Lucy called for "lights out" before darkness cloaked their vision as Lucy then called for "Eve number two."

Both felt a simulated cross breeze as they viewed live footage of a large waterhole at the Great Plains. Distant congregations of trees and bushes added to a natural splendor during a late afternoon. Scattered clouds along with a tinge of gold of Osiris gently demonstrated temperatures cooling as two rhinoceros-like mammals walked over to this waterhole for a drink.

"Look at the size of them!" Meena was fascinated to see how both herbivores stood at least eight feet (2.44m) at the shoulder and extended over fourteen feet (4.27m) long.

"That's *Brontops*." Lucy informed her.

"How do you know that?"

"Mack told me when he was at the scattered woodland he saw a larger group of them migrating."

"It must be a drag to carry such a nasal ornamentation."

"Both spherical attachments at each end of their Y shaped horn grow as large as a soccer ball." Lucy told her

"How much do you think they weigh?"

"Well…Mack told me they could be at least three or four tons."

"That's the mass of a young African elephant?"

"Huh…they're amazing. It's hard to believe how they became extinct."

"How did *Brontops* disappear?" Meena found it hard to believe that a bold brontothere could possibly vanish from Earth.

Lucy read a tabloid that revealed how the end of the Eocene epoch, which was approximately 34 million years ago was when *Brontops* along with their cousins known as *Brontotherium* browsed North America. One theory suggests that underneath Idaho, Wyoming, Nevada and Oregon lies a colossal pool of magma known as a plume, which fed several volcanic fields within these states. Lucy recalled when Dr. Netherland explained that these volcanic fields are massive craters known as calderas that were caused by a Supervolcano, which is at least 1,000 times more intense than any ordinary volcano. Yellowstone National Park at northwest Wyoming is also home to a Supervolcano.

Meena read a tabloid regarding the early 1990s when paleontologist Mike Voorhees excavated various gullies in Orchard, Nebraska to discover prehistoric rhinos, horses, turtles and lizards, which were in their prime phase of their lives when a cataclysmic event abruptly ended their existence around ten million years ago. Since no volcanoes exist within the Midwestern plains of the United States Mr. Voorhees decided to contact Professor Karl Reinhard of the University of Nebraska. Under careful analysis, Professor Reinhard discovered that such residual growth on their fossil bones only indicated a massive volcanic eruption that spewed volcanic dust and ash into the atmosphere which suffocated the region's wildlife.

Such a dilemma was brought to the attention of Professor Bill Bonichsen, of the Idaho Geological Survey who knew an extensive history of subterranean activities. He learned about one potential area located at the southern region of Idaho known as Bruneau- Jarbridge caldera. Professor Bonichsen recognized that this particular eruption coincided with the Orchard disaster and was most likely the sole cause.

Such a miraculous finding prompted Professor Bob Smith of the University of Utah and Professor Michael Rampino of New York University in Manhattan to investigate how such an eruption could impose devastating results. One event that occurred 74,000 years ago in Sumatra (Indonesia) occurred when a reservoir of magma erupted before a large area of terrain collapsed into a giant crater known as a caldera. This particular caldera formed Lake Toba, for which Professor Smith and Rampino accurately concluded that the Toba eruption was at least 10,000 times more devastating than Mount Saint Helens's eruption in Washington State that occurred in May 18th 1980. Lucy and Meena read more information on a tabloid displayed on the floor as they recalled Dr. Netherland's lecture about Supervolcanoes including the Toba eruption, which was one of the most devastating events in Earth's history and has a destructive compatibility to asteroid impacts such as the K-T boundary, which was the final blow to the dinosaurs.

Each brontothere took turns to drink from the waterhole while the other would scan the immediate area for possible danger. Most waterholes on Isis resembled those of Africa, which appeared like a small lake surrounded by weeds and tall grass. Meena looked over her right shoulder by chance and accidentally discovered a group of strange horses with white legs riddled with zebra patterned stripes and a brown torso. Both women noticed these patterns of stripes and a bright base faded as they traveled up their loins and upper flanks. By reading digital tabloids displayed on the floor, both of them were thrilled to find out that all eight horses are identical to a species know as

Equus sp., better known as the Western horse that inhabited North America from 1.6 million to 10 thousand years ago during the Pleistocene Epoch and was the last native horse species to exist at this region. Spanish settlers reintroduced domesticated horses into North America over 500 years ago. Lucy also read that the abbreviated sp. means species.

"So this is how ancient horses appeared?" Meena replied.

"They have a same pattern as an okapi or zebra of Africa, but are stockier than modern horses." Lucy observed.

"I wonder how western civilization would have evolved if the Western horse was domesticated instead of the modern horse?"

"That's a good question." Lucy responded.

One of eight members of this group of ancient horses led the others to the waterhole where *Brontops* initially analyzed their presence and intentions until their senses reassured their hospitable nature. Eventually the presence of all eight horses was accepted as they instinctively took turns with the brontotheres to drink and monitor the area.

As this informal arrangement was conducted by both species, Lucy noticed a group of giant robust cattle approaching the waterhole. All three appeared to be maturing males that possessed two short dense horns that curved and pointed forward. Each horn measured over three feet (1m) long as they stood six feet (1.83m) at the shoulder and extended 10 feet (3m) long.

Meena was impressed to see such a beautiful black coat shaded by a misty tinge of brown. A thick brown and white mane grew from under their jaw until it reached their stomachs and covered his former umbilical chord. Lucy continued to stare at all three bachelor males before she realized their similarity of an ancient breed of cattle that once coexisted with early humans.

"They look familiar." Lucy then read another printed tabloid on the floor in order to confirm her suspicion.

"That's *Bos primigenius!*" Both women witnessed a life form similar to one that lived during human history!

"I heard of this species." Meena replied to Lucy's findings. "One time Dr. Netherland told me how *Bos primigenius* also referred as aurochs were the ancestor of the vast majority of modern cattle. He told me that they were originally domesticated six thousand years ago, but human hunting activities contributed to their extinction until the last of the great cattle died in Poland in the year 1627."

Meena briefed Lucy of how an energetic species lasted almost two million years since the Early Pleistocene. She also told her how most of the Old World was populated by such a life form whose images reflect an adventurous existence on cave paintings in Lascaux, France. Reflections of their accomplishments continue to entice both women who observed their brawn and beauty.

While observing prized cattle grazing, both couldn't believe to see two other massive rhinoceros-like mammals with short bulky legs that carried a barrel of a body. Their stomachs nearly touched the ground as they moved slowly toward the waterhole and grazed on ripe grass. Although these living tanks were slightly shorter than *Brontops*, both women suspected that these hefty herbivores weighed the same as or even exceeded *Brontops*! It was noticeable to see a single short conical horn at their snout. However, when one of them opened their mouths wide, both were impressed to see two enlarged lower canines used to extract tough vegetation and fight rival males for mates.

"That's *Teleoceras*!" Once Lucy revealed the official name of an elite semi aquatic life form Meena wanted to learn more.

"How did you know that?"

"Mack told me that *Teleoceras fossiger* means complete horn, referring to their nasal horn. Although they're physically shaped like a hippo, they're a member of the Rhinoceros family.

"Tell me more."

"*Teleoceras* grows at least thirteen feet or four meters long and I estimate that they weigh the same as Africa's largest hippos or even match the weight of young elephants."

"I wonder that if they carry so much muscle and mass that they don't have any sore feet?" Meena and Lucy continued to observe both specimens capable of roaming great distances from rivers and streams to maximize their opportunity to graze similar to modern hippos (*Hippopotamus amphibius*) of Africa's savannah.

Each individual congregating around this waterhole recognized and accepted each other's presence. Although it was preferable to be the first to drink from at this precious place for hydration, it became evident that some individuals drank while others scanned and scented for any possible predators.

"Lucy what's that over there?"

Meena noticed an impressive warthog that was a member of the Suid family of pigs. This bachelor male's long brittle fur originating from the top of his head to the center of his spinal chord made him resemble a powerfully built wild boar. His enlarged upper and lower canine teeth curled out to make it possible for both women to see one smaller canine in front of the larger one at each side of this life form's thick muzzle.

Meena realized that this particular warthog was easily capable of growing five feet (1.5m) long and could stand over three feet or one meter tall at the shoulder. She also recognized since walking on two toes made this male's limbs more like a stout version of a cow or buffalo instead of a domesticated pig. This male's flattened snout indicated that he was a grazer with teeth patterns that could accommodate an omnivorous diet from grass to carrion.

"I remember Mack telling me about Alicia's exploration of the southern meadow near the bay." Lucy told Meena about how she discovered a life form similar to *Metridiochoerus andrewsi* based upon data from the Identification Detective. She also informed her of how such a giant male warthog resembled what was part of Africa's wildlife during the Late Pliocene to the Early Pleistocene, which would be from around 3,600,000 – 781,000 years ago.

Meena eventually became more impressed with Isis's biodiversity that revealed detailed clues of how Earth's prehistoric life appeared and behaved. She continued to watch *Metridiochoerus* graze nearby. Meena continued to indulge into viewing an active atmosphere until she noticed this giant warthog's snout rapidly twitching once a gust of wind blew in his direction. She recognized the warthog's ears standing upright before pivoting. He then looked vigilantly into all directions in suspicion of something threatening nearby. His tail rose, as a convincing sign of detecting something unsettling within this vicinity.

As they continued to monitor this male's conviction, one of two brontotheres looked ahead in recognition to the warthog's behavior. The male *Brontops* suspected pending trouble when his nostrils received a gentle breeze across the Great Plains. Lucy wondered what could possibly cause such concern as the other female brontothere raised her head before actively searching for what most likely would be troublesome.

"Something's wrong." Meena sensed pending danger as she recognized increased tension.

Without anticipation, Meena saw *Metridiochoerus* sprint in the opposite direction while Lucy observed how fast an ancient warthog could run. Once other acquaintances among this gathering at a natural basin witnessed *Metridiochoerus* running away from his original location, all eight Western horses instantly fled from the area. *Teleoceros* didn't appear much alarmed of this situation as they stood close to each other and stood their ground.

"Whoa…what are they?" Meena wondered.

From their left side of their view emerged a heavily built dog with shaggy black fur on top of this male's head. This pattern continued down this male's neck, back and tail. All four limbs along with his underside and throat revealed short smooth fur covered in a gold and white that spread across his throat, chest and stomach.

Judging from his speed, Lucy believed this life form was an active hunter that ran on their toes like modern African wild dogs rather than flat footed like bears. Such predators employ an endurance strategy to catch their intended prey. Instead of fast sprints that accomplish only a few hundred yards, a persistent chase is an option that involves wearing down potential prey to the point of physical exhaustion.

One distinctive advantage of this technique is because fatigue would make it more difficult for any dangerous prey to resist when they're subdued. Modern life forms such as Africa's hunting dogs (*Lycaon pictus*), the Gray wolf of North America and Eurasia (*Canis lupus*) and the Dingo of Australia and Southeast Asia (*Canis lupus dingo*) mastered this hunting strategy.

"I could see more of them!" Lucy recognized four more bear-dogs emerged from the left side of her view. All five individuals were at least five feet (1.5m) long and stood well over three feet of over 1 meter at their shoulders.

Meena requested the Identification Detective device inside the Clairvoyance projector room to reveal a tabloid, so she could read what would be identified as this pursuit continued. "Lucy, have you ever heard of genus called *Hemicyon*?"

"Once maybe," Lucy responded. "What does the tabloid say?"

A brown rectangular shaped holographic tabloid appeared on the floor next to them. Meena leaned over forward to read yellow words and numbers consisting of valuable facts of Earth's dynamic life form that is represented by a cunning pack of Bear dogs. Once Meena read and reviewed the contents, Lucy asked her enthusiastically of what she learned.

"*Hemicyon* lived during most of the Miocene epoch and was widespread in Mongolia, France, Spain and the United States." Meena explained. "The term half-dog is what the name of this species means because they're part of the Ursidae family, which consists of modern bears."

"Their Ursids?" Lucy wondered as they initially saw the giant warthog *Mertidiochoerus* running toward their direction. "They appear like dogs?"

Both of them noticed one of Isis's Bear dogs positioned close behind the giant warthog. Judging from a large circular pattern that resulted from the chase, each predator saved as much energy as possible and kept *Metridiochoerus* inside their orchestrated chase within a small perimeter of the open plains. Meena noticed how the most persistent individual in this chase, suddenly reduced his speed as a female member of this pack accelerated after their intended prey.

Both brontotheres lowered their heads and showed off their massive clubbed horns that were part of their skeletal anatomy made primarily of bone tissue. Although modern paleontologists debate of specific uses of their ominous ornamentation, it was evident that Meena revered their reassuring nasal arrangements that inspired full confidence in part of *Brontops*.

Bos Primigenius was capable of employing multiple defense tactics. All three males could either sprint away from danger or engage into a counter attack. Buffaloes, bison, cattle and most antelope evaluate danger and according to their own circumstances, then decide which strategy would be most suitable. Since all three males were bachelor bulls and the Bear dog was a smaller lighter predator, they lowered their heads and took a few firm steps ahead. A courtship of *Teleoceras* continued as they gently walked into the opposite direction apparently showing no concern for any vulnerability to such a threat as they approached a distant river. Meena and Lucy were impressed to witness an unforeseen array of life that they thought they'll never experience in their lifetime.

They were convinced that *Hemicyon* remained interested in their current pursuit of *Metridiochoerus* as they remained indifferent toward the larger herbivores. Once it became visually clear that they weren't in any real danger, the brontotheres and aurochs cautiously rejoiced back to the edge of the basin, but took turns to drink and monitor this nearby pursuit.

Another feature this telepresence projector possessed is an acute ability to zoom in further distances for, as long there are no obstructions such as trees bushes or tall plants. Lucy remembered Mack's instructions to extend one arm out and point her index finger to wherever she wanted to focus her attention to before saying "zoom in." Lucy acquired a closer view of this concerted effort of *Hemicyon* to capture their intended prey.

Since the giant warthog instinctively concluded that he couldn't outpace a pack of energetic Bear dogs, he suddenly decided to save his remaining physical endurance and changed defense tactics from fleeing to fighting. Meena realized that all five hunting pack members cautiously surrounded *Metridiochoerus* as he stood firmly against all five adversaries. Each pack member waited for their best time to launch an initial attack.

One of the pack members bit the warthog's right rear leg causing an intense male to rotate and swing his heavy head equipped with two pointed tusks on each side of his muzzle. This particular Bear dog's experience of hunting such dangerous life forms knew better by releasing his grip just in time to avoid being struck by these hardened tusks. Suddenly, a much younger male Bear dog attempted to bite the warthog's throat just as this agile *Metridiochoerus* rotated toward his opposite direction.

"Oh no!" Lucy felt a shock race through her nerves as she saw the giant warthog's head swing to deliver a pair of right side tusks into this youngster's neck before hearing a loud scream resonate across the immediate area of the open plain.

Meena could barely tolerate loud disquieting screeches that were heard as blood squirted out from a likely artery at the right side of the Bear dog's neck. "That's awful."

Meena suspected a deep puncture from thick pointed curved tusks ruptured a vital organ. Essential blood poured out from his wound as he withdrew his attention to his potential kill. Lucy was surprised when she observed the wounded male eventually leave his pack before watching him stumble away from the area. It became a challenge for Lucy and Meena to view this male's tragedy as he became weaker and wouldn't communicate with any of his companions for the remainder of his time alive.

While one male anticipated his fate, the outcome for four others proved to be within their advantage as they conducted a bobbing and weaving tactic used as one pack member attempted to distract *Metridiochoerus* while the others attacked from behind. Careful timing and positioning along with patience, endurance and persistence were imperative to wear down a dangerous herbivore into physical exhaustion. Loss of blood as well as torn flesh would impede this defending male's efforts to resist.

Collective team tactics continued to wear down a defiant male who fought until he wasn't able to maneuver anymore. Once another attack was imminent, *Metridiochoerus* finally collapsed before the remaining pack members embraced a rapid feeding frenzy by disemboweling the dying carcass. With the exception of waiting for an Alpha male and female or a genetically dominant male and female to claim their prime share, each hunter wasted no time to consume as much flesh as possible.

Although *Hemicyon* was not a part of the canine family, this pack demonstrated a feeding technique used by wild canines in Africa, North America and Australia. Dogs, wolves and dingoes in the wild commonly feed rapidly on their kills as a preventive measure of avoiding direct confrontation with larger predators. Smaller and more agile predators that hunt in packs are reputed to be the most efficient and spectacular hunters of all carnivorous mammals. However, larger predators such as bears, lions, hyenas and even smaller wolverines would detect a carcass then confiscate the carcass from accomplished hunters.

"Whoa!" Lucy became startled to see two gigantic felines moving from behind her view and moving toward the carcass.

"I should have been looking in the other direction." Meena turned over to her right side to see one more imposing feline moving rapidly to confront all four pack members for their prize.

Two marauding felines were at least ten feet (3m) long, while the third one reached eleven feet, six inches (3.5m) long and this male's shoulders matched the height of Lucy's shoulders. Almost standing as high as a pony, this lion most likely weighed at least 600 pounds or 272 kilograms or more.

"I remember observing them at the Osiris 4 Summit a long time ago." Meena recalled.

"Let me see." Lucy used the Identification Detective device of the Clairvoyance room only to confirm that they observed the same species they witnessed at the Osiris 4 Summit.

The legendary European Cave lion known as *Panthera leo spelaea* also once referred as *Felis leo spelaea* imposed their dominance that spread into Africa, Asia, and North America. They existed from the Middle to Late Pleistocene epoch ranging from 781,000 – 11,700 years ago. Meena suspected these impressive Cave lions were the apex predator of Europe that grew from 25% - 33% larger than the largest extant lions (*Panthera leo*) and noticeably larger than any existing tiger (*Panthera tigris*) known!

When Lucy looked over her left shoulder, she recognized that *Brontops* behaved more intense than before as they lowered their heads as an obvious gesture to stay away. She noticed *Bos primigenius* cautiously moving away as they kept a keen stare toward two of three invading Cave lions. When Meena looked over her left side she saw the pair of short horned aquatic rhinos identified as *Teleoceras* grazing further away. She thought about the Western horse heard that fled earlier was nowhere to be seen.

"I can't remember when rival predators interacted peacefully." Meena said while she monitored the giant European Cave lions approach the Bear dogs.

Both women focused their attention to an inevitable confrontation between two predators. Meena thought she'd never witness such a struggle. "Look at them clash."

All three Cave lions with white fur mixed with gray, stumbled upon the battered carcass before the pack of four relinquished it by running away from the immediate area. *Hemicyon* reluctantly fled while each feline held on to their portion of a mutilated carrion as Meena and Lucy viewed all three of them snarling and spitting as each individual tried to pull the carcass to their own direction making attempts to tear off a significant portion of their confiscated food source.

An agitated male made a stark growl when he noticed all four returning Bear dogs scanning for their opportunity to steal part of the carrion from the lions. A male *Hemicyon* actively utilized his nose to scent their patience, which would show how much meat they digested. As with any carnivore, the hungrier they are; the less tolerant they'll be toward rival competitors. Once a carnivore is full or even gorged themselves from overeating, then they'll be docile and more inviting. Some would even walk away from a rival if they were fully satisfied.

Both women heard greater volume of this male Cave lion's growl as *Hemicyon* continued their evaluation by circling them and searching for an opportunity to snatch any piece of the carcass away from them. Persistent rebuttal from *Hemicyon* convinced a snarling *Panthera* that his patience no longer served any purpose just before he pursued one of four Bear dogs. Judging from a swift mobilization of this male feline, both women realized that *Panthera* were biting cats similar to modern African lions rather than stabbing cats such as the Sabre-tooth cat. Lucy saw long sharp retractable curved claws along with a sheath membrane to prevent their claws from dissolving. Meena recognized that the Cave lion didn't evolve any typical male lion's mane but a pattern on longer fur under their jaws along the top of their necks and traveled in a wavy pattern down their spines and the top of their limbs with males growing longer hair than females.

Paleontologists continue to study what is believed to be the largest feline ever to exist! Debate continues in regards to whether the Cave lion is related to modern lions or tigers or were they an independent feline genus? Despite what various scholars conclude, all who study their great fossils are riveted from radio carbon dating that confirmed the Neanderthals and Cro-Magnons coexisted with this spectacular species!

Lucy noticed one of the four Bear dogs scurried from an enraged male that showed to be at his worst circumstance in terms of hunger. Enlarged canine teeth revealed a white row of flesh shredding incisors similar to modern living felines on Earth that also revealed a long day without a satisfying solution to an excruciating pain within his digestive tract.

Hemicyon stretched his legs as long as they could extend as he strode away from a ruthless feline struggling with famine. A steady snarl from *Panthera* forced *Hemicyon* to actively flex his spine as much as his anatomy enabled him to insure additional means to keep away from a relentless Cave lion.

Meena and Lucy noticed how *Panthera* reduced speed before he realized that there's a greater priority than to engage into this chase. Once this adult male looked over to the opposite direction, he immediately ran toward a depleting carcass. *Panthera* had only a few moments before he'll have an insignificant supply of meat. Both women were surprised to see a returning male almost as hostile to his companions as he was to the rival Bear dogs.

Individual attitudes and group tensions became surprisingly subtler one each Cave lion feasted on their satisfying share of their feast. Once they felt sated and felt reassured of fulfilling their nutrition demands, snarls and spitting of a subconscious feeding frenzy was superseded by a quiet purring expression emitting from three relieved Cave lions. Both women realized what greater effort various life forms on Isis and Earth would pursue to fulfill a significant demand especially if survival was ever in question.

"Now I understand why Mack is devoted to Isis." Lucy informed Meena.

Lucy explained her current observations and compared them to wildlife programs, Meena looked behind her only to find a tall heavily built mammoth approaching with full confidence of a mature male coming into season. "Lucy!"

Lucy took in a rapid and deep breath in as she shrieked to see a perplexing image of a bull mammoth the stood at least 13 feet (4m) off the ground and possessed a pair of 14 feet (4.27m) long enlarged curved tusks that arched forward until they crossed each other. These intimidating tusks were held by a massive body size surpassing 5 tons or 4.5 metric tons, while his longevity and maturity made him a full fledged adult.

Unlike most ancient mammoths, this species was less hairy indicating a long history of migrating south and adapting to a warmer climate. Their once shaggy fur that protected them from cold weather would shed when they settle into warmer regions. An enormous body size along with age, health, and a bold set of tusks along with an ever increasing dose of testosterone showed a primary candidate to attract suitable mates.

Both were startled to hear this male's groan as they felt a low pitched frequency resonated across the Clairvoyance telepresence projector room and penetrated their nerves. It appeared that he was staring at Lucy and Meena who continued to monitor his presence. Lucy initially suspected why this male focused his attention toward them. "I think he recognizes our probe."

"I hope he won't destroy it." Meena waited to observe what will happen next.

The male mammoth focused his attention toward the Eve probe that monitored and recorded this event. Lucy shared her friend's concern once he raised his dense trunk and pointed his nostrils toward their direction. Swift passages of air shifted inside his nostrils as he extended his trunk forward. As he examined a discreet probe, both women noticed that he scented something threatening once he withdrew his trunk.

"Uh oh, this male might knock it over," Lucy suspected as he initially waved his trunk and tusks.

Meena wondered what could generate such concern from a harmless probe. When the mature male peeked beyond the probe, he instantly and quite surprisingly walked around the Eve probe and charged toward where three Cave lions were feasting.

"Whew...that was close." Lucy felt relief. "I thought he'll destroy the probe for sure."

Brontops was the only group standing at the other side of the waterhole when this mammoth pursued the Cave lions. Although both species of giant herbivores acknowledged each other from their distances, *Brontops* felt some tension and concern as they monitored a male in season. Once they scented this male's true intensions, both brontotheres ultimately sympathized with the giant mammoth. Lucy and Meena were compelled to see a mutual defense between two herbivores.

Lucy verbally requested the identity of the pursuing bull mammoth eagerly confronting all three Cave lions. Once a match making process was made another holographic tabloid appeared on the floor next to them. Meena leaned over to read its contents.

"Whoa…this is identified as *Mammuthus columbi* referred also as the Columbian mammoth."

"What else does it say?"

"The Columbian mammoth lived during Late Pleistocene. However, there's one individual fossil in Nashville, Tennessee that was dated to be around 7,800 years old." Meena revealed.

"There's more!" Meena stated. "Their ancestors once ranged in the Siberian plains of Asia. Then the Columbian mammoth's ancestors migrated across the Bering Strait from the eastern tip of Asia into Alaska and continued to spread south through the western region of North America into Mexico and Florida."

"Wow, the Columbian mammoth accomplished a long and adaptive evolutionary history."

"The sure did." Meena confirmed as this male mammoth continued to pursue to confront three Cave lions that were more interested in feeding on a rare source of food.

Once a female Cave lion noticed the Columbian mammoth charge aggressively toward them she instantly took what she was consuming and held it tight inside her jaws before racing away with her share of what will give her energy for the near future. Soon after their female companions were chased away, the male Cave lion knew that rivaling an aggravated male bull mammoth in season would prove disastrous to himself and his pride.

The remaining male lion detected a heightened impulse of rage and resentment as two elongated tusks were deliberately aimed toward him. Meena also read that *Panthera leo spelaea* and their related subspecies of prehistoric lions such as *Panthera leo atrox* developed an intelligence to migrate across vast distances, which includes crossing the Bearing Strait from Asia before occupying most of North America, Central and the northern portion of South America. What's more is that many prehistoric lions developed an intelligence to realize the true danger of the tar pits by witnessing numerous herbivores and even rival predators become entrapped inside and dying either by sinking inside these pits, starvation or exhaustion. One likely reason why the European Cave lion lived up to historical times is by avoiding such danger that claimed many other lives.

Meena and Lucy realized so much could be learned by observing Isis's megafauna. She discovered how to interpret various behaviors of animals and their root cause. Meanwhile, Lucy felt a deep connection between humanity's distant past and the Central Continent. She thought how about how history repeats itself when she watched a brave male bull mammoth chased several fleeing felines. Lucy appreciated two extremely rare planets of Earth and Isis that reveal exceptional complexities of life in the known universe.

Monitoring three giant Cave lions retreat proves once again of such an unpredictable natural habitat. Both women never thought they'll be as excited and enthused of as Mack and Marcus, who were on their way to the orbiting flagship.

"Next scene," Lucy shouted out as their enthusiasm continued to grow inside a domed room.

"Wow! I could see for miles!" Meena was impressed to view an unobstructed view of open grassland.

She scanned in all directions to find a nearby forest opposite of her position. This simulator has taken them to the edge of the Great Plains! Only a lone tree stood near their location, but it never obstructed their view of this vast area along with various patches of trees, bushes, shrubs, bushels and weeds dotted across the open plain.

It didn't take much time to notice two different types of land birds they discovered. One of these two land birds appeared shorter and more heavily built than a taller sleeker one. The heavier moa evolved bald muscular legs but grew long strands of gold and brown plumage similar to the extant Brown Kiwi (*Apteryx mantelli*) of New Zealand. The lighter moa had short fine orange and red plumage that appeared to possess a smooth texture.

Meena was eager to find out what species on Earth could possibly compare to two fascinating flightless birds she monitored browsing at a thick batch of bushes for seeds and fruit. She made a verbal request for identity of both land birds that gradually walked in their direction. Once a match making process was completed, they leaned over to read the contents of both holographic tabloids displayed on the floor.

The shorter stockier moa they viewed was just like *Aepyornis maximus* of Madagascar, a large island off the southeast coast of Africa. The taller one was identified as *Dinornis giganteus* of the south island of New Zealand. Both species are believed to exist at some time during the Pleistocene epoch. *Aepyornis* existed until the 17th century. *Dinornis* lived up to around the year 1500.

"I find something very interesting about both of them." Meena claimed. "Isn't it a strange coincidence that both of the most impressive prehistoric land birds on Earth existed on an island near the southeast coast of a continent?"

"Since Madagascar is near Africa and New Zealand is close to Australia it would make sense if these islands had a land bridge that connected to the mainland, thus separating both species of land birds from their potential mainland adversaries." Lucy replied. "Since there were no predators and competition for food, these birds filled a niche by growing to their immense size."

Aepyornis was Earth's largest land bird ever to exist. Standing ten feet (3m) above the ground, fossil and historical evidence suggest *Aepyornis* weighed approximately 500 pounds (227kg) or more. Further findings suggest that they laid eggs that were over one foot (30.5cm) long and weighing 20 pounds (9kg). Such eggs posed a large interior that could hold 9½ quarts or almost nine liters. Three wide heavy toes on each foot supported their massive physique. When early explorers arrived at Madagascar during the sixth century of the Gregorian calendar, *Aepyornis*, which allegedly means greatest of the high birds, became commonly known as the elephant bird. Such a reference was originated by Arabian tales of the Rukhkh, which refers to how this massive primeval moa could carry an elephant over vast distances.

Dinornis was identified to be the tallest bird, which stood at least 11 feet, 6 inches (3.5m) and weighed 300 pounds (136kg) and behaved similar to the elephant bird. Human exploration and settlement during the tenth century in New Zealand hunted the elephant bird to their demise in the year 1500. *Aepyornis* suffered a similar fate in Madagascar two hundred years earlier in the 1600s. Viewing such valuable life forms that perished during historical times gripped Lucy as she felt a sense of regret about how these land birds vanished due to over hunting and deforestation activities. She reflected Mack's determination to preserve Isis's environment by refusing to make similar ecological mistakes made in the past and appreciated his efforts to contribute to Isis's well being.

"Lucy! Look at this!" Meena was captivated to sit before a flamboyant pattern of bony plates mounted on a domed shell.

"It's a turtle's shell!" Lucy realized.

"This turtle's magnificent!" Meena remarked. "This shell stands as tall as me."

Lucy stood up next to Meena. Both stood at five feet, seven inches (1.7m) tall. It was amazing to see a shell that stood only one inch (2.5cm) shorter than Lucy and Meena. Lucy's first response was to identify this spectacle.

"What kind of turtle is that?"

Lucy was amazed how the soul mate possessed data of a prehistoric legend existed in India and Pakistan around 2,000,000 years ago or within the Early Pleistocene. Further data revealed how this reptile was the largest land tortoise ever to exist in Earth's history. The Identification Detective device retrieved scientific estimation that large members of a species called *Colossochelys atlas* formerly known as *Testudo atlas* that grew eight feet (2.5m) long and weighed over a ton or 908 kilograms!

As Meena read additional facts, Lucy watched this shell before witnessing four limbs emerge from each socket before a long neck extended a large head. She saw four stocky legs with dense nails on his toes. This large male's legs arched and semisquatted stance that's common among reptiles. Protective cushioned pads underneath each sole of his foot enabled this giant turtle to travel considerable distances. His flexible neck enabled this titan of a turtle to consume grass, tall plants and even fruits. Lucy realized that a closest living resemblance on Earth was a massive tortoise of the Galapagos Islands known as *Geochelone nigras.*

"You know that the largest extant tortoise on Earth is the Galapagos tortoise. An adult could grow four feet long and weighed five hundred pounds." Lucy informed her.

"I've never imagine any turtle remotely like this."

"What's amazing is that since they're reptiles, the Galapagos giant tortoise could live well over 100 years!" Lucy added.

Both women continued to monitor the giant turtle walk across their view. It appeared that this male wanted to reach a destination where a group of stout plants stood. Both women realized this giant old male could be living well into his second century!

"Wait until we tell everyone what we've found." Meena was excited to discover three new species on Isis.

Lucy noticed shrubs and bushes bordering the woodland wiggle. Once she brought this to Meena's attention, both women witnessed these bushes and shrubs topple over by a large furry mammal swallowing leaves. It was easy to see four stocky legs supporting a massive body. This female's massive head and blunt stout resembled a giant wombat that grew an impressive array of claws on each foot and possessed smooth fur. Meena discovered two smaller mammals of the same species following her.

Lucy noticed their beige fur covering their legs, stomach, chest, throat and face. Rows of black diamond shaped spots were marked across their backs, shoulders, necks and heads. It became evident that both Meena watched a mother guide her maturing offspring. As they cautiously entered the open plains, Meena tried to identify this close knit group of healthy mammals, which grew up to ten feet (3m) long and stood well over six feet or two meters tall.

"It's *Diprotodon* of Pleistocene Australia." Meena explained how an awesome herbivore surveyed a large area of northern regions of this continent between 26 – 7 million years ago.

Although these marsupials generally appeared like giant wombats,

314

Diprotodon were an independent genus of the Diprotodontae family of marsupials whose fossils were found across Australia. Meena read how *Diprotodon* was the largest marsupial known as was an accomplished member of Australia's megafauna. Meena was shocked when she read that *Diprotodon* was estimated to have weighed over 6,000 pounds or exceed 2724 kilograms.

"This planet is full of surprises. I thought no such environment could exist in the universe." Lucy expressed her intrigue as she monitored this family of marsupials.

Both land birds observed *Diprotodon* with her offspring searching along the forest border. *Colossochelys atlas* behaved indifferently toward all three marsupials as the giant tortoise continued to chew leaves from ripe low level plants.

Although these massive claws of *Diprotodon* appeared threatening, Australia's prehistoric marsupials were herbivores that acknowledged both land birds. Lucy thought about Mack, Marcus and Derrick as they're approaching the orbiting flagship. "I hope we'll find answers to these flying spheres."

Meena also shared her concerns about future events unfolding as she continued to monitor activities of the open plains. "I hope so too...by the way, how are you and Mack getting along?"

"I think that when he comes back that I will propose to him." Lucy decided.

"You're willing to marry him?"

"Yes...I'm convinced that he's the one."

Meena paused for a moment and thought about how she felt towards Marcus. "I have the same feeling for Marcus...but, I'm nervous to tell him."

"We'll wait until they return."

Meena thought about Lucy's suggestion and decided that since this latest development should be the sole priority, she'd decided to wait until this issue is resolved before proposing to Marcus. "Not a bad idea."

Lucy smiled as she felt exuberance. "Just think, this matter will be resolved and we would be married as well."

"I think the best of times are clearly ahead of us." Meena claimed before both women happily embraced each other.

*   *   *

"We're ready to dock sir." One of two pilots informed all three passengers who sat patiently.

One pilot carefully positioned the shuttle craft until it was directly above a sliding hatch on top of the mother ship. When the ship's docking bay doors was opened the shuttle was successfully docked on to a landing pad inside the flagship. Mack contemplated various scenarios of what information this disk would reveal and how to respond accordingly.

A faint vibration was felt as this sealed hatch slid closed before supplies of oxygen filled the perimeter of the hangar. Once a panel light signaled sufficient oxygen, all three passengers unbuckled their seat belts and walked over to the front of the shuttle craft where a sealed hatch at the shuttle craft on the floor was opened before extending a portable ladder from a nearby storage compartment and slid it down until it touched the landing pad. Dr. Ryan then clamped both sides of the top of the ladder into a brace so it would remain stable as they left the shuttle craft.

"This way sir," one of the pilots guided them to a sealed door that led them out of the flagship's cargo deck.

After passing through a vestibule, Dr. Ryan and the others opened another sealed door that led them to a spiral stairwell that guided them one level down into an elongated corridor where they walked toward the front end of the orbiting flagship where they've noticed a slim man walking over to them.

"Gentlemen, I'm glad you could come on such short notice!" Dr. Gruber acknowledged. "Doctor Hollis will meet you at the vault room.

Dr. Gruber led all three men over to the same level where the command and control center was located. Once they arrived at their desired level, all four men headed the opposite direction to the vault room within the corridor. Two familiar men stood outside and guarded the front of a reinforced steel vault.

"Mike! Dave! How are you?" Dr. Nimbus greeted both men guarding the vault room.

"I haven't seen you for a while. How've you been?" Mike asked as Dave began unlocking the security door by pressing a series of buttons installed on an adjacent panel.

Once Dave's sequence was complete, this thick hatch opened revealing a pattern of vertical steel bars comprising of a sliding gate. Dave used his keys to unlock before sliding it open. Once they entered the vault, a single light inside the vault room activated as they got situated.

All vaults were locked before Dave used the once classified key that's designed to open vault #1. Inside was a carry case Dr. Nimbus, Dr. Grace and Dr. Gruber's names on them. They removed their assigned keys from the vault and used them to unlock vault #2, where the large key for Dr. Ryan was stored.

Dr. Ryan noticed red light above vault #4 indicating that X-rays are erasing the data from the disk stored inside, which possessed alternate information and directives. Dr. Ryan removed this small carry case securing a key meant for him to open vault #3. Mack then removed it from the vault before confirming this disk is authentic due to his long term memory. Before they gave back their designated keys to Dave, Dr. Hollis arrived before he guided them out of the vault room and lead them to a projector room where this specific disk would reveal all of its contents.

All five gentlemen entered a small room with a conference table with containing six seats. Dr. Ryan carefully removed the disk from its container as the others shifted their seats to one side of this small conference table so they could watch its contents on a flat screen LCD monitor inserted into a wall.

"I understand this is an intense moment for us." Dr. Ryan said before he added, "But we must learn the truth."

"What if there's a new mission directive?" Dr. Hollis asked.

"That's possible," Dr. Ryan responded. "If that's the case then we should obey all directives."

"I hope the video won't order us to travel back to Earth." Dr. Nimbus pouted.

"I hope not either." Mack replied.

"Well…everybody ready?" Mack asked his colleagues.

"I'm ready," Dr. Nimbus responded.

"We're ready," Drs. Hollis, Grace and Gruber confirmed.

Dr. Ryan then pressed a button to open a latch that slid out before placing this disk into its holding compartment before he pressed the same button again to close it. Dr. Ryan sat at his seat before the screen showed Dr. Netherland sitting behind a conference table with President Wilson and Dr. Mobutu.

Dr. Netherland sat at the center while Secretary General Mobutu sat at Dr. Netherland's left side while the President sat at his right. Judging from this room's setting, Dr. Ryan realized that this footage was taken at the federation's headquarters. All three gentlemen appeared grateful and felt optimistic to all who would view this presentation on this 50-inch (127cm) flat screen.

"Greetings, by now you would've settled on Isis." An image of Dr. Netherland stated. *"All of you made history by pioneering humanity into an interstellar civilization for the first time ever."*

Dr. Netherland informed each viewer that this presentation was made after the Osiris 4 Summit ended. He told viewers that it's likely that they've encountered unprecedented circumstances. Everyone was shocked to hear how Dr. Netherland accurately described spherical shaped aerial objects similar to what unnerved Dr. Ryan and his crew during their new settlement on Isis.

"How did he know about the existence of these objects?" Dr. Nimbus wondered as he continued to describe their behavior.

*   *   *

Lucy and Meena continued to monitor activities at the edge of the Great

Plains. All that remained was the giant land tortoise gently walking away. Both land birds known as *Dinornis giganteus* and *Aepyornis maximus* left the area searching for more vegetation to feed, while all three marsupials identified as *Diprotodon* traveled further to indulge into distant plants.

Lucy and Meena were studying what appeared to be a familiar prehistoric reptile with an enlarged arched shaped solar sail attached to the spinal chord from the rear of this male's neck and ended at the base of his tail. The structure of this finback reptile possessed long spikes from each individual vertebrae extending up to three feet and three inches or about one meter tall at the center. Meena suspected these sail attached to every spike to be a thick membrane, which contained an array of blood vessels throughout the sail on his back.

It was apparent that this male's sail was positioned toward the parent star Osiris. Meena noticed that daylight would penetrate his thick membrane and warm individual blood cells throughout his sail. A heavy skull with sharp brittle teeth along with tan scales made it easy for Lucy to identify the genus of this male to be *Dimetrodon* that mastered a strategy of rapidly warming up their body temperature by using this sail as an effective means to receive a sufficient dose of daylight in such a short period of time.

Extending ten feet (3m) long and weighing approximately 400 pounds (180kg) *Dimetrodon* grew as large as a Komodo dragon (*Varanus komodoensis*) of Indonesia. It was necessary for *Dimetrodon* to be able to raise body temperature within one and a half hours instead of over three hours for a similar sized reptile. This ancient reptile of Texas and Oklahoma was able to mobilize much faster than other reptilian life forms within their prehistoric fauna during the Early and Middle Permian, which ranged from roughly 299,000,000 – 260,400,000 years ago.

Reading information about *Dimetrodon* revealed that the name of this male's genus means, two measures of teeth, because it evolved more than one type of teeth in its mouth like mammals. *Dimetrodon* is the apex predator of their time and was able to scavenge. While this revered reptile continues to condition his body temperature, Lucy noticed a group of six in a herd that emerged from behind a distant batch of trees.

Lucy made a hand signal to activate a zoom lens to focus on six migrating herbivores. When Lucy found her best angle of view she noticed their bulky limbs to walk over to a collection of ferns. Meena noticed largest one grew nine feet (2.7m) long and weighed about one ton or 908 kilograms. Her careful analysis confirmed this mysterious reptile evolved bony plates within their skin as protection from predators and may well be efficient solar receptors riddled with blood vessels in order to rapidly warm up their body temperature.

Each individual carried a pair of canine teeth, which classified this prehistoric herbivore as a dicynodont or mammal-like reptiles. These herbivores fed on club-moss, low level ferns, roots and even tubers.

The most notable feature was their solid curved beak that was aligned with a pair short solid tusks emerging from behind their curved beaks and underneath each eye. Each tusk at either side of their cheeks extended at least several inches or centimeters longer than their curved beaks. Their thick gray and green leathery skin aided these gentle plant eaters' formidable appearance. Lucy suspected these tusks were also used for defense against lethal predators and a tool for maturing males to compete for mates.

Meena and Lucy used the Identification Detective device to discover what they could be. Lucy leaned over to read startling information. "Listen to this…a genus called *Placerias* apparently lived up to the Late Triassic, which their ancestors survived the Permian – Triassic extinction event also known as the Great Dying."

Lucy described how up to 96% of all oceanic life and 70% of all terrestrial inhabitants perished within a few million years. Meena remembered Dr. Netherland claiming that at least one massive comet or asteroid exceeding the size of Manhattan collided into southern region of Pangea. He suspected such an impact would've sent powerful shockwaves throughout the planet's crust before seismic energy focused its full force toward the impact site's antipode to trigger a possible plume eruption where the Siberian Traps would be today. Such an eruption that's worse than any supervolcano by far could've lasted for at least one million years. Such an event could've caused a sudden release of toxic methane hydrates from the ocean floor. These geologically devastating events may have even influenced the breakup of the supercontinent Pangea into all the existing continents Earth has today. Lucy became grateful to see extinct animals on Earth living on Isis. She realized a time machine would be the only alternative to see *Placerias* walking across the open plains.

Dimetrodon continued to bask in the sun and monitored *Placerias* while they indulged into low level ferns. Lucy watched both inhabitants conduct their daily routines of survival. Meena detected a strange bird-like creature searching for food. She analyze an elongated feathery tail that matched the length of the rest of this indigenous animal's body.

"Lucy! Take a look at this!"

Lucy was face to face with a life form similar to a legendary animal that altered the course of science since the nineteenth century. "That can't be *Archaeopteryx*?"

"Let's find out." Meena said while identifying this creature that matched the size of a European Magpie (*Pica pica*).

Once the results arrived, both women were excited to read the contents of *Archaeopteryx lithographica* that once existed in Germany during the Late

Jurassic or around 161,200,000 – 145,500,000 years ago. Scientists were baffled ever since they were first discovered accidentally in 1861 CE when laborers excavated a limestone quarry at Solnhofen, southern Germany. As craftsmen cut and shaped each individual limestone, one slab split open revealing a near perfect fossil specimen of what became known as a link between dinosaurs and modern birds!

Not only that these fossilized remains of *Archaeopteryx* were preserved, but impressions of feathers were also traced within the limestone slab interpreted as wings and a tail. Tourists from all over the world visit London's Natural History Museum to witness detailed anatomy of this spectacular specimen. Another more complete fossil of *Archaeopteryx* was discovered at a different slab at the same limestone quarry site in 1877, which was transported and currently exhibited at Berlin's Humboldt University Museum.

Both women continued to observe this female's blue base feathers as her wings showed a green haze along with black edges. She possessed large eyes and pointed teeth within her jaws instead of a sharp edged beak. Such a distinction led paleontologists to theorize a new perspective of how some dinosaurs survived beyond the K-T Boundary.

Since recent times, scientists analyzed similarities between modern birds and two legged bipedal theropod dinosaurs such as *Velociraptor, Deinonychus* and even others such as *Allosaurus* and *Tyrannosaurus rex*! Both, Aves (birds) and bipedal dinosaurs walked on three pigeon-toed feet connected to long legs along with extended bony tails for balance.

Most importantly both groups possessed similar hipbones, but *Archaeopteryx* developed a wishbone formed by two fused collarbones similar to modern birds. *Archaeopteryx* never developed a sternum like modern flight birds as a foundation for strong breast muscles. Available evidence showed that *Archaeopteryx* didn't actively flap their wings like birds, but were adapted to glide short distances from one area to another. Lucy recalled when Dr. Netherland told her that *Archaeopteryx* behaved more like the Southern flying Squirrel (*Glaucomys volans*) of North America, the Sunda Flying Lemur (*Galeopterus variegatus*) and the Flying Dragon (*Draco volans*) of Southeast Asia mastered this technique by utilizing their membranes or flaps of extra skin to capture gusts of wind to glide from one higher location to another lower location without ground contact. This technique serves two survival strategies of searching great distances for prey such as insects, lizards and small mammals and to rapidly escape from potential predators.

Lucy remember Dr. Netherland suspecting *Archaeopteryx* being capable of employing their extended fingers attached to their wings equipped with curved pointed talons to climb up trees before positioning themselves to glide over impressive distances. Such a unique evolutionary niche made it possible to travel long distances without consuming much physical energy. This female *Archaeopteryx* was covered with feathers except for her muzzle as a means to prevent infection while feeding, she was able to self regulate her body temperature like all aves to make it possible to engage into a physically active lifestyle. Dr. Netherland also believed *Archaeopteryx* could possibly be an evolutionary intermediary between bipedal dinosaurs and birds.

As soon as this female noticed *Dimetrodon*, she immediately used her long slender limbs to run toward the closest tree before climbing up to a high branch so she would not become prey. When *Archaeopteryx* eluded trouble, both women realized science would never be the same again and future exploration will be adventurous! Lucy was grateful that they could observe a host of animals living their lives instead of studying fossils. Meena also appreciated the fact that by observing fossilized animals of Earth living a pristine existence on Isis would test various research strategies that inspired past theories of life and evolution.

*   *   *

On board the orbiting flagship, the entrance door of this small conference room opened, a shocked expression was displayed on the faces of Dr. Ryan and his colleagues. Beads of sweat dotted Mack's face as he took a deep breath. He felt vastly different regarding these mysterious silver spheres. However, Dr. Netherland's video presentation provided enough assurance of its authenticity. Since he remembered this disk's code number embedded on its surface and the fact that this particular disk could only be recorded once and never be rerecorded, Dr. Ryan will abide by this mission's protocol unconditionally.

"Dr. Ryan, what do you want to do?" Dr. Hollis asked.

"The best solution is to conduct a news conference and broadcast it to the entire crew."

Dr. Gruber was excited about Dr. Ryan's idea. "I'll set up the auditorium while you prepare for your presentation."

Dr. Gruber then proceeded down the corridor and pursued to prepare the auditorium for a broadcast news conference. Dr. Hollis then assured them that he'd contact the entire ship and all who landed on Isis to schedule a broadcast conference so everyone would be informed of the true nature of these strange entities. Dr. Hollis activated his Watchdog device to advise all personnel to be prepared to receive breaking news.

When Dr. Gruber informed key crewmembers to distribute the information, Dr. Ryan contacted Dr. Weinstein to relay the truth to the Central Continent crew. Dr. Nimbus contacted Dr. Jordan Tyrell, commander of the Western Continent to prepare for a broadcast event. Dr. Hollis, who will become future commander of the Eastern Continent, will collect all of this data to bring it to with him when he departs the flagship. Once all necessary communications were completed all four gentlemen knew what they had to do.

"We should wear our dress whites since we're addressing this formal historical news conference." Dr. Nimbus referred to wearing their white formal attire with reflective silver single breasted buttons along with a silver ensign on each shoulder.

Once Dr. Nimbus made his suggestion, all three of them went to the dressing rooms where they'll prepare for this conference. Dr. Ryan was excited to wear the same outfit that members of the Chamber wore during special occasions, especially Dr. Netherland who wore dress whites often. Mack's excitement and exuberance escalated as they approached the dressing room while contemplating how he'll speak to the entire crew.

*   *   *

Meena and Lucy continued to observe the Great Plains until they were interrupted by Dr. Taina Kepa who just received news from Intelligence. "Ladies...come quick we're scheduled for a news broadcast from the starship Guardian!"

Both women suspected that the answers to their mysteries of these strange flying spheres would finally be revealed. Lucy verbally ordered the Clairvoyance system to deactivate before dull white walls of a domed room replaced scenes of the colorful Great Plains. Only a single light at the top of this domed room reactivated when all three women departed the room and headed for the main entrance.

All three women walked down two flights of stairs before they arrived at the main entrance where technicians assembled a large video projection screen mounted in front of eight rows of chairs. All three women took their seats at the front row as intelligence officials, medical personnel, explorers and engineers met before taking their seats. As soon as everyone was seated, Dr. Weinstein announced a broadcast transmission would be in effect.

Once they received the transmission, members of this audience were viewing a stage located inside the orbiting flagship's auditorium. Only a wide podium equipped with microphones was placed on stage. It was easy to them to watch an assembly of enthusiastic participants. The projection screen behind the podium was left exposed as spotlights lit up the stage. Dr. Grace arrived from the left side of this stage wearing his dress whites before he approached the podium. Everyone noticed his pinned metals draped over chest as the audience anticipated the most pivotal news in recent memory.

"*Ladies and gentlemen, please give a round of applause to Dr. Mackenzie Ryan and Dr. Marcus Nimbus!*" After Dr. Grace's introduction, he then waved to both men emerging from the right side of the stage before receiving a warm welcome from the audience as they walked over the podium.

Both men wearing their finest outfits with metals appreciated their warm reception by waving their white cotton gloves and thanking everyone who attended as cheers of applause provided additional encouragement. Once this lengthy applause receded, Dr. Ryan then initiated this historical presentation.

"Ladies and gentlemen, Dr. Nimbus and I wish to express our gratitude for attending this news conference. As most of you know, since we landed and explored the planet's surface, we've encountered an unusual set of circumstances."

Dr. Ryan added. *"As long as we both worked for the Humane Space Federation, none of us ever imagined we'll ever witness such a strange phenomenon from the sky."*

Dr. Nimbus revealed. *"After reviewing a secured information disk provided to us by Dr. Netherland and the Chamber, we've came to a conclusion that these UFOs we encountered are officially identified."*

The audience's attention intensified as Dr. Nimbus continued to provide their discovery. *"Dr. Ryan and I verified the authenticity of this information and concluded that all data contained inside this disk is legitimate and provides all necessary answers to our most recent dilemma."*

Dr. Meena Singh and Dr. Lucy Rosalila both held each other's hand as they braced for anticipated news from Dr. Ryan. *"I wish to present actual data provided by Dr. Netherland for everyone to witness."*

Dr. Ryan then requested to dim the lights and activate the projector before both men moved aside before the podium lowered until it was submerged under the stage so everyone could view the screen. The audience then recognized Dr. Netherland seated with President Russell Wilson and Secretary General Kufi Mobutu.

"Greetings Dr. Ryan, Dr. Nimbus, Dr. Grace and all who will view this presentation; the president and the secretary general both endorse the information I'm ready to reveal," were the words of Dr. Netherland as both President Wilson and Secretary General Mobutu knotted their heads in agreement.

When this introductory presentation ended, the image of three distinguished gentlemen was replaced by an image of Dr. Netherland wearing jeans and a buttoned shirt as he corresponded from a remote desert site near federation headquarters. While the audience watched his image, everyone was compelled to see two of these reflective silvery spheres descend toward the desert surface before hovering 30 feet (9.15m) above the ground.

Dr. Netherland's voice continued to be heard. *"As you can see, these identified flying objects have been with the federation for a long time. The abilities and effectiveness of each object presents a multitude of opportunity for the Humane Space Federation to accomplish some of our greatest challenges."*

The audience appeared confused because nobody suspected that these anomalous entities were functioning on behalf of the Humane Space Federation. As these objects moved freely around the immediate area, the audience saw Dr. Netherland come into view as he stood at the desert and pointed to both silvery spheres. *"What you're witnessing is nothing less than the most advanced prototype ever to exist in federation history."*

Daylight in the desert reflected off Dr. Netherland's face as he walked comfortably in a pair of boots. He twitched his eyes to prevent a mild cross breeze from blowing sand particles into his eyes. The audience then watched both devices hovering next to each other behind Dr. Netherland before he continued to speak.

"So far a total of twenty of these prototypes were developed, although considerable expense and effort was mandatory in order to produce these objects, however the federation and all of human civilization of Earth and Isis will be rewarded by our latest triumph."

Nothing more shocking and incredible could be revealed to the entire audience. Dr. Singh could barely believe such an object could ever be manufactured on Earth while Dr. Rosalila remained silent. Intelligence officials including Dr. Weinstein barely uttered a word as they focused all of their attention to the projector screen showing data that was once classified as top secret. Dr. Alicia Nevins, Dr. Fan Zhu and other explorers felt a sense of relief that these aerial crafts weren't hostile and could provide significant research benefits as it provided accurately detailed information of the Central Continent's topography and placed all this valuable data into the Soul Mate databank.

Dr. Malik al-Saud and his medical staff felt intrigued to learn how they could be actively working with these objects and could possibly decipher DNA compositions of each life form on Isis. Such capability could make it possible to decode accurate DNA strands inside chromosomes and ultimately be able to know the exact strands of each molecule within the cells of every living thing ever recorded without being subjected to feral hazards.

Engineers were intrigued to discover how these devices operated and wondered how they were capable of interstellar space travel and how they were able to travel great distances without consuming any fuel. Although most engineers were surprised by the news, enthusiasm for these objects' potential and their full benefits were shared among all engineers and technicians. All Chamber members who traveled to Isis such as Dr. Hollis, Dr. Grace, Dr. Gruber and Dr. Esther Weinstein were happy to learn about a cleaver ally instead of an intelligent adversary.

The audience inside the auditorium as well as all viewers noticed Dr. Netherland providing hand signals to both objects that instantly responded, convincing everyone that they were developed by the federation and would pose no harm whatsoever. Although concern for artificially intelligence was sympathized throughout the audience, Dr. Netherland informed everyone that each enlarged brain inside every craft is physically designed and programmed to respond to human needs through mental telepathy. It could detect when a person is worried and can decipher a solution to any individual's concern. The official name of these silver spheres was formerly introduced as Mindset, which was capable of transmitting telepathic messages across vast distances of space into a group of these massive brains inside a vast nanocomputer complex at headquarters so researchers on Earth could received messages from Isis and decode its contents of any latest situation.

Energy is supplied by various wavelengths distributed from all over the universe. From ultraviolet to radio waves is sufficient to provide enough power to activate these objects through minute receptor cells on its silvery surface. If maintenance is ever required, then it could be conducted in space where it could rest safely as it orbits Isis along with the Flagship. Dr. Netherland advised that the central nervous system at its center never needs maintenance and only its advanced circuitry would need occasional service. Once Dr. Netherland told viewers of how it could trace a planet's surface and relay accurate information to any Geographic or Planetary Indicator, Dr. Arnold Weinstein felt relief.

Dr. Netherland also stressed that each craft is capable of emitting various types of lasers varying from tracers to military weaponry. He also assured that none of these features would ever be misused by any of these new models for any reason. He also told everyone his estimation that these objects should last at least a century and advised those on Isis to make the best of this exceptional opportunity.

After he revealed the facts the audience then viewed the original scene of Dr. Netherland and his two distinguished guests seated at the original conference table. He then revealed that all 20 Mindset models were secretly stored into the Starship Guardian before Earth's departure and only two operatives referred as Mike and Dave, who guarded the vault room, knew everything about these prototypes. Mike and Dave knew how Mindset operated and when to activate them. Once he completed his basic description, Dr. Netherland promised that blueprint diagrams of these objects and how they operated would be available from the Soul Mate databank system and filed under the name Mindset.

"For all who viewed this data, I wish to congratulate each and every single one of you who handled this situation similar to how the federation wanted you

to handle such a situation, if there ever would be any extraterrestrial encounter." Dr. Netherland stated. "*The main reason why we sent these objects secretly and influenced your initial impression of these objects is to ensure every one of you would be qualified to handle the most unprecedented circumstances because the universe consists of numerous unprecedented circumstances.*"

Dr. Netherland began to sob before he delivered his final message. "*Since the discovery of Isis, I came to a conclusion that anything is possible within this incredible universe, which was why I was convinced that an encounter with an advanced scientific and technological civilization of sentient beings would not surprise me and other members of the federation. This incident assured us that we have the most talented, stable and most qualified people to handle such a challenge if it ever occurred.*"

Sympathy for Dr. Netherland was shared among the audience and viewers alike. "*On behalf of all world leaders including President Wilson and Secretary General Mobutu, I wish to tell everyone at planet Isis…may God bless you and we hope everyone will achieve peace, love, fulfillment, prosperity and happiness. Although this transition of humanity becoming an interstellar civilization will be completed, we will do everything necessary to continue our support and maintain communications. Farewell and I wish you all the best for you and planet Isis.*"

When all data of this particular disk was revealed, silence and sobbing was widely distributed among those who viewed this presentation. Once a subtle and supportive image of a mentoring Dr. Netherland and his distinguished constituents vanished into a blank screen, Drs. Ryan and Nimbus returned to the podium as lights of the auditorium illuminated once again. Drs. Rosalila, Singh and the entire group of observers at Town Hall watched both men poised and confident due to information stored inside a tiny disk that contained secret data. Not only did everyone's trials and tribulations finally come to a close, Dr. Netherland's message convinced the crew of their abilities to behave rationally if they ever experienced any anomalous encounters.

Dr. Ryan continued their presentation. "*Ladies and gentlemen, friends, colleagues and co-pioneers of this Era of Isis, now it's time to end our fear of the unknown and inspire a new beginning of hope and possibilities in human history!*"

Crowds inside the auditorium and the main entrances of Town Hall of the Western and Central Continents exerted cheers, whistles and applause as two reassuring figures waved from on stage. Both men acknowledged their favorable response before walking over to the right side of the stage. Tears traveled down Dr. Rosalila's face, while Dr. Singh sobbed as she continued to stare at a man she decided to spend the rest of her life with walking down the steps on the right side of the stage, greeting a delighted audience.

Observers inside Town Hall observed hugs, kisses and handshakes focused upon Drs Ryan, Nimbus and Grace. Members of the audience waited for their turn to express their gratitude to three gentlemen eager to embrace all. A standing ovation inside Town Hall resulted in cheer as viewers at the Central Continent embraced and congratulated each other for their contribution of the greatest accomplishment known within this euphoric crowd. After Drs. Singh and Rosalila exchanged their joy with their colleagues, both of them walked over to the edge of the main entrance.

A gold shade of daylight from Osiris reflected off their faces while they enjoy a wide panorama of the bay and ocean. Lucy and Meena contemplated their future exploration inside an inviting world. They viewed the sight of Osiris setting beyond the ocean's horizon, as they acknowledged fear coming to a close and a new day of optimism to commence when Osiris rises above the eastern horizon. Crescent reflections from two moons orbiting Isis showed a celestial symbol of humanity's open arms to embrace this new world and Isis's warm welcome to all who traveled three light years to reap the rewards of this cosmic treasure. A subtle gust of wind encouraged both women to gracefully enter their new phase in life, which will be changed forever.

"I could barely wait for them to come back!" Meena cried as they continued to anticipate their future.

Lucy shared her emotions as she decided that she'll become a spouse to a man who brought so much joy in her life and this entire mission. "Once they come back, I'll let Mack know that he would be the one."

*　　　*　　　*

God bless you Marcus! God bless you Mack!" One cheerful member of the audience shouted out.

"God bless you too," were the response of two dignified men who continued to greet everyone!

Friends and colleagues continued to praise all three gentlemen as they progressed up an aisle and headed to an exit. As they departed, more people continued to congratulate them as they walked down a long corridor. Attendees at this gathering followed Dr. Ryan and his colleagues as they approached the front end of the orbiting starship.

A passionate sense of accomplishment was shared among all three men when they entered the command and control center where helms people and navigators managed to successfully maintain a steady orbit around Isis. Enlarged observation windows show Isis's dark nighttime sky. As the starship continued to orbit Isis, a halo of light peeked from the other side of the planet. A quiet attentive crowd stared into the dark side of planet Isis.

Dr. Ryan continued to stare at an unveiling panorama as he felt his best days are ahead. "I think since our greatest challenge been resolved that I wish to become engaged with Lucy."

Dr. Nimbus raised his eyebrows when he heard Dr. Ryan's intention to spend the rest of his life with a woman who fascinated him since he first knew about her. "You're sure?"

"I'm positive…I was thinking it over and decided there's no other person who I want to be with for the rest of my life." Mack concluded as they continued to monitor their orbital path.

"I never thought you'll be so inclined to get married." Dr. Nimbus felt surprised by his best friend's intention.

"I've thought about it for a long time, but I've finally came to a conclusion, there's no other woman anywhere like Lucy, which is why I will tell her." Dr. Ryan added.

Once Dr. Nimbus heard his friend's affirmation, he paused to think for a few seconds. "When we return to Town Hall, I'll propose to Meena that she's the one who'll be my wife."

Dr. Ryan felt happy for his long time colleague as they continued to look out the observation deck where all 19 surviving Mindset objects instantly appeared outside the flagship directly ahead of their view. "Now what?"

Intrigue instead of uncertainty energized everyone inside the command and control center. Dr. Ryan wondered what their next task would be as they remained positioned in front of the flagship. Crewmembers at the bridge no longer felt threatened by Mindset, but were curious of why all of them appeared without any prior notice. One of the communications officers received an incoming signal displayed at the screen of his monitor.

"Dr. Ryan, we have an encoded message originating from one of these objects."

"Translate it on loudspeaker and record the message." After he received Dr. Ryan's orders, he flipped a switch before an English version of this signal was translated.

"Greetings for all who traveled to Isis to explore this new world; It is our obligation to reassure the entire crew that we're peaceful and will serve the Humane Space Federation. We wish to congratulate all who traveled three light years to settle on this new planet. We will continue to serve, protect and contribute to your new community and maintain our loyalty. Although we must return to Isis, we will always be with you. May we extend our best wishes to all who've departed Earth to live in this promising new world."

Once their message was completed, all 19 Mindset models simultaneously darted away from their original position directly ahead of the ship and raced toward the planet's horizon. As soon as the crew was no longer able to see any of these objects, Osiris peeked out from behind Isis revealing more unexplored regions to discover. All 19 Mindset crafts pursued to survey uncharted regions of this mysterious new world.

Once daylight revealed more details of Isis atmosphere and terrain, a sense of accomplishment was felt among this entire crew. A warm sense of friendship was felt among all who observed Mindset's departure. 19 prototypes, which are so sophisticated, it was conceived to be alien to the crew's conventional wisdom of aerial entities, will dedicate their sentient intelligence and social loyalty to the Humane Space Federation.

Like all mysteries that propelled humanity's curiosity and inspired enthusiasm to unravel the truth, this former mystery will forever be understood. Dr. Ryan will chart a new course for his crew before he thought about his future with his fiancé. Members of the crew reassured their rightful place within the federation and their contribution to human history. As for humanity, science will continue to change everyone for the better while civilization will survive, thrive and find an ever greater understanding of their place in the universe. In the minds of all who arrived at Isis realized humanity is gifted with many virtues that will overcome any social, economic and political challenges. As silence dominated inside the bridge, each person who settled on Isis came to a thoughtful conclusion that regardless of mounting challenges and imminent dangers, their settlement was worth every bit of their effort and action!

Welcome to:

"READERS' AIDE"

CAST OF MAIN CHARACTERS

Name	Position	Birthplace
Dr. Russell S. Wilson	President of the United States	Dallas, Texas (U.S.A.)
Dr. Kufi A. Mobutu	Secretary General of the United Nations	Nairobi, Kenya
Dr. Donald Netherland	Founder and Chairman of the Humane Space Federation	????
Dr. Julius Ramón Garcia	Presidential Advisor	San Juan, Puerto Rico
Dr. Deborah Reynolds	The Chamber	Miami, Florida (U.S.A.)
Dr. Mack Ryan	Mission Commander	New York, N.Y. (U.S.A.)
Dr. Lucy Rosalila	Psychology	Hope People, Mesoamerica, Arizona, (U.S.A.)
Dr. Marcus Nimbus	Vice Mission Commander	Los Angeles, California (U.S.A.)
Dr. Meena Singh	Engineering	Bombay, India
Dr. Karl Gruber	The Chamber	Bonn, Germany
Dr. Jordan Tyrell	Western Continent Commander	Detroit, Michigan (U.S.A.)
Dr. Daryl Hollis	The Chamber	Atlanta, Georgia (U.S.A.)

Dr. Arnold Weinstein	Intelligence	Tel-Aviv, Israel
Dr. Esther Weinstein	The Chamber	Tel-Aviv, Israel
Dr. Fan Zhu	Explorer	Shanghai, China
Dr. Ying Zhu	Engineering	Beijing, China
Dr. Derrick Grace	The Chamber	Ottawa, Canada
Dr. Julia Grace	Medic	Buenos Aries, Argentina
Dr. Malik al-Saud	Medic	Riyadh, Saudi Arabia
Dr. Ada al-Saud	Medic	Cairo, Egypt
Dr. Martin de' la' Vega	Explorer	Mexico City, Mexico
Dr. Angela de' la' Vega	Explorer	Rio de' Janeiro, Brazil
Dr. Art Remington	Engineering	London, United Kingdom
Dr. Doris Remington	Medical	Sydney, Australia
Dr. Harold Nevins	Intelligence	Chicago, Illinois (U.S.A.)
Dr. Alicia Nevins	Explorer	Cape Town, South Africa
Dr. Viktor Ivanov	Engineering	Kiev, Ukraine
Dr. Nina Ivanov	Intelligence	Moscow, Russia
Dr. Antonio Marino	Intelligence	Rome, Italy
Dr. Tracy Marino	Medical	Dublin, Ireland
Dr. Haru Nakamura	Engineering	Hiroshima, Japan
Dr. Taina Kepa	Intelligence	Suva, Fiji Islands
Dr. Claude Moreau	Intelligence	Paris, France
Dr. Zarina Ansari	Engineering	Tehran, Iran
Dr. Ozdem Yilmaz	Intelligence	Istanbul, Turkey
Dr. Natasha Aliyev	Intelligence	Astana, Kazakhstan

Chronology of the Humane Space Federation

November 7th 2015: Dr. Donald Netherland commanded humanity's first mission to mars, which was funded and operated jointly by the National Aeronautics and Space Administration (N.A.S.A.), the European Space Agency (E.S.A.), China, Russia and many other nations worldwide.

November 10th 2018: The entire Mars Mission crew safely and successfully returned to Earth declaring victory for humanity.

October 12th 2019: Dr Donald Netherland, Dr. Kufi Mobutu, Dr. Russell Wilson, Dr. Darryl Hollis and others officially founded the Humane Space Federation.

September 1st 2023: An orbital space telescope called the Illuminator discovered a unique planet orbiting around a solitary star system known as Osiris.

June 18th 2025: The Humane Space Federation launched the Adam & Eve probes from Earth to travel to this new planet.

February 21st – March 12th 2023: Dr. Netherland and other founders of the federation attended the World Peace and Progress Summit in Geneva. Topics such as demilitarization, collective environmental responsibility and global challenges to ban global terrorism and antimatter weapons while dismantling chemical, biological and nuclear weapons were resolved within this three week assembly of world leaders and experts. A new age of world peace was born when every world leader signed and declared a permanent alliance of people worldwide.

June 1st 2027: Hoi Kan Pao and Derrick Larson discovered a two mile wide spherical asteroid drifting toward Earth, which imposed grave consequences for humanity's existence.

July 1st – July 5th 2027: Dr. Donald Netherland assigns Dr. Mack Ryan and Dr. Marcus Nimbus to command a team of 50 scientists and engineers to travel and land on this threatening asteroid called; Hoi-Larson to place powerful retro-rockets to successfully capture and safely orbit the asteroid around the Earth before mining its surface and sub terrain.

December 28th 2030: The Adam & Eve probes reached Osiris 4 and initially transmitted data back to Earth, which would take about three years to accomplish.

January 1st 2030: Dr. Russell S. Wilson was officially sworn in as President of the United States.

December 29th 2033: The Hoi-Larson asteroid that threatened the entire world was completely consumed within six years after it was intercepted in space. The Humane Space Federation used and sold the giant boulder's precious metals and stone to develop the first Lunar research compound at the moon's North Pole region.

January 17th 2033: Confirmed data that reached the Earth from the Adam & Eve probes inspires the Humane Space Federation to develop an immanent plan and strategy to pursue this newly discovered extrasolar planet called Osiris 4. President Wilson and Secretary General Mobutu revealed this historic discovery to the global public.

TECHNOLOGY INFORMATION

Identification Detective (I.D.): A device that appears like a pistol, which holds a multi-wave projector at the front portion of this mock pistol. This projector can emit multiple wavelengths from infrared to X-rays to identify animals and plants. A four-inch crystal television screen displays the various references stored at the Soul Mate. A match making process will endure until the closest reference (based upon DNA, or skeletal structure). The reference will contain a video display and related information regarding any reference. Air molecules won't interfere with any intended detection attempts.

Soul Mate: This enormous data storage hard drive has a reference of over four million species of plants and animals. From insects to whales, the storage capacity is also an important educational device for future generations. The Identification Detective or I.D. sends data to compare the data inside and the most identical entity will be selected and sent back to the I.D. so it could display the reference and related information to the user.

Drifter: Two versions existed. The older version appeared like a three wheeled motorcycle, which was powered by solar energy and radio waves. A planet's magnetic field also provided additional power in case of an emergency. The newer version appeared more akin to the Jet Ski and extended eight feet (2.44m) long, over three (1m) wide and possessed multiple storage space including a trunk that held the Private Eye. Gravitational absorption rods take in a planet's gravity waves and harness this energy into a transducer reactor that would convert this energy into an emitting magnetic field to repel the planet's magnetic polarity from a host of deflection plates. A planet's magnetic field will deflect the craft to remain approximately three feet above the ground. Industrial strength turbo fans would propel the transporter forward and two smaller turbo fans would be able to shift this unit in reverse. The newest model could even float above water. The movement would feel like a speedboat moving across a subtle lake. Intake valves in the front would lead to the main propulsion engine while two smaller intake valves would be directed to the twin turbo fans mounted at the front. The smaller pair of retro engines at the front is also used as brakes.

Clairvoyance Projector: A four dimensional, 360-degree holographic projector. Similar to the virtue reality but no eyewear is necessary. The fourth dimension is time. The visual apparition would automatically convert any ordinary room into a visual display that covers the entire room. The appearance would place any spectator at the scene, as though they were really there. Data are stored on hard drive or disk.

Adam & Eve: The planetary probe is divided into two sections. Adam is designed to orbit an intended planet. It will probe the atmosphere of the newly discovered planet and compare it with the known data of the Earth. The data will then be compared and determined if the planet would be suitable for human habitation. Adam will also record the planet's speed of rotation, natural satellites, climate and noticeable weather patterns. Eve on the other hand, will descend to the planet's surface. Eve consists of four separate surface probes that will search for animal life on land and water. The valuable data will be sent back to Adam, which would send the signal all the way back to Earth as fast as the speed of light.

Geographic Indicator (G.I.): In conjunction with the Private Eye, Soul Mate Identification Detective, etc. The device consists of enormous amounts of storage space for data. The data will be transmitted from its counterparts and sent to the G.I. to compile and synthesize the bodies of water, elements, geographic features, weather patterns, and other valuable information and organize the data into a permanent four-dimensional holographic map of the habitation of the planet. A superb tool for future navigation, the device could display the map either on a flat twenty feet diameter circular table or use the Clairvoyance.

Planetary Indicator: This device is usually built-in the Adam probe satellite and the main orbiting ship such as the H.S.F.S. Guardian. It functions similar to the Private Eye and the Undercover. From an orbital position the device will emit infrared rays to the planet and receive returned signals. Although considerably dense clouds such as severe thunderstorms may limit the clarity of the data; however, this device is ideal for meteorology as well as geography. A satellite version and a built-in flagship edition could cover much of the planets surface.

Private Eye: This four-pound device consists of multiple infrared transmitters and video cameras pointed in all directions. The infrared lasers will be sent to the surface only to bounce off the surface and return to the module. The data will be sent to the Geographic Indicator or G.I., which would organize the data. The main set of helicopter blades on top will elevate the object up to fifty thousand feet. Each transmitter is pointed towards a different direction. The reason for this is because when the craft is elevated, the various transmitters will detect a wide area of a planet's terrain and send the information to the G.I. to permanently record and display specific land features for future navigation. When the maximum height is reached it will descend. Only one transmitter is designed to guide the Private Eye towards the Drifter it was originally stored. Even if the intended Drifter traveled a considerable distance after the craft was launched, the device will follow the beacon until it lands inside the rear trunk space of the Drifter to be stored for future use.

Undercover: Closely related to the Eve space probe and the Private Eye geographic terrain decipher. Using a sharp night visor would aid video cameras. The microphones will detect the faintest, background noise. What's more the Identification Detective receptors will detect and interpret various species.

Feral Sentry: This unique apparatus was designed to protect the Landers from any unwanted intrusions of potentially dangerous animals. Its role is to emit a repulsive but harmless scent and sound frequency to repel any intruder's effort to fulfill their curiosities or possible modes of attack. They appear like a narrow pole that's six feet high with an oval egg shape top, which emits a repugnant frequency of sounds and dreaded scent. Smaller versions are available for personal carry or to install on one of the Drifters. With the exceptions of the flashing lights, the signals emitted from the device are undetectable to humans and is equally harmless. What's more, the "Wild Watchman" as it means, was also designed to aggressively attract any member of the wilderness. The purpose of this was to carefully guide any animal to safety from catastrophic situations such as forest fires and floods.

Watchdog: A modern multiuse watch intended for every public official on Earth. A verbal command of the public official's name or the position of the individual would be called or identified once communication is established. The principal uses of the Watchdog are to call for conferences and to quickly organize meetings, summits, and parliamentary ratification procedures. The easy accessibility of public officials is also important for emergencies. The Chamber also uses this device to notify public officials of valuable information and to keep in touch with each member of the Humane Space Federation.

Good Samaritan: This six inch long device was a marvel from Engineers. Developed by Drs. Weinstein, Marino, Ivanov and Ansari; this device was made as a beacon for each explorer. It will send emergency messages to Town Hall and indicate the precise location. Originally designed as an electronic map, all an individual has to do is press their finger on the screen, and the blood pressure, heartbeat rate, temperature, and other valuable data regarding a person's physical and biological condition. It makes a great navigational organizer. The Geographic Indicator would send the detailed graphs of the terrain. What's more is the red arrows point in the preferred path to choose. Also, if an explorer is lost, then the red arrows on the four-inch screen will guide him or her back to safety.

Mercury-One: Specifically designed for long distance communications. The procedure utilizes the teletransport of light instantaneously over long distances. The Humane Federation Starship Guardian possesses a sending unit and a receiving unit and federation headquarters retain both units as well. A written message would be encoded into a series of flashing patterns of light sent through the sending unit while these patterns of light would be received before data becomes decoded and then translated into the same written message using the English alphabet and the punctuation marks. High frequency lights are necessary to deliver quality clear messages across the vast distance of space. This new procedure would send messages without signals traveling vast distances of space.

Clever Cap: Designed similar to any modern construction helmets or "hard hats" equipped with a high definition video camera along with a microphone. This device was made to transmit audio and video data to Intelligence who monitor and record data inside Town Hall. Since miniature broadcast equipment is built in each helmet, it made broadcasting much more convenient than any hand held device and promotes an explorer's attention to any local physical surroundings.

Dove: A small lightweight solar powered miniature airplane with a single ten-inch long propeller. The unmanned aircraft weighs approximately ten pounds and posses a three feet long wingspan, which matches the plane's overall length. Originally developed for search and rescue operations, the Dove is also designed to seek out particular places and objects. Using a collection of video cameras, infrared laser and sound receptors it could be used to find extremely dangerous inhabitants of Isis.

Condor: This fifty-pound double propeller miniature aircraft is similar to the Dove plane in ability and purpose. It scans large areas of land and sea. The two twelve-inch propellers installed on both wings enable the solar/magnetic-powered aircraft to travel long distances for well over one thousand miles.

Diver: A miniature unmanned submarine that extends up to 8 feet long and up to three feet wide. Similar in shape to the Los Angeles Class American Naval submarine, this device is controlled remotely from Town Hall while monitors at intelligence would reveal visual data ranging from video to infrared. Sonar reception could enable to produce a four dimensional (the fourth dimension is time) inside the Clairvoyance Projector rooms. This sub-aquatic device could produce a clear visual image of river or ocean debt similar in quality to protective eye goggles. The Diver submarine is primarily used for oceanic research.

Transcend Shuttle Transporter: The sleek design of this craft makes this 100 feet long miniature shuttle is easy to pilot that includes a built-in Clairvoyance projector. Specifically designed to accommodate long trips to the moon and Earth, an autopilot is commonly used when occupants travel long distances or when performing other tasks besides piloting and navigating the craft.

Illuminator: Designed by Dr. Ryan's father, this orbital space telescope is designed to find planets that have similar characteristics as the Earth. Each object would be detected and the densities of each object will display a color display. The dark colors such as blue and purple indicates a dense object. The color shift of the upper atmosphere must match the Earth's color shift in order to reinforce a planet's composition similar to Earth. Such accuracy of the Illuminator will encourage further research such as the Adam & Eve probes.

Aqua-Spring: The entire system of desalting water and detoxifying any form of poisons and biohazards. This finest water purifier is capable of removing clear water from any toxins including urine. Aqua-Spring will be a considerable importance aboard the H.S.F.S. Guardian and the Landers. Portable modules developed for extracting and purifying river or seawater for irrigation purposes, while units supplies drinking water.

Air Thief: Designed to fight fires on board the H.S.F.S. Guardian and the four Landers. The procedure starts off when the smoke and/or fumes are detected and them a brief warning alarm sounds off before all adjacent doors close and become sealed. The oxygen inside the room will be deprived and sent to a compression chamber. This process will suffocate the fire and deprive it of the essential oxygen. Air masks are available in every room of the starship in case someone is accidentally locked inside.

Geological Time Frame Chart

Ma = Million(s) or years ago.

± = Plus or minus any specified amount of time.

Holocene Epoch (0.0117 Ma – Present) or
11,700 years ago – Present

Pleistocene Epoch (2.588 Ma – 0.117 Ma) or
2,588,000 – 11,700 years ago

Pliocene Epoch (5.332 Ma – 2.588 Ma) or
5,332,000 – 2,588,000 years ago

Miocene Epoch (23.03 Ma – 5.332 Ma) or
23,030,000 – 5,332,000 years ago.

Oligocene Epoch (33.9 ±0.1 Ma – 23.03 Ma) or
33,900,000 ±100,000 – 23,030,000 years ago.

Eocene Epoch (55.8 ±0.2 Ma – 33.9 ±0.1 Ma) or
55,800,000 ±200,000 – 33,900,000 ±100,000 years ago.

Paleocene Epoch (65.5 ±0.3 Ma – 55.8 ±0.2 Ma) or
65,500,000 ±300,000 – 55,800,000 ±200,000 years ago.

Cretaceous Period (145.5 ±4.0 Ma – 65.5 ±0.3 Ma)
145,500,000 ±4,000,000 – 65,500,000 ±300,000 years ago.

Jurassic Period (199.6 ±0.6 Ma – 145.5 ±4.0 Ma)
199,600,000 ±600,000 – 145,500,000 ±4,000,000 yeas ago.

Triassic Period (251 ±0.4 Ma – 199.6 ±0.6 Ma)
251,000,000 ±400,000 – 199,600,000 ±600,000 years ago.

Permian Period (299 ±0.8 Ma – 251 ±0.4 Ma)
299,000,000 ±800,000 – 251,000,000 ±400,000 years ago.

Carboniferous Period (359.2 ±2.5 Ma – 299 ±0.8 Ma)
359,200,000 ±2,500,000 – 299,000,000 ±800,000 years ago.

Devonian Period (416 ±2.8 Ma – 359.2 ±2.5 Ma)
416,000,000 ±2,800,000 – 359,200,000 ±2,500,000 years ago.

Silurian Period (443.7 ±1.5 Ma – 416 ±2.8 Ma)
443,700,000 ±1,500,000 – 416,000,000 ±2,800,000 years ago.

Ordovician Period (488.3 ±1.7 Ma – 443.7 ±1.5 Ma)
488,300,000 ±1,700,000 – 443,700,000 ±1,500,000 years ago.

Cambrian Period (542 ±1.0 Ma – 488.3 ±1.7 Ma)
542,000,000 ±1,000,000 – 488,300,000 ±1,700,000 years ago.

Precambrian Times (4600 Ma – 542 ±1.0 Ma)
4,600,000,000 – 542,000,000 ±1,000,000 years ago.

ERAS

Cenozoic Era (65.5 ±0.3 Ma – Present)
65,500,000 ±300,000 years ago – Present.

Mesozoic Era (251 ±0.4 Ma – 65.5 ±0.3 Ma)
251,000,000 ±400,000 – 65,500,000 ±300,000 years ago.

Paleozoic Era (542 ±1.0 Ma – 251 ±0.4 Ma)
542,000,000 ±1,000,000 – 251,000,000 ±400,000 years ago.

Precambrian Times (4600 Ma – 542 ±1,000,000 Ma)
4,600,000,000 – 542,000,000 ±1,000,000 years ago.

BIBLIOGRAPHY

Books and Novels:

1. Turner, Alan and Richard L. Cifelli (introduction), National Geographic Prehistoric Mammals. Firecrest Books Ltd. Published by the National Geographic Society, Washington D.C., Copyright © 2004.

2. Bakker, PhD, Professor Robert T. Dinosaur Heresies: New Theories Unlocking the Mystery of the Dinosaurs and Their Extinction. New York: Zebra Books / Kensington Publishing Corporation, Copyright © 1986.

3. Maestro, Vittorio, ed. Mammals and Their Extinct Relatives: A Guide to the Lila Acheson Wallace Wing. New York: AMNH, Copyright © 1994.

4. Lambert, David & The Diagram Group, Midgley, Ruth ed. The Field Guide to Prehistoric Life. New York: Facts on File, Copyright © 1994.

5. Crichton, Michael. Jurassic Park. New York: Ballantine Books / The Ballantine Group, Copyright © 1990.

6. The New American Webster Handy College Dictionary, New Fourth Edition. Prepared by Philip D. Morehead. Edited by Albert and Loy Morehead. / First published by Signet, an imprint of the New American Library, a division of the Penguin Group (USA), Inc. Copyright © 2006 by: Philip and Andrew T. Morehead.

7. Asimov, Isaac. The Secret of the Universe. New York: Pinnacle Books / Windsor Publishing Corporation. Copyright © 1990.

8. Agustí, Jordi and Mauricio Antón. Mammoths, Sabertooths, and Hominids: 65 Million Years of Mammalian Evolution in Europe. New York: Columbia University Press. Copyright © 2002.

9. Burnie, David. The Kingfisher Illustrated Animal Encyclopedia. New York: Kingfisher. Copyright © 2000

10. Palmer, Dr. Douglas. Atlas of the Prehistoric World. New York: Discovery Books. Copyright © 1999.

11. Palmer, Dr. Douglas, ed., Professor Barry Cox, Professor R.J.G. Savage, Professor Brian Gardiner, Dr. Colin Harrison, And Dr. Douglas Palmer. The Simon & Schuster Encyclopedia of Dinosaurs & Prehistoric Creatures: A Visual Who's Who of Prehistoric Life. New York: Simon & Schuster. Copyright © 1988 and 1999.

12. Gould, Stephen Jay, ed., Peter Andrews, John Barber, Michael Benton, Marianne Collins, Christine Janis, Ely Kish, Akio Morishima, J. John Sepkoski Jr., Christopher Stringer, Jean-Paul Tibbles, and Steve Cox. The Book of Life. New York & London: W. W. Norton & Company, Inc., Copyright © 1993 and 2001.

13. Ronan, Colin A., ed. The Universe Explained: The Earth – Dweller's Guide to the Mysteries of Space. New York: Henry Holt and Company, Inc. Copyright © 1994.

14. Sagan, Carl. The Demon – Haunted World: Science as a Candle in the Dark. New York: Ballantine Books. Copyright © 1996.

15. Davies, Paul. The Mind of God: The Scientific Basis for a Rational World. New York: A Touchstone Book, Published by Simon & Schuster, Copyright © 1992.

16. Hawking, Stephen. Black Holes and Baby Universes and Other Essays. New York: Bantam Book, Copyright © 1980 & 1993.

17. Morris, Richard. Cosmic Questions: Galactic Halos Cold Dark Matter and the End of Time. New York: John Wiley & Sons, Inc. Copyright © 1993.

18. Sagan, Carl. Cosmos. New York: Ballantine Books. Copyright © 1980.

19. Pagels, Heinz R. The Cosmic Code: Quantum Physics as the Language of Nature. New York: A Bantam Book / published by arrangement with Simon & Schuster, Copyright © 1982.

20. Lambert, David, forwarded by John H. Ostrom, PhD. The Ultimate Dinosaur Book. New York: DK Publishing Inc. in association with The Natural History Museum, London. Copyright © 1993

21. Fraser, Gordon, Egil Lillestol Inge Sellevag, Introduced by Stephen Hawking. The Search for Infinity: Solving the Mysteries of the Universe. London * New York: Facts on File, Inc. Copyright © 1994 & 1995.

Magazine and Newspaper Articles:

1. Sloan, Christopher P. "Feathers for T. Rex? New Birdlike Fossils Are Missing Links In Dinosaur Evolution." National Geographic, Vol. 196, No. 5, November 1995: 98 – 107.

2. Shreeve, James. "Uncovering Patagonia's Lost World" National Geographic, Vol. 192, No. 6, December 1995, 120 – 137.

3. Achenbach, Joel. "Dinosaurs Come Alive: a new generation of scientists brings dinosaurs back to life flesh & bone." National Geographic, Vol. 203, No. 3, March 2003: 2 – 33.

4. Gore, Rick. "The Rise of Mammals: Adapting, Evolving, Surviving" National Geographic, Vol. 203, No. 4, April 2003: 2 – 37.

5. Dobb, Edwin. "What Wiped Out the Dinosaurs?" Discover, Vol. 23, No. 6, June 2002: 36 – 42.

6. Levin, Eric. "Dinosaur Family Values." Discover, Vol. 24, No. 6, June 2003: 34 – 41.

7. Keel, William. "Quasars Explained." Astronomy, Vol. 31, No. 2, February 2003: 34 – 41.

8. Filippenko, Alexi V. "When Stars Explode." Astronomy, Vol. 31, No. 2, February 2003: 42 – 47.

9. Schilling, Govert. "Stalking Cosmic Explosions." Astronomy, Vol. 31, No. 2, February 2003: 48 – 52.

10. Vettiger, Peter, and Gerd Binnig. "The Nanodrive Project." Scientific American, Vol. 288, No. 1, January 2003: 46 – 53.

11. Prum, Richard O. and Alan H. Brush. "Which Came First, the Feather or the Bird?" Scientific American, Vol. 288, No. 3, March 2003: 84 – 93.

12. Wilson, Jim. "Science Does The Impossible." Popular Mechanics, Vol. 180, No. 2, February 2003: 60 – 63.

13. Wilson, Jim. "Roswell Declassified." Popular Mechanics, Vol. 180, No. 6, June 2003: 80 – 85.

14. Lopez, Ramon. "The Revolution Will Not Be Piloted." Popular Science, Vol. 262, No. 6, June 2003: 60 – 67.

15. Gorman, James. "In Virtual Museums, an Archive of the World." New York Times, 12 January 2003, Sec 1: 1, 24.

16. Wilford, John Noble. "Experts Trace Whale's Family Tree to the Hippo Clan." New York Times, 2 October 2001, Science Times: F3.

17. Davis, Joel. "185 million years before the dinosaurs' demise, Did an asteroid nearly end life on Earth? Scientists may have found the smoking gun. Astronomy, Vol. 36, No. 4, April 2008: 34 – 39.

18. Sietzen, Jr., Frank. "To the Cosmic Edge." Astronomy, Vol. 32, No. 7, July 2004: 70 – 73.

19. Folger, Tim. "Nailing Down Gravity: New ideas about the most mysterious power in the universe." Discover, Vol. 24, No. 10, October 2003: 34 – 41.

20. Lubick, Naomi. "Goldilocks and the Three Planets." Astronomy, Vol. 31, No. 7, July 2003: 36 – 41.

21. Stover, Dawn. "Saturn Unveiled." Popular Science, Vol. 265, No. 1, July 2004: 65 – 72.

22. Spudis, Paul D. "Harvest the Moon." Astronomy, Vol. 31, No. 6, June 2003: 42 – 47.

23. Jayawardhana, Ray "Searching for Alien Earths." Astronomy, Vol. 31, No. 6, June 2003: 48 – 53.

24. Seeman, Nadrian C. "Nanotechnology and the Double Helix." Scientific American, Vol. 290, No. 6, June 2004: 64 – 69, 72 – 75.

25. Achenbach, Joel "When Yellowstone Explodes" National Geographic, vol.216, No. 2, August 2009: 56 – 69.

Videos or DVDs:

1. Walking with Dinosaurs. Video. Producer: Tim Haines and Jasper James. Narrated by: Avery Brooks, BBC Video, 180 min. Copyright © 1999.

2. Walking with Prehistoric Beasts. Video. Produced and Directed by: Nigel Peterson. Narrated by: Kenneth Branagh, Televised series narrated by Stockard Channing, BBC Video, 150 min. Copyright © 2001.

3. What Killed the Megabeasts? Video. Directed by: Chris Lent. Narrated by: Terry MacDonald. BBC Video, A Darlow Smithson Production for the Discovery Channel / Artisan Home Entertainment / Family Home Entertainment (F.H.E.) 92 min. Copyright © 2002.

4. Eternal Enemies. Video. A National Geographic Special. Produced by: The National Geographic Society, Filmed by: Dereck and Beverly Joubert, Narrated by: Powers Boothe, National Geographic Video. Approx. 60 min. Copyright © 1992.

5. When Dinosaurs Roamed America. Video. Produced and Directed by: Pierre de Lespinois, Written by: Georgann Kane, Narrated by: John Goodman,Discovery Channel Video / Artisan Home Entertainment / Family Home Entertainment (F.H.E.) Approx. 90 min. Copyright © 2001.

6. Sabretooth. Video. Produced by: Caius Julyan, Edited by: David Helton, Narrated by: Johnathan Price, Discovery Channel Video, 52 min. Copyright © 2000.

7. Zebra: Patterns in the Grass. Video. Produced by Dereck and Beverly Joubert, Written and Edited by: Dereck Joubert, Senior Producer: Nicolas Noxon, Narrated by: Brian Dennehy, National Geographic Video, Approx. 60 min. Copyright © 1991.

8. Allosaurus: A Walking with Dinosaurs Special. Video. Producer: Tim Haines. Narrated by: Tim Haines Televised version narrated by Avery Brooks, BBC Video. Approx. 60 min. Copyright © 2000.

9. Super Predators. Video. A Londolozi Film Production / Sable Enterprises, Inc. Research by: James Marshall, Predator Consultant Dr. M. Mills, Narrated by: Michael Richards and John Varney, Questar Video, Approx. 50 min. Copyright © 1992.

10. Crocodiles: Here be Dragons. Video. Produced by: Alan Root and Survival Anglia, Ltd., Written by: Alan Root Edited by: Howard Marshall, Narrated by: Richard Kiley, National Geographic Video, Approx. 60 min. Copyright © 1990 & 1995.

11. Valley of the T. Rex. Video. Produced and Directed by: Reuben Anderson and James McQuillan. Written by: Steve Eder and Steve Reich. Story by: Georgann Kane. Editor: Langdon Page. Narrated by: Jimmie Wood. Discovery Channel Video, Approx. 52 min. Copyright © 2001.

12. Chased by Dinosaurs. Video. Presented by: Nigel Marvin. Produced and Directed by: Tim Haines, Edited by: Andrew Wilkes, Discovery Channel Video. Approx. 52 min. Copyright © 2002.

13. Predators of the Wild: Grizzly Bear. Video. Filmed by: Joel Bennett, Written and Produced by: Malcolm Penny. Narrated by: William Hootkins. Time – Life Video, 52 min. Copyright © 1992.

14. Reflections on Elephants. Video. Produced by: Dereck and Beverly Joubert. Narrated by: Stacy Keach, National Geographic Video, 60 min. Copyright © 1994.

15. Lions of Darkness. Video. Produced by Dereck and Beverly Joubert, Written by Dereck Joubert, Narrated by: Keith David. National Geographic Video. Approx. 72 min. Copyright © 1994.

16. SuperCroc. Video. Written and Produced by: Simon Boyce, Presented by: Dr. Paul Sereno and Dr. Brady Barr. Edited by: Christine Jameson Henry Narrated by: Sam Neill, National Geographic Video, Approx. 100 min. Copyright © 2001.

17. Land of the Mammoth. Video. Written and Produced by: Adrienne Ciuffo, Directed and Edited by: Emmanuel Mairesse and Diana

DeCilo, Narrated by: Avery Brooks, Discovery Channel Video, Approx. 93 min. Copyright © 2001.

18. Africa: The Serengeti. DVD. Produced by: George Casey and Paul Novros. Written by: George Casey and Mose Richards. Directed by: George Casey, Edited by: Timothy Huntley, Narrated by: James Earl Jones. 40 min. Copyright © 2001.

19. From Here to Infinity the Ultimate Voyage. Video, Produced by: Robert H. Goodman, Written and Directed by: Don Barrett, Hosted and narrated by: Patrick Stewart. 43 min. Copyright © 1994.

20. Jurassic Park III. DVD Collector's Edition, Executive Producer: Stephen Spielberg (DreamWorks SKG). Based on Characters Created by: Michael Crichton Produced by: Kathleen Kennedy and Larry Franco, Written by: Peter Buchman, Alexander Payne and Jim Taylor. Directed by: Joe Johnston. Starring: Sam Neill, William H. Macy, Tea Leoni, Allessandro Nivola, Trevor Morgan and Michael Jeter. Amblin Entertainment Production, Universal Pictures. 1 hr. 33 min. Copyright © 2001.

21. Orca. Video, Produced by Paramount Pictures and Dino De Laurentiis, Directed by Michael Anderson, Written by: Sergio Donati and Luciano Vincenzoni. Starring: Richard Harris, Charlotte Rampling, Bo Derek, Keenan Wynn, Will Sampson, Robert Carradine. Paramount Pictures. 92 min. Copyright © 1977.

22. Flying Saucers Are Real (video collection). Produced by: J. Clifford Curley, Edited By: Guy Chaifetz, Presented and Narrated by: Stanton T. Friedman. UFO Central. Approx. 120 min. Copyright © 1996.

23. Wonders of the Universe (video collection). Produced by: Terrance Murtagh, Series Producer: David Taylor, Written by: Dr. William Gutsch, Narrated by: Michael Goldfarb, Produced for The Learning Channel by York Films of England. Executive Producers David Taylor and Bill Cosmas. Distributed by Ambrose Video Publishing, Inc. Approx. 25 min. Copyright © 1996.

Broadcasted Programs:

1. Giant Monsters. Created by: Charlie Foley. Presented by: Jeff Corwin. Produced by Alex West and Andrea Florence. For: The National

Wildlife Federation. Animal Planet. World Premier, Sunday, March 9th2003, 8 p.m. ET 2 hours. Copyright © 2003.

2. <u>Big Tooth: Dead or Alive</u>. Produced by: Moira Mann, Narrated by: Jack Roberts. Nigel's Wild Shark Week. Discovery Channel, Saturday, February 19th 2003, 9 p.m. ET. Approx. 60 min. Copyright © 2003.

3. <u>Supervolcanoes.</u> Written and produced by: Mark Hedgecoe,Director of production by: Bob Reid, Narrated by: Terry MacDonald, Discovery Channel. Sunday, April 11th 2004, 10 PM. ET. Approx. 60 min. Copyright © 1999.

Software / CD-ROMS:

1. <u>Microsoft Encarta Encyclopedia</u>, Standard Edition 2002.

2. Microsoft Corporation, Copyright © 2002.

3. Microsoft Network, <u>MSN Explorer</u> 8.0 for Windows.

4. <u>America Online</u> 9.0 for Windows.

5. <u>Zoo Guides: Prehistoric Animals</u>, Vol. 9, Prehistoric Animals, Version 1.0, REMedia, Copyright © 1998.

Websites:

www.nationalgeographic.com

http://animal.discovery.com

www.historychannel.com

www.Britannica.com

www.aolsvc.worldbook.aol.com

www.hydenplanetarium.org

www.about.com

http://coreshutdown.com/elite/starsystems.htm

http://cstl-cla.semo.edu

www.prehistoric.com

www.discovery.com

www.tlc.com

www.aetv.com

www.nhm.org

www.amnh.org/research

elib.cs.berkeley.edu/manis

www.wikipedia.com

www.mnh.si.edu/rc/db/colld.html

www.discoveryschool.com

www.rense.com

www.enchantedlearning.com

www.personal.u-net.com

www.paleocraft.com

www.Jsd.clairmount.edu

www.zoomschool.com

www.Encyclopedia.com

www.prehistorics.com

www.ceu.edu

www.personal.psu.edu

www.internetezy.com

www.prehistory.com

www.megalodonjaws.com/indel.html

www.aztecufo.com

www.iufomrc.org

www.popularmechanics.com

www.astronomy.com

www.bbcamerica.com

www.familyhomeent.com

www.paramount.com

www.amblin.com

http//news.bbc.co.uk/1/hi/sci/tech/193184.stm

www.popsci.com

www.letsfindout.com

www.science.nasa.gov

www.flmnh.ufl.edu

www.cbsg.org

www.stratigraphy.com

www.prehistorictimes.com

www.ebay.com

www.kheper.auz.com

www.alf.org/animals/

www.online.discovery.com

www.uic.edu/orgs/paleo

http://animaldiversity.lummz.umich.edu

www.museums.org.

www.planet-pets.com

www.discover.com

www.sciam.com

www.artisanent.com

www.universalpictures.com

www.dreamworks.com

www.beringa.com

www.ilm.com

SPECIAL THANKS

People:

Reuben Aaronson

Isaac Asimov

Joel Achenbach

Joel Achenbach

Dr. Larry Agenbroad

Jordi Agusti

Professor Leslie Aiello

Sylvia Arimaya

Johnny Arnet

Sir David Attenborough

Professor Robert T. Bakker, PhD

Dr. Ian Barnes

Dr. Brady Barr

Des and Jen Bartlett

Kate Bartlett

Professor Michael J. Benton

Joshua Berkeley

Paul Bibe

Gerd Binning

Rolin T. Bird

Professor Vladimir –
Prokorovitch Amalitzky

Professor Stanley Ambrose

Michael Anderson

Nick Anderson

Roy Chapman Andrews

Mauricio Antón

José Bonaparte

Professor Bill Bonichsen

Powers Boothe

Luis Alberto Borerro

Japeth Boyce

Simon Boyce

Dr. Bob Brain

Kenneth Branagh

W.W. "Mack" Brazel

Dr. Adam Britton

Avery Brooks

Barnum Brown

Alan H. Brush

Professor Michael Bisson

David Burney

David Burnie

Johannes von Buttlar

Paul Bybee

Hernán Cañellas

Andrew Carnegie

Rubén Carolini

Robert Carradine

George Casey

Guy Chaifetz

Dr. Bob Chandler

Stockard Channing

Karen Chin, PhD

Dr. Per Christiansen

Robert Christiansen

Adrienne Ciuffo

Joel Davis

Diana DeCilo

Brian Dennehy

Bo Derek

Edwin Dobb

Matthew Dodd Noble

Sergio Donati

Dino De Laurentiis

Steve Eder

Dr. Richard Farina

Professor Jim Farlow

Alexi V. Filippenko

Charlie Finn

Dr. Frank Fish

Peter Buchman

Richard L. Cifelli

Dr. Arthur C. Clarke

Dr. Sarah Cleavland

Dr. Robin Compton

Dr. Gill Cook

Dr. Margery Coombs

Edward Drinker Cope

Dr. Rodolfo Coria

Jeff Corwin

Bill Cosmas

Professor Barry Cox

Michael Crichton

J. Clifford Curley

Dr. Philip J. Currie

Robert Dalva

Keith David

Kent Fleet

Claire Flemming

Andrea Florence

Charlie Foley

Tim Folger

Dr. Mikael Fortelius

Dr. Scott E. Foss

Larry Franco

Dr. Jens – Lorenz Franzen

Stanton T. Friedman

Professor Brian Gardiner

Joby Gee

Jason Giles

Dr. Philip Gingerich

Dr. Daniel Fisher

Dr. Tim Flannery

Ken Goldman

John Goodman

Rick Gore

James Gorman

Dr. Mike Gottfried

Steven Jay Gould

Russ Graham

Dr. William Gutsch

Rebecca Hannan

Professor Harry Harpending

Tim Haines

Richard Harris

Dr. Colin Harrison

Stephen Hawking

Gary Haynes

Mark Hedgecoe

The Jarkov family

Ray Jayawardhana

Michael Jeter

Dereck and Beverly Joubert

Joe Johnson

James Earl Jones

Professor Lynn Jorde

Caius Julyan

Kan Chuen Pao

Vikki Kaisar

Professor Michio Kaku

Georgann Kane

Stacy Keach

Steven Godfrey

Michael Goldfarb

David Helton

Paul Hodgeson

Richard Holdaway

Simon Holland

Dr. Tomas Holtz, PhD

William Hootkins

Budd Hopkins

John "Jack" Horner

Dr. Gordon Hubbel

Timothy Huntley

Bill Hyme

Clare Imber

Dr. A. Inostrantzev

Steve and Terri Irwin

Jasper James

Christine Jameson Henry

Kathleen Kennedy

Richard Kiley

James Kirkland, PhD

David Lambert

Neil Larson

Chris Lent

Tea Leoni

Pierre de Lespinois

Eric Levin

Professor Andrei Linde

Dr. Adrian Lister

Raymond Lopez

Naomi Lubick

William Keel

Tim Kelly

Dr. Bretton Kent

Terry MacDonald

Professor Ross MacPhee

William H. Macy

Emmanuel Mairesse

Moira Mann

Major Jessie Marcel

Dr. Othniel C. Marsh

Howard Marshall

James Marshall

Dave Martill, PhD

Professor Larry Martin

Paul Martin

Dr. Tony Martin

Nigel Marvin

Octavio Mateus

Daniel C. Matt

Professor Bill McGuire

John H. Ostrom, PhD

Langdon Page

Douglas Palmer

Leslie Parry, A.C.E.

Nigel Patterson

Alexander Payne

Malcolm Penny

John Peterson

Ping Koy Lam

Johnathan Price

Floyd and Loretta Proctor

George Lucas

Dr. Herbert Luiz

Dr. Gregory MacDonald

James McQuillan

Dr. M. Mills

Dick Mol

Albert Morehead

Loy Morehead

Philip D. Morehead

Trevor Morgan

Dr. Michael Morlo

Flavio Morrisei

Terrance Murtagh

Virginia Naples

Sam Neill

Leonard Nimoy

Allessandro Nivola

Paul Novros

Barry Nye, A.C.E

Dr. Maureen O'Leary

Dr. Randy Reiches

Professor Karl Reinhard

Michael Richards

Mose Richards

Professor Holliston L. Riviere

Jack Roberts

Gene Roddenberry

Scott Rogers

Colin A. Ronan

Alan Root

Dale Russell

Professor Donald Prothero

Richard O. Prum

Charlotte Rampling

Professor Michael Rampino

Steve Reich

Dan Seeley

Nadrian C. Seeman

Dr. Paul Sereno

Christopher Shaw

James Shreeve

Dr. Carol Shoshkes Reiss

Frank Sietzen, Jr.

Christopher P. Sloan

Professor Robert Smith

Roger Smith

Professor Olga Soffer

Professor Steve Sparks

Steven Spielberg

Paul D. Spudis

Gary Starr

Jon Stephens

Dr. Mark Uhen

Dr. Peter Ungar

Professor Tjeerd Van Andel

Dr. Bass Van Geel

Professor Blair Van Valkenburgh

John Varney

Peter Vettiger

Sergio Vizcaino

Dr. Kent Vliet

Professor Mike Voorhees

Carl Sagan

Will Sampson

Barrett Sanders

Robert J. G. Savage

Govert Schilling

Professor Kent Stevens

Patrick Stewart

Professor Michael Stoskopf

Dawn Stover

Dr. Kent Sundell

David Suzuki

Kenneth Tankersley

David Taylor

Jim Taylor

Mark Thiessen

Dr. Hans Thewissen

Dr. J. G. M. Thewissen

Dave Thomas

John Thurley

Dr. Alexei Tikhonov

Alan Turner

Sheriff George Wilcox

John Noble Wilford

Andrew Wilkes

Jim Wilson

Professor Larry Witmore

Professor Carl Richard Woese

Douglas C. Wolfe

Jimmie Wood

Dr. Steve Wroe

Keenan Wynn

Professor Peter Ward

Henry Waters

Alex West

Dr. Charles Doolittle Walcott

William Speed Weed

David Whitehouse

Organizations:

A&E Networks

Amblin Entertainment

Ambrose Video Publishing, Inc.

American Museum of Natural History

Animal Planet

Artisan Home Entertainment

Astronomy Magazine

Audubon Center for Research of Endangered Species

BBC News, Sci /Tech section c/o BBC Online Network

BBC Video / BBC America c/o British Broadcasting Corporation

Benfield Greig Centre, U.C.L.

Big Bend National Park

Billabong Wildlife Sanctuary

Black Hills Institute of Geological Research

Calvert Marine Museum

Casper College, Wyoming

Center of the Search of Extraterrestrial Intelligence (CSETI) c/o SETI Institute

Chobe National Park

College of Eastern Utah Prehistoric Museum

Columbia / Tristar Home Video c/o Columbia / Tristar

Cranbrook Institute of Science

Darlowsmithson Productions

Discover Magazine

Discovery Channel c/o Discovery Networks

Encyclopedia Britannica

European Space Agency (ESA)

Facility of Science c/o University of Amsterdam

Family Home Entertainment (F.H.E.)

Florida State University

Fordham University

GEAL – Museum of Lourinhá

George C. Page Museum c/o la' Brea Discoveries

Glacier National Park

History Channel

Henry Waters & Brothers

Humboldt University Museum

Kennedy Space Center c/o National Aeronautics and Space Administration (NASA)

Idaho Geological Survey

Indiana – Perdue University

International Commission on Stratigraphy

John Jay Fossil Beds National Park

Johnson Space Center c/o National Aeronautics and Space Administration (NASA)

Krueger National Park

Liverpool John Moores University

Londolozi Film Productions

Londolozi Game Reserve c/o Masai Mara

Lucas Film, Ltd.
McGill University
Mesa Museum
MS Word, MSN & Encarta
Encyclopedia c/o Microsoft
Corporation
Museum of Mankind, London
Museum of the Rockies
National Museum of Natural
History c/o the Smithsonian
Institution
National Geographic Networks c/o
the National Geographic Society
National Wildlife Federation
New York Times, Inc.
New York University
New York City Public Library
North Carolina Fossil Club
North Carolina Museum of Natural
Sciences
North Carolina State University
Northern Illinois University
Occidental College
Ohio University
Oregon Health Sciences University
Oxford University
Paleontological Institute of the
Russian Academy of Sciences
Paramount Pictures c/o Viacom
Perdue University, Indiana
Peabody Museum c/o Yale
University
Penn State University
Popular Mechanics Magazine
Popular Science Magazine
Prehistoric Animal Structures
(PAST)
Prehistoric Times
Questar Video
Rancho la Brea Tar Pits

Rose Center for Earth and
Space (formerly the Hayden
Planetarium)
Royal Tyrell Museum
Russian Space Agency
Sable Enterprises
Saint Augustine Alligator Farm
Savuti National Park
Science Business and Public Library
(SBIL)
Scientific American Magazine
Serengeti National Park
Society of Vertebrae Paleontology
State University of New York,
(SUNY) at Stony Brook
Survival Anglia, Ltd.
Time – Life Video: c/o Time – Life,
Inc.
The Cincinnati Zoo
The Diagram Group
The Learning Channel (TLC)
Transvaal Museum, Pretoria
Tsalvo National Park
U.S. Geological Survey
Universal Pictures c/o Vivendi
Universal
University College, London
University of Bristol
University of California at Berkeley
University of California, Los
Angeles
University of Chicago
University of Colorado
University of Comahue
University of Florida
University of Illinois
University of Kansas Natural
History Museum and Biodiversity
Center
University of Maryland

University of Nebraska
University of Northern Arizona
University of Northern Illinois
University of Oregon
University of Portsmouth, United
  Kingdom
University of Southern California
Utah Geological Survey
Virginia Institute of Marina
  Sciences
Warner Brothers Home Video c/o
  Warner Brothers Pictures

"Most of all, I wish to thank every reader and

enthusiast like you who read Guardians"

— Verse Infinitum —

Made in the USA
Middletown, DE
19 September 2023

38807608R00222